MYSTIC SPRINGS

A COLLECTION OF ANOMALIES

WRITERS OF WARRENSBURG

INTRODUCTION

In literature and film, small towns and strange happenings go hand in hand, like ghosts and old attics, or ancient maps and the places they refuse to reveal. Why is this? After all, to most people, small towns represent safety and simplicity, where time seems to slow down—a place where everybody knows your name.

So, why are we so fascinated by unexplainable events that take place in small towns? Perhaps because of the stark contrast between a benign setting and a disturbing discovery. We expect small towns to be comforting, so when something strange happens, it disrupts that illusion in a way that captivates us. Regardless of the reason, our imaginations provide endless possibilities for fun stories.

Our group, Writers of Warrensburg, challenged members to create an anthology of short stories, with each story set in the same fictional small town, incorporating various businesses and landmarks as well as several universal characters. And with each story involving strange events related to the town's biggest attraction—a network of natural springs that supposedly possess all manner of healing properties. We're a diverse group of authors, writing in different genres—thriller, romance, science fiction, mystery, historical fiction, fantasy, and others. As expected and desired, these stories are as diverse as the authors.

Welcome to Mystic Springs. Stop in at the Deer Stand Café to grab a bite to eat and listen to Judd tell a few hunting stories. Visit Mystic Visions for a palm reading or to connect with a long-lost relative with the help of the mysterious Flaminia. Give a friendly wave to Police Chief Simpkins if she drives by—she has a knack for getting into perilous situations. And, of course, visit one of the natural springs. The water just might fix whatever's ailing you. Then again, you never know what else it might fix.

To learn more about our group, the authors contributing to this anthology, and how this short story collection came about, please visit our website:

https://writersofwsbg.weebly.com

We also have another short story anthology titled ***Hawthorn Creek: A Collection of Secrets***.

*To those who appreciate unexplained anomalies
and the thrill of reading short stories.*

CONTENTS

THE CAT'S PAJAMAS

WILLIAM SCHLICHTER

My body at least has the good sense to drop behind the bar as my little grey cells contemplate how four men wrapped in trench coats could obtain the password for entry. They aren't part of the band, and those sure ain't Stradivariuses inside their violin cases.

It's impossible to hear the clicks of those violin cases popping open over the loud, rapid beat of a jazz tune. The band is decent. Yet no matter how many patrons will rave about the musicians, not a one will speak to any of them on the street.

It is a good night. Everyone who knows their onions floods the dance floor at the first few notes of the *Maple Leaf Rag*. And those kittens are dressed to be hanged. My gin joint has the third-best jazz tunes in New York and the highest quality liquor. I never serve that woodbrew alcohol. There's a reason some places are known as blind tigers.

When constant repeating thunder interlaces with *boom* after *boom* to announce the evening's killjoys, I don't panic as most of my customers do. My practice with machine gun fire came while in France. I also know this is no official raid. That four-letter word always sends everyone scrambling for the exits.

Besides, I keep the fuzz in my pocket. If they must raid, they smash some of the cheap liquor I keep on hand for just such occasions. The coppers make out good in the newspapers, and I'm open again in an hour.

Brave or stupid, I take the same chance as every doughboy with a periscope over a trench and risk a peek from behind the bar.

It's reload time for the four men. Strange that not one body sprawls across the floor. My clientele's too busy shoving their way out the main entrance.

These goons came here to deliver a message by firing shotguns into the ceiling and a full Thompson drum into the bandstand. At least they gave the band a few seconds to vacate. The musicians are good people. It cost me a fortune to convince them to play this far away from Harlem.

The bar quiets now that the screams of the exiting dames and flaming youths subside. Until one of the men unleashes a few bursts from his Thompson into the wall of liquor bottles behind the bar.

"Not the Bacardi!"

"I have your attention now, Rexford?"

I know that voice. Hearing it tells me who sent goons to trash my gin joint. Freshly soaked from all that wasted giggle water, I glance to the heater mounted under the bar beside me, then behind me to the hidden dumbwaiter hatch I use to stock the bar in secret.

"You're operating without the required license."

Great. A thug with a sense of humor. I have no license of any kind. No one does. Selling distilled corn is illegal. You don't hop down to the courthouse and request the paperwork to open a speakeasy. No, this boob means I haven't been paying protection to the right crook.

"Is it too late to work out a percentage that will make Jimmy the Gil happy?"

Another short burst rains more rye whisky and glass down.

"Jimmy don't like it when people call him that."

I don't blame the guy. Jimmy came too close to getting a Harlem sunset. The shiv carved a scar on his neck that reminds people of a fish gill. No time for more insults, as I hear the crunching of boots atop the broken items scattered around the club's floor. The other three men will soon move to flank the bar. I again consider the heater beside me.

"So how much is this going to cost me?" This visit must be a warning. Jimmy's letting me know he means business.

"You don't got enough. Orders say to shut you down. That way everybody knows not to operate in Jimmy's territory without proper business arrangements."

I glance at the heater one more time and reach for the cigar box next to it.

I'd love to see all those faces when the men come over the bar. But by the time the goons find my escape route, I'll be gone.

There are miles—maybe hundreds of miles—of tunnels under New York. Some go back all the way to Revolutionary War times. Nowadays, these tunnels work well to smuggle booze into the gin joints, and for quick exits.

I stuff the spinach from the cigar box into a couple of different pockets, leaving a roll of bills cupped in my fist.

I elope.

Just inside the entrance to the tunnels, I find Herbert parked in his Ford. I know my supplier is not alone. At least two men wait out of sight in the dark, ready if someone attempts to high-jack the crates lashed to the bed.

"I need your truck."

"Are you crazy?"

When I am close enough for Herbert to see my hand, I hold up the wad of cabbage. "Payment for the load plus a thousand more. More than double what the truck costs new."

"We're just the delivery men. I'm keeping the truck."

"My place just got shot up by thugs. Shut my business down for good. Some beef about me not making purchases through the organization."

Nothing.

"It's Jimmy the Gil's men."

That gets Herbert out of the truck as fast as any man could move, even across a wartime no-man's-land.

"You got Jimmy's men after you?" He snags the fistful of cabbage. "Keys are in it." He calls out, "Boys, let's skedaddle." Herbert picks up speed on his run out of the tunnel and doesn't even turn around as he offers this advice: "For all that's holy, leave the city and tell no one where you're going."

While I drop a nickel in the machine, pop the Coke cap, and grab a road map, the gas station attendant pumps the fuel into the glass cylinder to inject into my automobile's tank.

The attendant, with "Bob" embroidered on his dirty chambray shirt, rubs permanently stained hands on a well-used rag. "Oil's fine, but your gas tank was about dry. Not a lot of stations along this road, so you need to fill up again at the next station."

"Company ought to invent some way to tell how much gas is in the tank besides that dipper stick. And another way to let me know if I'm really reaching my top speed of twenty-two miles per hour."

The man pats a crate covered by the tarp in the Ford's bed. "Doubt it with this load. But I filled your tires as well. We'll all do better on speed once the government finishes paving the main road."

"No time to wait on that." I hold up the map. "How much?"

"Says right on the cover. Thirty-five cents."

So it does. And with gas at eleven cents a gallon, I peel off two dollar bills from the lettuce roll and offer them to Bob. "Keep the change."

"Mighty generous of you." He tips his hat and stuffs the money into a pocket.

I drive a few miles, out of sight of anyone but a few cows, and cut the engine. Not much going on but a warm breeze and some soft munching of grass, which makes me miss the noise of the city. Adding radios in vehicles would help with long drives. Guess that will come after the paved roads people have been demanding, which, until I'm past the Bible Belt, I would avoid anyway. Still a good chance Jimmy's goons are on my tail. My escape will cause him to lose face, and he won't want that.

I determine my approximate location using the map. Plenty of know-nothing towns marked between here and California. What I need is to find a hamlet that Rand McNally forgot. Maybe lighten my load a bit without giving away that I'm not hauling Benny's Ten Penny Nails in all those crates.

Farther down the road, a different mechanic slides out from under my Ford. On his grease-covered shirt is the name "Bob" stitched in red. Are all mechanics named Bob? As the man speaks, he rubs his blackened hands on a grease-stained rag. "Axle's broken."

I kick the damn rattletrap's tire. "Can you fix it?"

"Parts need replacin' and they ain't on hand. Might could give a holler to Springfield to see if I can get 'em trucked in. That don't work out, then it's St. Louie. Gotta add charges on your bill for long distance calls and the mileage to Rolla to make 'em."

"This town doesn't have a telephone?"

"Nope. No hotel neither. Agnes, the widder-woman, takes in boarders. But if you want my advice, don't eat much of her cooking. Plenty around here believe that's what done her husbands in."

"Where exactly is *here*?"

"Mystic Springs, Miz-zuh-ree." Bob pats the side of the truck. "Cargo's gotta come out in order to change the axle."

"I'll need to store the nails."

"General store might take a few off your hands."

With my cargo, I will be better off with a pharmacy. Medicinal value and all.

"Drug store?"

"No, but our barber does a mighty fine bit of dentistry."

Did I travel back to the 1880s? "My teeth are fine. How does a town end up out here, Bob?"

"Name's not Bob. Owner said, 'Wear the shirt to work.' Gets a discount on 'em."

I clench my teeth at his explanation. I really may have to visit the town barber.

"Bob," as he doesn't give up his real name, scratches the side of his head. "Likely the town's here 'cause of the spring water. Far as I know, people been stoppin' over forever. Used to be Indian villages 'fore settlers moved on in. When war come and split the state, it became Graycoats territory." The mechanic nods. "People always need water. Lots of springs around to draw 'em in. The new paved road gets finished and there'll be more comin'—and plenty of their automobiles will need fixin'. Just like yours."

No, they won't. The road gets paved and there won't be hellacious ruts big enough to crack an axle. "I always respect a man of progress. Where's this widow woman?"

"Well, aren't you the cat's pajamas?" Plenty of birds flash their knees on the dance floor tonight, but this chick in front of me holds all my attention.

The young brunette titters at my remark as I place a glass before her. "The cat's pajamas?"

"Means you're even better than the bee's knees." I give her a wink. "All the rage in New York to be the cat's pajamas."

She flicks her eyes from the drink to me. Her bobbed hair reveals the soft curve of her neck, and a couple of beauty marks decorate her heart-shaped face.

"I hear you're from the big city. Been saving up my money to head there soon." She picks up the glass. "Teach me more slang. So I can talk to important men like you when I make it to New York."

Too bad that's not an invitation to join her. Like all kittens, she believes where she grew up to be the worst place to be stuck.

"Here's not so bad."

She swirls the amber liquid in the glass. "Isn't it? Isn't opening a speakeasy in a cave one step above using a hay barn next to the hog pens?"

I pat the top of the bar recently built from Benny's Ten Penny Nails crates. "Cave draws in plenty of customers," I lie. "Speakeasies in cities are all the same. Folks will sell their mothers to let loose in a place like this one." It's somewhat true, but all people really care about is a place to drink without interference from the fuzz.

She downs her liquor before she glances around the chamber lit with oil lamps. "Can I tell you a secret?"

Anytime a dame wishes to share a confidence, it's a promising sign. I slide a full glass into her empty hand, caught in the spell of her impish smile. "You can tell *me* anything."

She plays coy in a way I've seen on dames' faces a thousand times. "You'll think it's silly."

Country mouse or city mouse, dames are all the same. But something about this girl... intrigues me. I turn on my charm. "Nothing *you* say will be silly."

She gives a shy pause. "I shaved my legs for the first time to come here. My mother will burn my Ouija board if she finds out. She's so Victorian."

I give a laugh—the kind I offer women to placate them. With her, this laugh feels wrong.

"I'm sure, in her youth, your mother did something wild."

"What? Not wear the proper number of petticoats?" She holds out an unlit cigarette.

With a flick of my thumbnail across a matchhead, a flame bursts to life. I hold the dancing flame to the cig's end until she inhales, causing the tip to glow.

She releases a few puffs through rounded lips, but she only achieves messy little clouds. "How *do* people make smoke rings?"

I flash a grin. "Never could do that myself."

Two young men approach. They nod to... I'll have to get her name. I set both men up with fresh drinks and collect payment. After they return to a group of flappers, I slip the money into my waistcoat pocket.

"Why do you do that?"

"Do what?"

"Put some sales in the cigar box and others in your pocket."

Observant little vamp. "I'll tell you, but you have to do something for me."

She takes a drag on her cig. "And what's that?"

"Tell me your name."

She doesn't hesitate. "Florence. Florence Gale."

I lean on the bar. It needs more sanding to be smooth enough to wipe over and over—an old trick to create the illusion the bartender's always busy. "To escape with at least part of my earnings if the fuzz show up."

"No one's going to raid—"

I put a finger to her lips. "Never say that word. It clears a place out."

She pulls back—a little. "Nobody in this town will report you. Only law is one ancient constable, and I hear he can't hit the broad side of a barn—even wearing his cheaters."

I hear the same. Seems he's one of the few townspeople living with poor health. Even my old widow landlady is spry enough to keep up with all of these gyrating flappers.

Florence takes another puff. "I don't see how anyone in Mystic Springs can complain. So many people from the surrounding towns are spending dough on gas. Why, the station gets so busy it runs out of Baby Ruth bars." She leans in. "I hear someone's even building a hotel."

"I'm building the hotel."

She crushes out her cig, burning a spot on my bar. Her eyes drop in disappointment. "You're planning to stay *here*? Not return to New York?"

I bet you'll be my best gal until we get there. It's a shame she's set on leaving—I like this dame. Though not enough to share why this nowhere burg holds an appeal for me that the Big Apple cannot.

Florence makes a point of glancing at her watch among the bangles on her arm.

"Come now, it's still early and there's plenty of booze." She's still worth a little persuasion on my part.

She reaches into the fishbowl to snag a matchbook. "Yes, but my friends, who I've ignored all night to talk to you, are from Rolla. We have to be in bed before the roosters crow or our mothers will never allow us out again."

"I hear Rolla is growing." And the speakeasy's closest competition.

She flutters her eyelashes. "Nearly fifteen thousand people."

Flattery always works to get information.

"You're one smart cookie, Florence. How are the drinking places in a town that size?"

"Okay, but none are as big as this cave. And out here there's no chance of running into my mother's friends, who are staunch supporters of the Volstead Act banning liquor."

"Don't you worry. I won't let the cat out of the bag." I lean across the bar, hoping to steal a goodnight kiss.

She puts up her hands. "Not to be a killjoy, but this bank's closed on first encounters."

I hate for Florence to go. But if the connection between us is real, she'll be back. Besides, engaging in a too-close relationship can lead to visits from shotgun-toting fathers. And with this gal, I don't want to take advantage. She's got something magical about her.

The evening's fun at an end, I collect the stray glasses and bottles with care. Rock floors don't make it easy to keep my over-head down. Or the costs of bringing in and housing that cow-town jazz band, but they're worth the expense. I plan to build some rooms in back of the hotel just for them. Even in the sticks, everyone loves Black musicians and the tunes they play—but better if they're heard and not seen.

I leave the washtub near the cave entrance. I need to hire more help, to cut down on me driving back and forth to town. Takes the cabbage. My still, hidden in a cave chamber behind a quilt for a door, produces a new batch of money-making gin every three days. Soon, I'll get another still and add a whiskey operation.

I grab a tin cup for a taste. Something about the spring's water enhances the flavor. It's so good that I believe this is what heaven tastes like.

"The spring is not meant for your kind of firewater."

I spin at the deep voice. My hand pats my side for my heater —nope, it's back at the bar.

In the dim lantern light, my visitor—a Native man—glows a ghostly hue. Or maybe the hue means he's an actual specter. He's got obsidian hair and lined tan skin, and even sports a Union bluecoat over a breastplate a Spanish conquistador might have worn.

It takes more than this to frighten a born-and-bred New Yorker. "Let me guess. I'm encroaching on your sacred ground."

"No white man has ever concerned himself about our sacred ground."

"Can't argue with that. I've met people from all over the world. You're my first Indian."

"I am Osage."

I nod. Not sure what I'll do if he answers yes, I ask, "Is this your spring?"

"Water is a gift to the earth from Wa-kon-tah, the great mystery spirit. Not meant to be made into the firewater that ruins my people. And others."

"I could promise you I'll only serve the gin to my kind."

"You don't understand. Your people never understand. The spring offers powerful magic, but *only* if used for good."

This fella—or whatever—speaks pretty good English.

"Oh, I know the water is magical." I smirk. "It grows cabbage."

Not even a twitch. Guess the latest slang is lost on him.

The Osage shakes his head, an echo of the same disappointment in me my father has. "I give you a warning. The spring water will take care of you. But if you do nature's medicine wrong, it will cost you."

A cryptic message, but it's not convincing enough to prevent me from running my speakeasy. "Cost me how?"

The Native's eyes pierce into mine. "I live many summers when I am made scout for the Bluecoats. At the battle of Huzzah Valley, I am shot. Forgotten for dead by the Bluecoats, I follow Wa-kon-tah through forests for many days to this spring. I drink. My breath returns to me, and I promise to care for this water."

I don't know how much of his tale has truth in it. So far, he only asks me not to make booze from the spring water. It's possible considering, in a few more weeks, I'll have enough kale to bring in outside gin and some rye. But if the whisky made with spring water is half as good as the gin, it will beat out Jack Daniels's taste and their profits. True magic.

"What happens if I keep distilling?"

The Osage disappears before my eyes, but not before I hear a *thunk* as a tomahawk splits open the bottom of my pot. The hootch flows out with no time to save any.

But that hatchet? Having been a collector of unusual souvenirs during the Great War, I plan to keep this one.

Or will I?

The tomahawk is gone.

I crouch to examine the ragged gash. The damage points to the Osage being real and not a representative of ghostly spirits.

Now that's a good name for my speakeasy. Ghostly Spirits.

I've enough gin in storage to open tomorrow night. But the repairs on the still will require a few days and a trip to the hardware store in Rolla for supplies.

And there's that dame I'm digging. I find Florence's house, and I can drop by to "say it with flowers," as the ad says.

Mornings mean I meet the sun's brightness with a squint when I leave the cave. *This* morning, I meet the impact of a rifle butt crunching my nose.

My head pounds when I force my eyes open. Two men drag me through the woods, then dump me on the ground. Wetness covers my face.

One of the men kicks me in the ribs, forcing me to roll over. I hear footsteps before the unmistakable click of a Tommy gun bolt forced into the open position.

"Rexford, you think you can make a fool of me? You didn't learn your lesson back in New York. Here you are again, operating in a territory without paying the tribute."

"Forgive me if I didn't realize the Bible Belt was your territory, Jimmy." My sardonic tone earns me another kick in the ribs. Then a few more, until I lose count. Above me, Jimmy rambles on about how no one insults him like this, while I ponder how he found me.

That Osage sure meant business when warning me about punishment for my abusing the spring water. Damn, that was fast. Never even got to ignore my chance at redemption.

"Listen, Jimmy. This is a whole new untapped area. We can—"

This earns me a kick to the face.

"You still don't get how a territory works. Unlucky for you that my colleague, Mr. Capone, pays attention when he travels down here for relaxation. Unlike you, he respects the code."

Gotta love how gangsters have rules.

His two thugs jerk me to my feet.

Jimmy points his Thompson at me. "Want to blubber for your life like all the others?"

"Never." I wish for a mouthful of blood to spit at him.

"Then we make this slow." Jimmy the Gil trades his Thompson for a shotgun from one of his thugs.

"Jimmy, you kill me out here and no one back in New York will know. They'll all still believe I bested you."

The blast tears into my shoulder and upper chest. So much for logic and reason. The force throws me back into the pool. Sinking, I hear Jimmy's words.

"We'll wait until he drowns, or we'll fill him with enough holes to kiss the bottom."

I'm not sure what's more painful, the wounds from hot iron pellets decimating my shoulder or the biting chill of the coldest water I've ever been submerged in—and I'm a member of the Coney Island Polar Bear Club. I drift downward, arms akimbo with tiny blood ribbons marking my progress. My eyes gaze upward through the clear, freezing water, as the green of the forest overhead brightens.

Then there's no longer hot fire in my shoulder. No feeling in any of my limbs, really. Time ceases like magic as the water becomes comfortable. Even when my lungs remember I need to breathe, they don't burn. Mouth open, my body accepts the water. No struggle. No choking. My lungs fill with liquid, but I'm not drowning. My body merges with the water that has become my healer and restorer. As it returns life to me, I gain a new understanding.

A covenant can transpire. In exchange for what the spring offers me, I must protect it from evil purposes. From the kind of men who put me in this water—or men like me—with plans of illegal liquor.

Trapped in this state of not dead—and not sure if I can seek a life of righteousness—I sink into the depths. My only true regret is I will lose the opportunity of a life with my Florence. As I think of her impish smile, pain hooks me under my armpits. A jerk upward lifts me to the surface.

"Stand!" commands the Osage.

I fight for my footing to comply. Once I do, I wipe the water from my eyes. I float, my lower body hidden in the spring pool. I press a hand to my chest and then my shoulder. My suit and shirt are shredded from the buckshot, but I have no wounds. I look to the Osage, who waits next to me. "Where are the men who shot me?

The Osage remains stoic, as if the events of today are normal for him. "They leave and take all the firewater you make from the spring."

"And you let them?" I break for the shore, where I turn and ask, "Which way did—"

The Osage is gone without so much as a ripple in the water.

What a conundrum. I can't allow Jimmy to keep the spring water gin—I need that booze to open my speakeasy tonight. Also, the spring water in the gin makes people feel too good. The people from this area who drink in my cave may not notice it much. But what of people far from Mystic Springs? Once others imbibe and learn the water's true properties, they will flock here in droves.

I barrel down the road in my truck, wishing for my heater. Jimmy won't hand over the gin on a kind word alone.

I never think of the heart-racing speed of twenty-two miles per hour as slow, but I push the Ford past it, racing by cow pasture after cow pasture. At the fork leading back to the highway, I catch up with Jimmy's truck where it rests in the grass.

His two goons sprawl prone in the field as if they fell there and never got back up. The handle of the Osage's tomahawk peeks out from the smashed windshield on the driver's side. No Osage in sight, but behind the steering wheel I discover Jimmy the Gil. His skin has no color, and his hair is pure white. I see no visible wounds, but his open eyes see nothing.

I rifle through Jimmy's pockets and remove several large bundles of lettuce—a fitting inheritance.

My damp pockets bulging, it's time to handle the gin. I grab the tomahawk and go for the crates. I open the first crate of my homemade gin and toss the contents to the ground. What Mason jars don't break, I smash with the tomahawk. I repeat my sad process until nothing remains of what I've cooked.

I sink the hatchet's blade into the wood of the truck bed and return to my own contraption. Before I drive away, I offer a salute to broken glass, ruined hootch, and the now missing tomahawk.

I offer a rectangular box wrapped in butcher paper to Florence, who sits close to me on a bench in the town's park.

She takes the package and her demeanor shifts to that of an

excited child. "You got me a gift!" She tears the paper. "A Ouija board?"

"Just in case your mother burned yours."

"She did not, but if she catches me with two, she'll lock me in my room, thinking divination is more than my hobby."

"I couldn't stand it if she forbade you to return to Mystic Springs."

She looks up through her lashes. "There's no more speakeasy in a cave. What reason will I have to visit Mystic Springs?"

"I can think of one." I smile. "And there will be a speakeasy. A proper one, under my hotel, complete with secret access and password to enter. I've got an agreement with a supplier from Kansas City for the liquor."

"You're not going to distill your own giggle water?"

Not a chance... well, maybe an occasional batch for special occasions only.

"Safer to just have the products shipped in." I wink. "You up for a little transaction at the cave?"

Florence purses her lips. "What makes you think the bank's open to you?"

"Now, honey, I just thought we could try out your new Ouija board. Pretty sure we can find some spirits there protecting the spring."

"Oh, you saw the Indian."

Well, what do you know.

"He's an Osage, actually."

Florence remains playful, with a hint of seriousness. "I'll tell you another secret. The women in my family sometimes see apparitions no one else can. But if you see him too, he must be real."

"Not so sure what you mean by real. But after my encounters, I've a lot of questions about Mystic Springs." I grasp her hand. "Just the kind we can answer together."

"Come on, Rexford!" Florence tugs at me. "If we go to the cave right now, we can try to call forth your Osage friend."

Mystic Springs? Somebody got that right.

WILLIAM SCHLICHTER

William Schlichter is an award-winning screenwriter and author of science fiction and horror, who enjoys exploring the phantas-magorical world of the undead. Fan favorites include his popular *No Room in Hell* zombie series, *SKA: Serial Killers Anonymous* about a serial killer support group, and his fantasy noir *Sirgrus Blackmane*. His full-length feature script, *Incinta*, is a 2014 New Orleans Horror Film Festival finalist, while his TV spec script episode of *The Walking Dead* placed third in the 2013 Broadcast Education Association National Festival of Media Arts.

When not writing, William enjoys spending time on the convention circuit, and teaching acting, composition, and creative writing.

https://sandmenandzombies.com

BEETLESTONE

STAN C. SMITH

"LOOK AT YOU, *trying to blend in with normal people. You ain't normal. You're a loser. Just call it quits. Go back to the springs and end your misery.*"

Susana stared at the menu in front of her, trying to ignore Dark Susana.

"*You can't ignore me, loser. You know I'm right.*"

Susana raised a hand to flag down a fella who looked like he worked in this place.

He came to her table and raised his bushy brows.

She pointed to a battered jukebox in the corner. "Does that thing still work? I could use some noise."

He gave her a lopsided grin. "That's just for looks, darlin'. I got a decent sound system, though. This here's a honky-tonk, after all. But I don't ever crank it up over the lunch hour."

"*You're such an idiot,*" Dark Susana said. "*Even this lame fella can see it. Look at the pity in his eyes. Even he knows you don't deserve to exist.*"

Susana rubbed her forehead and whispered, "Just shut—"

"You okay, darlin'?"

She let out a breath and put her hands on the table. "Just having a turd of a day."

Without being invited, the fella spun a chair and sat down across from her. "Name's Judd. This here's my place, such as it is. Wanna talk about your turd of a day? I'm a good listener."

"Oh, he feels sorry for you. Because you're a loser."

The fella reached across the table and put a finger on her menu. "The Mystic burger is so good it'll curl your toes. Unless you ain't had breakfast yet—then the Deer Stand combo is the way to go."

She ignored this. "What do you know about the springs?"

He nodded, looking thoughtful. "About as much as anyone living in Mystic Springs. Why?"

"I think it's all a lie. That water don't work for nothin'."

He jutted his chin toward the side of her head. "Is that why your hair's wet? You took a dip in the springs?"

"I did. And I'm still having a turd of a day. That water don't work."

"Your whole life's one big turd. Tell this jerk to buzz off so you can get on with it."

"Shut up!" Susana hissed.

Judd squinted at her. "You got the voices in your head?"

She nodded. "One voice. Going on ten years." Susana used to keep this a secret, but she didn't care anymore. She'd lost everything because of Dark Susana, and coming to Mystic Springs was going to end one of two ways—she'd either kill the witch inside her, or vice versa. No point in keeping secrets, even from strangers like this Judd fella.

Judd puckered his mouth to one side. "Where'd you take a dip? In the public spring, where all the tourists go?"

"Isn't that where we're supposed to?"

He shrugged. "Most folks do. Some seem happy with the

results, others not so much. Most are just curious and expect nothing. There's more than one spring, you know."

This got her attention. "Really?"

"Sure. Plenty of others on private properties. The public spring is fine—it brings folks to town. That's good for business. People say, though, the private springs are where you wanna go if you really want the good stuff. I met one guy, came all the way from Boston. He was a mess, that guy. Too many years of stress and hard drinking. I sat down with him, just like I'm sittin' with you now. I could see he was at the end of his tether. So, I gave him a tip on where to go *besides* the public spring. Next morning, he's back in here again, ordering the Deer Stand combo and grinning like a cheese-shire cat." Judd flashed his teeth, maybe trying to share what a cheese-shire cat looked like. "That old boy thanked me about a hundred times." Judd's eyes gleamed. "I figure I saved his life."

"What a crock. Just tell this idiot it's too late for you. You're too pathetic."

Susana felt a tear welling in her left eye. "I said shut up!"

Judd puckered his mouth again. "You keep telling that voice to shut up, but I don't think it's listening."

Susana wiped the tear away. "Let me guess, you'll tell me what spring to go to for a price."

He scrunched his brows, looking genuinely hurt. "I don't want your money. In fact, your meal's on me. Just tell me what you're hungry for."

"I want to know which spring to go to."

He frowned. "What's your name, darlin'?"

"Susana."

"You thinking about suicide, Susana?"

She stared at her hands for moment. "Yeah."

He let out a long whistle. "You seen any doctors for it?"

"Three. Don't got insurance to pay them no more, and they were worthless... to me, anyhow." She leaned forward on her elbows, more tears forming. "Please."

"It ain't but spring water, Susana. Most people know it ain't really—"

"I don't care. Maybe I just need something to give me hope."

"There ain't no hope for the hopeless. Give it up, loser."

Susana's eyelids fluttered as she tried to keep her focus.

Judd sighed. "You got a phone?"

"Not anymore."

He pulled his phone from his pocket, tapped it a few times, and held it out. "See that pin on the map? That's Thomas Beetlestone's property. He's... well, he's an oddball. Stay clear of his house. But there's a spring on his land—might be what you're looking for." He zoomed in and showed her the spot, and where she could park her car without Beetlestone seeing her. He handed her the phone and told her to zoom out to see how to get there from the Deer Stand Café and Honky-Tonk.

"What makes his spring special?" she asked.

He shrugged. "Might be Beetlestone is immortal."

She blinked. "Huh?"

"Probably ain't true. Some people think he is, though. On account of him always looking the same." Judd pushed his chair back to stand up. "I don't tell many about *that* particular spring. But then, I don't meet many with voices in their heads and thoughts of hurting themselves. You wanted something to give you hope, so...." He got to his feet. "What'll it be, the Mystic burger?"

Susana also stood up. "Not hungry anymore. Got some-where to be."

Three miles out on a gravel road called Toad Suck Drive, Susana realized she'd gone too far. Thomas Beetlestone's house was now right in front of her, a dead-end property. She had no choice but to pull into his driveway to turn around. As she came to a stop, the man's house caught her eye. She lowered her grimy window to get a better look.

The house was simple, built out of thick cedar logs, but it was neat and tidy, with no trash on the porch or in the yard. Susana squinted. Nope, she wasn't seeing things—the logs of the porch and house were carved with fancy designs. Like one of those New Zealand Maori buildings she'd seen in a National Geographic at the shrink's office.

That Judd fella had said Beetlestone was an oddball.

"Go up and knock. Maybe he'll be a serial killer and put you out of your misery."

"I hate you!" Susana shouted, throwing the car into reverse.

"I beg your pardon?"

Susana froze. It was a man's voice—and there he was, coming around the side of the cedar-log house. Toward Susana's car.

"Oh, goody! Serial killer time."

"This happens to be private property, young miss," the man said with an English accent that seemed out of place.

Susana pushed the button to raise her window, but stopped. This joker looked harmless enough. She turned off her car, threw open her door, and got out. "Mr. Beetlestone?"

He came to a stop, looking like a black-haired, black-bearded Jesus. "And how would you know that?"

"I got a favor to ask. Can I go to your spring?"

"You are such an idiot. Do you even hear yourself?"

"Miss, do I know you?" Beetlestone tilted his head to one side as he stared. "You seem... familiar."

Susana pointed into the forest surrounding his house. "It's

that way, ain't it? I can find it myself." She started in the direction the spring should be.

"See here, young miss, this is private—"

She wheeled on him. "I don't care!" This outburst surprised even her—she usually only yelled at Dark Susana—but now there was no turning back. "I ain't no young miss. I'm thirty-eight. I just need to go to your spring. Please, I won't bother nothin'."

"*Please, I won't bother nothin',*" Dark Susana mocked.

The man looked flabbergasted. "You most certainly may not. Take your automobile and go away. I value my privacy."

Susana felt tears coming again. She was tired of crying, always crying. "Look, mister. I just need to—" She choked, unable to say more. So, she ran into the woods.

"Stop! It's not safe back there."

Susana was beyond caring. One way or another, her misery would end today. She ran, pushing through brush and thorns.

"*That's it. Run like a wounded deer. Serial killer will catch you and cut you into little pieces.*"

"Shut up! I'm tired of you ruining my life."

"*Oh, are you gonna cry again?*"

The spring couldn't be too far. Susana plowed through a stand of cedar saplings, which whipped and scratched her face. The ground beneath her feet disappeared. For a second, she was falling. She glimpsed water below. Her feet hit the water, then the rocky bottom, and her knees buckled. Her head slammed into something hard. Cold wetness engulfed her just before everything went black.

"Can you hear me, miss?"

Susana sensed she was dreaming, trying to get out of water thicker than molasses, but her arms wouldn't move. She wanted to wake up, but her eyes wouldn't open.

"Miss, are you aware?"

She struggled, but the molasses water wouldn't give up its grip. She managed to let out a moan.

"You *are* waking up."

Someone patted her cheek twice, breaking her free of the sticky water. Her eyes fluttered.

The man stared down at her. Black hair, black beard, serial-killer eyes. "You gave me a fright, young miss."

She swallowed. "I'm... thirty-eight."

"So you have said. You took a grievous knock to your head, thirty-eight-year-old miss. You're quite lucky, you know."

She blinked. "You gonna kill me?"

"Good heavens. It seems you hardly need help with that task."

"Who are you?"

"You already know who I am. The question is, who are you?"

"Susana. That's all you need to know."

"Lovely name. Susana, do you make a habit of trespassing?"

"I needed to go to your spring."

"Well, you certainly found it."

Susana turned her head. She was on a bed, in a room with polished-cedar walls. The furniture looked handmade. "How did I get here?"

"I carried you."

"How long ago?"

"Yesterday."

"And you didn't call an ambulance? You *do* plan to kill me." She started to sit up. "I'll scratch your eyes out, I swear!"

He stepped back. "My goodness! You are rather feral, aren't you?"

Feeling dizzy, she sank back onto the bed. "I don't take no crap off no one, if that's what you mean."

"Then I shall avoid offering you any crap." He picked up a cup that looked to be carved out of wood. "I can, however, offer more of the spring water you seemed willing to die for."

With effort, she sat up again, took the cup, and downed every drop. Best water she'd ever tasted. "Can I have more?"

He nodded, took the cup, and left the room.

Susana gazed at the cedar-log walls, the bookshelves filled with old and new books, the hand-carved doodads. She muttered, "See? He ain't no serial killer. You don't know nothing."

Silence.

Susana muttered again. "You don't have something mean to say?"

More silence.

"Dark Susana?"

Beetlestone came back in. He handed her the wooden cup, and she downed it again. "Dark Susana?"

Beetlestone frowned. "I beg your pardon?"

"Dark Susana, say something!"

Nothing.

"Are you alright?" Beetlestone asked.

She closed her eyes, listening. Nothing but silence. And calm. Could it really be possible? She opened her eyes. "She's gone."

"Who's gone?"

"The voice is gone! I call her Dark Susana because she wants me to kill myself. Always has, going on ten years. She's gone now."

He nodded like he understood something he could never understand in a million years.

"What?" Susana demanded.

"Is Dark Susana why you insisted on going to my spring? Did you believe the water would help you?"

"I wanted it to."

"Well, it did."

She stared. No. Good things like this never happened to her. "Dark Susana, say something, you stupid witch."

Nothing.

"Are you trying to convince yourself of the obvious?" Beetlestone asked.

"She's really gone."

Beetlestone stepped to a cedar dresser and returned with a hand mirror. "Examine your forehead, Susana." He held up the mirror.

She looked. Then she touched her forehead. There was a scar. A big one. But new skin had already grown over it. She turned to Beetlestone. "You lied. You said you carried me here yesterday!"

He pulled the mirror back. "I did not lie. You came here yesterday. You fell into my spring, ingesting the water. And I gave you more water just now. The water is healing you. Are these not the results you hoped for?"

She opened her mouth but didn't know what to say.

"Susana, where is your husband? Your family?"

She watched his face, looking for serial-killer clues. "I ain't made for husbands or families."

His brows shot up. "Care to explain?"

"*You* explain! Who are you? What's an Englishman doing here in the Ozark woods?"

"I am here for the same reason you are—the spring water."

He replaced the mirror on the dresser, then came back and stood beside the bed. "You see, I cannot leave this place. Oh, I've tried many times, but I cannot. Unless I wish to wither away and die."

"That don't make no sense."

He frowned. "I shall endeavor to ignore your butchery of the King's English. Listen carefully, young miss, for mine is a tale you've not imagined. I am telling you this because... well, because I assume you also cannot leave this place."

Susana threw the sheet back, ready to run from this crazy man's house, then she paused. She was wearing a long, white nightshirt. "Where's my clothes?"

He pointed to a neatly folded stack of clothes on a chair. "Susana, I am an honorable man. I did not impose upon your vulnerability. Your clothes were drenched, and I simply wished you to be comfortable."

Feeling dizzy again, she stumbled to the dresser. "Turn around, pervert!"

He turned away. "Would you like to hear my story as you get dressed?"

"You better talk fast," she said, pulling on her jeans. "Someone in town told me you was immortal. Start with that."

"Immortal, did you say?"

"Yeah, *immortal*! Why would people say that?"

"Oh dear. And despite my efforts to remain hermitic." He sighed. "Very well. I came from England in 1873."

"You're a liar! You ain't no older than me."

"A liar? This from the woman who no longer must listen to Dark Susana. Do you want to hear my story or not?"

Susana was pulling off the nightshirt. "You got about thirty seconds."

"I came to see America. On a tour of leisure, if you will. Riding the railways, viewing the sights—all that rubbish. On the fateful day of July 21st of 1873, near Adair, Iowa, my train was derailed and robbed by none other than the scoundrel Jesse James and his gang."

Without looking at her, he pulled a piece of wood and a knife from his pocket and started whittling. "Injured, I escaped the train with the few possessions I had. I was later found, delirious and at death's door, and taken to a hospital, where I partially recovered. However, to my mortification and discomfiture, I was plagued by intestinal distress. Thus began an exhaustive search for relief, leading me eventually to Mystic Springs. Here I found my cure, but here I must stay, as the cure vanishes upon my departure. Over the years, I have changed my forename occasionally, in hopes of convincing the townsfolk I have passed my property on to my son, then my grandson, and then my great-grandson. Apparently, some suspect this to be the ruse that it is."

Now dressed, Susana started tying her shoes. "You expect me to believe that crock of horse hockey?"

"I have no expectations, as I've not had the occasion to tell anyone before you."

"Then why dump that crap on me?"

He huffed. "I have my reasons. And I am certain I know what is responsible for this calamitous kettle of fish."

She rose to her feet. "I'm leaving. If you try to kill me, I'll gut you with my own teeth."

"Good God, woman! Please stop assuming I wish to kill you."

She pointed a finger at his face, warning him to stay back, then she walked out of the bedroom, through another room filled with more hand-carved furniture and doodads, and out the front door. She found her keys still in her car, and seconds later she tore down Toad Suck Drive, throwing gravel and dust.

Twenty minutes later, Susana came to a stop in Beetlestone's driveway again. Slamming her car door, she stomped onto the porch and yanked the door open without knocking.

"No need to go inside, Susana."

She wheeled around. There he was, sitting in a stupid cedar rocking chair on his stupid porch. She stomped over to him. "What the hell, man?"

He wrinkled his brows. "Please articulate your question."

"I get five freaking miles away, and my head starts feeling like it's in a microwave. And you know who came back?"

"Dark Susana?"

"Yes! So, it was either drive back here, or drive off the next bridge to make it all stop!"

"I warned you, did I not?"

"Why is this happening?"

"*It* doesn't want you to leave."

She glared at him, ready to spit nails. "What do you mean, *it?*"

He leaned forward, elbows on his knees. "I have not finished my story." He waved his hand to a second stupid rocking chair.

"I'm too mad to sit."

He shrugged slightly. "Tell me, Susana, before I continue, what exactly brought you to Mystic Springs?"

"Don't change the subject!"

"This *is* the subject."

Feeling like a trapped raccoon, she started pacing. "Fine. I came for the springs, just like you did in your horse-hockey story. I was done. Didn't have no job, no health insurance, *and* hardly no money. No family—haven't seen none of them since I ran away when I was a girl. No husband, no kids—like I said, I ain't made for that. Then Dark Susana showed up ten years back, and she commenced to hammering nails into my coffin. Couldn't get her outta my head. Finally, I came here. This fella in town told me about your spring. He could see I was driving on fumes." She turned to Beetlestone. "Now I'm here. Dark Susana's gone and my noggin don't hurt. But for how long?"

He nodded slowly. "For as long as you stay here, near *it*."

"Near *what*? The spring?"

"Indirectly, I suppose. *It* wants to be near the spring, and you need to be near *it*."

Susana growled and raised a fist. "You ever been punched by a hillbilly woman? I'll hit you hard enough to kill you three times over *if you don't tell me what's goin' on!*"

Beetlestone actually smiled. "You, Susana, are a veritable compendium of colloquialisms. I believe my long life is about to become more interesting."

"You think I'm staying here?"

"Well, there is that bridge you mentioned. Such a messy end, though."

Susana stomped her foot on the porch. Dammit, Beetlestone was right. Now she wanted to live, to see what life could be like without that witch in her head. And this was the only place where she could.

"I'm not a bad fellow once you get to know me," he said.

"You expect me to live here, in *your* house? You want me to be your sex slave or something?"

"Good heavens, no. I shall build you a hut in the woods. Or perhaps you would prefer a burrow or a nest, as other wild creatures do."

She raised her fist again. "Go on, keep insulting me. See what happens."

He held up his hands as if surrendering. "Point taken. My

offer to build you a hut is sincere, though. We'll call it a cottage. Seriously, Susana, you cannot leave if *it* wants you to stay. I am offering my friendship and service. I'm quite handy with wood and tools. God knows, this place could use a woman's sensibilities after a hundred and fifty years of gentlemanly inclinations." He extended a hand, like he wanted to shake. "I propose a cessation of hostilities. A truce, if you will."

She stared down at the hand. Was this guy for real? She sighed. Well, he *had* nursed her back to health. And Dark Susana was gone. She took his hand and shook it.

He nodded once and leaned back in his rocking chair, looking as happy as a fat groundhog.

"Tell me what *it* is," she said.

He studied her for a moment. "Are you sure? Some revelations can alter your ideologies, you know."

"Don't know what that means and don't care."

"Very well." He got to his feet and waved toward the other chair again. "Please make yourself comfortable. I shall return shortly." He went inside.

Still not wanting to sit, Susana paced the porch. She was mad, but also happier than she'd been in years. Somehow, she knew Dark Susana wouldn't be back as long as Susana stayed near the spring. Or near whatever *it* was. Thomas Beetlestone was more annoying than a cat in heat, but if he built her a cottage, maybe she could stay clear of him most of the time.

She stopped pacing. Her throat tightened. She could never leave this place, ever?

The door opened. Beetlestone stepped out, carrying a backpack—the kind kids took to school.

"If I can't leave this place, how am I supposed to get me a job? Or go to the store, or doctor?"

He placed the pack on one of the rockers. "If my hunch is

correct, you no longer need doctors. For employment, you can help me. I would enjoy the company, particularly if you refrain from threatening me with physical violence. For short outings, such as to the store, we will have to take *it* with us." He nodded toward the backpack. "However, *it* prefers not to be away for any length of time. Being a gentleman, I will accompany you, of course—if not for your sake, then for *its* sake." Again, he nodded at the pack.

She was almost afraid to ask. "What's in there?"

He unzipped the pack and hauled out a blue ball. This was all Susana could think of to call it. It was the size of a volleyball, but instead of being smooth, it was full of holes and crevices, like a long blue wire had been wrapped loosely. In some places, she could even see through it.

"What... is that thing?"

"I cannot say what *it* is, though I do know what *it does*." He held the ball cupped in one hand. "This, Susana, is what gives the Mystic Springs their renowned properties, bringing visitors from afar to seek their benefits. I found this object in the spring when I came here in 1874. *It* is the reason I purchased this property and have remained here since."

"You're talkin' nonsense, man."

"My spring is connected, by underground channels, to the other springs in the general area. When I remove this object from my spring, the other springs gradually lose their healing properties. When I put *it* back into my spring, the healing properties return. I have learned this by experimentation. Upon my visits to town, I listen to the folks talking, thus I learn of the springs' effects. If I remove this object from my spring for too long, visitors to the public spring become increasingly disgruntled, leading to fewer visitors, thus decreasing commerce and satisfaction among the townsfolk. I then return this object to my spring for a period of time. However, if I leave *it* in my spring too long, I fear the health benefits will become so pronounced as to draw too much attention to Mystic Springs, embroiling the town in power struggles that may not end well for the good townsfolk. You see, I am a guardian of the town's good fortune, though no one knows this but myself, and now you."

Susana just shook her head. Had Beetlestone lost his marbles?

He went on. "When I venture to town, I take *it* with me in this rucksack, and *it* keeps me from suffering as I would without *it*. However, if I linger too long, *it* becomes insistent to return. I have learned the hard way not to resist." He stared at Susana, then frowned. "You do not believe a word I am saying, do you?"

She stayed quiet.

"I see you need proof." He turned the ball in his hands, like he was looking for something, then he pointed to a certain spot. "Insert your finger there."

She eyed the hole. "Why?"

He waited.

"Fine." She held her middle finger up to him, then turned her hand over and shoved the finger into the hole.

Susana felt like she was falling off a cliff. Her stomach churned, and her feet lifted off the porch. With Beetlestone grinning, she floated there, her toes dangling inches above the cedar planks. She yanked her finger back, then dropped to the porch, barely catching herself before falling. "What the heck was that?"

"Proof that this object is extraordinary."

"Where the heck did that thing come from?"

He shrugged. "I have theories."

"*It* must be from space. Aliens musta brought *it* here."

"I prefer to imagine kind folks from far in the future have brought *it*, placing *it* in the spring in order for *its* healing properties to benefit their distant ancestors. Perhaps this is why *it* refuses to be taken far from my spring. *It* belongs here, where *it* can influence the water, thus helping people like you and me."

She stepped closer and pointed. "What happens if I stick my finger in *that* hole?"

He yanked the ball back. "No! I do not recommend it." He turned the ball in his hands again, searching. "Here. I do, however, recommend you experience this." He pointed to a different hole. Then he paused, like he wasn't sure. His pointing finger even trembled.

"What?" she asked.

He held the ball out, still pointing at the hole with a shaking finger.

Susana was too curious to not try. She pushed her finger in.

She was no longer standing on the porch. Instead, she was kneeling in a garden, picking green beans. Thomas Beetlestone knelt beside her. They weren't speaking, but Susana felt comforted by him being there. The garden disappeared. Now she was in a cedar-walled workshop. She and Thomas were assembling a rocking chair, next to a row of others they'd already made, ready to be sold in town. Holding the frame steady, she glanced at him. He smiled at her as he fitted a chair leg into its hole in the seat. His smile made her tingle inside, and she threw a handful of sawdust at him, making him laugh. The workshop vanished. Now Susana was on a cedar-post bed. She was warm, comfortable, waiting. She heard water splashing from someone washing up, then Thomas stepped into the bedroom, wearing the same long, white nightshirt he had put on Susana that day long ago when she'd fallen in the spring and busted open her head. One scene after another flashed through her mind, scenes of her and Thomas Beetlestone, extending far into the future.

Finally, the scenes faded, and Susana pulled her finger from the strange object.

Beetlestone was watching her. "What did you see?"

She took several seconds to shake it off. She had been so happy in these visions, as if Dark Susana and the rest of her miserable life were only faded memories. "Was that our future?"

He shook his head. "I don't believe a future can be written in stone. But I believe you saw a *possible* future."

"What did you see when *you* tried it?" she asked.

"Exactly what you saw, I imagine. However, it was long ago when I first put my finger into this particular hole. I had almost forgotten what your face looked like until you appeared yesterday."

Susana gazed into his eyes. She didn't feel the same passion now that she'd felt in her visions, but she assumed the visions were at least possible. Flustered, she turned away from him, staring off into the woods. She pointed. "That's where I want my cottage. By them big oaks there. For now."

From behind her, he said, "So, you will stay?"

She faced him again. "Better than driving off a bridge, ain't it?"

He nodded. "Wise decision." He held up the strange ball. "It will be most refreshing to have someone else here to help me look after this temperamental thing."

She eyed him for a moment. "Mr. Beetlestone, can I call you Tom?"

"Absolutely not." He grinned. "I am Thomas."

She rolled her eyes. "Do you even know how annoying you can be?"

His eyes sparkled. "Indeed, I do. I have been annoying myself for many years."

STAN C. SMITH

Stan's secret formula? Create strange worlds filled with even stranger creatures. Drop in unsuspecting characters. Shake vigorously. The results are always fun. Stan lives with his wife Trish deep in the Ozark Forest of Missouri, where creatures are more docile than those in his novels. His goal is to stimulate your sense of wonder, get your heart pounding, and keep you reading late into the night. His books are for anyone who loves adventure, discovery, and mind-bending surprises.

Want a new short story every two weeks?
Subscribe to Stan's newsletter: http://www.stancsmith.com

THE FAIRY'S SPRING

ARIA LANGRIM

October: **Full Falling Leaves Moon**

Pamina breached the surface of the spring. A breath, then she sank back under, surrounded by a silence so complete she could hear the blood rush in her veins and by a dark so deep it felt like she hung suspended above an endless void.

Pamina kicked until she surfaced again, this time closer to the edge—damp soil over stone that dropped away in sheer, water-smoothed walls. She grasped at whatever she could reach —grass, roots, reeds—to claw her way out. Her arms, her legs, and her pale blue sundress were covered in mud by the time she dropped to the ground, coughing up water and shivering on the grass.

She'd lost her shoes scrambling out of the water. Her locket was missing, too. And something else she couldn't name, but the loss of it ached. Warmth trailed down her face, and Pamina lifted her hand to wipe it away. The mud she smeared across her cheek didn't stop the tears, only forced them to find new paths.

When she sat up, she saw the full moon reflected in the Fairy's Spring, a perfect bright circle—a pale eye, watching her.

It was late. She shouldn't have been there. *Do not go after dark.* She had disobeyed at least two of the spring's rules. *Do not touch the water.* The spring didn't give back what it was given—she'd been lucky.

Pamina stood to leave, and the world, disjointed and distant, blinked in and out in disconnected moments.

She stumbled among trees so tall they blocked the moonlight. Sticks and stones cut her bare feet.

She stood in a street, red and blue lights flashing nearby. The cold pavement stung. Someone draped a blanket over her shoulders. Pamina turned. Chief Bagshaw and a policewoman she didn't recognize stood nearby. The woman was talking to her.

A familiar door opened. Pamina's mother wrapped her in a hug, despite the damp and mud. Her mother pulled her inside, and Pamina left dirty footprints on the carpet.

She lay tucked into her bed, warm and clean. Her mother stroked her hair as if she were a child instead of nearly eighteen. She felt echoingly empty.

Pamina closed her eyes. When she heard her mother leave at last, she cried herself to sleep.

She dreamed, and it felt like a memory fluttering just out of reach.

April: Full Awakening Moon

Eddie was hours late. He hadn't answered any of Pamina's calls or texts since she'd surprised him with the news after the basketball game Thursday, but surely if she waited a little longer....

Pamina tried to talk herself into leaving. If this weren't so important, she would be gone already.

"Just a few more minutes. He promised he'd be here."

October: New Moon

"Hey, viewers! Ricky C here!" Rico Cerna lounged in an armchair against a nondescript beige wall and grinned for the camera. His teen-to-young-adult viewers liked his dimples. Rico liked giving his biggest demographic what they wanted. "Welcome to another episode of *Mystic Mysteries*, a series digging into mysterious happenings in small-town Mystic Springs. Today's mystery involves a resident we'll call *Pam*. Now, on *paper*," Rico held up an overstuffed folder, "Pam is practically perfect. She volunteers, sings in the church choir, and at school she's teacher's pet. Then, she vanished." Rico tossed the folder away carelessly.

"Police searched for three months without a trace. *Until,* in early October, a newly hired *lady* police officer found Pam wandering the streets in the dead of night—soaking wet, unresponsive, with no memory of where she'd been. Or so her family claims. But c'mon, really?" Rico smirked. "You *can't* be serious!"

The view cut to a street with Rico center-screen. "We're going to get to the bottom of this mystery! In a moment, we'll interview Pam in person."

Rico dashed across the street, camera jiggling as he weaved through parked cars and trucks to reach his goal. He turned the camera to a worn, gray junker.

The shot whirled before settling on Rico leaning against the car. A school bell rang. "Time to get some answers." The sounds of chatter and crunching gravel swelled as teenagers passed Rico's chosen perch.

"Um..." a hesitant voice said from off-screen. The shot flipped, showing Pamina, who took a step back. She shifted uneasily, tightening her grip on her backpack. "Can you get off my car?"

"Pam!" Rico said from behind the camera. "You're on *Mystic Mysteries*, and we have a mystery to solve!"

"That's not my name." She took another step back, followed by the camera.

"Rumor has it you disappeared for a while. What in the *world* were you up to *all summer*?"

Pamina flushed. "None of your business."

"You *can't* be serious!" Rico said, smug.

Pamina took several more quick steps back, Rico and his camera keeping pace. Then she turned, dashing toward the school.

Rico chased her. "Where were you? Were you kidnapped? Did you run away? We won't stop until we know the truth!"

Pamina pulled on the door, and Rico's hand slammed into view, keeping it closed. The camera was too close to get a good shot, catching flashes of hair and limbs.

"I don't know! Leave me alone!"

Thwack!

The scene whirled before settling on the edge of the roof against the sky.

"¿Qué *chingados*?" Rico swore. "Does she keep *bricks* in her bag?" He lifted the camera, using his image as a mirror. He prodded a red mark on his face. "Did she give me a concussion?"

Hinges creaked, and Rico's gaze darted upward. "¡Mierda!"

He scrambled to his feet, view moving wildly as he ran, showing glimpses of an angry teacher by the door.

"Rico Cerna!" the teacher shouted. "I don't know what you think you're doing, but your mother is going to hear about it!"

May: Full Budding Moon

Pamina had driven to Mystic Spring's rival school in Spirit Cliff for Eddie's last game of the season—the last place Pamina knew he would be. He'd ghosted her, blocked her on all his social media, but he wouldn't miss a chance to show off for recruiters, even with the basketball scholarship he'd already been awarded.

The cheerleaders gathered around the water fountain at half-time, and Pamina overheard them from her post by the locker rooms.

"Is that the Mystic Springs slut that cheated on Eddie?"

"She cheated on Eddie Hart?"

"Must have. They were together ages, and now suddenly he's single."

Pamina's face burned. She pretended she hadn't heard the painful lies. She and Eddie had their future planned out—college together, then a winter wedding, him joining his father's business, her freelancing and a stay-at-home mom. They'd promised each other forever. This was just a hiccup.

She didn't see Eddie that night.

October: Waxing Gibbous

Pamina's costume was simple—an empire-waist bridesmaid's dress from her aunt's wedding and a pair of fairy wings she'd bought in the city. She'd outgrown trick-or-treating, but Mystic Springs hosted Halloween events for the nearby high schools, attempting to prevent teenage mischief.

Pamina carpooled with her best friends, Sunny and Birdie. She hadn't fit into their old dynamic when she'd returned, and the weeks since hadn't changed that. Hopefully, tonight would help. It was Halloween. Halloween was *always* fun.

Pop tunes and heavy beats blared from the gym speakers. Teenagers—not all locals—whirled through fog and flashing lights. Sunny and Birdie didn't seem to notice how many recent songs Pamina didn't know, and she wasn't about to point it out. She didn't need to know the songs to dance to them.

The evening wore on and they were joined by an ever-changing cast of other girls, few staying long.

"I'm getting a drink," Birdie said when a slow song started. "Anyone else?"

"I'll come," Sunny said, adjusting her angel halo. "I want more mini-mummy-weenies."

"You and those weenies," Birdie huffed. "They're fancy pigs-in-a-blanket." She tucked her secret-agent sunglasses into her pocket so she could see where she was going. "You want anything, Pamina?"

"To dance!" Pamina said, twirling.

Birdie laughed. "We'll be back in a minute." They wandered toward the snacks, leaving Pamina with the unfamiliar girls they'd been dancing with.

As soon as the others were out of earshot, two girls dressed in Spirit Cliff High's cheerleading uniforms turned on Pamina, their previously friendly expressions icy.

"*You're* Pamina?" the blonde asked. "The snot-nosed cow who faked her death last summer?"

"No," the brunette said, glaring. "She just took a spontaneous vacation and destroyed Eddie Hart's life."

There were so many gaps in her memories that Pamina couldn't be sure of anything about her disappearance. "Who's Eddie Hart?"

They stared at Pamina, mouths agape.

"What the hell?" Blonde put a hand on Brunette's shoulder. "Hold me back before I do something that'll get me suspended."

"*Who's Eddie Hart?*" Brunette echoed, indignant. "Eddie's a damn *treasure,* is who he is."

"He broke up with you." Blonde sneered, jabbing a finger at Pamina. "So, you *stalked* him."

"I wouldn't...." They were *wrong,* though Pamina couldn't explain how she knew.

Blonde flipped her hair. "*Everyone* heard you showed up at his house and wouldn't leave until his mom threatened to call the cops. After your vanishing act, they were all over him trying to prove he did something. He almost lost his basketball scholarship!" She scoffed. "Obviously you're fine, though."

Another girl, wearing a more elegant fairy costume than Pamina's own, shoved herself between Pamina and the girls harassing her. "Cease this drivel!"

It was too much. Pamina felt a panic attack building. The fog machine's smoke scratched at her throat, choking her. The flashing lights stabbed into her eyes. She fled, barely hearing the other fairy continue scolding the cheerleaders. "Harridans! Termagants! You are no more than vipers—wagging tongues and wagging tails, spitting poison and snapping at your betters! You—"

The cool autumn air wasn't any easier to breathe. Pamina

ducked into an alcove and slumped to the ground, head between her knees to stave off her nausea. She wished the suffocating panic had as easy a solution.

Pamina could *picture* it—a two-story house at the edge of Spirit Cliff, redbud trees in the yard. She could almost hear the shouting from the open door.

June: Full Windy Moon

Pulling into the drive, Pamina suddenly realized she'd never met Eddie's family. She'd been to his house, but never when anyone else was around.

If Eddie wouldn't talk to her, maybe his parents would help? Hopeful, Pamina got out of her car.

The front door opened before she reached it. A woman with Eddie's face stood scowling like an angry mother bear.

"You!" the woman shrieked.

Pamina flinched. This was a lost cause.

"Just because my son was nice *to you doesn't mean he owes you anything."*

"I need to see Eddie. It's important."

"Hah! This behavior might sell romance novels, but it doesn't fly in real life, young lady! You have two seconds to get back in your car. If I see you again, I'm calling the police."

November: Full Frost Moon

The sound of shifting gravel pulled Pamina back to see two black streaks dart into the grass. She'd have thought they were snakes if the weather hadn't already turned chilly.

"Art thou well?"

Pamina turned.

The other fairy hovered uncertainly by the corner of the school. The moonlight made her look beautiful in a way that didn't match her drawn brows or the nervous way she bit her lip, waiting for an answer.

Pamina shrugged.

The fairy came to crouch beside her, close enough that Pamina could feel the heat of the other girl's skin, making her realize how cold she was. It was after midnight—no longer Halloween—and she sat on the ground, wearing a dress designed for a summer wedding. She was *freezing*.

The fairy must have seen Pamina shiver—she gently tugged loose the ribbons of Pamina's wings and put them aside. Then she unfastened her long cloak and draped it over Pamina, tugging the edges closed and settling the hood over Pamina's head. It felt light but surprisingly warm.

"Thou shouldst be wary of the chill air. It would not do to fall ill."

"Thank you," Pamina said, voice barely a whisper.

The fairy wiped away Pamina's tears, her hand warming the icy tracks left behind. Pamina couldn't stop herself from leaning into the touch, letting it soothe the knot left by the recent memory.

"It is nothing, dear," the fairy said.

"Still." Pamina pressed her cheek against the other girl's hand. It felt almost familiar. "I heard you defend me."

The girl's moon-pale eyes widened, a rosy blush spreading over her cheeks. Her smile turned gentle. "Mind not the prattle of the ignorant rabble. They ought not to have spoken to thee so. I have dealt with them."

Pamina laughed, her heart lighter. "I hope you didn't do anything that will get you in trouble."

"None hold me accountable save those to whom I give leave to do so."

She sounds like she's reading Shakespeare, Pamina thought, smiling. She took the girl's hand from her cheek, holding it between her own. "You probably heard, but I'm Pamina Reisen. What's your name?"

The girl's gaze bored into Pamina's eyes so intensely it was like a weight pressing on her soul. Then it eased, and the fairy drew her lips into a pout. "Call me Brooke."

Pamina thought the name suited her. "Hello, Brooke."

An icy gust of wind chilled Pamina everywhere Brooke's cloak didn't cover. Brooke must have been even colder.

"We should go inside," Pamina suggested. "Don't want you to get sick either." She smiled at Brooke, her stomach twisting and lurching in a strange, not entirely unpleasant way.

Brooke waved dismissively. "The fête is nearly ended."

"Oh! Then I need to find Sunny and Birdie." Pamina tried to stand, stumbling awkwardly halfway up.

Brooke frowned. She wrapped an arm around Pamina and stood, startling a squeak out of Pamina and lifting both of them easily to their feet. "Unnecessary. I will escort thee."

Pamina hesitated. "I at least need to get my things and let them know I'm leaving."

"Wait here." Brooke was around the corner before Pamina could object, and returned almost as fast. "Thy companions have been informed," Brooke said, holding Pamina's purse and jacket. "And I have retrieved thy possessions."

"Can we trade numbers?" Pamina fished her phone out of her bag.

"I— have no such thing to give thee," Brooke admitted.

Pamina frowned. "Not even a landline?" This would make keeping in touch difficult. She didn't recognize Brooke from town. She was probably from Spirit Cliff or some other blink-and-you'll-miss-it place nearby.

Brooke scowled at the ground, fiddling with Pamina's green jacket.

Pamina's emotions tangled and welled—sad and protective and so, *so* soft for the other girl. She retrieved a pen and notepad from her bag. "Then I'll give you mine—if that changes, you can call me."

Pamina tore out the page to offer Brooke. The girl stared, cheeks red, and glanced aside when their eyes met. She took the paper and solemnly tucked it away. "Thank you."

"I should give this back too." Pamina started to remove the cloak, but Brooke's hands on hers stopped her.

"Keep it."

"Then *you'll* be cold."

Brooke shook her head.

Pamina took her jacket from Brooke and wrapped it around the girl's shoulders. "You keep mine, then." It wasn't nearly as nice as the cloak. It was old and ragged, shiny green fabric worn dull in places. Her mother had wanted to throw it out for years, but it was familiar and comfortable—soft and puffy and warm. Warmer than letting Brooke go bare-armed.

The blush on Brooke's face darkened, but she didn't object as Pamina threaded the girl's hands through the jacket's sleeves. When Pamina finished, Brooke pulled the edges around herself like a blanket.

"Thy kindness shall be my undoing," Brooke murmured softly.

Pamina didn't think she was meant to hear. She pretended she hadn't. "You wanted to escort me home?"

Shaking herself, Brooke smiled mischievously and offered her arm. Pamina grinned and played along. Too soon, they stood at Pamina's door, stalling for a few more moments together.

"I can't even check that you get home safely," Pamina complained.

Brooke scoffed playfully. "Nothing can kill me in a way that matters."

Pamina grinned, delighted at the reference to one of her favorite memes. "No phone, but you know *mushroom* memes?"

"They amuse someone precious to me." A sad edge crept into Brooke's smile.

Silence fell between them.

Pamina squeezed Brooke's arm. "I should go inside."

Brooke nodded but didn't move.

Pamina trailed her hand down Brooke's arm to lace their fingers together. "I hope I see you again."

Brooke raised their joined hands and traced her thumb lightly over the racing pulse in Pamina's wrist before she let go. Brooke stepped closer, cradling Pamina's face between her hands. She placed an almost reverent kiss on Pamina's brow. "This is my wish also."

Breathless, Pamina watched Brooke walk into the night.

July: Full Thunder Moon

Pamina ran into Eddie by chance at the state fair. He looked anywhere but at her—at her hands resting gently on her belly.

"Isn't this everything we wanted, Eddie? A family?" Pamina reached for him, missing the steadfast comfort of his hand in hers.

He pulled away, running his hand through his hair. "Look, I don't want to keep it." Eddie finally met her eyes, his brow creased and gaze cold. "If you do, then I don't want you."

Tears gathered in Pamina's eyes.

"C'mon, don't cry at me like that'll change anything. Get over yourself."

Pamina watched Eddie walk away until she lost him in the crowd. The future they'd planned together drifted away like dust in the summer heat.

December: Full Little Spirit Moon

"Hi, Garrick," Pamina called over the meowing, a dog's frightened whines, the scolding tones of Flaminia's bird—the usual noise of the veterinary clinic. "Anita texted about kittens?" Pamina liked helping socialize cats for Anita's grant-funded project—a catch/neuter/home program to prevent feral cats from decimating local wildlife.

"Yeah, go on back," Garrick answered, staring steadily out the corner of his eye at Samuel, his and Anita's slate-gray kitten. Samuel's ears lay flat, tail twitching, staring directly back. Business as usual, then. Samuel couldn't stand Garrick, despite his efforts to win the cat over. Pamina thought it was hilarious.

Anita was moving hissing kittens into a pen when Pamina found her. "Oh, you're here! You know what to do, so I'll leave you to it. Flaminia's bringing in her 'raven' again." Anita attempted air quotes with a kitten in each hand.

"I heard," Pamina said wryly. "It's scaring the minister's dog."

"Shoot, they're here already?" Anita dashed toward reception. Pamina could tell when she got there by Garrick's yelp. Soon, Samuel ambled in—smug, like he'd made Garrick bleed again.

Pamina shut herself into the pen with the kittens and settled down, waiting for them to decide she wasn't too scary to investigate. Samuel yowled at the door, and Pamina let him in as well. He sniffed at the younger kittens as they waved their tiny claws at him, hissing and spitting like hot oil. Samuel ignored their threats and settled into a purring loaf beside them. The kittens calmed almost instantly.

Pamina huffed. "I'm not even needed here, am I, Samuel?"

"*Mrrrp*," Samuel answered, aggressively washing the nearest kitten's face.

Pamina had hoped the kittens would be tame enough to cuddle, but she was content to watch, her presence more important than interaction at this stage.

Once the kittens were sleeping, Samuel abandoned them to hop into Pamina's lap.

"Yeah, okay." Pamina scratched under Samuel's chin. "You're a baby. You're forgiven for hogging the babier-babies."

Samuel purred and rubbed his face across her stomach. And *kept* rubbing against her front, purring loudly.

Pamina lifted her arms out of the way, watching the kitten rub from her right side to her left.

"What are you up to, kitty?"

Anita poked her head in to check on them. "How's everyone doing?"

"The kittens are asleep. Samuel's obsessed with my shirt."

"Oh, he's scent-marking you."

"*Why?*"

"So other cats know you've got a clowder," Anita said. "Our old cat would *constantly* do it to me when I was pregnant with Cecilia." Her face scrunched. "Then she started bringing me dead animals."

"Gross."

"Yeah. It went great with the morning sickness. She got worse after Cici was born."

"Worse?" Pamina couldn't imagine, her stomach already twisting in sympathetic nausea.

"She brought me *mostly* dead animals."

"Ugh!"

Anita shrugged. "Gotta teach the baby to hunt, y'know?"

Pamina picked Samuel up. "Samuel, I do not need dead animals." Samuel meowed, loud and plaintive.

Anita laughed and took Samuel from Pamina, gathering the purring cat against her chest. "Unless you're pregnant, you're probably safe."

"I guess," Pamina said. But her stomach kept twisting.

July: Full Thunder Moon

Pamina knew she shouldn't have come to the Fairy's Spring so late, or talked to the stranger who now held her and carded gentle fingers through her hair. She was breaking all the rules that the schoolgirls taught each other for staying safe when they came here. Pamina didn't believe, not really, but she knew the stories. They said that sometimes, if you gave the right gift, some-

thing at the spring would grant wishes—and Pamina needed a miracle.

"I don't know what to do," she sobbed. "I just wish it didn't hurt so much!"

"I could fix it for you," the other girl said, rocking Pamina like a child. "I could take the memories, the heartache... the cause of your woes." She laid a gentle hand on Pamina's abdomen. "It could be like it never was."

Pamina's breath caught. "No!" She wrapped her arms defensively around her belly. "I love them."

"Such a little spark? It's not yet even as big as a sprite."

Her breath still ragged, Pamina sat up, glaring at the fairy. "Yeah. But it's my sprite!"

December: Full Little Spirit Moon

Pamina's stomach still twisted with nerves when she slipped out of the house. She'd broken the spring's rules before. If it got her answers, she was willing to risk it again.

When Pamina arrived, someone already stood beside the water, wearing a familiar green jacket.

"Brooke?"

Brooke turned and gave the same sad smile she had worn on Pamina's front steps. She looked different now. The angles of Brooke's face were somehow not quite human. She glowed against the darkness with an inner light like moonlight reflecting on still water. She looked otherworldly in a way Pamina hadn't remembered.

Pamina was *tired* of forgetting! Tired of forgetting her past, no matter how painful. Forgetting Eddie and Brooke and—her stomach twisted again, sharp and insistent, and for a moment, Pamina couldn't breathe. "Brooke, please! What's happening? Why can't I *remember*?"

Then she was cradled in Brooke's arms, head against the other girl's shoulder, slick green fabric beneath her cheek. Pamina choked back a sob, her whole body tense.

"Brave heart, dearest." Brooke pressed a kiss to the crown of Pamina's head.

August: Full Lightning Moon

"Brooke, come quick!"

"Dearest?"

Pamina grabbed the fairy's hand and pressed it against her stomach, where she'd felt pressure a moment before.

The feeling came again, and Pamina grinned at Brooke. They stared at each other in wonder, eyes wide and teary.

"You felt that, right?"

Brooke nodded. She leaned forward, pressing a kiss to Pamina's stomach beside their overlapping hands and resting her forehead there. "What a strong little sprite."

December: Full Little Spirit Moon

Pamina stood gasping in the middle of a street, red and blue lights flashing nearby.

"Lord, are we doing this again?"

Pamina turned to see Officer Simpkins approaching, steps slow, like she was trying not to spook a wild animal.

"Ms. Reisen? Can you hear me?"

Pamina nodded.

"That's a step up from last time I found you out here." The policewoman looped an arm around Pamina, guiding her toward the cruiser. "This gonna be a regular thing, kid?"

Pamina shook her head, teeth clenched against pain.

"Good. It's not great, finding you wandering around wet and dazed in the cold. You okay?"

Another wave of pressure washed over Pamina and she cried out, fingers digging into Officer Simpkins' arm to stay upright.

Eyes wide, Simpkins glanced down at the dampness on Pamina's skirt and leggings. "Kid? Did you just have a *contraction?*"

Pamina nodded, not bothering to keep from crying anymore.

Simpkins stared a moment before letting out a string of curses and scooping Pamina off her feet, setting her down only long enough to open the car door before shuffling the girl into the back. She slid herself into the driver's seat, arguing with someone over her radio.

Pamina shrieked as another contraction washed over her.

"The hell was that?" Chief Bagshaw's tinny voice demanded.

"I *said* ten forty-nine," Simpkins snapped.

"Sam, we ain't *got* ambulances."

"Chief, I've got a teenager *giving birth* in the back of my squad car," Simpkins replied. "I'm kind of freaking out about it."

"What? Who?"

"The Reisen girl."

"Damn."

Simpkins suddenly threw open her door, shouting, "Doc! Anita!"

Anita jogged over. "What's up, Sam?"

"Get in back. I'll explain on the way."

Anita opened the door but paused when she looked inside. "Pamina?"

Pamina let her head fall back against the window with a pained cry, spurring Anita to scramble in and slam the door.

Samantha Simpkins, wasting no time, flipped on her siren and took off.

"Where are we going? What's wrong with Pamina?" Anita leaned over to smooth the hair away from Pamina's face. Pamina only cried harder.

"She's in *labor*."

"*What?*"

Pamina howled through another contraction, confirming it.

Anita stared at Pamina before turning back to the police-woman. "What do you want *me* to do about it?"

"I don't know! Whatever it is you do!"

"I'm a *vet*, not a doctor!"

Simpkins gestured frantically. "It's basically the same though, right?"

"I am not qualified for this!" Anita shouted.

"Well, you're the best we've got between here and the hospital."

"Oh, God."

"I want my *mom*," Pamina sobbed.

"You and me both," Simpkins muttered. Louder, she said, "Chief'll get your parents and meet us there."

"Everything's going to be fine," Anita added, awkwardly patting Pamina's knee.

September: Full Song Moon

They lay together like two pieces of a puzzle. Pamina wove Brooke's hair into tiny braids, while Brooke sang softly, her head resting on the curve of Pamina's belly to feel the baby react to her voice.

Brooke laughed quietly. "Our little sprite is in a dancing mood."

Pamina frowned, tugging the braid in her hand. "Makes one of us."

Brooke winced. "Sweetheart."

Pamina released the incomplete braid and hid her face behind her hands.

Brooke levered herself up on her elbow to better see. She sighed, sharp-edged sorrow showing through her unearthly beauty. "Dearest...."

"Do I really have to go back?"

Brooke scooted up to wrap her arms around Pamina, tucking Pamina's head beneath her chin, holding her close. "I have grown —attached," Brooke admitted. "If I could keep thee by my side, I do not know that I could allow thy return. Yet I know my realm is no place for a mortal to live, much less the little one."

Pamina flung her arms around Brooke, looking up at the fairy with teary eyes and wobbling lips. "I don't want to forget you."

"Then perhaps thou wilt remember," Brooke whispered. "But if not, I will remember for us both."

December: New Moon

Pamina held her daughter, humming a lullaby that brought to mind cool stone and deep water.

She still had gaps in her memory, but had remembered enough to make peace with those she'd given up. She'd lost her perfectly planned future, could hardly remember loving the boy who had dreamed up those plans with her.

But Pamina wouldn't wish away this future with her daughter for anything.

January: Full Greetings Moon

The doorbell rang on New Year's Eve.

"I'll get it," Pamina called. She opened the door to moon-pale eyes and a hesitant smile on an otherworldly girl wearing a ratty green jacket.

Pamina laid a protective hand on her daughter, sleeping in a sling against her chest. "You're not here for my firstborn, are you?" she asked, not quite joking. "I remember refusing to give her up."

"No!" Brooke blurted. "Though I would treasure any child of thine." Her hands flew to cover her mouth, then her whole face, as her cheeks reddened at the blunder.

Pamina laughed.

"Dearest, do not tease me so," Brooke pleaded, peeking between her fingers.

Pamina pulled Brooke's hands away, revealing a pout.

"I have acquired a cellular telephone," Brooke offered, glancing nervously at Pamina.

"And you didn't call me?"

"I am—unsure how to operate the device."

"Do you want to come in?" Possibly it was dumb to invite an actual fairy into her home, but Pamina didn't think it was the *most* reckless thing she'd done in the past year. "I can show you how your phone works. You can meet my parents. And Brooklyn."

Brooke's smile turned teary. "The little sprite is named for me?"

Pamina shrugged, cheeks warming. "Maybe." She tugged Brooke past the threshold.

In the next hours, Pamina introduced her parents and showed Brooke how to text. Brooke returned a locket, lost half a year ago now, the old pictures replaced with tiny portraits of the two of them gazing at each other. When Brooklyn fussed, Brooke soothed the baby and adoration shone in Brooke's moon-pale eyes.

Pamina kissed Brooke at midnight—a perfect start to a new year.

ARIA LANGRIM

Aria Langrim believes most stories would be better with a few more dragons, and that poetry is an inevitability of human language. Growing up pre-internet, she fell in love with her parents' fairy tale and poetry books.

When not writing, Aria can be found working her it-pays-the-bills day job, reading, making art, or napping. She dreams of one day owning a fiber farm, including animals like silk moths, angora bunnies, and sheep. Aria is a mid-Missouri author living with one of her besties and more books than she has space for.

Aria's Website: https://aria-langrim.weebly.com

SAMUEL

P.N. HARRIS

Spring, 2020 - The Kitten

"No one wants *him*!"

Those are the last words the kitten hears before he is taken from his mother. At only a few weeks old, the kitten has started to pick up the language of the people around him, but he does not understand what he just heard. He only knows it did not sound good.

The kitten meows loudly when he is picked up by a bad-smelling man with angry hands. The frantic meows of the milk-giver who cleans and cuddles him become muffled as he is dropped inside something. It becomes dark as this thing closes in around him, leaving just a sliver of light at one end. The dark thing is not solid, but sways. He is scared, and he wants his milk-giver, called Mama by the person with the soft voice and gentle hands who sometimes holds him.

He also sometimes hears a loud, angry voice that shouts words like "shut up," and "dumb cat," and other words the kitten would later learn the small people called "children" are not allowed to say. He wonders if the loud person is the one who has picked him up and has him trapped.

From inside his dark encasement, he feels himself dropped onto something firm but not as hard as the wooden box where he and Mama sleep. The swaying stops. He hears a thud, followed by a soft rumbling, like purring. Although he feels cold and scared, the gentle rumble and soft vibration soothe him to sleep.

He jerks awake to the sensation of flying. The soft rumbling sound fades, as he comes to a sudden and painful stop that knocks the wind out of him. He aches all over, and it is colder now. He meows for Mama as loudly as he can, but she doesn't come. He is alone.

After a time, the kitten once again feels someone pick him up. A sliver of light begins to widen, and he sees part of a face—a people face—the part people use to look at him and Mama.

The person peering at him begins to peel back the dark thing, and the kitten feels a rush of cool air against his face. He musters as much strength as he can to squeeze out a pained "meow," and the person ceases trying to free him. Weak and in pain, he remains in his cloth casing with only his head sticking out as the person carries him to a small room and gently sits him down on another firm surface. He hears another thud, and a familiar soft hum, then sees the person's hand reach across a strange wall and move something in the wall to point toward the kitten. Warm air caresses him, even while he remains encased. The warmth of the small room puts the kitten at ease, and he rests quietly near this new, gentle person.

The purring of the small room and the flow of warm air

stops. He is lifted. The gentle person carries him into a place that is unfamiliar except for a faint scent like that of the mean man with angry hands. He is placed on a hard surface that seems far above the floor. Another person appears and removes him from what they call a "little bag." His head and body hurt, and his muscles are weak. He is confused when he hears multiple voices now. It mostly sounds like mumbling to him, but he understands two words: "warm" and "eat."

Spring, 2022 - Life with the Dunstans

Two years ago, a stranger pulled over onto the shoulder of a road to pick up a small blue drawstring bag after seeing it thrown from the window of the car in front of him. The bag had a kitten inside, which he took to Anita Dunstan, the veterinarian, and her husband Garrick, the business manager at their veterinary clinic in Mystic Springs. When their then-five-year-old daughter, Cecilia, met the kitten, it was love at first sight. They kept the kitten, and Cecilia named him Samuel.

Today, Samuel sits atop his cat tree by the front door in the Dunstan's house. He observes Anita leaning against the kitchen counter drinking her morning coffee when Garrick enters the house with their dog Sawyer. The man removes his jacket and Sawyer's leash, then places them both in the closet next to the front door. Garrick doesn't notice Sawyer greet Samuel with a quiet "ruff," meaning "'Sup, Sam?" before running straight to Anita for pets.

Garrick closes the closet door and turns to greet Anita, when Samuel leaps from his perch onto Garrick's chest and bounces off, landing on the floor—on his feet, of course.

"Ahh, dang it, Samuel! Why must you torment me?"

Anita forces back a chuckle, then tries to sound like she's sympathetic. "Sweetie, Samuel's just being playful."

A frustrated Garrick responds, "No, Nita, your cat attacked me just now, because he hates me." Garrick glares at Samuel. "I took care of you when you were just a patchy-furred, yellow-eyed little—"

"Garrick!" Anita interjects.

Garrick responds, "I was going to say *kitten*."

All true once, but as Samuel matured, his smokey-gray coat thickened and gained a silvery hue. His now jade-green eyes glare at Garrick for a moment, then he snarls a loud "mmr-reeoow!" The house cat version of a roar.

Garrick is right. Samuel does not like him, though he cannot explain why. Even if he could, Garrick would not understand him anyway. Only other animals, like Sawyer, understand what Samuel says in his meows.

Anita tells Samuel and Sawyer to enter their car crates for a trip, and the whole family settles into what Garrick calls "the Dunstanmobile." Cecilia is dropped off at school. Parents and pets head to the Dunstan's veterinary clinic, where Garrick handles the business and Anita treats patients. Sawyer and Samuel spend the morning napping and playing quietly with their toys. Garrick occasionally gives them a treat with a pat on the head and a "good boy," even for Samuel.

Samuel relaxes in his cozy bed on a bench in a corner of the vet clinic. It's perfect for naps, especially when the mid-morning sun beams in through the large store-front window. Passersby often peer in, and though Sawyer's bed is on the floor nearby, Samuel is certain he's the main attraction.

Samuel wakes from his nap to find Sawyer in his dog bed, contentedly chewing a fake bone. He hears Anita escorting

Flaminia Tempest, the town psychic, from an exam room to the front desk. From his bed he spies Flaminia carrying a golden cage with a raven inside. *Is she going to eat that bird?* he wonders.

"Flaminia, her wing is healing well. Let Lenore out sometimes, so she can strengthen it. I know she showed up at your house in Maine long before you came here, but it's illegal for you to keep her. When she's ready, you must let her go."

"Anita, I've tried, but Lenore just keeps coming back to me. I can't help it if she wants to be my friend."

Samuel puzzles, *Friend? You've caught it. Why wouldn't you just eat it?* Samuel daydreams about hunting birds while the humans continue speaking. He snaps out of his bird-hunt daydream in time to hear Flaminia say, "Thank you. Goodbye. I'll see you both tomorrow at the barbeque." She stops at the door, turns to Samuel, and says, "I have a feeling we'll see each other again today." Flaminia walks out the door, raven cage in one hand and blue velvet drawstring purse hanging from the bend of her other arm.

Samuel stands up, enjoys a lovely slow stretch, then jumps to the floor and approaches the front door.

Garrick says, "Going out on your rounds, Samuel?"

Samuel looks back to see Garrick grinning at him from behind his desk and thinks, *Yes, Garrick, of course I'm going on my "rounds," as you say. I do this every day.* After a moment of glaring at his nemesis, Samuel continues toward the door. Through the glass that runs along the side of the wooden door, he confirms nobody is coming in before exiting through the cat flap.

A few blocks from the veterinary clinic, Samuel arrives at the vacant lot where he likes to frolic. He stalks birds and insects in the tall weeds. *Whew, this is hard work!* His efforts soon pay off when he catches and eats a dragonfly. *That was fun and yummy. I am an excellent hunter.*

The Word Around Town

Samuel leaves his hunting ground and saunters to Classy Cuts Hair Salon. He sits outside until a woman approaches and opens the door to enter, then he quickly slips into the salon behind her.

Samuel slinks toward a row of three tall chairs next to a wall on which hangs a large mirror that nearly spans the length of the salon. Samuel sits on the floor directly in front of the middle chair and faces the clients. The owner, Maggie, is cutting someone's head fur at the farthest chair from the front door.

"Here's Mr. Man himself!" says the lady in the first chair from her round face under mounds of head fur with tubes stuck in it.

What are those things stuck in her head fur called? Coner... no, curtains! No, no, those are the playthings in front of the living room window. Curlers? That's it!

Maggie says, "Good morning, Samuel."

Samuel knows Maggie. He often visits her shop. He says, "Good morning," but he knows she only hears, "Meow."

"See how he looks at her when she talks to him?" says the skinny-face lady with the short head fur in the middle chair. "Sometimes I think he knows what she's saying."

Samuel thinks, *I do know what she's saying. I know what all of you are saying.* After he moved in with the Dunstan's, Samuel picked up people-language quickly.

Maggie shares town gossip with the ladies in the shop. "Anyway, as I was saying before our little visitor arrived, Michelle's got a man. Found him online, on some over-fifty dating website."

Samuel's ears perk up. Normally, Samuel is not a curious cat, but the mention of Michelle's name caught his attention. Michelle teaches at Mystic Springs Elementary, and Samuel visits her almost daily when school lets out. Michelle adores him, and Samuel loves adoration.

Samuel listens as Maggie continues, "They've been texting, and they've been doing that thing where you call but you also see each other on a computer screen. But Michelle doesn't really seem to know anything about him. I asked her where he's from—she doesn't know. I asked her does he have kids—she doesn't know. I asked her what kind of house he has—and she doesn't know because he always talks to her from a hotel room!"

Round face, curlers-in-head-fur says, "That is sketchy!"

"Michelle claims he travels for work, so he's hardly at home. She doesn't know exactly what he does for a living."

Short head fur chimes in. "Is she sure he's not calling from a prison common room?"

When the ladies' conversation turns to reality TV shows, Samuel moves to the door and waits to be let out.

His next stop—the Deer Stand Café. Someone there might share their food with him if Judd, the owner, doesn't shoo him out, spouting some nonsense about animals and food safety regulations.

The Deer Stand Café

Samuel bounds up the four wide, wooden steps leading to the large front porch, where the door is left just enough ajar for

Samuel to spy inside. A couple inside walks his way, and he steps aside as they open the door to leave, then hurries in before the door closes.

Samuel immediately locks eyes with the owner. Judd shouts, "Hey, git outta here, ya dern cat! I can't git shut down again 'cuz of live critters in here." When the man stomps forward, Samuel bares his claws and teeth, ready to attack if Judd tries anything. Instead, the door opens and a command is given. "Go on, git!"

Samuel leaves and runs down the porch steps. He looks back to see that Judd is back in the restaurant and out of sight. He then hops back up the steps of the porch, leaps onto the porch railing, and rests there. He likes to observe people coming and going from the café. He sees all kinds of people: farmers, mechanics, families, and Dottie the insurance lady, who stares at Judd a lot and giggles when he looks back at her.

Garrick has an opinion on that relationship and shares it with others. "That woman is forty years old! She's too old to act like a schoolgirl."

Why am I thinking about anything Garrick has to say?

Samuel soon hears the rhythmic click-click of Dottie's three-inch heels on the sidewalk as she draws near.

I do not know what insurance is, but selling it must make a person's feet sound strange when they walk.

Samuel does not recognize the man and woman who accompany Dottie as she arrives today. He decides to not pay attention to the trio, until he hears Dottie say, "Did you hear about Michelle Tuttle?" Once again, Samuel's ears perk up at the mention of Michelle. Dottie continues with a squeal, "She's got a beau!"

A bow? That thing Cecilia ties to Sawyer's neck?

Dottie mentions Michelle's man.

This is the same old stuff they talked about at the head-fur shop.

Samuel gives himself permission to nap. He wakes to find Dottie and friends gone and four ladies standing on the porch talking. Samuel drifts in and out of sleep, only occasionally catching parts of what one of them is saying.

"Yesterday, my boy... wet shoes... said he lied to me... actually frog hunting... ended up in the spring."

Samuel yawns, but is lucid in time for more from the same lady. "This kid lies a lot, but it's weird he would confess like that."

Another of the ladies pipes up. "It's the springs."

"Here we go again with the magic powers of the springs!" one lady complains.

Samuel loses track of who says what after that. He has a hard time seeing whose mouth is moving. All of these ladies look alike to him, with the same long, straight head fur and similar clothes.

"I'm telling you, the springs around here can do things to people, and she just said the boy fell into the water of the springs!"

One woman says in a loud whisper, "Look there, it's Flaminia Tempest. What's wrong with her dress?"

Samuel hears another voice. "She is so weird."

The four women—and Samuel—spy on Flaminia, who is now a few feet from the porch. Her long dress is wet and her cloth shoes with the rubbery soles make squishy sounds as she walks by the café.

"Hello, everyone." Samuel notices Flaminia sounds more pleasant than the porch talkers, who echo their hellos back. He thinks these ladies are either annoyed by the psychic's presence, or they don't care that she exists.

Samuel moves from the railing to the porch floor and looks

up at each woman. All have what Anita calls—*wait*—*what does she call it? Something face. Itch face? Kitch face? Whatever it is, they have it.*

Samuel and Flaminia

Samuel hops down the porch steps and joins Flaminia. She talks as they walk together back to her shop, which is also her home.

"Hello, Samuel. I told you I'd see you again today. I wish I could speak cat so you could tell me what those women on the porch said about me. Never mind. Even if I weren't psychic, I could guess." Flaminia chuckles. "I must look a mess—they already think I'm strange. I took a walk by the springs, but I stumbled and ended up in the water."

Upon reaching Flaminia's shop, Mystic Visions, Samuel leaps onto Flaminia's favorite armchair and has a lie-down as Flaminia kicks off her shoes just inside the doorway. Samuel gives his best innocent kitty face when Flaminia, her dress and feet still wet, walks to the chair and says, "Oh no you don't. That's my chair. Here, come sit on my lap."

Samuel thinks he's about to get scratches and pets, but when she picks him up, she gasps and immediately drops him.

Samuel expels a string of loud meows, saying, "Hey! You dropped me! Good thing I always land on my feet!" He knows Flaminia does not speak cat but is pleased to accept her unso-licited, yet appropriate, apology. "I'm sorry I dropped you, Samuel. I felt a shock just now when I picked you up. And I had a vision." Flaminia strokes Samuel's back and puzzles, "Why a vision right now, though?" She stills. "It's the springs! I'm dripping with spring water."

Okay, Flaminia, if you say so.

"Samuel, just now in the vision I saw you as a baby, I mean a kitten. A man—I couldn't see his face—threw you out of a moving car. Wait, I smell something. I don't know what it is, but it's familiar. Samuel, I don't know if you understand what I'm saying, but for a long time, I've felt like maybe you do."

I do understand what you say, but I don't smell anything besides the usual weird smells that come from your house.

"I think the vision and the smell are somehow connected. I smell something kind of metallic, like medicine, similar to mouthwash, but also like wet dirt, but not quite either of those things."

That's what Garrick smells like.

Flaminia stands and begins to pace. "I smelled this scent recently, but I don't know where."

Samuel's head turns to-and-fro to follow Flaminia pacing.

"Where have I been recently?

Samuel wonders, *Is she still talking to me, or to herself?*

Flaminia continues, "I was here, of course. Before that, I was outside, then I fell into the spring water. Before that, I was here with a client after I picked up Lenore from—that's it! I'm smelling the vet clinic!"

Yeah, 'cause Garrick stinks up the front office.

"Wait a minute. It just smells like that at the front desk. Could it be Garrick? Good gracious! Garrick must wear the same cologne as the horrible man who threw you away. Samuel, no wonder you don't like Garrick. His scent triggers you!"

Samuel no longer has any memory of being thrown out of a moving car, or of the man who did it. He does not want to think about a scent being the key to his disliking Garrick. That would mean admitting that he's been wrong to dislike him. Samuel wasn't sure he could admit that. Uncomfortable with this new revelation, Samuel heads for the door to leave when Flaminia adds, "Wait! You are about to do something important for someone. A truth will be revealed."

She opens the door, and as Samuel exits, she says, "Samuel, one more thing. You do love us, the people of Mystic Springs. Your little visits to people aren't really about what you can get from them. You care for people, even Garrick. This isn't from a vision. It's just an observation."

Samuel and Michelle

Samuel peers into the open door of Michelle Tuttle's classroom.

"Hello, handsome. Come on in."

Yes, I will come in. I like it when you call me that, because I am so very handsome. Samuel saunters into the classroom, straight to Michelle's desk where she sits in her chair with the wheels on the bottom. *Why don't people have wheels on all their furniture? Wait a minute, something's different about her.*

"Come here, you handsome boy. I'll give you your head scratches." Michelle picks him up and places him on her lap. She places her fingers in his fur and begins.

Yep, the scratches—that's what I came here for—nothing else. Then again, maybe I do care about people. No, Flaminia was wrong about that.

"You almost missed me. All the kids have been dismissed for the day, and I was about to go home." Michelle pauses midscratch. "I have something to tell you, sweetie."

No thank you. Just the head scratches, please, and a bit under the chin.

"I can't stay as long as usual for our afternoon chat and scratches. I have a sort of appointment. You're not the only man in my life anymore, handsome." Michelle squeaks out a giggle. "I met someone. He's sweet, and he makes me laugh. I haven't felt this good in years. Six years, actually, since my husband died."

Samuel looks up at Michelle.

Her face looks weird. She's got stuff on her mouth and her eyes. Like Anita does sometimes when she leaves the house with Garrick and the neighbor lady comes over to stay with Cecilia.

"Anyway, I'm supposed to have dinner with him tonight. He's in a different city, but we see each other on our computers when we video chat.

I don't like computers. I don't know what they do, but when people pay attention to them, they stop paying attention to me.

"I put on a bit more makeup than usual to look nice for Barry. That's his name. A couple of people told me I look nice today." Michelle lifts Samuel from her lap. In a moment, her colorful face is directly in front of his. "What do you think, Handsome? Do I look nice?"

Samuel blinks. He doesn't know how to respond to this line of inquiry. *What are you supposed to look like with that stuff on your face?*

Michelle cradles Samuel and rocks side to side, scratching under his chin. "Well, handsome, I have to put a few things away in here and hurry home." She gives Samuel a gentle squeeze, holds her cheek next to his face, then places him on the floor.

Samuel stalks to a row of windows opposite the door. He leaps up onto one of the student desks and exits through an open window. He makes his way back to the vet clinic to be taken home for the evening. He's still thinking about what Flaminia said.

The Big Day

The next morning, Samuel wakes up in his bed in Cecilia's room. He's slow to get up, but he can hear the Dunstans downstairs.

"Mama, can we light candles and sing, even though Daddy already opened his birthday presents?"

"Yes, baby, if he wants to."

"Can we eat cake too?"

"We'll have cake after the barbeque, but we can sing *Happy Birthday* now."

Samuel hears Cecilia's screechy, excited voice add, "I'll get the matches for the candles!"

What is machez? Samuel ponders as he rises and has a good stretch.

He hears Garrick say, "Whoa, honey, not those! Those were my grandpa's. His mom told him years ago there was a man tryin' to hide out from some gangsters—"

Anita interrupts, "Garrick, I think that's a story for when she's older." Anita setting Garrick straight always amuses Samuel. She announces, "I'll get the lighter."

Samuel walks toward the staircase and hears singing, then clapping. He smells something new in the house, something pleasant.

After more clapping, Anita says, "Cecilia, go pick out the barrettes you want, and I'll come upstairs in a minute to braid your hair."

Cecilia passes Samuel on the stairs as she's going up and he's going down. Samuel walks into the kitchen and looks on as Garrick kisses Anita on the cheek and says, "Thanks again for the fishing pole and the cologne, Nita. It will take getting used to after wearing my old stuff for so long, but I like this new stuff."

That's what I smell. Not the birthday cake, it's the cologne. Nice, like the clean sheets Anita won't let me roll around in.

"I even like the bottle, kind of art déco, like my matchbook."

Samuel at the 'Que

The Dunstans arrive at Mystic Springs' largest park, Dentsel Park. Townsfolk all wear their "Mystic Springs Annual 'Que" T-shirts, set up their grills, and roll their coolers around. Pets, kids, and adults run and play games, and the park smells of grilled meat.

Garrick and Anita toss a Frisbee for Sawyer. Nearby, Cecilia pulls and bounces a cloth mouse on a string for Samuel to chase. Eventually, families begin to sit down at picnic tables to share a meal, and Michelle arrives with a covered dish and her boyfriend, Barry. Michelle and Barry join the Dunstans and Flaminia at their table. Samuel and Sawyer are poised to pounce on any scraps that may accidentally fall, or are intentionally dropped for them by Cecilia.

Samuel meows at Flaminia, seated next to Cecilia. Flaminia whispers back, "Hello, Samuel."

Samuel turns to Sawyer and says in their usual animal speak, "I don't trust this Barry guy. We have to keep an eye on him."

Samuel hears Barry's cell phone ring and looks on as he answers. The man tells the others, "It's work. I have to take this."

He walks past the grills and picnic tables to the far end of the park for some privacy, not realizing Samuel and Sawyer are behind him, listening in on his conversation.

"Yes, hi... No, I'm in a park. I finished the audit early and I'm here for a concert in a park... It's, um, Mozart."

Liar.

Barry finds a spot to stand, under a tree and away from the crowd. He continues his conversation, so engrossed in it that he still doesn't notice Samuel and Sawyer. "It's fine, the concert hasn't started yet... Yes, of course I do. You're my wife."

Samuel hisses to Sawyer, "Did you hear that? He's married, like Anita and Garrick. Michelle has to know! I have an idea. I'll make him drop his phone, and you grab it."

"Okay, Samuel. What's a phone?"

"That thing he's holding up to his ear. Be ready to grab it when he drops it. Run with it to the springs behind the movie house just across the street. Make sure you get all the way in the water, so he has to follow you. Do you understand?"

Sawyer nods his affirmation.

Unseen, Samuel climbs up the backside of the tree where Barry stands. Samuel lines up on a limb that gives him the perfect angle for the maneuver he intends to use. He jumps from the tree onto Barry's shoulder, then to the ground.

Barry is so startled he drops his phone, which is exactly what Samuel wants. Sawyer grabs the phone, as instructed, and takes off for the spring, with Barry and Samuel in pursuit. They run through the picnic table area, past the Dunstans and Michelle and Flaminia.

Michelle screams, "Barry, where are you going?" She jumps up to chase him, and Flaminia jumps up to chase Samuel. Garrick grabs Cecilia, and he and Anita chase the whole lot of them.

They all soon arrive at the spring where Sawyer stands, belly deep in water with Barry's phone still in his mouth. Barry tries calling Sawyer to him with no success. He yells, says some more loud words, then Barry kicks off his shoes, steps into the water, and slowly moves toward Sawyer. The group, including Samuel, stand at the edge of the spring, watching Barry's progress toward Samuel's buddy Sawyer.

Michelle asks, "What's going on, Barry?"

Barry blurts, "I was on the phone with my wife when the cat attacked me from a tree. It made me drop my phone, and the blasted dog took it and ran to this creek, or whatever it is."

Samuel hears soft murmuring from the Dunstans and Flaminia. He notices tears welling up in Michelle's eyes.

"Wife?" Michelle asks.

Barry kicks at the water. "Yes, I have a wife, and a girlfriend in Cleveland, and another one in Wichita. Barry pauses and his face pales. "Uh, I don't know why I told you all that."

Sawyer looks to Samuel, then drops the phone and lumbers back to the family.

Flaminia looks at Samuel. "I know this is all your doing. You knew the spring water would do things to people. You knew it would make Barry tell the truth."

Denouement - Summer, 2023

Samuel lies on the floor next to Cecilia's chair in the Dunstans' dining room. The family has just finished enjoying dinner with Michelle and her new beau, Robert, whom she met online.

With a smile and a head shake, Robert says, "Imagine my surprise when Michelle told me she lives in Mystic Springs."

Michelle chuckles. "Imagine my surprise when Robert told me he had been here before, to leave a kitten he found on the road with our town vet."

"Your cat sure turned out to be a fine-looking animal," says Robert. "Once upon a time, I worried he wouldn't survive a week."

Anita offers dessert to Michelle and Robert, but they choose to leave to catch a late movie. Samuel gives them both an affectionate rub around their legs as they say their goodbyes to the Dunstans at the door.

After Michelle and Robert leave, the Dunstans go to the living room to watch an old movie on TV. Anita and Garrick sit on the sofa with Cecilia between them, and Sawyer lies on the floor in front of the sofa. Samuel curls up on Garrick's lap and quietly purrs as Garrick gently strokes his fur and occasionally scratches his head. Anita smiles at them both.

"I'm glad you two are friends now."

Garrick smiles back and says, "Me too."

Samuel thinks, *Me too,* and drifts off to sleep.

P.N. HARRIS

P.N. Harris was raised in small-town middle America, where she earned a Bachelor of Science degree in Public Relations and a Master of Arts degree in Mass Communication. Her essay, "Prolific Stereotypes of Black Men and Images of Black Masculinity in Tyler Perry's 'Diary of a Mad Black Woman'", was published in the anthology, *Interpreting Tyler Perry: Perspectives on Race, Class, Gender, and Sexuality*. Ms. Harris enjoys fantasy, science fiction, whodunits, and comedies, both in print and on film, as well as classic films and TED Talks. She also enjoys music and musicals.

THE SCARLET OAK

B.A.L. MCMILLAN

LETITIA ARRIVED at her family's cabin in Mystic Springs late afternoon, bringing in only the box containing the urn, preferring to appraise the cabin before disturbing it with her own belongings. The two rooms were scantily furnished, neat but dusty, shining from the afternoon light and perhaps from her love for Darcy. A few items were personal: a basket of pencils and pens, a worn terrycloth robe, a pair of overalls, and two drawstring cotton slacks, all for a petite frame. Darcy's. Stored under the sink were a zipper bag of soil, another bag holding small stones, a trowel, and hand rake—maybe the makings for a serenity garden? The night-table drawer held a Bible, and the space below a worn book with a dark gray cover, *Myths of Greece and Rome*. Meaningful? She worried, shivered, felt a thrill. She was an old lady, but her nature hadn't changed.

Letitia brought her one suitcase in, left her clothes inside.

She unpacked the urn, trying to brush aside the Styrofoam pieces. They clung to her hands, which spooked her, though she understood static electricity. The urn was beautiful, but still! Oh, how lovely her niece had been. How young not to be here now. Letitia saw bits of color among the floaty packing. Little books. She opened one, then others. Journals, six of them, in Darcy's handwriting, and with her delicate sketches. Letitia would wait until she was settled and could read them all in one unbroken space of time, a precious visit.

The August twilight outside looked bright and hot, but the cabin's interior was shadowy and cool, one of its mysteries. She exited through the cabin's rear door and walked to the low fence separating the family's lot from the springs proper where, at this northwestern area, a tangle of greenery, trees, ferns, and flora thrived and hummed with the wonder of small life. The nearby soil appeared firm, the air rich with blossom scents. Nostalgia waved through her, and she nearly swooned. From grief perhaps. She felt singled out and incapable. As she stared, the west horizon of the springs seemed to waver, like ripples of green. Letitia rubbed her eyes, blinked for focus. Yes, it wasn't an illusion. There was a glow. That was where Darcy wanted her ashes taken if possible, and without anyone, even family, knowing. Letitia only knew where, not why. Or how.

Turning away, Letitia stumbled, and, catching herself, glimpsed a flat stone at her feet. A line of black marks down its center formed an arrow. She picked it up, dusting the bottom. Closer, the black marks resembled elongated letters and could read as "Letitia." She glanced in all directions. Darcy did this? She took the stone inside, placing it on the fireplace mantel. Not for anyone's eyes but hers. She was supposed to destroy all clues, but she couldn't destroy a stone, could she?

She needed to visit the springs, see how she fared on the ground and in the atmosphere of doing something outside her nature and maybe outside her values. She was a simple woman. Yes, she once had fancies. Outgrew them. Maybe. She was seventy now, not spry, not delving into daydreams of turtles who traveled in little homes that somehow held a larger space when they drew inside, a whole mini house of rooms for even turtle children; and of fairies who lived in tulips which closed at night over a smaller, beautiful, colorful, airy world, and who drank honeysuckle juice. They were safe from any predator. That was then, when she was a child.

Letitia drove to the main springs, interested in the quaint signs here and there. A huge sign on weathered and cracked wood, remindful of notices on haunted tunnels or abandoned mines, marked the tourists' entrance. She visited a legend kiosk shaped and covered like a cistern, offering a sketched map of the better-known springs. She asked an attendant if she might just follow one path back and return, or was she to follow a printed guide? Ambling toward the far reaches would be best, just for a general feel of the place. Her family owned an adjacent lot, and had, in fact, donated part of the springs to the city.

The attendant allowed her free rein but added, "Just be careful and don't put anything in the water or the soil. We're keeping them pristine. I'm sure that's what you want, too."

As far as she could see, the paths were similar, occasionally a plank bridge, a stretch or pool of water, ripples of ferns and creeping blossoms, some hugging the earth and growing around and through the gravel. Continually heading west, Letitia came to the end of her open path. The tree canopy, though spacious enough for sun, hung low enough to impede movement, and the undergrowth grew closer, vines wrapping around stems. No path to the left or right. But when she retreated, the earlier path was gone, too. A little yelp escaped her lips, and she thrust herself forward, realizing with the act that she had panicked. She wasn't lost at all. She recognized plants she had seen earlier and the tiny turtle resting on the rise of soil from sunstruck water. "I'm glad to see you," she said, relieved, but disappointed, too.

She was hungry, but unwilling to enter Balm and Brimstone Café, or the Deerstand Café and Honky Tonk. How many worlds in one were there? Who were the denizens of those cafes? Of Mystic Springs? Why would Darcy want her remains to lie eternally here? Letitia found a normal-looking grocers with a green door, and there purchased cheeses, bread, crackers, peanut butter, fruit, and coffee, her favorite fare.

Inside the cabin again, that sweet warmth, Letitia said, "I'm back," and busied herself with storing the purchased items, fixing herself a cold supper but hot coffee. Although night had not yet fallen, she donned her cotton pajamas, and, propped by two pillows, she gathered the journals close and studied Darcy's entries. The early ones noted Darcy's simple activities and appointments, like library or church or dentist. They became increasingly detailed sketches of something Darcy had seen, surrounded by her miniscule, perfect script—a spring's name with its qualities or a major feature, such as:

"a ladder into blue water. I wanted to descend beneath the surface. If only."

"White flowers lacing the shoreline."

"Shortleaf pines."

"Walking fern everywhere. I waited to see it move. It didn't."

"Blue lobelia."

Three plants appeared often: fern, hydrangea, and iris. Then another shift and trees dominated—their leaves, the veins, colors, berries. The colored pens and pencils came to the fore here. So many images, scaled from seedling to adult.

As Letitia stacked the journals in order, a card fell from one of them. At first, Letitia thought it was a tarot card, though she had never held one, but she realized it was an advertisement for a palm reader. She felt strange just holding it, especially at night and in bed. She put the journals and card on the night table but then rose to move them into the main room by the urn. They belonged together. She considered the texts *in* the night table but didn't move them. They were positioned rightly. In her own home, she never put anything on top of the Bible. She loved fairy tales, too, though. Myths, legends, grand things.

In bed again, Letitia closed her eyes momentarily, and Darcy's sketches and script flitted like memories, settling to be her dreams. Dreams were the mind's way of sorting and storing knowledge for conscious or unconscious use. She turned off the lamp, waited for her eyes to adjust in the darkness. The moonlight through the burlap curtain lay a muted sheen over the small room. Here, Darcy had slept, dreamed, possibly grieved, feared. She had been the sweetest person. Despite a twisted body, she had appeared graceful in movement and stillness, draping herself in loose and flowing clothes. Letitia patted the cover drawn near her breast. "Ah, honey," she muttered. "Poor girl. Love you." She wondered if Darcy heard her, maybe longed to respond.

She turned to her right side, facing the window. She wondered why a person was more comfortable on one side or on the back or needed a different kind of pillow or temperature. Or world. Needed something special. Every person alive needed something special. To *be* special, too.

The early morning air was a bit cool, the night breeze fading. Letitia, dressed in beige slacks and yellow shirt for the day, surveyed the cabin's grounds, a patchwork of dirt, clover, chickpea, and bursts of flowering plants, which, though lovely, could be weeds. At times, who could tell the difference? She noticed a gray stone near one plant and found "curly endive" painted on it in a fine print. Another stone identified "felicia daisy." Darcy had found a good way to protect plants from hasty or ignorant land keepers.

The paraphernalia of folklore filled the shelves and bins of Mystic Visions: oils, stones, amulets, candles, masks. Meeting a mystic was offering a handshake to the devil, at least had been in Letitia's childhood community, and in the back of her mind now. The world was sharply divided by what God favored and what he didn't, between his overwhelming mercy and love, and his eternal condemning wrath. He was like a crochety, predictably mean grandfather.

"I'm nervous about being here," Letitia told the dark-haired proprietor. "I really don't want a reading. I want a consultation, but not about me."

"All right. I've done consultations for writers and performers. Is it for something similar?"

Letitia shook her head. The woman's voice was pleasing, husky and concerned. She was pretty in a kind of overblown way, accenting too much, like a country western singer or a circus performer. "No. Honestly, I want to talk with you about my grandniece, who may have consulted you for herself."

"Oh. I see. Darcy Thurbridge?"

The accuracy gave Letitia goosebumps. "Yes. How did you know?"

"I'm not sure. Maybe there's a similarity. Come with me."

She led Letitia past a room with black walls, a great round table, and six chairs. Letitia smelled candle wax, oils, flowers. "I'm uncomfortable," she said, stopping.

The woman turned, took Letitia's right hand. "I don't want you to be uncomfortable in any way. If you want to leave, that's absolutely fine. Don't you worry about it. We're going to the small room where I spoke with your niece. It's dark, but that's just for privacy and intimacy. I'm not in league with any evil forces. I belong to a Christian church. I don't attempt communication with the dead or predict the future or read palms. I respond to people. We'll use tarot cards, but they don't have any power." She tilted her head and squeezed Letitia's hand. "Will you come with me?"

Letitia nodded. While the woman's high-piled thick hair, arched eyebrows, and black eyes were certainly those of a witch, her tone and touch were convincing and welcome. And she had known Darcy.

The room was large enough for a five-foot-long rectangular table, a chair on either side. The walls were black velvet, displaying, in all, six colorful posters. The one behind the woman's chair showed a silk-clad woman embracing the planet Earth in the foreground of a vast universe. "Don't be alarmed. I have to feel comfortable with my image, too. The posters are just enlarged tarot cards. They're art, you know, some ancient, some current, but with common themes. Now," she crossed her forearms on the table and leaned forward, "tell me what you need from me."

"I want to know why Darcy contacted you. What she might have been planning. If you can tell me. Her state of mind, maybe."

"Could I explain how I might have determined those things? Without frightening you?"

"Yes."

"Okay. Be patient." She brought a black box from beneath the table, took five cards from it, glancing at Letitia as she did so, and placed them face up on the table. "I'm not doing a reading. I'm demonstrating a process. Each of these cards does have a name, but the name doesn't indicate the meaning. Each card offers myriad possibilities, positive and negative, depending on the person who responds to them. That doesn't have to be the psychic. It's the client who wants a meaning. You understand?"

"I think so."

"Now. This card," she touched it with a fingertip, "is Death, but any of the other cards can also mean death, not necessarily physical, but an ending or a beginning, death of a habit, of a love, of a fear."

"Was Darcy consulting with you about her death?"

"No. Nothing negative. She wanted to know her affinity with natural elements. Some people are comfortable around the ocean, you know? Some in a forest setting, or a farm. They feel in place, safer or just more integrated. Some people like stones, feel peace or empowered—Don't worry. I'm not talking occult power, though some people do believe that, and there's evidence. But as we visited, I learned that Darcy felt most at home away from cities, in the woods, particularly. She loved the secrecy of them, shifting leaves, droopy branches under which a person could hide. A friend of hers had painted a scene of a young girl hiding under fall branches, and the sunset seemed to get caught there. She described the painting, how she wanted to be the child in the painting, and had been, when she was younger."

"Did she talk with you about her plans, what she intended to do? Or her health? Her family?"

"No. We talked about what she enjoyed and why that might be. She was a lover of life but somewhat restricted. She didn't like crowds, but she liked people. I felt that she was a loving observer. No names, ever. No negativity. I wondered about her myself. I gather you're dealing with her . . . estate."

"You knew she was ill?"

"I'm certain everyone did. She wasn't unknown, just private. I think people loved her."

The last was spoken in an even softer voice, hinting that the speaker herself was fond of Darcy.

Letitia watched Flaminia scoop up the cards with her beautiful hands, each slender finger tipped with a long, vividly red fingernail. Her physical presentation was a role play, the arched brows, the jet-black hair, so thick and unruly Letitia longed to brush and braid it.

"I truly thank you," Letitia said, rising. "I read online that a good . . . session with a psychic should be acknowledged with a generous tip. I would like to do that, because you have been helpful to me, and to Darcy."

"You paid for the session, and I would rather return that payment to you than to accept a tip."

Flaminia escorted Letitia to the front, nodding to a waiting customer who was searching through a black bin of amber pieces. At the door, Letitia hugged Flaminia wordlessly, then stepped into the street. A good deed was a good deed, no matter the source. Charity was charity.

In the sunlight, one of Mystic Springs's restaurants now struck her as appropriate. Balm and Brimstone. The restaurant fare hadn't yet switched to Cajun, so Letitia ordered biscuits and gravy. Plain food, good, as real and wholesome as her upbringing. She dallied, having coffee with three sugars. A woman attired in a brown uniform entered just as the waiter approached Letitia's table. "Is that your sheriff?" Letitia asked the black-haired young man. "I saw her photo in the paper."

"That's Samantha Simpkins, our police chief. Good one, too."

Letitia believed that, but, to her own embarrassment, she wanted police officers to be men. The same requirement for ministers. And God. The idea of a female God was disquieting.

Not all women were loving natured, and she was accustomed to dealing with men.

The cabin was lusciously warm from the fall sunshine. The old oak floors were a burnt honey, the shadows soft. She walked to the room's window, looking south to the springs proper, and to her right the western region, where Darcy wanted her ashes buried or scattered—which was against the regulations and thus against Letitia's own ethics. How could she do it? She couldn't cross this long swath of land at night. Not only was it likely filled with snakes and skunks and other creatures, but it might be marshy enough she could get trapped. She was old. Pretty nimble, but not that kind of nimble.

Trees. Darcy wanted to be among trees. Letitia sat at the round table with the little journals. She leafed through slowly, Darcy's fairy-like script running from page to page. She paused for a while at the blue water and ladder, but finally went on. Trees. She slowed down as the sketches became intricately detailed, colored. Then, in the sixth journal, she saw it. Why had she not seen it before? The colors didn't match! Bits had been added at a different time, with newer pencils. Several oak copses, with young trees in the foreground, space among them, like traveling light and sky. And nearest, the smallest of all, a sapling, with Darcy's fine print, "scarlet oak." Growing by it were the plush white flowers of a "wild hydrangea."

She went into the bedroom, peeked into the drawer holding the Bible, but shut it. She took the book on myths to the table. A sliver of space invited opening, and the pages parted, a small leaf between them, at "Dryads and Hamadryads." She chilled, not from fear, but from the unexpected expected. Paganism. Lesser divinities, a subject most people had studied at one time or another. Not much different from fairies, elves, hobbits, warlocks. Letitia had once wanted that world to be the real one and sometimes could see that it was—people resembled dwarves and wizards, and gnomes, and even giants. She had seen photos of skeletons, huge, nine and ten feet tall. Modern giants weren't so big, and weren't well, maybe a sign of something going awry. She wondered if there was a world *in* this world, secret perhaps, where giants thrived, peeking in windows at night as Roald Dahl had envisioned. Darcy's fancy was more a belief. It was a hope for, or maybe a knowing of, a different kind of afterlife. Dryads and oak trees. Darcy wanted to be a dryad and to protect their world—what might be their world. This was not just a matter of keeping one's word. This was one of honoring a deep faith and maybe helping it to be true. Life sometimes offered a touch of grandeur in a gesture, and this could be one.

Letitia had always felt that she needed to hide from God, or at least not attract his attention, because she was a dreamer and a doubter. She liked best to sit in churches alone, during the week, sort of sneaking up on God, without a minister to take her as his charge and ask questions and give directions she wasn't ready for. But she much enjoyed sitting in an empty church. *"It's the house of a friend,"* her mother had said many times. *"They're all his, and thus all yours."* Letitia felt welcome in most churches, but the doors were usually locked. Not so in the old days.

She drove by the Mystic Springs Methodist Church and was relieved to see no sign designed for tourists. It was a small church, too, which was promising. To her surprise, the big double doors opened, and she slipped into a long and deep foyer, disappointedly offering a counter with a coffee pot, sweeteners, napkins, and—probably—sweet rolls on Sunday. Too modern for Letitia, who thought beauty more appropriate for a loving and powerful God. She didn't want a coffee-klatsch friend. She went on, almost dipping in the aisle since she did feel a reverence for God in any of his houses and wanted to acknowledge his superiority in a way she could manage. Not total subservience. She advanced to the third row, close enough to be embraced by the aura and far enough not to intrude. There was no kneeling rail, so she took up one of the Bibles at the pew's end and sat, eyes closed, holding it. She didn't feel condemned. Didn't feel like a heathen. When she opened her eyes a long-boned, middle-aged, and rather pasty man stood in the doorway leading to and from the sanctuary.

"May I help you?" he said. "I'm Pastor Sweeting."

"I just want to sit here a little while. I don't need anything."

Still, he was advancing, which she didn't really want. He was so pale, and almost chinless, more like a weakling elf or failed wizard. She was sorry for her thoughts, but they weren't going to stop. Which God would know. If he were there.

"I won't intrude," the minister said, "unless we need to talk and you're just worried about imposing, or about not being part of the congregation."

"No. I sometimes visit churches. I'm new here, but the habit is old. I like to avoid crowds."

"And ministers?"

Letitia smiled, though she was startled. *And thus one knows she's been found out.*

"Yes. And ministers. I do like your church. It's small, and it's lovely here with the stained-glass windows. They look old."

"They are. One of the members inherited them and donated them to the church. Installing them cost a pretty penny. But they are beautiful. We have a nice congregation, giving and open-minded. There's an early service for people who like more modern praise songs and a casual gathering, and a more traditional service on Sunday.

Was he a wizard? Had God sent him the words? Did he know how apt he was? Letitia felt weak in the chest and legs, and very tired. "I'm here because I'm trying to make a decision about a burial ritual. I've made a promise to someone I love, and I want to keep it, but I'm afraid to. It's going against the way I was raised."

"Is it anti-Christ? Are you talking about something really opposing God?"

"No. It's not even a burial ritual, not one of any particular faith, pagan maybe, reincarnation. It's like scattering ashes into the sea or over mountains."

"That's common, even among Christians. Some people believe they can't be reincarnated if the body isn't intact. Voluntary cremation would be denying oneself the possibility."

"I don't believe that, and, honestly, I don't know what I believe. I'm a big doubter. This planet has been around for at least three billion years. I can see why we need God. We're so small."

"If you're not doing anything to harm anyone, or overtly against your own faith, I can't see the harm in keeping a promise you want to keep." He gestured at her pew. "May I?"

Letitia scooted back, made room for him.

"You're related to Darcy Thurbridge?"

"I am! I'm her great aunt. How did you know?"

"She sent a card to me a few months ago, telling me she had lasted about as long as she could and she was at ease with dying. She used to come here, as you have, just sitting alone. I didn't press her."

"She talked with you privately?"

"At times, about the beauty of the world and the unity of faiths, how most of them are working toward the same end, probably the same god. She was a charming young woman. She would sit in the pew over there, nearest the green window. It was her spot. Do you always sit in the same pew when you visit a church?"

She glanced around. "I guess I do."

"I think Darcy was and is one of God's favorite people."

How could this man be weak? Be a failure? His statement was her own belief. Darcy should be one of God's favorite people if she wasn't. "So do I. And I'm glad to hear you say it."

"Come any time." He rose, moved away so she could exit. "There's a special place for you."

She curtsied toward the sanctuary, nodded to the minister. "You have a lovely church here and you are a lovely person."

"Not so very," he said, and thereby solidified her fondness for him.

Outside, doubts assailed her. It was too strange. What pastor is named Sweeting? How could she take anything serious with a seer named Flaminia, a town thriving on lies and superstitions and made-up miracles, restaurants that touted killing and devils in their names and the titles of their food? Maybe she herself had crossed some mystic boundary and was at risk of never leaving. Something like Brigadoon, only Brigadoom.

An urn of ashes. A scarlet oak. Potting soil. Stones. A shimmering land part of yet separate from the main springs. She wasn't capable of crossing the field at night, but could she scatter the ashes in daylight? Were there cameras? She didn't want to reveal what Darcy wanted concealed. That was part of the commitment. Did everyone see that faint glow? Or only certain people who had activated a part of their brain, a secret-self brain, activated by hope, maybe another's hope, a primitive brain, or the more advanced. She didn't know. She turned back to the table and the urn, the scattered wee journals. She picked up the little white stone and the larger one with her name. The other would have to read as "Darcy." No doubt there.

In the morning, after a hasty shower, and dressed in a gathered skirt with pockets, and a drapy cotton blouse with a drawstring waist and three pockets beneath, with a small sketch pad in one, a handkerchief folded around a tiny bit of Darcy's ashes in another, and a stone with Darcy's name on it in the third, Letitia drove to the main springs. She wore a wide-brim, woven-reed hat which covered her eyes—to hide deceit. She did three hasty sketches as she strolled west. When she was at the end of the path she had taken last time, she pressed a finger into the ashes and looked pleadingly ahead. She had no key, no code, just love of Darcy and a longing to do right. Her vision or the world itself blurred, but she stepped forward. She sensed people moving and the whisper of voices, like a light overlay life where the other was. She was in a grove of trees in various stages, singles and groups, the path broad now, diverging in different directions. She could move only to the right and did so. Bending without kneeling, believing this the very place where the scarlet oak and the wild hydrangea grew, she scooped a shallow depression in the ground and gently opened the hanky to let the ashes drift down. She smoothed a bit of soil back in place and dropped a bit into the hanky, which she folded and returned to a pocket. Then she set the white stone on the earth covering her grand-niece's ashes. She stood erect, eyes watering, and looked around. "This is Darcy," she said. The whispering stopped. Letitia faced where the path to the front and her world should be. She knew when she crossed because the air was heavier and her presence firmer, and she was an old woman, a bit shaken by her own breaking of rules.

In the cabin, Letitia transferred the spring soil from the hanky into the urn. Now Darcy was in both places, and so was the soil. She laid a fire in the fireplace for later in the evening, then reread the journals, recalling Darcy's nature, such a sweet girl, never giving in, always striving to be active and pleasant, learning. When the night shifted into true dark, Letitia carried the urn outside, aware of the moon above, and of the earth and sky, and unity and tugs of the heart and the universe. She set the urn on the ground and opened it. With a final look at the night above and around her, she returned to the cabin. After the fire was burning steadily, she tore pages from the journals and put them in the flames first, then the covers. She couldn't bring herself to burn the book on myths, and returned it to the night table.

When she woke the next morning, she fixed coffee on the narrow range, and, shortly later, with a cup of coffee in hand, she looked out the rear window. The urn was there. Heart heavy, she turned away, finished the coffee, washed the little cup, and went outside. She had done her best. She picked up the urn. Lighter. Empty! She clapped the urn to her chest. The western spring wasn't shimmering. The sky above was a steady blue. She heard birdsong, heard a car in the distance, smelled the scent of grass and broken soil, and flowers, and water. Darcy, dear!

Mystic Springs, all around her, probably all around the world.

B.A.L. MCMILLAN (R. M. KINDER)

Whether writing realism or fantasy, McMillan explores the mysteries of everyday characters—their concept of good and evil, their personal choices, strengths, and passions. She writes about factory workers, musicians, children, animals, ghosts, angels, witches. Through traditional and indie presses, she has published four collections of fiction, three novels, a novelette, and co-authored a biography of a Missouri fiddler. Her most recent book is *Ghost House*, available through major bookstores. Her current project, near completion, is Plum and Crow, a fantasy.

Websites: www.rmkinder.net and www.balmcmillan.com. Please visit and correspond.

THE NARROW TRAIL

AMYE WEBSTER

THE OLD DODGE dually crept down the winding road, approaching the town of Mystic Springs, Missouri. Retired school teacher, Bonnie Hollister, gripped the wheel firmly at ten and two. She prided herself on being a good driver. Entering a curve, she rode the brake, then stomped hard on the accelerator climbing the next hill. The Dodge engine groaned in protest, pulling a heavy living quarters horse trailer.

Bonnie sought the healing waters of Mystic Springs. Some people claimed the water was magic, but she knew that was a bunch of malarkey. However, her arthritis was getting worse every day, and she had to admit she had been in a bad mood for —well, several years. It was worth a try. Maybe Mystic Springs was the answer. The elderly mule in the trailer was also a big part of the reason for this trip.

Bonnie and her husband used to trail ride together. He rode the ornery mule and she rode a gentle mare. Then her husband ran off with the neighbor lady, and Bonnie's mare up and died from a 'bout of colic.' Bonnie was left alone and resentful to contend with the hard-headed mule named Clyde. For a couple of years, Bonnie would take Clyde out on trial rides by herself. Unlike the infamous couple, this Bonnie held no affection for this Clyde, as she always referred to the animal as her ex-husband's mule. It had been a long time since she had ridden him at all.

Old Clyde was as standoffish as she was. He didn't care for human companionship. He didn't particularly care for other equines either. He and Bonnie were actually a lot alike. They were each crabby loners, forced together by happenstance. Like her own, Clyde's joints were stiff. His back had grown bony while his belly was bigger with age. He was an oddly shaped animal at best and had clearly outlived his usefulness.

Bonnie had decided *not* to nurture him through his later years. She was staunchly opposed to the expensive upkeep. Oh, she did the basics. His hooves were trimmed twice a year whether they needed it or not. She gave him dewormer each spring and fed him a handful of senior grain every morning—not to mention what a hay burner he could be. These costs all added up in a hurry. Besides, her trail riding days were long since over. He wasn't *really* her mule anyway. She rationalized her decision as she drove. This was going to be a one-way trip for Clyde. It was all she could do to afford her own life. She sure wasn't paying to maintain her ex-husband's mule forever.

In the late afternoon, Bonnie rolled to a stop in front of the Deer Stand Café and Honky Tonk. It had the look of a local gathering place. She noticed trucks outnumbered cars three to one in the gravel parking lot. She slid stiffly out of the pickup and hobbled to the trailer. Opening the center door, she allowed Clyde to shove his massive head out into the sunshine. He blinked his enormous eyes and flopped his giant ears forward, surveying his surroundings.

"You ugly beast," she said with a sigh. Dutifully, she laid a flake of hay into his manger. She walked around the trailer and headed for the front porch of the cafe. Glancing at the sign, she rolled her eyes. You might as well just call it *Uneducated Hill-billy Joint*. Bonnie had always been a bit of a professional college student. She hadn't actually finished her PhD, but she had accumulated a lot of college credits over the years. She considered herself to be quite well educated. She had developed a strong disdain for common folk. It was hard for her to hide her contempt as she opened the front door of the dimly lit cafe.

The place grew quiet, and all eyes turned toward Bonnie. She slipped into the closest booth for privacy and in hope of a late lunch. The proprietor of said *Uneducated Hillbilly Joint* was coming her direction. He was wearing a camouflage apron. He introduced himself. "Judd Rusbridge, and what brings you to town?" The man was all smiles.

Bonnie ordered coffee and took the menu grudgingly. "Just trail riding," she told Judd with a sniff, lifting the menu high. Making it clear there was no more conversation to be had.

Judd stood his ground. "Figured you were here for a dip in the ole magical springs. That's what brings most folks to Mystic Springs." He was met with silence. He shifted on his feet and muttered, "Well, you look that menu over and I'll be back."

"What a bunch of malarky," Bonnie said under her breath as Judd walked away. Her thoughts wandered, the plan for Clyde weighing on her mind.

She had checked into putting him down with her local vet. The farm call to her place and the euthanasia would set her back $400 or $500 easily. Not to mention, in her county, there was an ordinance against burying dead livestock on private property. Rendering services to get his old carcass hauled away would be at least another $1,000. Bonnie had convinced herself that the only affordable thing to do would be to ride him into the hills, bid him a fond farewell, and help him into an eternal sleep herself. No one would ever be the wiser.

Bonnie folded her menu smartly, glancing around for the head hillbilly. Her decision about Clyde was final. So was her decision for dinner. She was going to have the special. It just wouldn't be right to spend any more money than she had to in this sorry excuse for a business.

Judd walked over, no doubt eager to take her order. He lingered at the table, asking about trail riding. Bonnie tried to sidestep the conversation, but Judd rambled on about local gossip and geography. Bonnie began listening more closely. She did need a place to camp tonight. Plus, her map showed an endless network of trails. There were over a million acres in the Mark Twain National Forest. She needed an easy trail. It had been years since she had been in the saddle.

Judd was delighted that she was listening and told her about the hot spot in town. "Mystic Visions." He rolled the name out slowly, as if it were of great importance. "It's the headquarters of magic here in Mystic Springs. Flaminia Tempest runs the place, and she is a tourist attraction all by herself." Judd flashed a crooked smile at Bonnie like he had just shared the town's most top-secret information.

What did this have to do with her? Bonnie wondered.

"Flaminia is what we like to call *gifted*, and the more you pay her—the more *gifted* she becomes. If ya' know what I mean." Judd winked as he turned away. "Oh yeah," he added, "Flaminia has a place behind her shop where you can plug yer camper in, too."

After a very filling, rather greasy meal at the Deer Stand, Bonnie drove her truck and trailer slowly to Mystic Visions.

Parking behind the rustic shop, Bonnie stepped stiffly from the truck. Loosening her belt a notch, she studied her surroundings.

Bonnie gasped as she realized she herself was being studied. A tall, dark-haired lady, who could only be the mysterious proprietor of the place, stood on the back porch, seemingly waiting for her.

"Damn," Bonnie whispered under her breath. "Mystic Vision, alright. Mystical and she's a vision... of something."

Dressed in a floor-length gown, the elegant woman glided toward the trailer. Brilliant colors swirled softly around her legs.

"Ma'am," Flaminia acknowledged, draping long fingers toward Bonnie, who shook her hand awkwardly.

"I'm Bonnie Hollister," she stammered. "The gentleman at the cafe said I might find a camper hookup here. I also need to tie this mule out somewhere, if that's okay?"

Flaminia nodded. "Thirty dollars per night," she said flatly. "And he wants to be on the grass under those trees." She gestured toward the small, wooded yard beside her shop. Then she strolled right past Bonnie toward Clyde. The head door of his slant stall in the trailer was still open, and his ears flopped forward with interest as he watched the goings on.

"What a grand ole soul," Flaminia cooed, reaching him to rub his giant forehead and stroke the long ears. "What brings you to Mystic Springs?"

Bonnie hesitated. She didn't know if this unusual woman was directing the question to Clyde or to herself. "Trail riding," she stammered, "and I've heard about the magic water of the springs."

"I see," Flaminia answered, eyes flashing as she stared directly at Bonnie.

Bonnie instantly felt uncomfortable and looked away. A dark

image arose in her mind—the two syringes, all drawn up and waiting in the glove box of her truck. The first syringe would provide a nice, deep sleep, the second would deliver a fatal dose. Coyotes and turkey vultures would take care of the carcass. No one would be the wiser. She would just say he died—with the saddle on. Actually, it was her husband's saddle. It had always been a pain in the ass, literally. Bonnie felt flustered, dragging her thoughts back to this moment. Shaking her head, she realized Flaminia was still looking at her—looking through her.

"Uh, I'm interested in a Tarot Card reading when I return from my ride," Bonnie stammered. "I would love for you to tell me my fortune." Promising to spend a little money with Flaminia might be the right approach.

Flaminia ignored Bonnie but leaned in close to Clyde, bending one giant ear down as if to share a secret with him. "When you hit the water, remember, you *know* how to swim."

"What did you say?" Bonnie demanded. "I don't think I heard you correctly."

Flaminia arched one slim, dark eyebrow at Bonnie. "I was talking to Clyde," she said simply. "Actually, I would have loved to read your palm." Flaminia turned away, laughing. To Bonnie, it sounded more like a cackle.

Would have?

"What do you mean would have?" Bonnie called after her. "And how did you know his name?" But Flaminia disappeared through the door of Mystic Visions without so much as a backward glance.

Early the next morning, Bonnie fed Clyde his breakfast in the trailer. Soon, she was driving up Ridge Road. It was easy to find on the map. The head hillbilly at the cafe had shown her on his phone when he recommended this route. A wooden arrow guided her into a large parking area. She found a place to park her rig, and held the door frame as she stepped from the driver's seat. She shuffled around to unlatch the trailer door. Dutifully, Clyde slowly backed out.

As if on cue, Bonnie heard a motor bike approaching. Judd Rusbridge rode toward them on an ancient Hiboy motorized pedal bike. It had definitely seen better days. The bike was outfitted with bulky, black leather Harley-Davidson saddle bags that were modified to fit over the fender of the rear wheel. They were bulging, full of something heavy. Bonnie studied the cargo on the back of the bike but didn't say anything. Whatever it was, it made the whole contraption awkward and heavy. As Judd leaned the bike over onto its kickstand, a bit of cracked corn trickled out onto the ground. He glanced at Bonnie nervously, as if hoping she hadn't noticed.

Bonnie turned toward Clyde, stiff brush in hand, half-heartedly brushing his withers where the saddle would sit. Strategically, she kept her back to Judd.

"Beautiful morning for a ride." Judd grinned. "You'll like this trail. It's got some awesome views." Judd pointed toward the top of the bluff. "At first the trail is wide and easy to follow. Then it gets really skinny. See there?" Judd gestured. "Follows right along the edge of the cliff."

Bonnie turned to look at the trail. She could see the narrow line, clinging to the mountain edge. Beneath it, a long, slim waterfall tumbled into the waiting limbs of colorful trees below. She whistled, surveying the incline and the steep, dangerous trail. "You pedal *up* that trail?" she asked incredulously.

"Naw," he answered with a grin. "I just pedal 'til this little motor kicks in." He patted the bike affectionately.

Judd went on to explain the name of the trail, Seldom Seen.

"At least that's what the folks around here call it. 'Cause it's so high and scary, most people close their eyes when they go around that curve. Get it? It's seldom seen."

Bonnie turned away from him again, placing a thin Navajo blanket on Clyde's bony back.

Judd seemed to get the message. He gave up on trying to visit and pedaled away. A thin line of yellow crumbles trickled out beside the bike as he went. Bonnie heard his engine kick in. Judd squeezed the throttle, and it whined in protest, climbing the slope. "Enjoy your ride, Ma'am," he yelled over the noise of the bike. "And be careful!"

Bonnie was grateful to be alone again. Well, alone with Clyde anyway. She pulled the saddle out of the back of the trailer. It was heavy. She groaned as she dragged it over to Clyde. Judd's bike rattled loudly in the distance. Judd was no small fellow, and his cargo of corn for the deer had to be a load. She snorted to herself. Of course, he would be illegally feeding the deer in the woods. "Lawbreaker. Deer shooter. Hillbilly." Bonnie had listed the labels she could stick on him to herself. She would be glad to finish this unpleasantness and go home.

Bonnie gripped the saddle with both hands and also boosted it with her knee, successfully hoisting the heavy saddle onto Clyde's back. She pulled the girth tight. Then she buckled the back cinch, breast collar, and britchen. Mules were a lot of work. Her saddle bags were tied behind the cantle of the saddle.

Bonnie retrieved the two syringes from the glove box and placed them carefully into the nearest bag. Riding up the mountain and administering both injections needed to help Clyde along with his dirt nap might take a while. She had already packed trail mix, a bottle of water, and a flashlight. Almost as an afterthought, Bonnie slipped her phone into the nearest saddle bag along with a small bottle of scotch. Her hands were shaking as she buckled the saddle bags tightly closed.

"I'm gonna need that scotch," Bonnie said, trying to calm her own fears. "Bye-bye to Clyde," she whispered. "Bye-bye last reminders of my rotten marriage." She pulled her bridle from the tack compartment of the trailer.

Finally, she reached out to slip the bit into Clyde's mouth. He shoved his muzzle straight into the air, above her grasp. She cussed him. He turned his head to the right, well beyond her reach. Bonnie smacked him smartly on the shoulder. Slowly, Clyde complied, lowering his head and accepting the bit. This was their routine from way back. Nothing happened where Clyde was concerned until he was good and ready.

Bonnie locked her truck. Then she pulled her handy mounting block from beneath the saddle rack. She locked the back tack compartment and dragged the step close to Clyde, so she could reach the stirrup. Clyde played his part, moving far away from her. She cussed him again. He moved farther away, making himself impossible to mount. Bonnie whacked him on his shoulder again. "Dammit, Clyde!" she said through her teeth. At long last, he sidled over close enough for her to step into the stirrup.

"Difficult right to the end," she murmured, gathering the reins. Then she clucked to him and drummed her heels upon his sides. "Daylight's burning," she scolded.

Clyde ignored her and plodded forward with the slowest walk he could muster. He continued unperturbed and steady on the upward trail. One narrow hoof was placed after another until gradually the terrain became steeper. Clyde breathed heavier. Sweat shined on the sides of his neck. Bonnie sat still, holding the horn of the saddle. She was feeling much less confident about her plan as they actually made their way higher up the mountain.

Eventually the pair came to the curve on the cliff's edge, Seldom Seen. Bonnie's stirrup nearly brushed the rock wall to her right, and her left stirrup hung over what appeared to be eternity. Daring to test tradition, Bonnie peered ever so slightly, past her left boot toe. Tree tops clad in rust-colored leaves reached upward toward her stirrup. Far below and crisscrossed with leaves and branches, she saw the silvery glimmer of water. She could hear the loud rushing sound of the waterfall beneath them, but could not actually see it. She gasped—turning her head away from the cliff and closing her eyes. She drew a ragged breath and struggled to calm her trembling hands. When she opened her eyes, that's when she saw him.

Judd was hurtling down the trail toward her. Engine off, he held his long, gangly legs above the pedals. His rickety old bike freewheeled down the steep slope. The ignorant hillbilly's focus was below, his face hidden by the brim of his hat. The collision was inevitable on the narrow trail. Bonnie opened her mouth to scream at him. Her voice stuck in her throat. The loud, rushing of the waterfall drowned out all else.

Clyde's head hung low as he chose each step with care. That's how the handlebars of Judd's bike caught him square across the bridge of his long nose. The front wheel jammed directly between his front legs. Clyde's old arthritic knees buckled with the impact and down he went. Bonnie flew forward onto the mule's neck, then over it. Judd launched over the handlebars of his bike and flew forward into the space between the mule and the rock wall.

Clyde scrambled for a foothold on the crumbly edge of the cliff. His hard mule hooves met only shifting rock, then air. Bike and mule clung to the trail's granite rim for a long, terrible moment. Then they went over, tangled together, a cartwheeling blur of mule legs, wheels, long ears, pedals, saddle bags, and stirrups.

Down and down!

Tree limbs cracked loudly and exploded into pieces as mule and bike crashed out of sight. The shattering sounds of destruction were deafening as beast and machine tumbled to earth, and the roar of the waterfall paled in comparison. Clyde brayed a final terrified mule scream—then a muffled, double splash far, far below.

Judd groaned and gasped for a breath. He had landed flat on his back in the middle of the trail. Bonnie Hollister laid full length on top of him. Her pointy boots rested on either side of his head. Bonnie moaned, trying to untangle herself from between his bony knees.

"You! You... hillbilly, redneck, sorry excuse for a man." She berated him further as she tried to rise, rolling to one side. She caught a glimpse of tree tops and seemingly endless expanse below. Silence. Bonnie couldn't breathe, or speak. She crab-crawled back and sideways, pressing herself against the rock wall, as far as she could maneuver away from the edge while still entangled with Judd.

After a few moments, Bonnie drew a ragged breath. "Why didn't you watch where you're going?"

"If you hadn't landed square on top of me...." Judd threw up a hand. "Well, you'd have gone right over the cliff with that old mule." He said the next through clenched teeth. "And my Hiboy bike is gone... Damn. Damnation!"

Slowly and awkwardly, the two struggled to untangle themselves and stagger to their feet. Bonnie's jeans were torn at the knee, exposing her skinny white leg. Judd's eyes watered and his nose was scraped raw. A whale of a shiner was darkening under one eye.

In spite of it all, he helped her off the ground. Judd held Bonnie's elbow as they began to hobble down the trail together. She was stiff with insult, injury, and anger. She wanted to tear her arm away from him, but thought better of it. Her riding boots were not good for walking, and honestly, every inch of her body was bruised and sore. Her toes were pinching, and she was sure her ankle was swelling. Even though it was downhill, it was slow going. All because Judd had caused this wreck, as she pointed out repeatedly as they made their way down the steep trail.

"Damn you all to hell, Judd Rusbridge—this is your fault." Bonnie then cussed him one more time, wobbling as she walked. Her ankle began to throb even more, and her wrist was beginning to turn a funny shade of purple.

It seemed to Bonnie they were moving at the same speed as the sun. The farther down the trail they went, the lower the sun settled beyond the mountain. Shadows were long and the air was cooling. A chilly wind had come up. She stumbled in her narrow boots. Judd held her aching arm firmly. Although furious he had caused such a wreck, she knew he was the only thing holding her vertical.

At last, the two of them reached level ground at the bottom of the trail. Judd guided them around a rugged outcropping of rock and brush. They were no longer on any kind of trail. Judd was picking their way. Bonnie was worn out. She was still so angry. The waterfall was loud now. At last, they reached the pool at the bottom of the falls. She braced herself, expecting to find Clyde floating dead in the water.

She stared in surprise. The dark water appeared empty. She looked to the bank where it was scraped and scarred with narrow hoof prints. The wet ground told the story. Clyde had obviously fought his way up and out.

"Lawd, I can't believe it," Judd gasped, also reading the signs. Deep mule tracks made a straight line before disappearing into the woods. "Nary a sign of my bike," Judd muttered, peering into the pool. "But look there."

Bonnie followed his pointing finger with her eyes. The saddle was under water—just a few feet from the bank. It lay in shambles: mangled leather, broken rigging, cinches torn loose. Smashed and soggy on the bottom of the pool.

"Get me that saddle," Bonnie commanded.

Judd did as he was told, wading into the cold depths. It barely resembled a saddle anymore, and with the bags still attached, it was *heavy*. Still, Judd dragged all to the edge of the water.

Slipping and sliding after Judd, Bonnie reached for her saddle bags. She ripped the nearest wet leather bag open and impatiently groped inside. "My phone," she said, searching. Bonnie jerked her hand back, dropping the bag.

Something had bitten her, hard.

She blinked. She couldn't understand the sharp pain. She looked to Judd in confusion, holding up her hand. A syringe stuck out of her palm—the needle completely impaled in the fleshy part of her hand just between her thumb and her wrist. Bonnie jerked it out, dropping it to the ground, now empty. She blinked again—hard—studying the syringe. *Which one was it?* she wondered. It didn't matter. Either mule-sized dose was the end of her.

She stared at her hand. A thin red stream trickled from where the needle had been. She blinked, studying the tiny wound. "This was supposed to happen," she mumbled, shaking her head. Slowly, Bonnie sank to her knees. She leaned back, breathing deeply, and reclined on the wet ground. She could feel the damp earth, soft beneath her.

Bonnie's hand burned. She gathered a handful of cool mud to hold. *Much better.*

"Are you okay?" Judd asked. "What happened? What was in that syringe?"

Judd sounded far away. His voice was strangely high-pitched. He was talking a lot. He was on his phone. He was stammering. Very upset.

Why is he so worked up? she wondered.

It was odd to lie on her back beside the pool. Bonnie could see a portion of the trail high above. But her eyes were drawn to a slice of brilliant sky. She studied the view—colorful leaves framing the little patch of vivid blue. White fluffy clouds floated along. She felt as if she were falling up—up, into the beauty of it all. Bonnie held her handful of mud tightly. It was soft and cool. The leaves of the trees rustled in the breeze. There were all the colors of fall. Crimson, gold, dark orange.... Why hadn't she noticed before? It was an incredible day. Not too cool. Just perfect. The crashing waterfall was close. What a wonderful sound.

Bonnie dropped the ball of mud onto the grass. She felt so relaxed, content to absorb the details of her exquisite surroundings. Judd was still around—somewhere—his voice just barely heard over the sound of falling water.

Motion caught her eye high on the trail. Bonnie squinted and focused. *Could it be?*

"My god," she mumbled. "Clyde?"

The mule's coat was glossy, glinting in the sunshine. There was no doubt. It was Clyde—but different. He looked young. His body was strong and beautiful. He stood still, swinging his massive head toward her, long ears flopped forward.

Bonnie lay motionless on the cushioned ground. Absorbed in this moment—in the smells of water and earth, the sounds of the waterfall, the vivid colors of autumn in the woods, and at the center of it all, Clyde.

Above, the mule turned and began to walk away. Then he broke into an easy, ground-covering trot to climb the steep incline effortlessly. At the bend in the trail—and without so much as a glance back—he disappeared into the trees.

AMYE WEBSTER

"Born in a barn" is a figure of speech until you spend time with Amye Webster. A horse barn is her natural habitat, and she has dedicated her life to raising, training, riding, and showing great horses. She is also very devoted to her second love, which is writing. Amye now resides on a beautiful horse farm near Kansas City, Missouri. There, she divides her time between the saddle and her writing desk. Her literary endeavors are always well-flavored with her own personal experiences within the world of all things Equine.

SILK MAN

JACK VENTIMIGLIA

THE MORNING SUN glares at the worst angle. Hoàng Tử R ồng's left eye squeezes shut. He cups a hand over his right eye and stares up the street at the red, wooden bench outside Happy Hair, his shop in downtown Mystic Springs. When not fishing in one of the area's enchanting springs, he and his best friend Ben often sit and talk on the bench. Someone sits there now. Not Ben.

Pronounced "Wrong" by friends, R ồng half groans, half sighs. *Small towns can't do much for unhoused folks.* He considers the twenty and the six ones in his wallet. He needs most of the twenty for lunch at the diner across Meditation Avenue. He'll give up the ones to send away the man on the bench. *That'll buy a short stack and coffee. Or shooters. His choice.*

Closer to Happy Hair, R ồng gets a better look at the stranger. *That's not a person. What is that? Shredded and curled strips of ribbon pasted all over a white mannequin?*

R ồng reaches the bench and stares. *Is this a big-city-type art project? They used to do that—put life-size, fiberglass animals in public places—pigs in Cincinnati, cows in Kansas City, dinosaurs in... People painted them. Is that what this is?*

R`ông rubs his eyes. *Those art pieces weren't like this, a duck ready to pluck. I gave no permission to put a dummy on my bench.*

Searching the street, R`ông finds no paper people in front of the diner, psychic parlor, or Springs and Things gift shop. Not anywhere. *Is this a joke?* Then, suspiciously, *An insult?* He brushes his fingers across the dozens of strips of paper. *No, not paper. Silk ribbons.* The thin fabric reminds his fingers of sua blossoms and home. He notices words hand-written in curlicue style in pale pink ink on the underside of a coil. He considers pulling off a strand. *It's on my property. I've got a right.* Still, he feels nervous when he peels off a strip and reads: "Family is forever."

R`ông grunts a laugh. "This belongs in a fortune cookie."

A truck eases between vehicles parked diagonally in front of Balm and Brimstone diner. R`ông longs for crispy bánh xèo, but the diner specializes in biscuits and sausage gravy for breakfast and burgers and Cajun dishes for lunch and dinner. The food is tolerable, but not bánh xèo.

Ben gets out of the faded red Ford F-150 and waves to R`ông.

Just seeing Ben causes R`ông to sense something, a feeling almost hidden just below the surface of Ben's eyes—like a feral kitten too timid to come out. Ben hides his feelings well.

"How 'bout those Cardinals last night? They—" Ben pauses. "Hey, what's that?"

"Don't know. Found it when I got to work."

Ben wears a handsome smile without trying. A moment later, standing next to R`ông, Ben frowns at the sculpture. "Damnedest thing I've seen in a month of Sundays."

"Ain't it a sight?" R`ông speaks formal English better than most Mystic Springers, but uses their Ozarks style of talking to fit in. He learned the when-in-Rome concept from Jarhead Jimmy while working decades ago as an interpreter at the American Embassy in Saigon. The Marine helped R`ông through the chaos and onto one of the last Hueys to leave the embassy roof in 1975.

Ben gives him a friendly hug, then spots the ribbon in R`ông's hand. "What's that?"

For reasons he can't explain, R`ông feels guilty, like he's defaced the flag or spilled a beer. "I pulled it off Silk Man. There's writing on it."

"That's what it's called—Silk Man? And it's got writing, like a fortune cookie?"

R`ông smiles, not because he made the same comparison, but because of Ben's eyes. They are blue like the morning sky over the Black Virgin Mountain northwest of Saigon.

Ben cocks his head boyishly. "Mind if I tear one off?"

R`ông does not want to say no to Ben. But Silk Man must belong to someone, and R`ông tries to steer clear of trouble. "I don't know. What if it was put here by mistake?"

Ben gives a mischievous smile. "What if it was?"

R`ông notices Dil and Agnes Lackey—she calls her husband by his last name—leaving the diner. In her yellow, broad-rimmed sun hat and flowered, shin-length dress, Agnes licks a paper napkin for use in wiping the corners of Lackey's mouth.

He protests. "Agnes, don't be doing that in front of people."

Agnes brushes crumbs from his salt-and-pepper-and-biscuits beard. "Honestly, Lackey, if you... What people?" His gaze takes her to where R`ông and Ben smirk. Agnes then notices Silk Man seated on the bench. "Who's the mummy, dummies?"

Ben smiles at being teased. "R`ồng found it sitting here when he got to work."

Agnes takes her spic-and-span husband by the arm and crosses the blacktopped street. She sizes up Silk Man. "That's really something. Don't know what, but something."

Lackey nods. "Yep, something."

Ben drapes a friendly arm over R`ồng's shoulders.

Being a head shorter, R`ồng feels gripped by a bear—the huggable, stuffed kind. He sighs. He wants this feeling of acceptance, of mattering to someone, to last.

"Our buddy R`ồng here doesn't know what it is, either." Ben hugs R`ồng closer, then releases him. "But he tore off a piece and found writing on it."

"Writing?" Eyebrows up, Agnes seems intrigued. "What's it say?"

R`ồng reads the silk slip: "'Family is forever.'"

Lackey laughs. "Sounds like a fortune cookie."

Ben cocks his head at Lackey. "Dead on. I said the same thing."

R`ồng wipes his hands back along his temple and over his scalp, a habit developed when he had hair, wavy and shiny black. Doesn't seem right to him—being an almost bald barber. People make bad jokes. One customer, Newt Limbaugh, calls R`ồng an "air stylist."

Agnes sails right past R`ồng and up to Silk Man. "Can anybody pull off a fortune?"

Ben shrugs. "R`ồng says no. Doesn't want to ruinate it."

Agnes crosses her arms, reminding R`ồng of a righteous *bà ngoại* catching her grandchild's little fingers in a bowl of sugary Tet holiday lotus seeds. "That right, R`ồng? You tore one off, but we can't?"

R`ông doesn't want to disappoint Agnes, or Ben, or anyone. "It's just that Silk Man isn't rightly mine. I found it—"

"On *your* bench, which is *your* property." Agnes is quick. "Possession's nine-tenths of the law, and quite a bit more in *our* little corner of the world."

His thumbs wrapped in overalls straps, Lackey parrots Agnes. "Quite a bit."

R`ông has made the same argument to himself about the figure being on his property. Still, he's uncomfortable. "What if the owner comes along and wants it back?"

Agnes seems to have all the answers. Always. Right or wrong. "We ain't planning to snatch it bald like a chicken. There's near a thousand fortunes glued there and we'd just like one for each of us."

Ben gives R`ông a gentle shoulder nudge. "That'd be fair, wouldn't it, R`ông?"

Lackey grins. "I'd like a pull, too."

R`ông and Ben share a goofy gaze that collapses under Agnes's fiery green eyes. She won't tolerate such a devilish look from them. Neither does she explain how a good church-going woman knows what that look means. She then gazes at Lackey. He smiles for her.

R`ông believes he sees what Agnes finds in Lackey's brown eyes—childlike innocence in a face turned leathery from years of tending a southern Missouri farm. Lackey is just a bit smarter than a mule, but honest as the day is long, and pure as the driven snow, as folks say. Often sarcastically. But not about Lackey. He's the real deal.

Agnes returns to R`ông. "So, one tab each? What do you say?"

Feeling pressured, he tells himself, *You'll give in. You always do. And Lackey's a regular customer. But try to sound magnani-*

mous. "Okay, one each. I hope you do better than 'Family is forever.'"

The past flashes in R`ông's head. He recalls men and women in stalls and at tables lining the Big Market's streets after a summer rain. They sold cinnamon, pan-fried basa for which his mouth waters, yellow apricot blossoms, and much more.

Diesel fumes burned his eyes. The pleasant aromas and stench of Saigon, now Ho Chi Minh City, are memories in his nostrils. He almost hears motorbikes, a fixture day and night on the streets, like those crooning calls from painted "butterfly" women and other vendors.

Good memories mix with those involving worse sights, smells, sounds. Explosions. Blood. Screams. Sirens. Gunfire. The thump-thump of Huey blades.

"Here goes." Like a bright-eyed kid, Ben yanks a tab. When unfurled, the pig-tailed silk strand is as long as R`ông's forearm. "Whoa. Take a gander at this."

Agnes raises mostly plucked eyebrows, the remnants penciled in red to hide gray. "Dang, Ben, whatcha trying to do— pull the whole blasted thing apart?"

"Agnes, ain't like I knew it was gonna happen."

The bald spot, like a white scar upon Silk Man's chest, horrifies R`ông. *Someone made a terrible mistake leaving him out in public so his secrets could be laid bare to the world. Or was it a mistake? What if it's interactive art? Maybe people are supposed to tear it apart. And if it's not interactive, then that's not on me.*

Or Ben. Or any of us. It's on whoever left it here. Rồng brightens a bit while looking at Ben. "Well, what does it say?"

Ben offers a full-faced smile. "It says, 'The Dragon Prince found love, but his mother, the beautiful and wise fairy queen, Au Co, warned the marriage would be doomed if he left their homeland.'" Ben looks up from the scroll. "That's one weird fortune, if that's what it is."

Agnes snorts a laugh. "A head scratcher for sure."

Lackey scratches his head. "An unfortunate fortune?"

Rồng's eyes fill. A tear falls. *Who sent this Silk Man to me?*

Ben puts a hand on Rồng's shoulder. "Does it mean something to you?"

A beeping horn startles Rồng. Pickups driven in opposing lanes stop dead in the middle of Meditation Avenue, between Happy Hair and the diner. Windows slide down. A woman and a girl jawbone.

Looking straight through the cab of the girl's old Chevy, the woman calls, "Hey, Agnes, whatcha doing there, hon?"

"Hey, Zee. We're pulling a man apart one bit at a time."

"Ha! Sounds like fun. Mind if we help?"

"More the merrier."

In his head, Rồng repeats what Ben had read: "The marriage would be doomed." He recalls Mother spoke those exact words. He loved her, his brothers, and sisters, and still does, but fifty years ago he followed his heart to America.

"My turn." Lackey touches a piece of curled fabric on Silk Man's head. Another on the right elbow. He considers dozens of coils from nose to toes.

Nellie, sixteen, livestreams Silk Man the moment she parks her truck next to Zee's. "Maybe I'll scoop Rico."

"He doesn't do stuff like this. He's a supernaturalist. His followers only want to know about weird, bizarre stuff. This is too normal." Zee is tactless, and Rồng knows she, like most women in Mystic Springs, is crushing on hunky Rico Cerna, a social media influencer. While Lackey takes his time inspecting each strip, apparently looking for just the right one, Zee appeals to Agnes. "What's he doing, picking out a new combine?"

Agnes takes the hint. "Step it up, Lackey. I gotta *go*."

Lackey rips a strip off Silk Man's leg. As Rồng watches, furrows almost deep enough to plant soybeans cross Lackey's forehead. The farmer reads the script to himself.

"Well?" Ben asks. "You gonna share?"

"Okay, okay. 'The journey of fifteen thousand miles begins with a TWA ticket.'"

Nellie's face goes blank. "What's TWA? Like texting? Trouble Went Away?"

Zee rolls her eyes. "Hon, TWA's an... *was* an airline. Big one, long time ago."

While Zee and others over-explain, Nellie stops listening. And livestreaming.

Rồng bows his head. He recollects, after Saigon's fall, taking a TWA flight to reunite with Jimmy at LAX. He can still picture the Marine wearing a midnight blue uniform with a new addition to the sleeve, a "smile" stitched under a three-bar chevron— staff sergeant. Rồng recalls feeling proud of Jimmy, but confused when people at the airport point and scream ugly words. Rồng remembers asking Jimmy, "Why are they yelling at me?"

Tears welled in the Marine's eyes. "No, that's all for me. The uniform."

"Isn't it *their* uniform?"

Jimmy wiped his eye. "It's complicated."

R`ông and Jimmy's bond, formed during Vietnam, meant more than any sheet of paper stamped by a government. More than any law written to keep them apart. R`ông's heart soars to recall settling on the coast of Louisiana and making a good living fishing. Jimmy owned the boat and R`ông owned the luck, never failing to know exactly where to haul in the biggest and best catch.

They lived as princes, working, playing, and loving hard up until their last night in New Orleans. Three young sailors at a jazz bar didn't like R`ông. Not his bronze skin. Not his walk. One called him ugly things. R`ông pleaded with Jimmy to go. Not Jimmy's way. He got in two punches and a kick before a pistol flashed. Jimmy went down. He died choking in R`ông's arms. Neither NCIS nor the police ever found who did it. R`ông wonders, *Did they even try?*

In the months that followed, R`ông spent a bit of his savings on barber school—a noble, useful, calming profession to take his mind off Jimmy, though never entirely. After graduation, R`ông drove his rusting Rambler American north, hopscotching from town to town until he discovered Mystic Springs. The name soothed his heart. And right off, at the diner, he met Ben, who told him the town's old barber had died. Ben captivated R`ông with stories about some of the town's many myths: Otoe-Missourian spirits hunting deer in Mark Twain National Forest; a hidden spring promising eternal life; tree dryads, beautiful green folk who slip into sleeping bags to make love to young men and women; and, just a year earlier, two angels with swords flaming banished a demon—howling creature of oil, creature of latex—after an epic battle that left a park restroom ablaze.

A cheerful, "Hey, y'all," comes from Mrs. Alice Fleck at the diner. She and other Rotarians spill out, blinking in the sun after their weekly breakfast meeting.

Agnes answers, "Old R`ồng the barber found an oddball dummy covered in fortune cookie notes and we're reading 'em. Oddest things you ever did hear."

Curiosity leads several more men and women onto the sidewalk in front of Happy Hair. R`ồng steps off and out onto Meditation Avenue to give them room.

"My turn!" Agnes rips off a strip.

Nellie again livestreams.

Because of the crowd, R`ồng can no longer see Silk Man, but he hears Agnes. "Got me a long one. Whoa! Hair-ribbon long." A pause follows. "What's it mean?"

Ben suggests, "Read it for us."

"'Like tears for a loved one, rain runs down upon green mountains. Rivers overflow in brown torrents, flooding fields. But in time, the rain ceases. Like puffs around drying eyes, clouds fade. At last, the golden dragon, the great prince who had left his people, feels sky and land and family urging his return. His mother waits, expectant arms wide. Her love is eternal.'" Agnes frowns. "Does that make a lick of sense to anyone? R`ồng? Is this something you know about?"

R`ồng is evasive. "You know fortune cookies aren't from Vietnam, right?"

Zee bites on that. "Yeah, hon. They're from China, not Nam."

R`ồng shakes his head. "San Francisco, actually. A Japanese man created them to—"

Agnes interrupts. "Don't want a history lesson. Can you tell us what it means?"

R`ông recalls an embassy room. Lights off. Bamboo blinds half closed against the sun. A black-suited man, imposing, nameless, face obscured briefly by cigarette smoke, shoved a manila folder stamped "Top Secret" across a dark mahogany table. "They say you're the best. Can you tell us what this means?"

R`ông tried several decoding systems. None worked. Then, while using an old Hill cipher, he recognized a word from North Vietnam's ancient Vietic dialect. "Clever. If you didn't know Vietic, you'd never get this, just like the North doesn't get our use of Navajo for field communications. But deciphering this will take time."

No smile. "We stay until it's done. I've got to keep eyes on you the whole time. It's going to make taking a piss uncomfortable, at least for me."

After twenty-six hours and nearly as many cups of egg coffee, R`ông finished. "This means the CIA's March 5 view that ARVN can hold Saigon through the dry season and into 1976 is wrong. The VC are advancing quicker than even they imagined. They expect Saigon to fall by May." R`ông asked the big question: "What happens to the people of Saigon?"

The man reached under his black jacket and placed a Browning Hi-Power muzzle against R`ông's forehead. "*This* happens if a word, just one, about anything heard here is spoken to anyone. And if your mama-san, favorite bar-girl—bar-boy, in your case—or anyone hears any of this, they'll take a helicopter ride over the jungle. Got it?"

The black-suited man said many more things. Never "thank you."

People stare at R`ồng. None have the stone-cold look of a CIA killer. R`ồng believes Mystic Springs folks are salt of the earth— some scruffy, even crude, but good at heart.

Agnes folds her arms. "C'mon, R`ồng. What's it mean?"

"The words remind me of a story from my homeland about the fabled fairy queen, Au Co. She weeps for the son who left his family to follow an ill-fated love that broke his heart. She misses him and feels his grief as only a mother can. After years of separation, Au Co decrees the time for tears at an end. She calls the prince, her firstborn son, home."

Agnes snorts. "The Golden Pánzi in Branson's got better fortunes."

R`ồng sees the "low-battery" light flashing as Nellie turns off her camera phone.

Newt Limbaugh, a Rotarian who gets one of R`ồng's standard crewcuts every two weeks, holds a chaw of Skoal in his cheek and a red plastic cup in his right hand. In a gravelly voice, Newt grunts at R`ồng. "I served in Nam. There during Tet in '68. Spent lots of time among your kind. And I know y'all got a thing for dragons."

R`ồng reminds himself that Mystic Springers are good at heart. "Dragons are significant in Vietnamese culture, like *our* American eagle. Both symbols stand for power and noble spirits. Dragons further represent intelligence and talent. In literature, Vietnamese think of themselves as children of the dragon."

Agnes shrugs. "So, it's just storybook stuff, not a proper fortune like Flaminia tells with her cards and crystal ball."

R`ồng suggests, "It's art. Interactive, storytelling art."

Lackey strokes his beard, and a biscuit crumb tumbles loose. "What's that?"

Saying "what's that" could mean Lackey either didn't understand or didn't hear what R`ồng said. Maybe both. Or maybe he referred to the loose crumb. R`ông speaks louder and slower. "Interactive means you don't just look at the art, you engage with it."

Nellie offers an impish smile. "Marry it?"

Zee patronizes her. "No, hon. It's not *that* kind of engaged."

Nellie huffs. "I was just kidding—obviously."

Mrs. Alice Fleck, the Rotary Club president, puts her fine arts degree and teaching experience to work. "It's like this, Nellie. At Boardwalk Aquarium over Branson way, did you see where there's the bottom half of a fiberglass mermaid? You step right up to it and your body becomes the top half so you can get a photo of yourself as a little mermaid."

"Yeah, I done it." Nellie's face reddens as everyone stares, imagining. "I was ten."

"You and maybe a million others, Nellie." Mrs. Fleck is in teaching mode. "Me, too. It's called a photo stand-in, basic interactive art. You don't just look at it, you join with it."

"I'm next," Nellie decides, and peels a tab from Silk Man. "Oh, heck, it just says, 'The one you love is closer than you think.'"

In a way that suggests longing to R`ông, Ben says nothing while gazing at him.

R`ông matches the look, also saying nothing.

Mrs. Fleck rips a long strand from Silk Man. "This one's too big to fit in a cookie."

Ben urges, "Don't keep us in suspense. Some of us have to get to work."

Agnes blurts, "And I gotta pee."

As if talking to her high school class, Mrs. Fleck answers, "All righteee. Here goes: 'My firstborn, light of my life, far from home but ever in my heart, your fifty sisters miss you. Their eyes shine like stars in the heavens. Their luxurious hair flows as waves on the midnight sea. And, dear son, your forty-nine brothers look for you to lead them. None in all creation have truer hearts or mightier limbs. Your brothers and sisters are brave and powerful beyond compare, and in each I take pleasure only a mother can feel. But our family cannot become whole until you return home, my son, my prince. We miss you."

Lackey laughs. "What a load of hog flop."

Newt gives a self-satisfied nod. "Yeah, they sure like their dragons."

Mrs. Fleck shakes her head. "It sounds sweet to me."

Agnes agrees. "That's what a good mother wants—all her kids together."

Zee folds her arms. "Until Thanksgiving dinner's over and they leave her alone in the kitchen to wash dishes while they watch football and have a fart fest."

Ben, Lackey, and some of the other guys look like guilty little boys.

Newt spits in his cup. "Thing is..."

Nellie whispers, "Gross."

"... the Vietnamese *are* simple folk. Peasants working barefoot in rice paddies. Conical hats on their heads. Barely making enough to feed themselves or—"

"Hey," Ben cuts in. "Folks in south Missouri right now work in rice fields, ballcaps on their heads, and that don't make them—"

Newt raises his hands in surrender. "Don't go all cancel culture on me. I guess I was taking the long way around to say folks are the same all over. We all want to make our mammas happy, and we all think of them as magical queens who care for us."

In the middle of the street, Ben now at his side, Rồng says, "We children of the dragon *are* simple folk in some ways.

Complex in others. Newt's right, folks *are* the same all over, and we all want to make our mammas happy."

Rồng backs a few steps farther away from the crowd gathered on the shaded sidewalk outside his shop. In the morning sunlight that bathes the street, he feels his body growing warm, and sees his skin starting to shimmer like a highway heat mirage.

Ben's eyes remain trained on his friend. "What's going on, Rồng?"

Rồng cannot answer. His jaw tightens. Racked by sudden pain, bones snapping, Rồng feels his body undulate, expanding slowly, like a massive mylar snake balloon fed by a helium tank. His head rises atop a neck that stretches six, ten, fifteen feet over the street. As his clothes fall in tatters around him, the rest of Rồng's body also lengthens, morphing into an elegant, eel-like form covered in shiny sun-and-gold scales.

While pulling Lackey away, Agnes squeaks, "Rồng!"

Rồng continues to swell. His body inflates along the blacktop from the barber shop seventy feet south to the main intersection. Replacing what he has always considered frail human limbs, Rồng feels his four powerful, stocky legs take shape. They end in long-clawed feet that support his muscular, serpentine body—a body he has missed after spending decades as a man. His tongue rolls across rows of spiked teeth, perfect and white, filling crocodile-shaped jaws. Six-foot-long whiskers —Rồng enjoys how they resemble polished copper cables—stand out on each side of his face. He observes shocked people scattering beneath him.

As the pain of transformation fades, Rồng's smile spreads back to where his ears dissolve into his skull. He sighs, at long last revealing his true self to everyone, with predictable results. Almost predictable. Ben does not run like the others.

In the middle of Mystic Avenue, Ben stares up at Rồng.

"You're beautiful! Those eyes—vivid jade. Your whole body's golden, almost blinding in the sun. Magnificent!"

Rồng blinks away a tear. "No more than you."

"I'm guessing all those fortune cookie messages were meant for you, old friend."

Rồng nods. "Mother calls me home."

"Folks here would miss you if you leave. I'd miss you. You know that, right?"

"Au Co is family, Ben."

"And after all these years, I'm not?" Ben's eyes fill. "Would it matter at all if I said, you know?"

"Know what?"

"You know. I think, deep down, you've known since the day we met. But I'm not Jimmy. I could never replace him."

"I never wanted that, Ben."

"I'm nothing to look at. Or smart like you. Got nothing to offer. So, I've just tried to be the best friend I could be, hoping maybe someday you and me—"

"We've known each other a long time, Ben. When would someday ever come?"

"Today. Now. If you'll have me."

Rồng's neck drops. He is face to face with Ben. "Do you mean it?"

Ben strokes Rồng's smooth-scaled nose. "You know I do. With all my heart. I do."

———

Three weeks later, after a long day spent controlling rains in the north and sunning crops in the south with his brothers and sisters, Rồng sits side-by-side with Ben on the couch in the family castle atop Mount Fansipan. They focus on the computer monitor, watching Zee and Nellie mic'd up under the lights in Rico Cerna's studio.

Cerna offers a practiced stage smile for viewers and asks Zee and Nellie, "You still dispute the findings? Even though experts at the Centers for Disease Control and Prevention described how a unique strain of bird flu infected the Balm and Brimstone Diner's egg dishes to cause a mass hallucination?"

R`ồng and Ben smile at each other while Nellie answers, "Like we said, *we* didn't eat at the diner and we saw what we saw."

Almost frozen, Zee mumbles, "Uh-huh."

Ben laughs. "She's stagestruck." He squeezes R`ồng's hand.

Cerna returns to Nellie. "Too bad no one thought to livestream what happened."

"Yeah." Red-faced, Nellie's jaw locks. "Listen, no matter what the CDC or anyone says, what I saw will stay with me forever—old Ben riding over the springs and tree-covered hills, then disappearing into the sunrise on the back of a golden dragon."

While watching, R`ồng rests his head on Ben's shoulder.

"Quite the image, Nellie, and no one who was there that day disputes it." Cerna turns to the camera. "The CDC has their story and our eyewitnesses have *their* story. What really happened? Bad eggs or good magic? You decide."

A camera zooms in on Cerna. "It appears Silk Man is destined to become another one of the many fascinating stories folks tell their children at bedtime and around campfires in the sleepy little town of Mystic Springs." After a strategic pause, Cerna concludes, "Until next time, I'm Rico Cerna, your host for all things mysterious, bidding you a super supernatural day."

R`ồng nudges Ben. "Hear that?"

Ben grins. "Yep. We're fascinating."

JACK "MILES" VENTIMIGLIA

Some writers build worlds. Jack builds people—fantastic characters who interact realistically with each other and the world around them. Experience informs the characters he creates. Jack's background includes high school dropout, carnival game clerk, Mississippi River barge hand, natural gas roughneck in Oklahoma, journalist in Illinois, Missouri, and Kansas, and a 2021 Missouri Press Association Hall of Famer. He has received scores of writing awards, and prizes a Missouri State House proclamation in "deep gratitude" for his public service. Jack and his family live in Missouri with a shaggy mutt and more books than shelves.

THE GHOST WRITERS

JASON MEUSCHKE

ANSON ALLYNE CHECKED his phone again. "Eight minutes till," he muttered, setting it on the table before him beside his laptop. His eyes immediately went to the clock on the screen, verifying again it was almost midnight. He moved the ebony-black summoning candle more to the middle of the table before moving it back again. A red, plastic lighter lay beside it. He reclined in his seat, observed his setup, then burst into laughter.

"This is ridiculous!" he cried and began pacing his room. He couldn't help but feel conned by Flaminia, the strange gypsy woman who had greeted him when he arrived in town that afternoon. Granted, there was an exotic, mysterious quality to her, and she somehow knew he was there seeking inspiration for his writing career.

But how?

He continued pacing his small, third-floor room in the Atlantis Bed & Breakfast, also where the gypsy woman had insisted he should stay. The Atlantis, he'd discovered, was built to house distinguished visitors to the town in the late nineteenth century. The mystique of Mystic Springs did indeed bring visitors. Over the decades, this historic building had housed numerous travelers from around the world, celebrities, and even a politician.

Like Anson, their curiosity had brought them here. But interest had waned after a new interstate bypassed the town in the 60s and, until recent years, much of the world had forgotten about the town and its mysteries.

"I can't believe I'm even considering this," he said, still pacing the faded green carpet. But he had little other choice when recalling his recent berating from Grandpa.

"I don't care, Anson," Grandpa had bellowed, pointing an arthritic finger at him. "Your father coddled you too much when he was alive and running things. Allowing others to do everything for you. Did you even write any of your college assignments?"

"Yes!" Anson lied.

Grandpa's yellowed, bloodshot eyes stared Anson down, eventually forcing him to turn away. He never could meet Grandpa's gaze.

"I mean, I had some help occasionally, but only because I'm not a fast typist."

"Excuses!" Grandpa huffed, scowling. "Always an excuse. Well, it ends now. Starting today, you're cut off."

"You're throwing me out on the streets? How am I supposed to live?"

"I suggest getting a job."

Anson placed his hands on his head. "But I have a deal in place with a publisher! Surely that—"

"Don't try that on me, boy!" Grandpa barked. "I've spoken to your friend's boss in Seattle, at Hawthorn Books. He tells me you're nowhere near ready. Says most junior-high students can write better than you. And none of your articles have been printed, either." Grandpa steepled his fingers under his chin, eyeing Anson. "Did you learn nothing during all those years of college we paid for?"

Anson bit back a harsh response, knowing it wouldn't help him. Instead, he inhaled deeply and exhaled before answering. "Grandpa, please listen. I understand the writing rules. I'm just struggling with the story, is all. Besides, it's not unusual for writers to start slowly early in their careers. If you take away my money, I—"

"You graduated six years ago and have published exactly zero! You're as flighty as your mother. Meanwhile, you're regularly exceeding your monthly allowance of $15,000 your father arranged for you to *get by on*." Grandpa said this last bit with finger air quotes.

Anson kneeled at his grandpa's side, peering up at him, eyes glistening. "Grandpa, I promise I'm working hard. I just need a little more time."

Grandpa gave him a blank stare before shaking his head. "When I retired, and your father took over, he spoiled you after your mother ran away. And in the six months since cancer took him, forcing me out of retirement, I've observed first-hand how much of a leech you are on the belly of this family. That ends now. This month's allowance is the last. I suggest you either make something of yourself with your chosen career path or get a real job."

Anson bowed his head. "But, I'm a writer. I *need* to be a writer."

Grandpa stood on wobbly knees and hobbled to his office window. A nasty cough rumbled in his chest and he dabbed at his mouth with a handkerchief. Without turning, he said, "Show me something a publisher has accepted, and I'll consider it. Otherwise, maybe this isn't your calling. Like they say. Those who can't write, teach."

Anson's phone alarm chirped, notifying him it was one minute to midnight and bringing him out of his memories. He gritted his teeth, ran a hand through his wavy, chestnut hair, and forced a deep, calming breath.

"Okay, let's see what kind of voodoo BS this lady is pushing."

He sat at the table, woke his laptop, and cracked his knuckles. Keeping an eye on the clock, he flicked his lighter. At the stroke of midnight, he touched the flame to the wick.

A persistent knock woke Anson from a deep sleep. "Ugh," he mumbled, reaching for his pillow, only for his fingers to fumble against a hard surface. Opening his eyes, he discovered he'd fallen asleep at the table. His back and neck complained as he pushed himself upright in a confused stupor.

The knock came again.

"Oka—" he began, but his throat constricted, and he was suddenly aware of the extreme dryness in his mouth. A raspy cough erupted from his lungs, and he wobbled on unsteady legs to the bathroom. His tongue felt like sandpaper as he turned on the water and dipped his head into the cool stream. He gulped as if he'd gone days without water. He let it flow over his pounding head, then drank some more. At last, his throat eased enough to answer the persistent knocking.

"Hang on," he barked, dabbing his head with a towel. Moving unsteadily, he opened the door. Standing before him was the gypsy woman.

"Mr. Allyne," she said. "You are awake at last. We talk now." Without invitation, she brushed past him into the room. Her black, jewel-inlaid, silk robe whisked silently about her as she made her way to his table.

Anson closed the door and had to clear his throat twice before he could form a sentence. "What are you doing here?"

She tilted her head as if contemplating his laptop. "I'm here to ensure you remember the rules."

Rules? Anson thought, unable to expel the question from his dry mouth. Instead, he threw up his hands in a shrug.

Her fingers caressed his laptop, which woke from sleep.

"Hey!" he cried hoarsely, pushing her hand away. He started to close the device but stopped when he saw what was on the screen.

"You've had a successful writing session, it seems," she said with a hint of sarcasm as she glided to the window.

Anson stared at paragraphs of words on the screen. He sat down and ran the cursor over multiple open tabs, revealing even more writing.

"I don't believe it," he said, massaging his temple. "How did I do this?"

She turned from the window and approached Anson. "Do you still doubt your abilities?" Her left hand disappeared into the folds of her dress and produced a tiny vial, which she placed on the table.

"What's this?" he whispered.

"Drink," she said flatly, then once again returned to the window.

Anson raised the bottle, removed the stopper, and sniffed. The aroma of cool, clean water filled his nostrils, making his throat ache. Without another thought, he tipped it into his mouth, swallowing the contents. Instantly, his mouth felt cool and refreshed, and his headache subsided. Like a wave moving over him, the sensation washed down his throat and through the rest of his body, leaving him revitalized within seconds. Anson closed his eyes, relishing the moment and feeling as if he'd had a full night's sleep.

He opened his eyes and stared at Flaminia. "What *was* that? I feel incredible!"

She shrugged without turning away from the window. "Just water."

He shook his head, marveling that his pounding headache was gone. "Yeah, sure, but what was in the water?"

Flaminia turned to him, her eyes boring into his. "It is water. Now you tell me what you experienced last night."

Anson wanted to argue, but her words triggered a memory. Something he couldn't quite make sense of. Almost like a... "I dreamed a lady visited me! What was her name? Oh yeah, Wilder. Laura Wilder. She was giving me writing advice, like writing-from-my-heart kinda stuff. Crazy, right?"

Flaminia narrowed her eyes. "Laura Ingalls Wilder visited you for inspiration and you think it crazy?"

Anson blinked curiously. "Umm, well I dreamed it, and who's Laura Ingalls—"

"Dreamed?" Flaminia interrupted, waving to the laptop. "And do you *write* in your sleep also?"

Anson considered her insinuation, but struggled with it. After all, it had to have been a dream, right? He scrolled through his writing as if it might hold the answers, then a popup alerted him to a new email marked *Important*.

Anson opened the email. He read it, rubbed his eyes, and re-read it. It was an acceptance letter for an article he'd submitted. *What article?* He tapped into his mailbox and found two more emails from publications, both of them acceptance letters. "What's going on?" he whispered.

His phone buzzed, startling him. He grabbed it, recognizing the name of his editor friend, Stan. "Hello?"

"Where have you been?" cried Stan.

"What do you mean?"

"I've only been trying to reach you all morning about those articles you sent me last night. Where'd you come up with this old-timey angle, anyway?"

Anson's lips moved without sound. Finally, he said, "Stan, let me call you back." He hung up and stared stupidly at Flaminia. "What's happening?"

The slightest of smiles danced at the corners of her red lips. "Is no mystery, Mr. Allyne. You lighted a summoning candle and inspiration came to you, just as I say it would."

He pointed to the computer. "But how could I have done so much in one night?"

She huffed. "Willpower can be quite strong when properly motivated. Now listen." She placed two more tiny vials on the table. "Remember what I say. Only three days for inspiration. Too much risk beyond that."

"What risk?"

Flaminia slapped the top of his head like an old schoolteacher punishing a student. "Do you forget already how you feel this morning? The summoning has a cost! Just as you are learning from the spirit, the spirit feeds from your very life force to feel alive again. A few hours with a spirit can cost you days of your mortal life. The water can replenish you, but it cannot quench a selfish heart!"

The day after his third night, a buzzing sound dragged Anson from a deep, dead-like slumber. He'd dreamed he was buried to the neck in the desert sand below a blazing sun. He pried his eyes open to discover he was lying on the floor. He tried to speak, and his throat constricted with the effort, threatening to collapse like a depleted coal mine.

The water! his mind screamed around a jackhammer headache. His legs felt useless. So, using his arms, he slowly dragged himself to the table. His elbows creaked with the strain, and the bones of his fingers popped like bubble wrap. His skin stretched taut over his body like old leather on the verge of tearing.

At last, he reached a trembling hand over the table's edge and grabbed the remaining bottle. Opening it, he downed the contents greedily. Rolling onto his back, he shook the empty bottle over his mouth and ran his tongue over the end, craving every drop. Gradually, he allowed his arm to fall aside as the water coursed through his veins, washing away every ache and pain and refreshing him better than dousing his head in ice water. His bones felt strong once again, his skin soft and supple.

"Holy cow, that's incredible," he gasped. He got to his feet and woke his laptop. Waiting for it to come alive, he recalled that on his second night of writing, he had been visited by none other than Mark Twain himself. Their chat had rewarded him with another article, an articulate opinion piece on the price of fame. Additionally, he had written two short stories of more than five thousand words each, and a twelve-page outline for a novel along with the first three chapters.

Stan had been ecstatic and quickly made deals for all of it by late yesterday morning. He added that two publications had inquired about first-look rights of whatever he wrote next.

Anson smiled at the thought, but when the laptop screen finally lit up, a joyous laugh erupted from his core. "I don't believe it!"

Typed on the screen before him was a science fiction novel of over seventy thousand words, and just shy of three-hundred pages.

"I'm amazing!" Anson bellowed to the empty room, jumping from his seat. He tossed the empty vial into the trash. Laughing, he went to the fridge, suddenly realizing how famished he was. He retrieved a bottle of orange juice and a granola bar before returning to the table.

He took a swig of juice and racked his brain, trying to remember the name of the third night's spirit. "Robert Heineken? Hemline? Heinlein? I think it was Heinlein, wasn't it?"

He had a vague memory of hearing the name in college, but he couldn't be sure.

"Oh well." Anson took a bite of the granola and settled into his chair to look over his story when his phone buzzed. He recalled the phone had been what woke him earlier, and he had a feeling he knew who it was.

Anson grabbed the phone and spoke around another bite of granola. "Footure best-sheller shpeaking! Tell me shomething good, Shtan!"

A woman's voice on the other end stammered, "Er, I'm trying to reach Mr. Anson Allyne."

Anson coughed, choking on the granola, and sat up straighter in his seat. He glanced at the phone screen but didn't recognize the number or the name. "This is he."

"Mr. Allyne? Oh good. I've been having a difficult time reaching you today."

Anson checked the time on his laptop. *Holy crap, almost four in the afternoon?*

The woman continued. "My name is Sharon Rivers. I'm an

associate with the Caspian Bay group. We're the legal team behind the Allyne Foundation."

"Okay," Anson said slowly with a shrug, reaching for his juice.

"Mr. Allyne, I'm very sorry to be the bearer of bad news, but your grandfather passed away early this morning."

Anson's hand froze halfway to his mouth. Slowly, he placed the juice back on the table and struggled to find his words. "Um, what? Are you... are you sure?"

"Yes, Mr. Allyne. I'm afraid so. Do you need a minute?"

Anson cleared his throat. "No, I'm okay. Thank you."

"Of course," she said. "Now, I've already spoken with Mr. Brooks, your grandfather's assistant at the Allyne Foundation. Are you familiar with him?"

"I... I'm not sure. Maybe?" An image came to mind of a portly, bald man he'd seen occasionally, but he'd never bothered to remember the man's name.

"Mr. Brooks handles much of the day-to-day goings-on with the foundation. He requested that we contact you with the news and arrange for your return. He'd like you to return by tomorrow if possible."

Anson frowned. "You mean for the funeral?"

"I'm sure that's part of it, Mr. Allyne. I believe he'd also like to make certain arrangements with you, as you are the sole heir."

Anson bolted up from his chair, knocking his juice bottle to the floor in the process. "The sole *what?* Hang on, lady. Are you saying my grandfather kept me in his will after all?"

There was a frustratingly long silence on the phone. Long enough Anson nearly said something before she spoke again.

"I'm unaware of any recent changes to the will, Mr. Allyne. There will still be a formal reading of it after the funeral, but I have ascertained that you are the sole heir to your family's foundation."

"Holy sh—" Anson clapped his hand over his mouth. A thousand jumbled thoughts raced through his mind, and he began to pace. "So, uh, okay then. What do I do now?"

"Mr. Brooks has made arrangements for a car to pick you up and take you to the nearest airport, where he'll have the jet waiting for you. Your car rental will be taken care of for you."

"That's great!" Anson said, louder than he'd intended. He couldn't wait to get back to his beloved jet, already imagining using it for book tours with his newfound author fame.

"Very good then," Ms. Rivers continued. "Mr. Brooks also requests that you write a piece for the paper about your grandfather."

Anson's mouth gaped. "Me?"

"Yes, sir. He said your grandfather would've wanted it that way, given your recent success."

Anson grinned. *Of course. Grandpa kept tabs on my progress. I bet he knew about my article sales from that first day!* A tear formed in the corner of his eye, and he wiped it away. "I'd be honored to."

"Very good. Mr. Brooks will email you the factual information, and you'll put your own creative spin on the rest."

"I'll do my best."

After they hung up, Anson sat back at the table. He allowed himself a few minutes to peruse his sci-fi book, marveling at the details. Next, he checked his emails, first finding one from Mr. Brooks with the family history he'd need, then another from Stan, who was over the moon for the new book.

"This is gonna be huge!" Stan's email read, mentioning how the book lent itself perfectly to a series.

Anson beamed.

He realized what crap he'd been writing before these past few days. If he had to be honest, he'd never really put in the effort before, which Grandpa had recognized. But now things were different. Now, he knew he could do this, just as he'd always believed he could.

Anson cracked his knuckles and opened a new document. He read over the information from Mr. Brooks, then began typing his grandfather's piece for the paper.

Eight hours later, Anson slammed his head on the table. "Argh!" The afternoon had melted into darkness, and the laptop clock read 10:47 p.m. During that time, Anson had toiled away at writing something—anything—resembling the quality of his work these past few nights. Of the eight attempts to write the newspaper piece on his grandfather, not one had any feeling or flow to the words. Rather, they all read like something an elementary-aged child wrote for school. As Grandpa had said, a junior-high kid could do better!

Anson then switched gears, attempting to find his flow by writing something else. He tried to start the sequel to his sci-fi book and realized he didn't remember enough to continue. Next, he used his novel outline from the second night to try writing just the next chapter. Instead, he spent nearly an hour staring at the blank page and writing less than a paragraph.

Now Anson raised his head from the table, only to plop it into his hands. He knew the experience of the past few days had been something to learn from. Something he could build from if he took the time to do so going forward. After all, he could still hear the spirits' voices echoing in his mind.

"Except their advice is all jumbled right now!" he yelled at the room. Anson slammed his fist on the table, shaking the laptop and the summoning candle. He stared at the black candle for a long moment before getting up.

"Screw it," he said. He went to the trash and dug out the tiny vials from Flaminia. He took them to the sink and filled each from the tap. This water was a little clearer than hers, but what other choice did he have? He placed them on the table beside the candle, then grabbed two bottles of water and two bottles of Gatorade from the fridge. He went back for a third Gatorade and began chugging it on his way to the table.

"I can beat this," he said, pumping himself up. "I just need to hydrate ahead and I'll be good to go."

He sat down, finished the drink, and opened another.

"Besides, I just need one more night for a buffer. This should give me more than enough work to buy me time to study what I've learned in between book tours and events."

He chugged half of the new drink before stopping for a breath. "Once this book comes out and I get a movie deal, I'll have plenty of time to prep the next book. It's not like I'm gonna R.R. Martin this thing! I'm Anson Allyne, sole heir to the Allyne Foundation, and we make stuff happen!"

The clock showed 11:59.

Anson clapped his hands together and took a deep breath. He twisted his head to one side and got a satisfying crack, then repeated it on the other side. As he'd done the previous three nights, he picked up his lighter and held it near the candle.

He stared at the old vials now refilled with tap water and a pang of worry curled in his gut. The gypsy woman's words echoed in his mind. *The water cannot quench a selfish heart.*

The clock turned to midnight.

Anson pushed away his doubts and lit the candle. The flame turned from yellow to blue, with a black outline. Anson watched it curiously as he drank from one of the vials. He didn't remember the flame changing colors before.

The flame grew in both size and intensity. Despite the blue color, its vibrancy illuminated every corner of the room.

Anson felt a trickle of perspiration on his forehead, and he drank from another vial.

The candle erupted into a torrent, like a tiny flamethrower. Wind began to whip and wail within the room, throwing papers and food wrappers about.

Anson covered his eyes with one hand, reaching for the candle with the other. This was too much. He needed to snuff it out.

Suddenly, the wind stopped, and the candle calmed to a small, steady yellow flame.

Anson tried rubbing the spots from his eyes.

"Good evening," said a voice behind him.

Anson turned to find a well-dressed gentleman.

"Hello," Anson said with a smile.

The gentleman bowed. "I am T.S. Elliot."

"And I am William S. Burroughs," said another voice.

Anson spun the other way, surprised by a second spirit. "Whoa, two of you?"

"My name is Maya Angelou," a woman's voice sounded right beside him.

"Holy crap!" Anson said, startled. "Three?"

"What's going on?" grumbled a new voice. "Why am I here?"

Anson turned again, this time finding an older, gruff-looking man.

"Good of you to make it, Hemingway!" said Burroughs.

"Why have I returned?" said Heinlein, strolling past the others and looking about the room.

Anson squeezed his eyes shut. He felt dizzy. He opened his eyes and waved a hand for everyone's attention. "Why are there so many of you?"

"Excellent question, my boy!" announced a new arrival, John Steinbeck.

"Oh man, not this again," said another voice.

Anson searched out the voice and stared dumbly at a familiar face. "Stephen King? But you're not even dead, are you?"

King leaned closer to Anson and grimaced. "You never saw me."

Anson blinked and King was gone, replaced by even more ghosts. A shudder racked his body and Anson covered his eyes, crying out, "It's too many! There's too many of you!"

With more appearing by the minute, their voices blurred together as they began giving Anson advice.

Anson watched as his room filled with spirits. At one point, he swore he saw the black silk robes of the gypsy woman, but she was gone when he looked again.

"I didn't want this!" he moaned thickly. His mouth was parched and felt full of cotton. He reached for the remaining vial but stopped. He didn't recognize the now weathered, bony-looking hand trying to grab it.

The spirits gathered around the table, speaking to him in a blustering cacophony.

Anson threw his head back to scream, but nothing came out.

Mystic Springs Police Chief Samantha Simpkins climbed the stairs of the Atlantis B&B, where her deputy greeted her in the hall outside one of the third-floor rooms. "What have we got, Shad?"

The young deputy tipped his hat back on his head and nodded to an open door. "Missing person, I guess."

She squinted at him as she passed, entering the small room. "You guess?"

Shad followed her. "Well, I don't really know what to make of it, ma'am."

Chief Simpkins stopped just inside, having spotted another man in a suit and tie speaking on a cell phone.

Simpkins raised an eyebrow to her deputy, then spoke to the stranger. "Can I help you?"

The man held up a finger, as if asking for patience, and went back to his call. "Yes, sir, that's correct. I don't know where he is. No, I'm in his room now and he's not here."

Simpkins turned to Shad and crossed her arms.

Shad winced. "I know, I know. He shouldn't be in our crime scene, but since we don't know what this is yet, I asked him to stay."

"Who is he?"

The man ended his call and approached. "My name is Waters. I'm a representative of the Allyne Foundation, here to pick up Anson Allyne, except he's not here."

Simpkins shook his hand, giving him a skeptical look. "Allyne. Sure, I've heard of them. I take it this Anson fella is kin?"

Waters's brow shot up. "As of yesterday, Mr. Allyne is the heir, and CEO, of the Allyne Foundation."

Shad whistled.

Simpkins nodded. "And I take it he's the one we're looking for?"

Shad nodded. "Yes, ma'am. He hasn't checked out and no

one's seen him since yesterday evening when he had a bunch of sports drinks sent up from the Deer Stand Café." He pointed to a table in the middle of the room.

Simpkins approached the table. Empty Gatorade bottles, and a half-full one, sat next to an open laptop. But what truly drove her curiosity was the dust-covered pile of clothes on the seat and floor by the table.

"Are these his clothes?" she asked the two men. Neither had an answer. She squatted beside the chair for a closer inspection of the shoes. They were full of the same dust, with the socks still inside.

She rose. "Well, either the rapture happened, and I wasn't counted worthy, or I'd say your friend has a strange sense of humor."

Waters cleared his throat and spoke, somewhat under his breath. "Honestly, Mr. Allyne has always been a bit flighty, but why would he run off now?"

Simpkins cocked her head. "Maybe the pressure of taking over the company? Maybe he wanted to do something else with his life?" She put on a blue latex glove and touched the laptop's trackpad.

The screen came to life, showing an open document.

Simpkins leaned closer to read it.

A selfish heart has a thirst which cannot be quenched.

A selfish heart has no cure.

No cure! No cure! No cure! No cure!

Simpkins shook her head. "I don't know your friend, but this has all the hallmarks of a mental breakdown if you ask me. This last part about *no cure* repeats for another three pages."

"Oh dear," Waters sighed, looking back and forth between the laptop and the chief.

Shad turned to the window. "What's going on outside?" He

opened it and a gust blew past, scattering the dust as if a vacuum had exploded.

"Shad!" Simpkins yelled as the deputy slammed the window shut.

"Sorry!" he said sheepishly while Simpkins and Waters patted the dust from their clothes.

"What was so important?" she asked.

Shad hooked a thumb toward the window. "Looks like news of the mystery is getting out. I even saw Rico with his camera."

"Great," Simpkins muttered, not at all anxious to face the imaginative questions from the town's famed podcaster. She waved both men toward the door. "For now, I want everyone out of the room. Mr. Waters, give Shad your number and we'll keep you updated as we go."

"I need to call my boss back," he said. He removed his phone from a pocket while patting the dust from his pant legs with his free hand.

Once everyone had left the room, Simpkins began closing the door behind her when something caught her eye. She reopened the door and scanned the floor by the table. She stepped inside and spotted something glimmering in the remaining dust pile beside the shoes.

Simpkins bent down and, using her gloved hand, removed the object. She inspected the tiny glass vial for a moment, recognizing it as one used by half a dozen shops in town to sell the so-called magical water of Mystic Springs.

She sighed, disappointed. "Darn, I was hoping for a clue."

Simpkins sighed again and tossed the tiny bottle into the trash on her way out the door.

JASON MEUSCHKE

Jason A. Meuschke is a U.S. Air Force Veteran who writes thrillers with various sub-genre elements like Paranormal Mystery, Crime, and Science Fiction. He's currently expanding the world of his first series, which he labels Retro-80s Sci-Fi, called *The Bandit Chronicles*, with book three coming soon. Jason also hosts *The Sample Chapter Podcast*, a weekly show where he interviews authors from all around the world.

Links for Jason's books and show are at:
https://www.jasonameuschke.com

GETTING NAILED

G. A. EDWARDS

"I'M GOING to check on the minister's wife in the mud-bath room, and then I'll be in my office." Galina Turner looked around her new beauty and wellness salon, The Glamour Grotto, for an acknowledgment. Nothing.

Petros, the nail technician, hid behind the latest copy of the *Mystic Times*. He wasn't likely to speak, even if she could understand his thick Eastern-European accent. He was still miffed from earlier in the morning. She'd spilled his sorting tray of acrylic nail tips when he was applying her new nails. Her nails looked good, but what a fit he'd thrown.

Galina moved to the designated hairdressing area of the salon. Rhoda, the ancient, hard-of-hearing hairdresser, backcombed a lavender-tinted bouffant. Her customer, Miss Ovaline Parsons, the even more ancient and proudly self-proclaimed town spinster, demonstrated the mastery of sleeping upright. At least, Galina hoped she was sleeping.

As a business owner, Galina planned to utilize the services of the vendors renting space from her. In addition to the two working, she had hired a Mystic Springs local as a masseuse. The problem was the woman only worked when her *chakra* circle was favorable. The empty table indicated today wasn't one of those days.

Galina twisted her neck from side to side. She would schedule a massage soon. From the style emanating from Rhoda's teasing comb and arthritic fingers, it would be a while before Galina risked her smooth brunette pageboy with an appointment.

A certified esthetician, Galina had used her skin product know-how to develop a special facial and body mud using the mineral-rich water surrounding the town of Mystic Springs. Locals had claimed all sorts of mysterious properties of the waters, from granting people's wishes to punishing others who did bad things. Galina only wished her use of the waters would encourage enough people to love her Mystic Mud and keep the business afloat. Her investment money had been spent to update the spa building's interior and build a walkway to the stone grotto.

Galina stopped outside the door of the mud-bath room. Rumors claimed Minister Sweeting's wife was looking to add a little spark to their marriage. Galina wanted her best customer content as she rested in a tub of mud, her brown hair tucked in an absorbent terrycloth turban, relishing the soft sounds of an artificial rain shower.

Knock. Knock. "How are you doing in here, Mrs. Sweeting?" Galina peeked around the door of the mud-bath room.

"Now, Galina. Just call me Myra. The Lord sure blessed Mystic Springs when he called you here from that heathen-hole Houston. Your great-uncle Floyd—bless his heart—performed an act of glory by passing this building to you."

"Well, I didn't really know him, but... Is there anything I can get you, ma'am?"

"No, dear. These moo-mosa drinks are wonderful. I've had tree from the pitcher already. I mean *three*." She giggled, waving her hand about, flinging tiny mud chunklets. "I can't wait to tell the ladies at the All-turd—'scuse me—I meant Altar Society all about them tonight."

"Uh, okay. It's nice to see you so... relaxed."

Just what Galina needed in this wacky, backwoods town—rumors that she got the minister's wife drunk.

At her desk, Galina entered another amount in her bookkeeping program. The good news was that each time a customer had booked a service, she'd been able to upsell her Mystic Mud. But the figures weren't enough to cover the renovations inside the stone grotto. Set behind the salon at the water's edge on the chilly public spring, the grotto promised spa-friendly combinations of reviving cold-water plunges and stress-relieving hot-yoga sessions around the center platform's propane firepit.

Galina rolled her neck from shoulder to shoulder. Too bad yoga was her best bet to relieve her own stress. An extended romance dry spell hadn't allowed for her favorite type of stress relief.

Ding.

The front door. She stood to go greet the new entrant when the sound of angry voices came from the front of the salon.

Crash.

Galina jumped at the sound of glass breaking. Guttural shouts were exchanged in a foreign tongue. She stuck her head out the office door to see past the hairdressing area. Two figures flailed back and forth across the front section of the salon. One was Petros, her cranky nail technician. The other looked to be a large man.

Galina stepped into the hall when Rhoda popped into view between her and the silhouettes of the wrestling men. Headed for Galina, Rhoda ushered the ancient Miss Parsons, who was tightly cradling her large handbag to her sagging chest.

Galina rushed forward, then guided both women into her office, the only room besides the front that had a landline phone. Once inside, she shoved and stacked office chairs in front of the door. "Rhoda, call the police!"

"Did she say she's going to Nice?" Miss Ovaline Parsons asked. "That's Italy. My neighbor took me to one of those I-talian restaurants with the soup, salad—"

"Rhoda! The police." The hairdresser nodded, still focused on backing Miss Parsons into the only chair Galina hadn't stacked in front of the door.

"I had wine, and for dessert—"

Before the woman could continue, and amid the chaos out front, a knock came on the office door.

"Shush!" Galina ordered.

Knock. Knock. "Honey, are you in there? I'm out of the mud bath, and I've got some in my eyes. I can't see a thing."

Mrs. Sweeting? "Oh no!" Galina tossed the chairs she'd just set in place to the side and opened the office door to tug the minister's wife inside. Galina slammed the door and began rebuilding the chair barrier.

Mrs. Sweeting said, "I swear that grotto construction work sounds like it's inside the building. And those words said in anger? Well, my husband has been preaching in vain on the use of our Lord's name."

Rhoda moved to use the edge of her smock to dab at the mud covering Mrs. Sweeting's eyes.

Every head in the room turned in the direction of the build-ing's front when a mechanical whirring screeched before revving up. Then came agonized screams.

Galina backstepped from the door, pulled Miss Parsons off the chair, and herded all of the ladies into the storeroom connected to the office. "Okay, everyone grab something to arm yourselves. No, Miss Parsons, not the toilet paper."

"I wish I hadn't left my Bible in the other room," Mrs. Sweeting said, mud chunklets flying from her arms. "Someone out there needs a good thumping."

"Am I going to die?" Miss Parsons dug in her handbag and pulled out a compact. "Or..." She pursed her wrinkled lips, "be vi-o-lated?" She took a swipe at her hair. "My stars! I haven't had a man try that since 1967 on Tuesd—"

"No dying, no violating," Galina interrupted. "The police will be here soon."

Focused on the noises up front, Galina could have sworn she heard another ding or even two from the front door.

But she was all ears when Rhoda said, "Um, Galina. I forgot to phone the police."

Now they were ready. Galina had called and been forced to leave a message on the police station's answering machine. With only two officers in town, there was no telling when help would arrive, but she had taken point with a gallon jug of Mystic Mud in each hand. Rhoda flanked her with tubes of rainbow-colored hair tint for squirting into the intruder's eyes. Next to Rhoda, Miss Parsons leaned on a broom that she could use as a club or possibly fly on. Mrs. Sweeting had refused to weaponize on the basis that the Lord protected those who were mighty of heart.

The buzzing of the saw and the screams had stopped.

Ding. Either someone had left or someone had entered. The band of beauty salon vigilantes still waited in the storeroom.

Zane Hillard watched his step down the crooked sidewalk of the main drag. He'd already stopped by the town's police station to speak with Chief Simpkins, who'd recently solved a big murder case. Simpkins's uncle—back in Chicago and Zane's most recent boss—had requested the courtesy visit. Zane hadn't minded, since Mystic Springs was mostly on his way to the Gulf of Mexico. After a year and half undercover to infiltrate a group selling drugs and illegal arms, Zane was on extended leave and primed for fun in the sun.

And to get this long, straggly hair off his neck. When Zane had asked where to get a haircut, a man outside the honky-tonk had told him some far-fetched tale of the missing barber and a dragon. The man then suggested Zane head down to the fancy new spa.

Wait, is that blood? Zane studied the sidewalk just outside the doorway of what the overhead swinging sign identified as The Glamour Grotto. He reached for the weapon he usually carried, but he'd left his gun locked in his motorcycle saddlebags at the hotel. Grabbing his phone instead, he hit the emergency number for the police station only to reach an answering machine, where he requested assistance. Then he crouched close to the ground to spy into the salon's large window. Overturned furniture and supplies sprawled across the floor in disarray. More blood decorated the floor, walls, and chairs.

Could be someone is inside and hurt.

Zane moved to the door and entered, taking care to step over shattered bottles of nail polish, cutting shears, teasing combs, and the biggest cans of hairspray he'd ever seen. And blood. A lot of blood. Farther in the salon, there were piles of some dark substance that tracked from one door to the other. Sliding along the wall down the hall, he pressed his boot's toe in one of the piles. Some substance that was thick and slimy.

He shoved a door open. Clear, but the tub full of mud explained at least one thing. He moved across the hall to the door labeled *Office*. He twisted the handle—not locked, but resistant to opening. Cracking the door open with a push, he saw stacked chairs.

Someone is inside. Maybe the source of the blood—or the reason behind it.

Zane muscled the door open to reveal papers strewn across a desk. That was all he had time to determine when another door flew open and released his very own banshee Armageddon.

A pretty-faced brunette woman led the charge, followed by two older ladies sporting towering hair, with some kind of earth monster bringing up the rear. Stunned, Zane failed to notice their weapons.

Turned out a jug of beauty mud might be great for complexions, but not so great for his nose. Or for maintaining consciousness.

———

"That's him. The big city cop who got beat up by women at the salon."

Zane hobbled to the bar, sporting mask-like bandages over his nose and cheeks, his entire body sore as hell from the beating. Every single soul in this God-forsaken room stared. Probably hoped he'd shed some light on the biggest excitement for Mystic

Springs—in oh, a month or two—a crime missing both perpe-trator and victim. *Heck, all that blood in the salon would be big news anywhere.*

Zane wanted to slam back a beer. Lots of them. Then again, the label on the pain pills the doctor had prescribed stressed alcohol was a no-no. Maybe he'd just hold a cold one against his face like a boozy ice pack. Probably wouldn't help, but it couldn't make him seem more ridiculous, with his reputation as a lawman in shreds. He'd stopped by the police station and the chief had let him read the file. A couple of items were listed as missing—some of that mud stuff and the salon's appointment book—but the blood and the missing employee suggested more than a simple robbery. As for Zane's part, he'd learned three ladies had taken him down. Another had prayed over him. Now, he just prayed this place served some kind of soup.

Someone slid onto the stool next to him. He didn't even look up.

"Mr. Hillard, I'm Galina from The Glamour Grotto."

He was about to tell the woman to clear out when he recalled that brunette who had been the one good memory of his trip so far. He turned and was not disappointed. Same pretty face, and he now saw her eyes were hazel. Even better, her lanky body in jeans and a top revealed curves where he liked them.

Please, don't let her be wearing boots.

For Zane, a woman wearing boots called to him like the fiery spice of a jalapeno. With his aches and pains this night, he wasn't up to even bland bell pepper action. Still, he looked down.

Yep, boots.

Hoping his silence meant he wasn't angry with her, Galina leaned in, then pulled back when the man turned to reveal a striking set of aquamarine eyes. They were sort of bloodshot around the edges, and maybe the contrast of the white bandage crossing his nose and cheeks exaggerated their beauty, but Galina felt a spark of attraction for this man. She looked the rest of him over. Nice. "Uh, as I was saying, Mr. Hillard, I am just so—"

"My name is Zane." His voice was deep. Dreamy, even if his pronunciation was off.

"Oh, I know. Zane Hillard, and you're a big-time police officer who mostly works undercover." Galina shrugged one shoulder. "Everybody in town knows. It's in today's paper."

Zane winced. "Sounds like you know my bidness." *Bidness?* He swallowed, then cleared his throat and tried again. "Why don't you tell me about your business?"

"My salon has only been open for a couple of weeks. I've always wanted to have my own business." She smiled.

Zane nodded. Cracking a smile back would hurt too much. "Who all did you have working for you that day?"

"My nail technician, Petros, but he's disappeared. And Rhoda Carmichael, the beautician." She grimaced. "You actually met her the other day at the salon."

"Is she the reason I'm wearing a mask, my clothes look like rainbows, I'm traumatized by the broomb—uh broom—lady with towering hair, or that my nightmares will feature the scary dirt-faced-praying-towel-wearer?"

"Rhoda's the rainbows. And watch what you call dirt. I hit your face with a gallon jug of my patent-pending Mystic Mud!"

Zane leaned back at her little outburst, wary of catching an enthusiastic elbow to his already broken nose. "I see. Tell me about this missing guy Petros."

Galina's face sobered. "Oh yes, Petros, the nail technician. He had just been working for a couple of days. All of that blood —I so hope he's okay."

She sounded teary, so Zane ripped off a paper towel from a spindle, used in place of napkins, and placed it on the bar just in case.

"This Petros got a last name? And what was he like?"

Galina swallowed. "Popvov. Quiet overall. He seemed a little jumpy and kind of cranky. But I had him do my nails for me and they turned out okay." She extended one hand for Zane to inspect.

He grasped her hand, holding it, then holding it more, before he ran his thumb over the side in a caress. Galina leaned in. Zane leaned in.

"So, what'll it be?"

Galina jerked her head, hand, and body away.

"Big Junior Wayne Lee cooked up a batch of deer meatloaf tonight." The man, whose folksy demeanor screamed property's owner, leaned forward. "Secret is he adds the heart, kidneys, and such, then a scoop of the raw liver right before it's served." He grinned. "Tells everyone his recipe is *organ-ic*—get it? I say it's organs with a little *ick*."

"I'm going to pass, Judd." Galina's voice shook. Likely from laughing at the repulsed look on Zane's face—well, the parts that showed.

"But I will take a slice of Bernice Ellen's chocolate pie." She asked Zane, "Do you like broccoli?"

"Hate it."

"He'll have the chicken noodle soup."

"Alrighty then. You're missing out." Judd scratched their order down on a pad and shuffled off.

"Just pie?" Zane asked.

"Life's short and then you…" Galina's face looked troubled, like she just figured out Petros could be dead.

Zane changed the topic. "What if I don't like chicken soup?"

"Only kind offered other than broccoli and cheese. The good news is soup only comes premade in cartons. Big Junior Wayne Lee doesn't add his culinary flair. Another tip—don't ever order the chili."

Zane bit the bullet and smiled at Galina. The pain was worth it. "I'm going to trust you on this." The word *trust* reminded Zane he was helping the law of the town gather information. Not flirt with this woman. Or kiss her. Definitely not sleep with her. He sighed. "So, back to this nail tech guy."

"Petros just showed up one day. Said he saw my ad in a trade magazine. Do you think he's—"

The door of the bar flung open with a *whack,* and a man strode in.

"Ya'll ain't gonna believe this one. You know that *fur-rin* guy working at the new beauty place?"

Galina and Zane whirled, waiting to hear more.

"Well, two fishermen came across him down in ole' Perry Jenkins's fishing shack."

"Is he okay?" Galina asked, her quiet voice betraying her concern for the man.

"Is he dead?" Zane asked, his voice steady, betraying it wasn't his first time to ask such a question.

"No, he ain't dead!"

"Oh, thank goodness!" Galina said.

Zane reached over and clasped his hand over hers.

The man continued his sharing. "I ain't even told the real kicker."

"Well, get to it," a bar patron ordered.

"He's missing a body part."

With leery looks, Zane and Galina asked at the same time, "What part?"

The man assumed the position of a cheerleader about to deliver the big finish. He threw his arm straight up and yelled, "His whole hand!"

Zane and Galina slid off their barstools. Dinner was over.

"Rico Cerna, live from Mystic Springs. If it's mysterious, it can happen here. I'm outside The Glamour Grotto, the site of a grisly attack. One man's hand was cut off with what was likely a medical-grade bone saw. Reports are coming in of a large man wearing a long coat with a reddened face confronting town citizens and grabbing at their hands. So far, victims have escaped, fighting back with whatever weapons were close at hand—golf club, leaf rake, bone-in ham, and an aggressive, three-legged Chihuahua named Zippity-Do-Dog. This is Rico, signing off with this warning—keep your hands in your pockets and your eyes open for the Bone Saw Butcher."

Galina was worried. Petros was healing, but still refused to give any information. The police had looked with no results for the big man that everyone now called the Bone Saw Butcher. That sensational name had encouraged the people of Mystic Springs to act even more crazy than usual.

Maybe she was, too—*crazy*—to think she could make a go of the spa.

The office clock showed five minutes until Galina's usual opening time. Not expecting any business, Galina trudged to the front of the building, but stopped. A line of faces were pressed to the salon's windows, looking in.

How dare they come to gawk!

Wasn't it enough that poor Petros was missing a hand, and his career as a nail tech was over? And her dream of a successful salon was likely kaput?

Wait, was that Myra Sweeting out there? And that traitor Rhoda!

Galina stomped across the salon and flipped the locks, ready to do battle. Instead, she was gobsmacked when the crowd let out a cheer.

"I, uh, what is happening?"

Rhoda bustled up to her. "Everyone's come to support you, Galina."

A woman hustled forward wearing a long floral dress and huge hat. "Hi, dear, I am Mrs. Beau John Taylor, Chamber of Commerce president, and we're here for your surprise-ribbon-cutting! Don't worry about a thing." The woman pointed and ordered, "Alan, set up the table. Anita, roll out the ribbon and get the big scissors. Myrtle, be a dear, and set out dessert napkins." The woman turned back to Galina. "The Deer Stand's cook seasoned the summer sausage on the charcuterie plate himself." She stepped closer. "I hope you're ready for appointments. Several of us can't wait to try your Mystic Mud."

Rhoda offered, "Galina's wonderful, even hires staff members for her own beauty needs. Petros did this manicure before... well, before." She held Galina's hand up to display the painted nails. "I can't wait to get my own hands on that flat hair of hers. Poof it right up!"

Mrs. Beau John Taylor squealed. "A business woman who supports her staff and isn't afraid to take risks? We'll plan a full photo feature in the newspaper."

Zane should have left town before now. Instead, he, Officer Shad, and Police Chief Simpkins sat in the two-room police station staring at a rolling bulletin board covered with case details on 3x5 cards awaiting connections by yarn.

Hadn't helped, because the three of them still had nothing. The only information confirmed was that a bone saw really had been used to remove the nail technician's still unrecovered hand.

Zane lamented, "I wish somebody in this town had real cameras, trained on the front of The Glamour Grotto."

"People here are trusting," Shad said. "Even with all the strange stuff that happens with the springs."

"Stranger than somebody cutting off a man's hand?" Zane asked.

The two local officers looked at each other and shrugged.

Shad said, "We could try a sweep for new witnesses."

"We could," Chief Simpkins agreed. "But everyone in town that day was interviewed. Even some from out of town who wanted to be part of the action."

Shad looked down at the floor. "I hate to suggest this, but could Galina be involved? She hasn't been in town long."

Zane felt himself bristle. "So? I'm from out of town. Do you need to pat me down?"

The chief smiled. "Well, you were at the salon when we showed up."

"Unconscious," Shad added in an undertone.

Zane took a breath. He should be relieved he was being hazed, since it showed he was accepted. He hated the thought, but Galina's involvement wasn't impossible. Maybe he'd been too focused on her... *boots.* "I don't get that vibe."

Shad said, "If we could get Petros to talk—"

"I don't see that happening," Zane interrupted. "Too afraid."

"Don't blame him," Shad said. "I wouldn't want to lose a hand. Or anything..." he glanced down, "important."

Both men shuddered. Chief Simpkins rolled her eyes.

"You guys notice Petros wears clear nail polish on his remaining fingernails?" Chief Simpkins asked. "Advertising his services?"

"Maybe." Zane answered. "Remind me again what was missing from the salon."

"Well, a hand," Shad said. "And beauty stuff and an appointment book."

Zane stood and paced. "Did we establish connections between the people the possible perpetrator has grabbed?"

"No. Mostly women." Chief Simpkins stood too.

Zane raised an eyebrow. "The kind who would go to a salon?"

The chief frowned. "Don't get where you're going, but yes."

"Think he's using the appointment book to target certain clients?" Zane asked.

"Could be." Shad joined the others.

"Then we need to talk to Galina about what she remembers about who had appointments." Chief Simpkins glanced down at her watch. "But tomorrow. First thing. It's getting late."

A few minutes later, outside the police station, Zane watched the officers drive off. He knew better than to ask Galina about her clients before the chief did. He also knew he still planned to leave town for fun in the sun. And he really knew it wasn't a good idea to take a walk by her salon just to see if she was working late.

But he'd never claimed he was all that good.

Galina guided the long pole of the paint roller into the tray, then added another swath of paint on the inside wall of the grotto. Based on the current décor, the previous owners had used this place for naughty swinger parties. Everything inside was covered with some form of gold finish. Included were some sturdy stone statues of Greek gods and goddesses that had adorned every nook. It all had to change. A sultry Mount Olympus was not copacetic with the health and wellness theme Galina sought.

In spite of all of the tacky décor, the grotto was pleasant. Soothing water lapped against the inner circle of the structure. A spiral ramp allowed people to lower themselves into the water for more of a full-body soak. Overhead, hidden exhaust fans sucked out acrid mineral smells. And paint fumes. The blush-colored paint was potent.

"You will pay tonight. Look what ze mud has done to my face! Once perfect, like baby's behind."

Galina spun to see a behemoth. Dressed in a long suede dress coat that in another setting would have led her to call the man dapper. It was the red, blistered skin of his face that screamed of some danger.

With the man blocking the only doorway to escape the grotto, Galina thought of another way to describe him—deadly!

"How can I help you?" Galina lowered the painting pole to her side to appear friendly. "Uh, I can't talk long. My boyfriend is meeting me here."

"Ze out-of-town cop? He is busy at the police station." This man's accent was thick, and spittle flew out with his words.

Wait, I know that accent. Oh crap!

Galena raised her dripping paint roller to an *en garde* position. He looked like a man who would want his coat to remain pristine. "What do you want?"

"You. You, very a bother to me. I, Yasbecki Haig, am a professional. Always get jobs done. Nail man stole boss list when at house to paint wife's nails. Took microchip that name all in group. Try to sell to other groups for big money. Get drunk at bar and brag he would put microchip under fake nail on his hand later. Left hand. I come for microchip."

So far, Yasbecki held his position between Galina and an escape. Her only chance was to keep him talking until she could find a way past him.

"You cut his hand off!"

"Refused to give microchip. Tried to stab me with nail file. Heard noises in back and knew no choice. Leave quickly with hand. I take book on front desk to know who come to salon and be witnesses. Then I see jars of your face mud. Yasbecki proud of his fine face. But you have ruined it!" He strode down the ramp, coming closer.

She extended the painting pole and asked, "Wait, why didn't you leave town? You had..." Galina gagged, "the hand."

"Because Petros lie. Microchip not on his hand. I look at your book. Find clients to search their nails. They all scream and try to hurt Yasbecki. Not friendly at all. Tiny rat-dog bite me!"

"Can you blame them? You *did* cut off a man's hand."

"So? Was clean cut." He smiled, then frowned. "Newspaper say you have employee do your nails. Had to be Petros."

Galina wobbled and lowered the paint roller. No wonder

Petros had been so upset when she'd spilled his nail tips. One must have held the microchip.

"I not know which hand, so I take both." Yasbecki unbuttoned his coat and pulled it open to display a variety of weapons inside. "This one bone saw. But first, I torture you for what you do to my face with your *magic* mud."

Galina's eyes narrowed. She might be about to be handless, but no way would she allow this man to malign her product. "Now, you listen! My *Mystic* Mud is made from the best quality ingredients along with genuine Mystic Springs water. Just like this!" Galina plunged the roller into the spring below and flung paint and water on his face.

In the midst of extracting a sharpened ice pick, Yasbecki shrieked, "You burn me with water!" He dug his fingers in the splattered areas of his face. "I'm melting!"

"Oh, please! This isn't the Land of Oz. It's just water." She flung some more, then the door burst open.

Zane stood there, taking in the scene.

There was no time for a warning as Yasbecki charged Zane. The two men grappled. The bigger man soon had the smaller pinned on the center floor area, Zane's head dangerously close to being shoved under water.

Galina dropped the paint roller and grabbed a stone statue from the Greek gods-and-goddesses collection. She positioned herself on the ledge. She moved the statue back and forth, hoping to hit Yasbecki. The men shifted again. The statue flew from her hands and clocked Zane's head. He opened his mouth to speak then fell back unconscious.

But it was Yasbecki who had Galina's attention. The tenor of his earlier screams changed to those of abject terror. She watched, astounded, as frothing waters flowed upward to grab hold of the man before plunging his face over and over beneath the spring's depths.

When Yasbecki's screams stopped, the water deposited him on the grotto's ramp before receding. The parts of his body she could see were torn and raw—blood seeping. He twitched—still alive.

"Cuff him."

"Zane!" Galina turned at the sound of his thready voice. She jerked him into her arms.

Zane winced. "Cuffs are on my belt."

Galina wrestled Yasbecki's limbs together to cuff him. She then embraced Zane. "I thought I was going to lose you."

"Not a chance. This town offers a lot that interests me." He peered over her shoulder at Yasbecki. "Whoa! What happened to him?"

She gazed to the water below. "Pretty sure Mystic Springs happened."

G. A. EDWARDS

G. A. Edwards spent her earlier years as wife, mother, and public educator. Today she's added grandmother, professional editor, public speaker, and published author to her daily mix. She hasn't yet added independently wealthy, jet-setting world leader—but hope remains. Whether her current work is a humorous contemporary, young adult romance, traditional who-dun-it, or a thriller featuring a young protagonist attempting to navigate both high school and a hometown terrorized by a serial killer, she remains committed to her number one goal—*spreading the joys of literature one word at a time.*

You can learn more at gaedwardspresents.com

THE UNDYING SCHISM OF ANA KANE

DAN BRIGMAN

Ana gazed downward. Her ancient smartphone lay at the edge of her right knee, the phone's cracked screen positioned to avoid the glare of the setting sun through her truck's windshield. Ana pulled up an app and let it play in the background. A prominent social media influencer, Rico Cerna, who delved into the supernatural, lulled Ana out of a familiar despondency. She struggled to recall a time in her nearly 150 years of life when a mild winter's darkness had interwoven with death so casually. Losing her brilliant grandson Tolver harried Ana's mind, yet his unification theory would have freed her from this funk.

Rico's voice pulled Ana back to the phone. As Rico stared at his interviewee, he lowered his dark sunglasses. "Flaminia, you're telling me you can speak to the dead here at your shop? You *can't* be serious." Rico and the woman sat at a round table covered with a variety of occult trade ephemera: lit candles, a small crystal ball, a brass singing bowl, a Ouija board, and an unfamiliar animal skull.

Intrigued, Ana smirked as this Flaminia person took the bait. Through the screen cracks, Ana watched her every movement.

Flaminia's mass of long black hair swayed in the white light positioned to accentuate her face. Her dark eyes glimmered, and her cheekbones glowed. *Based on the lighting alone, Rico knows his business.*

"I don't just speak with the dead," Flaminia replied with a generic, yet practiced, European accent. "I confide with dearly departed loved ones of those seeking my unique talent."

Ana's smirk slipped to a grin. *Her accent's a good attempt at sounding foreign.* Based on Flaminia's accent, she must have lived in nearly every Eastern European country before the Iron Curtain fell. As Flaminia continued, Ana silently thanked her for the reminder of her homeland of Northern England. Ana's own accent had faded long ago, and she sometimes forgot she had carried one for decades.

Ana's smile fell. In the buried ruins of her mind, she heard the ancient witch, Kane, laughing. *Kane doesn't fail to remind me of my lineage, though.*

Rico interrupted Ana's thoughts, his straight, white teeth refocusing her gaze. "Do people in Mystic Springs seek your services?" At Flaminia's nod, Rico continued. "What about those touring the springs?"

"I help anyone willing to seek out loved ones," Flaminia said, her tongue rolling across most of the words.

Rico's grin shone. "Excellent. How do I reach you if I'd like to talk to my grandpa?"

Flaminia turned from Rico to stare at the camera. "When someone desires my assistance, I gain the departed person's trust *first.* That can take time. I implore you to reach out to me early. I'll be more than happy to speak with *your* dearly departed. All who remain on our plane of existence await our interaction. They long for it. It only takes your faith *and* my skill to link the conversation. Sometimes, enough faith will offer a chance to *see* your dearly departed."

"Again, excellent," Rico intoned, as the camera switched to him. "That's all for today, you fine people. Mystic Springs is full of mystery, but you can find the *most* mysterious activity at Flaminia's Mystic Visions. In the liner notes, you'll find Flaminia's contact information and website. Thank you, Flaminia."

Ana muted the app, then Googled the contact. Mystic Springs was little more than a backwater town next to a national forest. Kane's gleeful laughter resumed in Ana's mind as she checked Flaminia's website and reviews. After decades of enduring the witch's laughter, Ana knew it served as a prelude to her voice. Ana's finger froze on the screen as the creature whispered in her mind.

You know that woman is a load of bollocks? Kane asked.

After countless failed attempts at ignoring Kane, Ana simply confronted her head on. *Likely. But after what* you *made me do in Hawthorn Creek, it's well past time we parted ways.*

Kane's laughter erupted again. *You've never minded taking bodies at my behest. My failed curse gives ample opportunity—*

Ana mentally shushed Kane to little more than a whisper, then selected Flaminia's address. She set the phone in her passenger seat and adjusted the rearview mirror. In the fading sun's light, Ana's amber eyes became two fiery orbs—no matter how many years passed, she still appeared in her early thirties. She turned the key in her Toyota, then followed the navigation app's verbal prompts to begin the six-hour drive.

Ana's eyelids flitted open when the sun began glaring through her truck's windshield. She repositioned in the bucket seat, then groaned due to the long hours behind the wheel. Ana froze. At the other end of Mystic Visions' small parking lot, a tall person, concealed by a wide hat and brown coat, stepped out the front door. As he strode away, his boots crunched on the gravel. Flaminia stepped onto the door's threshold, her black hair swayed, her gaze remained locked on the departing figure.

Flaminia turned to step back inside until she spotted Ana's vehicle. The psychic motioned toward Ana. Ana scanned the lot. Her Toyota's solitary presence confirmed Flaminia's intended target. Ana groaned. *I wanted to become presentable before speaking with this woman.* Ana glanced at her wrinkled black shirt and pants, then back at Flaminia, who motioned again. Ana reached for her sunglasses but hesitated. *She should see my eyes.*

Halfway across the parking lot, the seemingly absurd plan abruptly bristled a surge of foolishness up Ana's neck. Kane's taunting laughter erased the surge. Ana stepped up to Flaminia. *I must at least talk with her.* In the sunlight, without the advantage of strategically placed studio lighting, Flaminia appeared years older.

Flaminia's gaze met Ana's before she asked, "What can I do for you?" Flaminia stretched out a wrinkled hand. The psychic frowned when Ana disregarded the offer.

"I understand you do seances." At Flaminia's nod, Ana continued. "Good. How soon could you do one for me?"

Flaminia smiled, forcing wrinkles outward from her eyes and up to her brow. "For *you*, my dear, I could do one during tonight's waxing gibbous. At no cost."

Ana crossed her arms. "*Everything* has a cost."

Flaminia smirked, then turned. Within the shop's darkened entryway, Flaminia said, "I'll see you at midnight, my dear."

Turning around, Ana strode to her truck. When she stuck the key in the ignition, the dash clock lit up. *Fourteen hours to kill.* She frowned, checked her eyes in the rearview mirror, then decided to tour the town of Mystic Springs.

Like every small Midwestern town, Mystic Springs turned out to be a blended soup of Americana. Tolver's favorite soup had been *caldo de pollo,* so Ana found a Mexican restaurant. The aroma of enchiladas and tortillas, coupled with the view of an older man sitting alone sipping a margarita, pulled Ana's mind back to grandson Tolver's favorite meals. Ana avoided attention by slipping on sunglasses and ordering two meals to go. Minutes later, she pulled into a nondescript city park full of well-manicured lawns, mature oaks, and disc golf baskets.

The day's remaining hours passed in a blur. Ana enjoyed the two meals, walked the short paths within the park's boundaries, and people-watched. Long after the streetlights flickered to life, Ana departed the park to reach Mystic Visions just before midnight. Not bothering to lock up the Toyota, Ana strode to the door and knocked. Her gaze narrowed while the door swung open at her third knock. A voice deep within the shop beckoned her inward.

Ana slipped inside the darkened storefront. Radiant moonlight streamed through the windows, and candlelight peeked through two curtains. Her eyes absorbed the ambient light, and she smiled while avoiding the storefront's tables and counter. *This must be part of Flaminia's ambiance. Any other customer would be blind in this seeming-cave.* Ana swiped aside a curtain and stepped into Flaminia's domain.

Large pillows lay at the wall's outer edges, with a curtained exit at the opposite wall. In the room's center, Flaminia sat on the floor atop a wide blanket next to a circular wooden table. The wooden walls and patterned-copper ceiling soaked in the light of the few red candles placed equidistantly along the table's middle. Ana turned her gaze to Flaminia, who motioned her to sit. She removed her boots and sat cross-legged across from Flaminia. Ana flexed her stockinged feet. Days of pent-up stress released into the cushions.

The candle wicks' slight crackling filled the room's silence until Flaminia asked, "Are you ready?"

Ana nodded and reached for Flaminia's outstretched hand lying atop the table. Ana gasped, reflexively pulling back at her thoughtless gesture. *I can't let this woman touch—*

Flaminia pursed her lips into a frown at Ana's movement until Kane's screeching wail undulated in waves within Flaminia's mind. Her fingers locked around Ana's flesh like a lightning rod absorbing a bolt from a storm-charged sky.

Ana and Flaminia's minds shunted out all external stimuli. Kane's presence flooded their now-mutual consciousness.

Memories flashed through them like a film set on fast-forward.

Kane haunting a village far to the east of Mystic Springs over a century ago. Her sending hexed rats to permanently poison the village's spring. Ana attempting to stop Kane. Kane's backfired curse intended to cause Ana's instant death, yet instilled her with long life. And Ana's long path to sever the curse that accidentally kept them both alive *and* together. A path fraught with failure and death, despite Ana's grandson, Tolver, formulating an experiment that would have hopefully severed the connection. And finally, Tolver's death despite all his experiment's precautions.

Until just a few months ago, Kane had been an entity borne of chaos and contradiction. Despite the witch's simmering hatred within Ana's brain and the desire to break free, Kane understood that Tolver's theory of unification held validity. And it meant Kane's death.

These thoughts suddenly provoked the witch to a reverberating scream, causing Ana and Flaminia to stiffen. Ana's eyes narrowed, their amber glow fixed on Flaminia. Flaminia gasped as Ana-now-Kane unlatched from her still-grasping hands. Kane leapt over the low table, cackling in delight as her rough hands seized Flaminia's neck.

For a seemingly eternal second, the combined consciousnesses grappled. Kane latched onto Flaminia's mind, Ana ripped at Kane's focus, and Flaminia staved off the sudden insanity scratching at her rationality.

Flaminia's finally seemed to relax when Ana-now-Kane's glowing eyes dimmed. Kane screamed in an unfamiliar language, until Ana finally broke Kane's hold on her and Flaminia.

Ana lay staring at Flaminia, her dimmed eyes meeting the psychic's darker eyes. Their lungs bellowed as if they'd just run a sprint. Kane's whispers renewed at the back of Ana's mind.

"Magnificent!"

Ana shot up straight up like a cat startled from a deep sleep.

Flaminia coughed and motioned toward a man near the curtain, a man Ana hadn't even noticed until this moment. With a raspy, distressed voice, Flaminia said, "That's Xavier. He watches all my seances. You never can be too careful these days."

Ana stood and shook her head. "This was a mistake."

"On the contrary, my dear," Xavier said. "You are in the *perfect* place. We can trap whatever is binding your mind, then reach out to your grandson." With long, red hair accentuating his handsome features, Xavier stood considerably shorter than Ana.

"We?" Ana asked, wondering how he knew about Tolver.

Flaminia stood and nodded. "Yes. He and I can work

together to help you. Although, if you don't mind, please don't touch either of us until we bind that witch."

Ana gave a wan smile and shrugged.

Kane's mutterings shifted to shocked silence at Xavier's grin.

Ana rubbed her neck as she sank naked into one of the locale's small springs, and her eyes closed of their own accord. After leaving Mystic Visions, she had found a rare warm spring—one far from any volcano's proximity. Flaminia had said the necessity of two days' rest, coupled with the full moon, would give Ana enough respite.

Steam wafted up, brushing Ana's cheeks and neck. She sank deeper and felt sleep scraping away the nightmare at the shop. An occasional owl hooted, complementing the spring's silence.

Crack! Thud!

Ana jolted at the noises on the spring's other side. She listened and remained still. Her clothing, belongings, and tactical knife waited in a neat pile a few yards away. *May as well be on the moon.*

The cloudless sky gave Ana enough ambient light to notice a massive creature with shaggy fur. Its white claws and eyes offset the hide's inkiness. *A black bear?*

Unsure of what to do, Ana remained in the pool. Her control drained away with each passing second. She groaned when Kane tugged at the levers controlling her body.

The slight sound pulled the bear's attention directly to Ana, prompting Ana to groan again. The bear sniffed and clawed at the ground until its muzzle pointed toward Ana. Each of the bear's breaths pushed up puffy clouds. In the spring's still water, the moon reflected near Ana's exposed chest. Despite the low light, the bear's dark-eyed gaze locked with hers.

Only two puffs issued from the bear's nostrils before a growl rumbled deep in its throat. Ana tensed—time slowed as she waited for the bear's attack. Decades of self-defense training and knife fighting had easily stopped numerous human assailants. But a black bear's claws and teeth would rip through her naked flesh like scissors across rice paper.

The bear lifted its head and sniffed before rushing off into the darkness. The bear's bulk smashed saplings and branches, each sounding like a shotgun blast. Within seconds, even her amber eyes lost the bear's fleeing form.

Kane's animalistic laugh rumbled out of Ana's mouth, replacing the bear's deep growl.

Well, you've ruined this, Ana thought as she left the water's warmth, dressed, then slipped into her red, two-person tent. She had set up camp near her truck, which was parked at a lot alongside a narrow gravel road. The camp was far enough away from her truck to escape notice, but she would move if a forest ranger required it.

As Ana glided to sleep within her sleeping bag, Kane's thoughts intruded into her mind. *Soon, my dear.*

Ana trekked throughout the forest for the next day and a half to help stifle the witch's renewed taunts. Kane's deep satisfaction mirrored Ana's at knowing the curse might end soon. They had both been disappointed so many times. Her most recent sorrow from the deaths of her grandson and great-granddaughter helped Ana focus past Kane's chaotic stream of thought bubbling within Ana's consciousness.

Yet some uncertainties remained undiscussed.

What would *really* happen when Kane's curse was severed? Their mutual death, *or* just Kane's banishment into oblivion? Or something worse? The prospect had always bubbled when Ana's control loosened, yet they dared not openly discuss it.

By the end of the second day, Ana had consumed her food and fresh water. Pulling away from the parking lot, she flipped on the headlights and drove into Mystic Springs. Her phone's map guided her to the Deer Stand Café and Honky-Tonk. It had mostly positive reviews. A grin slipped in, helping reduce Kane's moaning. Ana could almost feel the witch's mental hand-wringing, but even that could not reduce Ana's renewed positivity.

Twenty minutes later, Ana pulled into the café's crowded lot. She debated for a moment whether or not to wear sunglasses. Her eyes never failed to raise curiosity. She shrugged. *Let them think what they may. Might give this little town something to talk about. If my eyes don't give me away as a weirdo, my clothing probably will.* She couldn't recall the last time she had worn anything but a sleeveless shirt, tight-fitting black jeans, and boots. The dark garments hid stains well, no matter what Kane forced her to do. Ana brushed away images of piled corpses.

The café's windows offered Ana a preview. The open floor had tables full of folks enjoying dinner, with a few servers frantically trying to keep up. A hum of laughter and talking filled the air. Ana stepped inside. She flashed a smile at a few of the patrons' double-takes. She swung her gaze wide until a middle-aged man motioned her toward the bar. A solitary double-taker kept staring at her as she passed by his table. Ana sat on the barstool and shrugged, knowing the man's gaze remained on her.

With an unlit cigarette hanging from his lips, the bartender studied her for a breath, then asked, in his thick Southern drawl, "Stranger, what can I get ya?"

"I'll take the special with your best ale."

The bartender laughed, his teeth flashing in the café's fluorescent lights. He stared at her exposed eyes. "You want to know what it is first?" At Ana's head shake, he smiled and strode to the order window. "One venison stew, French fries, and a Honky-Tonk." He paced back to Ana and stared into her eyes with fascination.

She flitted her gaze to the mirror directly behind him, and her glowing amber eyes still seemed odd. Her eyes had once been as brown as the bartender's. *Before Kane's mark.*

"Only seen that kind of eyes twice, ma'am. Both times they set in an *animal's* eye sockets. Those eyes come with a past life or two, I reckon. How'd you earn such beauty?"

Beauty? Ana smirked. "You saying I'm not human?"

The bartender's eyes widened, and he held a palm up. "Not at all. Didn't mean that, ma'am. Just meant such beauty is usually found out in nature, not in some ol' bar at the edge of the woods."

Ana laughed. "That pickup line is refreshing, but I'm not looking for companionship."

The bartender's tanned face flushed fiery red. "No, no, ma'am...." He turned away, removed his stained cap, and ran a hand through his full mop of curly brown hair.

Ana chuckled, pulling the bartender's focus to her. "Listen, I'm just kidding. I don't get around people much, but I'm hoping to change that soon. What's your name?"

He swallowed as some of the redness faded. "Judd, ma'am."

"Okay, Judd. I think my meal's ready." She glanced at the order window's counter. A plate with a steaming bowl of stew and golden fries waited along with a glass mug filled with a dark brown ale. "What do I owe?"

He retrieved her meal, then said, "Nothin', ma'am. Just

havin' someone like you here is payment enough." Judd's cheeks blossomed red again, and he pulled his cap lower before asking, "Let me know how it is, okay?"

Before Ana could reply, Judd turned to help another customer. Ana shrugged and enjoyed each bite of the meal. *I'll need to leave a positive review.* After slipping a twenty into the tip jar, she exited the café. Halfway to her truck, she heard gravel crunching behind her. When she reached her truck bed, she dipped her right hand down to unlatch the tire iron. Spinning to face whoever stood there, Ana gripped the iron in one hand and formed a tight fist with the other.

Two men in plaid shirts and jeans, one with a black beard, both shorter than Ana, stood near the truck. Both were strangers, yet the patron who had stared at her stood closest while his buddy waited, scanning the lot with wide eyes, obviously second-guessing their decision. Black Beard held both hands in tight fists.

"You don't need to do this," Ana said, holding the iron higher.

Black Beard growled and took one step closer. "Sure we do—"

Ana's iron caught Black Beard across the head, dropping him in a heap. She glanced at the other man. "I imagine you're ready to take your friend inside and explain he had one too many drinks."

He gulped. When Ana motioned with the iron, he reached for the downed man's armpits and dragged him away. She scoffed, waited for them to be out of range, then slid inside her truck.

I'll still give Judd a good review. She smiled on the drive to Mystic Visions.

Flaminia stared at the wizard, Xavier Houx, where he stood in her fortune-telling parlor. His reddish-white staff lay against the wall within arm's reach. The staff seemed cut from a pristine piece of marble. She had rarely seen him without it. *It makes him look so wise.*

Xavier caught her eye. "My dear, do you know how lucky we are?"

Flaminia shifted on the floor cushion. "I'm not so sure about this, Xavier."

Xavier turned and sat on the cushion Ana had used. "Can't you see it? The woman is possessed. And you said she is old. *Very* old. By freeing Ana of her demon, we can sacrifice both beings to reach our goal."

"*Our* goal?" Flaminia muttered.

Xavier tilted his head questioningly. "Considering what your path is, and what we've discussed these past few years, yes."

"But we've never *sacrificed* anyone." Flaminia shuddered. Her skin crawled at the thought of killing. Yet, this wizard of great repute and power burned with zealous passion. "I just didn't think it would ever come to this, Xavier."

His stare could have melted iron. "Flaminia, the power we have been seeking is finally within reach. We must strip away this piece of the wall blocking the Ancient One."

This Ancient One must have unlimited power. All of Xavier's power and influence stems from it. Whatever 'it' is. "I just don't—"

"Flaminia, listen," Xavier said, laying a hand on her shoulder. "We love each other, don't we?" At her nod, Xavier continued. "Then trust me. Within a day or two, we will be more powerful than either of us can imagine. You must convince her to go to the cave." He turned toward his staff, then wrapped a hand around it. He stared down, and his lips moved soundlessly for a moment before he pushed through the curtained exit.

Flaminia frowned. *I'm just not sure about this.*

A knock at the front door pulled her attention away.

Ana held her hand up to knock again, but let it fall when the shop's front door opened. Flaminia smiled and motioned Ana inside. A tightness, absent at their initial meeting, now pulled at the edge of Flaminia's eyes. Ana stepped inside the shop's foyer. Watching Flaminia don a long maroon coat, Ana asked, "What are you doing? I came *here* for the séance."

Flaminia placed a hand on Ana's bare arm and grimaced as Kane laughed at their resulting reunion. "*This* place," Flaminia said, "doesn't have the energy I need. The time since I met your friend helped my understanding that ley lines are *needed* to guide me to your grandson."

Ana nodded. "Where is the lines' convergence?" Ana squirmed at Kane's mental prompt. Much of her occult knowledge stemmed from Kane, despite years of keeping the witch buried behind a mental shroud.

"Within a cave hidden from the main spring. Far from the prying eyes of tourists." Flaminia removed her hand from Ana's arm as Kane thrashed in protest. "I'll ride with you, dear. Easier to give you directions."

Kane shouted about this deceitful fraud.

Anything that can rid you of me is worth trying, Ana thought, then said, "Know this, psychic, if you try anything...."

Flaminia motioned toward the dark parking lot.

After Ana pulled onto the roadway, Flaminia stared ahead

while only offering directions. Ana silently took each turn, as Kane had quieted, an apparition waiting at the edge of Ana's mind. After numerous winding gravel back roads, Ana pulled into a drive walled in by cedar trees extending past the headlights' beams.

"Stop here," Flaminia said. "Give me ten minutes to prepare with Xavier." As she stepped out, the truck's interior light shone on Flaminia, highlighting her drawn lips and green pallor.

Is she sick? To Flaminia, Ana said, "This better *not* be a trap." Her threatening undertone fell on deaf ears.

Flaminia smiled, shut the door, then paced in front of the headlights and into the darkness beyond.

Ana opened her door and clicked off the headlights. A concert of spring peepers and crickets filled the creeping time while the dashboard's clock ticked off eight minutes. Her eyes had gradually absorbed light from the near-full moon. She followed the psychic's path to a wide opening in the side of a cliff nearly fifty feet from the truck. The cedars offered the perfect privacy fence.

Within the empty cave, an oversized campfire burned, its smoke pouring upward to a hole in the rocky ceiling. Almost-invisible lines of energy tapered away from the fire's edge, reflecting off the water of a spring bubbling up from a corner of the cavern. The fire's flickering light highlighted carved, red symbols covering the cave's smooth walls. Tiny, brown bats dotted the ceiling's highest points. Tapestries with star patterns hung on either side of a small passageway in the back, extending into darkness. Ana placed her boots carefully along the slippery rock floor and opened her hands for defense. Kane's blessed silence shifted to a hum of anxiety.

Ana approached the fire, and a robed figure clutching a red-white staff strode from the passageway. Flaminia followed behind, the paleness of her face exacerbated by the fire's brightness. She stared ahead, her eyes wide, shimmering with tears.

"Xavier?" Ana asked.

Ana froze in place while Xavier spoke. "Ancient One, I beseech you, take these elder ones and bless us."

The chant drove Kane into a flurry—she beat against her self-inflicted mental prison.

"*Another* witch," Ana whispered. Any thoughts of speaking with her grandson faded. As Xavier held his staff straight up, Kane and Ana synchronized their thoughts solely to defend. Fleeing held no reality in this cavern while Xavier lived.

With the staff, Xavier drew a wide circle ahead of himself, then paced to one side of the cave while repeating his chant with each circle. At the third circle, the staff's end ignited, leaving a trail of smoke. With the next rotation, Ana gasped, mirroring Xavier and Flaminia's shocked exhalations.

Within the circle's interior, a field of blackness appeared, punctuated by stars and galaxies. The circle's boundary wavered as energy emanated from what could only be a gateway. To where, exactly, Ana could not imagine, until an apparition coalesced in the blackness, blocking points of light. *A gateway to something, not just somewhere.*

At Xavier's completion of the gateway's fourth circle, he turned to face Ana. His hood slipped down, and his lips formed a rictus grin.

Ana stepped back, Kane's frantic screaming overwhelming Ana's hearing. When Xavier lowered the staff's end to the level of Ana's chest, he stepped forward, and Ana shifted onto the balls of her feet. Still unable to hear his words over Kane's mental panic, Ana's initial alarm faded, and her smile blossomed.

Xavier flinched, confusion pushing his brow down. As he

pushed the staff toward Ana, a blurring Flaminia shouted, "No!" and slammed into Xavier's back, knocking him to the cave floor.

From the floor, Xavier growled, "*You* dare to stop me? Let the Abyss take you first!" He swung the staff toward Flaminia.

The blurring red-white arc froze a foot from Flaminia as Ana's hand locked around the staff. The cold marble removed Kane from Ana's brain like an ice block extracted from a frozen river. Kane's cry of relief held in the cavern's air until her aggrieved groan overwhelmed all other sounds.

Xavier's confused shock grew into a wide-eyed stare.

Ana shifted her focus from his eyes. She intoned, "Enjoy your *new* master, Kane." Knee rising, Ana snapped the staff across her thigh.

Xavier stared at the broken staff in disbelief. Rage erupted in his eyes, now glowing amber. In a blur, he growled and lunged toward Ana's neck, eliciting a surprised cry from Flaminia.

Ana braced herself, then kicked at Xavier's rushing form. Her boot connected with his stomach, forcing him closer to the still-open gateway. Ana's second kick forced Xavier into the gateway's opening, instantly cutting off his growls.

Xavier-Kane floated in the darkness of outer space until the still-coalescing apparition reached him. An appendage of the apparition struck out, and Xavier-Kane's thrashing filled the gateway's view.

Ana grasped Flaminia's hand. "Thanks." As the gateway shrank, the apparition's appendage shredded Xavier-Kane into ribbons of flesh. Ana ripped her gaze from the closing gateway, then pulled the psychic from the cavern to the truck. Flaminia sat in the truck and stared outward, her shock mirrored by Ana's face.

The drive back to the shop filled Ana with tentative relief. She searched her mind for the tiniest sliver of the cursed witch.

When they reached Mystic Visions, Ana's urge to weep in relief washed away upon glancing at Flaminia.

The psychic's head rested against the window, her eyes closed. Ana shook her. "Flaminia?"

Flaminia smiled, then laughed. "I'm fine, my dear. Wonderful. Finally free of Xavier."

Ana smiled. "You really can't talk to the dead, can you?"

Flaminia shook her head, her smile fading. "But the living talk to me much more than I realized."

Ana opened her mouth, but Flaminia held a hand up. "Your grandson, Tolver, isn't dead."

"What?" Ana's mind—her *solitary* mind—whirled.

"His being is trapped within another person. Much like what happened to you. *All* those years ago."

Ana's mind raced. "Of course! He would do that." Ana latched gently onto Flaminia's wrist. "I can't thank you enough."

After a short nap and driving many miles from Mystic Springs, Ana pulled out her ancient smartphone. She punched in Hawthorn Creek, her grandson's hometown, then checked the rearview mirror.

Ana grinned at her still-glowing amber eyes—the only remnant of Kane. *I'm coming, Tolver.*

DAN BRIGMAN

Dan has lived in Missouri his entire life and resides near the town of Knob Noster. Fantasy and science fiction are his focus, yet he's published in the field of history. He loves writing stories which speak to humanity's essential relationship with nature. In his books, Dan uses magic, technology, and intellect to overcome challenges, unite devastated nations, or to restore separated families. When he's not writing, he serves as a park superintendent and teaches martial arts.

Find more about Dan at https://www.danbrigman.com, on Substack @danbrigman, or on Facebook

WILL-O'-THE-WHISKER

STEPHANIE FLINT

Ash lunged over a lumpy, overgrown sycamore root, then hissed as a thorny branch from a stealth locust tree caught their belt. A tiny, gleaming object flew into the underbrush as they crashed through the twigs. Branches snapped underfoot, and only by luck did their long legs find balance between two brambles. Sweat trickled on their forehead and they patted their belt.

They froze. Where there should have been multiple smooth pins—the spoils collected from numerous conventions and festivals—there was an empty spot.

Panic rose in their throat. Which pin had they lost?

They turned the belt, frantic. The missing pin was one Meena had given them. But they couldn't lose anything else of her. Not with her missing for the past week.

Ash dropped to the ground, scanning fast until the tiny, yellow, purple, and white *they/them* pronouns pin caught the sunlight, sending a flash of sparkles through the leaves. They snatched the pin and shoved it, muddy underside and all, into their cargo pants pocket as they plunged deeper into the forest. They could clean the pin later.

Who knew how much longer their girlfriend could wait? Everyone else thought Meena had gone vacationing with her college friends, but she would have told Ash. And she wouldn't have left behind her favorite tarot deck.

Leaves squelched underfoot, victims of the summer's hundred-degree weather, as dew rose in hazy wafts of steam from the morning sun. Ash's T-shirt clung to their shoulders, sticky with humidity and sweat. It wasn't even ten o'clock. But the sweat wasn't entirely because of the heat. Ash pressed their hand against their chest, where their heart pounded too fast, too nervous. Hopefully Meena was all right, wherever she was.

They ducked a maple branch with scores of yellowed leaves and picked up their pace as mosquitoes buzzed into action. A swat here... there...

Ash sprinted wherever the bushes weren't too dense. Couldn't the heat have driven away those stupid mosquitoes? Instead, the swarms had intensified. One more thing to worry about—

A black blur dashed past. Ash shrieked, hop-skipping to avoid tripping, and skidded to a stop, mere inches from a cluster of prickly blackberries. They spun around.

What had they almost stepped on?

Ash waved away a persistent mosquito and peered between sycamores. A long, fluffy black tail flicked under a bush. Ash squinted. A cat?

Something sharp pinched Ash's neck.

Smack!

Dead mosquito. Ash grimaced and wiped their hand on their pants. Beyond the sycamores, the cat had vanished. They swallowed hard. Hopefully, the cat would be safe out there, what with the owls and coyotes. Ash bit their lip, wishing they had time to investigate. But right now, they needed to find Meena, which meant they needed to get to the spring.

Onward they plunged to a tiny, private spring away from the one the tourists frequented in their town of Mystic Springs. This one was a burble between rocks that Ash and Meena escaped to for shared picnics and cuddly naps, since the forest stayed cooler than their treeless yards during the heat of summer.

Except, this time, the spring wasn't a tiny burble among a pile of slick brown rocks. Swampy, ankle-deep water spread across the forest floor, as if there had been a recent flood at the park and all the pipes had overflowed.

Strange.

There hadn't been rain for weeks.

Ash slowed their pace. If what the town's psychic, Flaminia, had told them yesterday was true, they needed to get to the center of the spring, to the burble that supposedly lent this spring power. With the spring's magic, they might be able to better pinpoint Meena's location.

If it had any power.

Ash scoffed. Honestly, while they *had* encountered other springs with unusual properties, this one's only blessing seemed to be a refreshing taste. Ash hadn't minded that lack of power, though, since they preferred not to dabble in magic after that incident where they'd found themselves being chased by fire-breathing imps. Since then, they had been *very* careful to only break rocks that were definitely geodes. Thankfully, only a few of the townsfolk knew about that incident, and Ash hadn't had to explain what they'd seen.

Until now, Ash had thought Meena's dealings with magic had been different.

Absently, they removed a velvet pouch from their cargo pants—a deck of tarot cards. Ash normally didn't ascribe magic to Tarot, but today they hoped they were wrong. If they understood the internet articles they'd scrounged in their desperate search before speaking with Flaminia about Meena's disappearance, then they needed to cleanse the deck with water from the spring. A few sprinkles were all. Nothing that would hurt the cards.

Still, they'd been careful to choose a deck with a plastic coating. No need to ruin their girlfriend's favorite deck in the process of their search.

Cards clutched in hand, mud squelched under their tennis shoes. Icy water soaked into their socks, numbing their toes. Hopefully, this really was water from the spring and not some backed-up sewer. If sewage, they were going to want new shoes.

And a shower.

But it didn't smell weird. Besides, was sewer water ever this cold?

Their fingers tightened over the cards. What if they dropped them? Then it would be *sploosh!* No more cards. No more options to locate Meena. They had tried to buy a new deck from Flaminia's shop, but she had insisted that a more familiar deck might help them locate Meena faster.

Ash swallowed hard, nervousness beading on the back of their bare neck despite their short hair. They slid the deck from the velvet pouch and into their hand. The pouch's charms—silver paws and fish—glinted in the sunlight that danced between the leaves. Slowly, they fanned the cards. Sleek, plastic-coated paper, gilded in silver and designed with rich detail—cat people instead of the usual Rider-Waite-Smith designs. They flipped the cards to the paws and astrological symbols of the backing, shuffled them, and then dipped their free hand into the burbling water. Their fingertips tingled in the frigid spring.

"Please work," they whispered, sprinkling droplets across the cards. "Please help me find Meena." They waited as long as they could stand before drying the deck. To complete their ritual, they shuffled the cards once more, and then drew a single card.

The Page of Swords. This deck's design featured a tabby cat in a flouncy tunic, tights, and boots, his sword held aloft as if he was the cat from the "Puss in Boots" fairy tale. His boots, however, were probably more watertight than Ash's waterlogged shoes.

Ash scowled at the card, wishing they'd brought the deck's explanation booklet. Tarot reading was Meena's practice, not theirs. They knew a little from watching her, but it didn't come so naturally to them.

What they *did* know was that, as one of the pages, this card represented youthful passion, energy, and newness. As part of the swords suit, there was conflict or action, and if Ash remembered Meena's previous readings, it had something to do with a truthful reveal.

At the very least, the card represented enthusiasm.

How that was supposed to help, no idea. Whenever they weren't sure about a reading, they usually drew a second card to try to clarify the first—

Light flashed in a blackberry bush at the far edge of their vision, like the reflection of a shiny phone screen in the afternoon sun. They froze. Was Rico, the town's self-proclaimed social media influencer, out here, snooping around for that sleazy show of his? That gossiper always had been nosy. This spot belonged to Ash and Meena. They didn't need him bringing visitors. Especially now.

Thankfully, the forest remained devoid of further flashes. Since Flaminia had warned Ash that their emotions could affect the spring, they took a deep breath. Calm. Better not to let anger at Rico poison the spring. Besides, now that they'd cleansed the cards, they might as well return to their air-conditioned home before the day got hotter.

Ash spread the deck on their bed with the backs faced up, and then shuffled the deck by spinning their hand through the cards, turning them this way and that. This was Meena's favorite way to ensure that some cards were reversed and some were upright, the better to add more meaning to the reading.

The more *confusing* to make the reading, in Ash's mind, but since they were looking for Meena, they figured they ought to give Meena's method a try.

Ash had already covered the foot of their bed with a pair of pebbles the two of them had collected at a beach deeper in the Ozarks, a rubber duckie in a witch's hat Meena had gifted Ash for Halloween, a sandalwood tiger for prosperity, and a necklace she'd accidentally left behind in Ash's bathroom.

"What do I need to know to find Meena?" Ash swiped their hand over the cards and selected the one that felt right to them. They flipped it, revealing the High Priestess, an elegant Russian Blue cat in pale blue robes with sunflowers gathered around her.

"Flaminia," Ash murmured. Who else would be the high priestess with the knowledge they sought? Granted, they'd already visited Flaminia's Mystic Visions shop yesterday, but that was before they had cleansed the cards.

It would be a hot drive, though.

Ash sighed. They'd better get the car's air conditioner running at full blast. Give it a chance to cool, then maybe the steering wheel wouldn't be hot enough to burn them by the time they made it out of the bathroom.

They gathered the cards and, on their way to the door, a flick of movement drew their eye to the window. A fluffy black cat, too fine-boned to be a tom, sat on the brick ledge in the shade, tail flicking lazily across the side. She opened her mouth in a giant, toothy, pink yawn. There was something familiar about her that Ash couldn't place, but simply *knew.*

A neighborhood cat? Or was this the same cat from the forest? She was small. Cute. Had muddy paws. If Ash could catch her, they could see if she had a collar. Ash grabbed the keys from the hanger by the door and hurried outside. But the cat was gone, leaving only a rustling, crispy bush to suggest she had been there at all.

In her place on the windowsill was a rusted nail.

"Weird." Ash twirled the nail between their fingers. Crude. Pitted. This hadn't come from the house. At least, not from any of the nails they'd seen lying about. It couldn't have come from the cat... could it?

They pocketed the nail, filled a bowl with water and left it under the bush, and then slid into their still-sweltering car.

Lavender incense filled the hazy interior of the Mystic Visions psychic parlor, a cramped set of rooms brimming with book-shelves and glass cabinets that held too many craft books to count. Everything from herbal remedies and astrology, and how to forage for mushrooms that could be eaten without dying, to how to crochet tiny monsters with beady eyes. Crystals and bundles of sage interspersed the shelves, along with numerous boxes of tarot decks in every style and size.

In the next room over, a giant round table displayed flick-ering candles. Flaminia's manicured nails rested against a deep violet tablecloth, weaving it with wrinkles. "The Page of Swords, you say?" Her accent tended to vary with her readings, and this time, the European influence was slight.

Ash passed the card to her. "This one."

Flaminia peered down her nose at the card, her eyebrow arched over-enthusiastically. Unlike Flaminia, Meena never got theatrical. The Tarot reader at the healing crafts fair hadn't been terribly theatrical, either. But theatrics were what tourists came for at the parlor, so the practice must have stuck for Mystic Springs' resident psychic.

"I also drew this when asking what I needed to know." Ash placed the High Priestess on the table, their foot bouncing on the carpet. "So, I came to you."

Flaminia's gaze flicked to Ash, a smile briefly crossing her lips. Ash suspected she was flattered, even if she didn't want to show it. "Given that the suit of swords is one of communication, perhaps you should find a way to communicate with Meena."

"You're psychic, aren't you?" Ash leaned against the table, hands clamped between their knees to stop their foot bouncing. "Can you contact her? Or ask a spirit where she is?"

Flaminia's amenable smile faded to a frown. She shifted in the chair, one hand drawn to her chin. "I don't..." Her attention slid to the curtained door leading into the back room. "Better not to tempt anything."

"Tempt anything?" Ash echoed. What was that supposed to mean?

Flaminia shook her head, her face pale under the shop's dim lights. "Has anything else happened? Any other cards, or odd circumstances?"

"Well, I almost tripped over a cat in the forest. And I *think* I saw the same cat sitting in my window later. I went to see if she had a collar, but she ran off. Only thing left behind was this." Ash dug the nail from their pocket and added it to the table's knickknacks.

"A nail..." Flaminia's eyes widened and her mouth shaped into an O. "Iron, maybe?"

"Iron?" Ash prodded. The tourists might have enjoyed her cryptic answers, but Ash didn't have time for that. *Meena* didn't have time for that.

"Has the cat brought you anything else?" Flaminia asked, her voice urgent.

"I don't think so."

"Let me know if she does. Next time you see her, see if you can get her to let you follow. Maybe she knows something we don't."

"The cat?"

"Indeed. The cats about town hear things, you know. And they see what we cannot. At least, those not gifted with the Sight." She winked.

"Mmhmm." Ash forced a smile. Sometimes they weren't sure when Flaminia was joking and when she honestly believed what mystic mumbo-jumbo she spouted. But maybe the cat *did* know something. "I'll try that." Ash stood. "I'll grab some cat food at the store. See if I can get her to trust me."

"Tuna does wonders, dear." Flaminia sighed. "Good luck."

I'm going to need all the luck I can get, Ash thought, *especially if I'm resorting to chasing cats for answers.*

After stopping for a small bag of cat food and a couple cans of tuna—one for the cat and one destined to be tuna salad for Ash's lunch—Ash replenished the water and cracked open the can.

They left it on a shady part of the porch, then returned to the air conditioning to scout from the window.

The cat didn't return.

That evening, as the sun set and cast everything in a golden glow, Ash nodded off on the couch... only to wake with the faintest of whispers teasing their mind. Whispers too soft to understand.

They opened their eyes. The noise hadn't come from the TV, which had powered off from disuse hours ago. This whisper niggled at them. Pulled them away from the couch to the window. They pressed their nose to the still-warm glass. Something was out there. A nagging something that called them outside.

They *needed* to go outside.

Uneasy, Ash grabbed their keys and stepped onto the porch. Humidity flooded through their shirt. Crickets screamed like the band Ash's shirt referenced. Louder and louder, drowning out that whisper they'd heard while asleep.

But they *had* heard a whisper. Still did, like the hum of a window unit unable to compete with the evening heat. Ash started toward the forest. They needed to follow, needed to learn where that whisper came from—

A dull pain shot through their big toe.

The whisper silenced.

Ash cursed, fumbling to right themselves over whatever object they had tripped on. Their toe throbbed, but as they bounced on one leg to grab the other foot and coddle it, they caught a glimpse of a flickering light bobbing between the silhouetted trees. Ash stopped bouncing, stunned, as the light bobbed twice more, then vanished. Golden-black fur flashed through the underbrush.

They let out their breath.

The cat.

Their toe still smarted, and when they turned to see what they had stubbed it against, they found a railroad spike shedding flakes of orange rust. How strange. There weren't any railroads nearby. They hefted the chunk of metal to examine it closer. Heavy. Not something that could have easily been moved by a cat....

Not that a cat would have moved odd objects. That'd be absurd.

Granted, it was about as absurd as that whisper they'd heard earlier.

Goosebumps tingled down their spine. Had they really heard it calling them? They couldn't remember what words had been spoken, if any. Just a feeling. A *need* to follow and explore. And yet....

A line of dirt led to the railroad spike, as if it had been dragged here. And where the dirt hadn't completely disintegrated to dust, faint paw prints remained.

Follow the cat.

If they waited until morning, the night winds might blow away the trail. Then they wouldn't be able to see if it led to Meena.

The sun's golden light faded, plunging the forest into deep blue twilight.

Soon there wouldn't be any light to see by.

Ash turned on their phone's flashlight and followed the railroad spike's trail. At first, the single track led toward town, maybe toward the museum, or the antique shop. But they hadn't reached the main road before a bobbing light drew their attention once more.

The orb of light dipped and dove, dancing through the trees

like an unsteady lantern swinging in a ghostly miner's hand. Or a mischievous will-o'-the-wisp, leading them into the unknown. Ash wandered after it, toward the trees, toward wherever it led. They half-remembered lowering their phone's light so they could see the orb better, and they stumbled through the dry grass in the evening heat, the taste of a storm brewing in the night.

The shimmering light led them to the edge of the forest, and then between the first few maples and past a giant sycamore with dead branches waiting for the right storm to send it toppling. Ash's arm hairs stood on end as the weaving light drew them deeper and deeper into the wood, to the high trill of flutes, and singing, ethereal and enchanting—

Something bumped their leg.

They screeched, jolted to alertness. The singing stopped. Ahead, lit by the edge of their phone's wayward light, a ring of mushrooms popped up through the forest brush.

Their heart skipped a beat. Something about the ring... too mysterious and perfect.

Part of them knew there was nothing to be afraid of. Mushrooms were prone to creating such rings, after all. Simply how they spread.

The other part remembered the singing, the flutes, and that bobbing light as a fever dream, stirring in their mind like the electric brewing of a summer storm that left their arms tingling. And, sitting beside their feet, a black cat, her tail flicking anxiously as she caught their gaze before she ran, vanishing once more into the trees.

Something was terribly, terribly wrong.

Ash bolted. Away from the fairy ring of mushrooms, away from where the cat had been sitting seconds before. Away from the forest. Dirt flew from the soles of their tennis shoes as they raced into town, all the way to Flaminia's house. Seemed unlikely she'd still be at the shop, so her house was their best bet, though they *knew* no one ever entered her house but some strange man Ash had never seen but heard plenty of rumors about.

Ash didn't care right now. They had seen something they shouldn't have, and Flaminia Tempest was the only person they could trust to have answers. The only person who could confirm if what they had felt had been magic, or nothing more than a too-anxious person missing their girlfriend.

A bird's shrieking cry sent Ash flying faster to the door. They didn't check to see if the bird was the fabled raven that hung around Flaminia's house and brought her odds and ends.

"Flaminia!" Ash pounded on Flaminia's door and was still pounding when the door swung open. They toppled inside, nearly into the arms of a lady wearing a night robe, her dark hair down in frumpy ringlets with a thick aroma of sage about her.

Ash didn't wait for her to kick them back out before they blurted everything they'd seen, everything they'd felt, everything they'd heard. They told her that they had an awful feeling that this thing they'd seen was fae—hadn't there been an incident recently? One Rico had mentioned about a fae stealing away some pregnant girl? Anyway, Ash had also seen a fairy ring, and could that flickering light have been a will-o'-the-wisp? It certainly wasn't swamp gas, or the ghost of a dead miner.

Despite Flaminia's surprise and occasional nervous glances toward the back of the house, as if maybe that strange man waited in the shadows, her expression softened. "Make yourself comfortable. I'll bake a pan of cookies." She gestured to a blanket and the couch, across from a TV playing some guided meditation soundtrack to a rainy forest view.

Ash took the blanket, their muscles frozen despite the summer heat, and followed Flaminia into the kitchen. Outside, evening thunder rumbled, rattling the window. Flaminia lugged a tub of cookie dough from the fridge and dropped it on the counter with a resounding *thud*. A tap of her long-nailed finger, and the oven beeped the pre-heating chime. "Does seem suspicious." She knelt and selected a rust-stained baking sheet from below the oven. The pan's hollow rattle reminded Ash of thunder. "The fae have been active lately."

Ash pulled their blanket tighter. Details might have been nice, but knowing those might make the whole situation feel more real.

"Still, it seems you have someone watching over you. Hand me a spoon?" Flaminia rapped her knuckles on the drawer closest to Ash.

They handed over a spoon as she peeled the plastic lid from the tub.

"Hmm... thicker handle, please?"

This time, Ash rummaged for one unlikely to bend in the dough.

Flaminia scooped uneven balls of cookies and plopped them onto the pan. "That cat sounds like a familiar. Or a friend." She paused in mid-scoop. "Keeping you from entering the fairy circle. Providing you with iron... that'll definitely keep the fae away. They've never been fond of iron."

"The nail and the railroad spike?" Ash hedged.

Flaminia tapped her nose. "Exactly. What cat would drag a railroad spike all the way from who knows where unless they knew what it could do?"

Ash gnawed at their lip. "Is it possible the fae drew Meena into the forest, the way they almost...." Their voice trailed. What

would have happened if they had stepped into that ring? "Are...
are you sure you can't try talking to your spirits for help?"

Flaminia stiffened, then shook her head and dropped the
final ball of dough onto the pan. "Why don't you ask the cards
for advice? Let the universe guide your hand and use your own
logic to figure out the answer. Spirits can be... Well, they'll give
you an answer, but it might not be an answer that's good for
you." She clicked another button on the oven. "Go on. You've
got twelve minutes before the cookies are done."

Ash sighed and entered Flaminia's living room. They settled
into the plush couch, which attempted to swallow them as they
tucked their feet under. With the blanket wrapped around their
shoulders, only their arm stuck out from the fabric. They shuffled the cards on the psychic's coffee table. This time, they drew
the Six of Coins, in which a regal Burmese cat offered a pitcher
of milk to the bowing cats before him, the other paw holding up
scales sloshing with more milk.

An offering....

Ash stretched backward on the couch and craned their neck
to where Flaminia watched from the half-step in the raised room
above. "Do the fae like gifts?"

Flaminia tilted her head, black ringlets falling to one side as
she got a better look at the card. "Coins, huh?"

Ash nodded.

"There's a little fae in the garden who I leave milk for in the
morning. She gets testy if I don't. So yes, some might. There's all
manner of fae about. Some friendly, almost as human as you or I.
Others... less kind. Less caring."

Ash let out their breath. The cat offering milk in the card...
"If I make them a peace offering, maybe they can tell me what
happened to Meena." Ash started to untangle themself from the
couch, but Flaminia shook her head.

"Wait. Stay for a cookie, at least."

"But I need to find—"

"I'll get you something to help protect you."

"Protect me?" Ash blinked, not sure how to respond.

Flaminia disappeared into another room. When she returned—right as the timer beeped and Ash automatically stood to pull the cookies from the oven—the psychic had acquired a weathered cardboard box.

"These are wind chimes. Not the best solution, but the best I have at the moment. The fae don't like the deep sound of bells. If you run into trouble, ring the chimes. Also, here's milk, which they *do* like." She poured a glass for each of them and then passed the remainder of the gallon to Ash. "So you don't have to run back home. I can get more at the store tomorrow."

Ash eyed the wind chimes. Unwieldy, but better than nothing. They still had that rusty nail, too, though they'd lost the railroad spike at some point while chasing the glowing orb.

"Lastly, a cookie. To lift your spirits." Flaminia passed Ash a plate. "Might want to let it cool."

Ash waited as suggested, their leg bouncing the whole time, and snagged a second cookie before returning into the night, the distant flashes of lightning illuminating the trees and their quivering, restless branches.

The edge of the forest loomed as a silhouette against the twilight, illuminated only by the brief flashes of lightning streaking the sky. The storm would pass Mystic Springs, judging from the growing intervals between each flash and the thunder. Still, it brought a chilled wind to the hot day. Ash's arm hairs stood on end.

They held the box of wind chimes pinched under one elbow, ready to extract if necessary. In that same hand, Ash clutched the rusted nail. Their first line of defense. In the other hand they lugged a half-filled gallon of milk.

Only a little way into the forest, they wished they could reach for their phone without lowering the rusted nail from their defensive stance. Without their phone's light, they could barely discern a low tree branch or tall bush. Hopefully, they'd be able to avoid a ring of mushrooms.

As they drew closer, a faint, golden glow overtook the darkness, spilling onto the leaves like morning light. An orb weaved and bobbed at its center. Ash tightened their fingers around the rusty nail.

Despite the storm's already cool wind, near the circle the temperature dropped further, like that of an autumn morning. Damp mulch and wet leaves, a taste of cinnamon and apple cider on their tongue....

Like an entrance to a different world.

They swallowed hard and then, careful not to crush any of the mushrooms or to step inside the fairy ring, they offered the gallon of milk. They held it up for whomever was here to see, then sat it within the circle.

"This is for you." Their voice shook. "A gift. In return, could you help me find my girlfriend, Meena? Or, if you have her already, could you return her?"

The orb sprung to Ash's left. They jumped, but the orb undulated and bobbed, and then oozed around the milk, causing the whole carton to glow.

For a brief, unbelievable moment, a pearlescent man knelt in the light of the glowing milk. Long, unkempt hair spilled across his emerald tunic. Ivy wove through his hair among dried twigs. His long ears tapered to a point. He took the milk to his chest, and when he turned Ash's direction, his eyes were wild and as beautiful as backlit amber. His skin had an opalescent sheen. He scowled as he caught Ash's gaze, and suddenly those eyes seemed less like warm amber and more like sunlit ice on a frosty morning.

Lightning illuminated the trees and the mushrooms. Then the man, the *fae,* was gone. In his place was a fluffy black cat whose purr was so loud Ash could hear it from where they stood.

"Meena?" Ash whispered.

Let us awaken, their girlfriend's voice responded.

Ash swayed, dizzy, and sunk into unconsciousness.

Thunder rumbled through the house. Gray storm light filtered through the half-closed curtains. Curled against Ash was Meena, her black hair tickling Ash's chin.

"The cats say such strange things," Meena murmured, and nuzzled closer.

Ash blinked, then snatched their phone from the nightstand. Their attention caught on the date: five days from when they'd gone searching for Meena. They had no memory of anything that had happened between then and now. Had they lost time when dealing with the fae?

Meena snuggled closer and wrapped her arms around Ash's shoulder. She smiled. "Thanks for listening. Also, for future reference, I don't like tuna."

Ash pulled Meena's arms tighter. "Glad to have you back. By the way, we need to stop by the store."

"Why's that?" Meena asked.

"Because I'm pretty sure the milk I have is expired, and I

don't want either of us getting stolen away again. Unless you *like* being a cat...." Ash booped her nose.

Meena chuckled. "Meow." She kneaded Ash's shoulder playfully.

"Too soon," Ash mumbled. "Way, way too soon."

STEPHANIE FLINT

Stephanie Flint (she/her) loves reading and writing stories about sprawling worlds, uprooting oppressive societies, and awesome LGBTQ+ characters. When not writing, she creates digital 3D art, builds skybridges in Minecraft, and plays table-top games with her husband (who makes sure she doesn't break their story universes with one-too-many shiny new magic systems). Originally from Missouri, she graduated with a degree in photography and creative writing from UCM before moving to the snowy Upper Peninsula of Michigan.

Find Stephanie on her blog (stephanieflintbooks.com), and subscribe to her newsletter for a free short story (infinitaspublishing.com).

BENEATH THE SURFACE

R. A. WESLEY

Mr. Flores's frail, clammy arm was draped over my shoulder as I guided him toward the Mystic Inn's kitchen. He was dehydrated from our mid-Missouri heat, and was the latest victim of the town's magic-springs-will-heal-you scam. We shuffled so slowly that I fought the urge to pick him up and deposit him in a chair. But in my experience, men didn't appreciate being manhandled by a woman.

Over the last few years, Mystic Springs had become a popular destination for the elderly due to claims that our springs held medicinal properties. False ones, considering, so far, the tourists were as gray-haired when they departed as when they arrived.

Still, the rumors had changed the town when the first tour bus from Branson arrived. Shops ran out of items such as insoles and Bengay. Locals adjusted by stocking walking sticks, lots of pain relievers, and small battery-operated fans.

All great things for the town, but extra work when Deputy Shad and I had to develop a search-and-rescue team for tourists who veered off trails in quests for a holy grail of springs. If I had known this would be a regular duty of mine, especially now as police chief, I wouldn't have accepted a job in Mystic Springs.

Claude, the day clerk of Mystic Inn, pushed through the swinging door and froze. "Chief?"

"Mr. Flores needs to sit down with a glass of water. Don't worry, I know my way."

Claude didn't move. "Hold on, I'll get the water. Just... take him to the sitting room by the front door."

I narrowed my gaze at Claude's back as he vanished through the swinging doors. Why would Claude suggest we backtrack?

Unless... he was hiding something.

Maybe it was the lunchtime mess in the kitchen. Ridiculous. I didn't care what it looked like.

I had Mr. Flores shuffling toward the sitting room when Claude returned with a bottled water and a straw. "I've got this, Chief." He helped Mr. Flores sip the water.

Then it dawned on me what was strange about Claude's reaction—no eye contact. Suspicious, but maybe Claude was acting this way because everyone acted strange around the town's police chief.

"There is no need to waste your time," Claude said. "I'll take care of him."

I was skeptical that he could do much for Mr. Flores. It was nothing personal, but Claude was pint-sized. Still, I needed to get back to the station. "Okay."

As I lowered Mr. Flores onto the couch in the sitting room, an older woman entered the inn. She glanced at my uniform and began to prattle.

"Oh good, I'm glad you're here, officer." She waggled her bony finger. "I didn't get a lick of sleep last night. I heard loud arguing outside my window. Is that the kind of town you run? If something isn't done, I'll have to leave a bad review. I hate doing that, but what's the point of paying a premium price if I can't sleep?"

I didn't care about a bad review for the inn. I was more concerned with tourists or teenagers roaming the streets and woods at night. Too many caves and crevasses where someone could get hurt. "I'll look into it."

In the sitting room, Claude had paled. Why would a desk clerk care so much about one bad review? I shook my head and departed for home.

After a shower and uniform change, I longed for a shooting therapy session. Accuracy was vital, even though I hadn't pulled a firearm in the line of duty since I moved here. I paused at the door to the basement and promised myself I would shoot after my shift, then headed for the station.

At the department, Shad glanced up and gave a nod toward my office. I inwardly groaned as I crossed the space to deal with one of the challenges of my job.

Mayor Coyle reclined in my chair with his hands behind his head, his polished loafers digging into my keyboard. "Sam." He flashed his capped teeth.

In the doorway, I casually rested one hand on my Berretta. The cold metal helped ease my irritation. "Call me Chief Simpkins."

He ignored my comment. "Stopped by to check on my police force."

I didn't respond.

The man was the most self-centered human—everything he did was for his personal gain. He'd been mayor for years because no sane human would run against him for fear of retaliation.

As for why he was in my office, from experience I knew it had nothing to do with department needs.

His expression sobered. "What are you doing regarding these silly accusations?"

Most people avoided friction with the mayor. I was not most people.

"Who said they were only accusations?"

Mayor Coyle's feet dropped to the floor and his face reddened. "Someone is trying to frame my son. He didn't paint that graffiti on the coffee shop's exterior."

"He signed his artwork."

Evan Coyle wasn't the only teenager trying to get attention from a parent by causing havoc on the streets and trails at night, but he was, without a doubt, guilty of this crime. Witnesses saw him in the act, and then the boy had bragged. But his father wouldn't admit his son wasn't perfect.

The mayor stood abruptly.

I put a hand up. "I'm not done with my investigation. But I can promise you the guilty party will clean up the graffiti."

The mayor's reddened face relaxed. "Thank you, Sam."

"Chief Simpkins," I corrected. Again.

He flashed his teeth and crossed the room to lay his hand on my shoulder before exiting. My fingers twitched to grab that hand and twist it behind his back.

It twitched even more when Mayor Coyle stopped at Shad's desk and ruffled my deputy's hair. "No more buckets of grasshoppers in the town square, ya hear?"

Shad pulled away from the mayor's reach. "I was six years old."

But the mayor was already out the door.

"Grasshoppers?" I asked.

"That was twenty years ago."

I crossed my arms and leaned against the doorframe. "How long did it take to collect a bucket of grasshoppers?"

Shad grinned. "Three days."

I could easily imagine Shad working tirelessly, even as a child. He was one of the few people I really liked in this town. Dedicated to any task he was assigned. I also appreciated that he was a computer genius. Computers and I didn't get along as a general rule.

My phone buzzed, and I excused myself to my office. When I saw the St. Louis area code, my heart sunk. The number wasn't saved, but it could be her.

Indecision warred through me. I tossed my phone on the desk. Whoever it was could leave a voicemail.

Except the unanswered phone made me feel like I had abandoned my baby sister, Toni. Again. Before I knew what I was doing, I had the phone to my ear.

"Chief Simpkins."

"Chief?" a familiar, but male, voice questioned.

"Hatch?"

Liam Hatch had been my first—and only—partner on the force in St. Louis.

"You made chief? That's great!"

"Yeah. Thanks." I didn't mention I only got the job because my predecessor went missing, or that I was grossly underqualified.

Hatch must have sensed my hesitation to elaborate. He had always been good at reading the room and pivoting. Instead, he filled me in on his life over the last four years. How he got married and had a two-year-old daughter named Mavis, which they shortened to Mav.

"Two syllables are a mouthful." He laughed.

Some of the guilt I carried regarding my time in St. Louis lightened, and my chest swelled with joy at the sound of his laugh.

"Hey, Simpkins. The reason I called is I've got a case. Your town came up during our investigation."

Hatch went on to describe a missing person. Jason Bassinger was a social media influencer from St. Louis, who had been diagnosed last winter with terminal cancer. The man's YouTube channel once catered to gamers, but the content switched to alternative medicine, featuring miracle cures like the kind supposedly found in Mystic Springs.

"So, what do you need from me?" I asked.

"I hoped you could ask around if anyone has seen him," Hatch said. "I know this isn't an easy one for you—being a missing person case."

Old feelings of heartache, fear, and worry washed over me. But this was Hatch. "I'll do everything I can to help."

Before hanging up, Hatch added, "Simpkins, if you wanted to come back, there's a position coming open. You'd fit in great. No street patrolling."

No street patrolling meant I wouldn't have much chance to get anyone else hurt.

Like when I got Hatch stabbed.

"Just think about it." Hatch said before ending the call.

We had chased a perp down an alley, where, instead of having my partner's six, I froze at the sight of an unconscious girl sprawled on a soiled mattress with a needle in her arm. For a second, I thought she was Toni.

In the years before Hatch's stabbing, I had realized my sister didn't want to be found. Her need to find the next high was all she cared about. Nothing had stopped me from searching for her until my hesitation to act landed Hatch in the hospital.

Once I knew Hatch would make a full recovery, and even though he said his injury wasn't my fault, the next day I applied for every position as far as I could get from the city. I took the first offer.

Hatch was wrong. It was my fault. As long as I was in St. Louis, I would be a liability.

I wished Hatch hadn't called. His voice reminded me of my old life and brought memories of Toni to the surface.

I knew exactly what it felt like to wonder if your loved one was safe—or even alive.

If Jason Bassinger was in Mystic Springs, or even close by, I would find him.

Shad's computer knowhow would be a big help with research right now, but I needed time to myself to unfurl the knots in my stomach.

Over the rest of the afternoon, I clicked through the missing man's YouTube channel and watched his health decline. When I saw a comment from a Mystic Springs local under Bassinger's latest video, I knew where to start my questioning.

I opened my door. "How well do you know Rico Cerna?"

Shad looked up from his computer. "Pretty well. We went to school together since kindergarten. How come?"

"Because he is suspect number one in a missing person case."

Shad's eyes widened.

I grabbed my keys. "C'mon, I'll fill you in on the way."

Rico took a dubious look at me when he opened his door. Then he spotted Shad. "Hey man. What's up?" The two clasped hands and proceeded to run through an intricate handshake.

I glared at Shad from the corner of my eye.

On the way over, my deputy had explained all the reasons Rico couldn't be involved in a missing person case. Reasons such as "I know him" and "we played ball together" were why we decided it would be best if I took the lead.

I forced a smile. "Can we ask you a few questions?"

Rico opened the apartment door wider. "Yeah, of course."

In the living room, we sat on metal folding chairs, surrounded by the camera equipment Rico used as the local YouTuber.

I pulled out my notebook. "Just have a few questions."

Rico's eyes bounced between Shad and me. "Okay."

"Have you heard of a YouTuber named Jason Bassinger?"

He shrugged one shoulder. "Sure."

"What is your relationship with Jason?"

Rico's dark brow furrowed in confusion. "Relationship?"

"How do you know him?"

He shook his head. "Never met him."

"Hmm." I continued, "Do you comment on many YouTuber's videos?"

He shrugged again. "Sure. It's normal practice to share likes and comments. You know, if you scratch my back, I'll scratch yours."

I had hoped Rico would be a solid lead but the confusion and responses seemed sincere. My gut said he was telling the truth.

"Did you know he was missing?"

"No." He paused and seemed to consider his words. "What does that have to do with me?"

I leaned forward. "Well, in a comment on one of his videos, you recommended he visit our town. Then he posted a video mentioning Mystic Springs. Twenty-four hours later, Bassinger was reported as missing."

Rico's eyes widened in shock.

Shad leaned forward in his seat. "We're just gathering information." Shad was still a rookie, and it showed.

I closed my notebook and forced a smile.

Rico's shoulders relaxed. "I swear, I don't know the guy. I've always suggested people visit Mystic Springs. It's what my channel is about. The more interest, the more likes and subscribers I get, which drums up more revenue. Jason's channel focuses on alternative medicines, so I figured the healing springs were right up his alley. More followers for both of us. That's it."

I nodded, told Rico to call if he heard from Bassinger, and we let ourselves out.

Back in the truck, Shad asked, "What do you think?"

"Rico is telling the truth."

"I thought so, too. Where do we go from here?"

I didn't have an answer. Rico was my only lead. Then a thought struck me. "Let's find Sebastian."

The local bus driver drove Branson's tourists to Mystic Springs for the day and back. It was well known Sebastian loved the pancakes at the Deer Stand Café. He was easy to spot with his usual hunter-orange ball cap and the beer belly wedged between the bench seat and table.

Shad flipped a chair around to straddle it at the end of the table, while I slid onto the bench opposite Sebastian.

The man paused with a fork-full of pancakes halfway to his mouth. His gaze darted around the diner, as if seeking help.

Shad grinned. "Hey."

Sebastian grunted, then swallowed.

I laced my fingers on the table. "Mind if we ask you a couple of questions?"

"Am I under arrest?"

"Should you be under arrest?"

He stabbed at the stack of pancakes and shoved another huge bite in his mouth. "Nope."

"Then, no."

He swallowed. "Fine."

I pulled up a photo of Bassinger on my phone and slid it toward Sebastian. "Have you seen this man?"

His jaw tightened as he stared at the photo. His eyes flicked up at me, then back at his plate. "Never seen him."

"Are you sure?" I asked.

"Yep."

My gut told me to dig. "How is your health, Sebastian?"

He sneered. "Why? You selling insurance or somethin'?"

"I wondered if you ever watched YouTube videos on alternative medicine. Reiki, shaman, crystals, or maybe healing springs?"

Sebastian's jaw tightened again. "Naw. That stuff's for quacks."

Shad asked, "You ever get people from St. Louis on your bus?"

He shrugged. "I don't ask, and they don't tell."

This was going nowhere, so I tapped the table. "Enjoy your meal."

As Shad and I were on our way out the door, my attention was caught by the quick movement of a menu jerked up to cover a face. I stalled my exit and focused on the dark hair showing above the menu. As I stepped outside, I saw Rico's profile through the window. Eating at the diner wasn't suspicious on its own, but I didn't like coincidences. I had to wonder if I'd missed something. Why would he follow us? The worst part was, now I doubted my gut feeling. The investigation had hit a wall.

I directed Shad back to the station to begin his research magic on Rico and Sebastian. If there was a connection, I was confident the deputy would uncover it.

Since I had an evening planned of searching for destructive teenagers, I was headed home for a quick bite to eat. On my way, I called the inn to check their records for a guest named Bassinger. No luck.

Armed with bug repellent and my Beretta, I reached the trails with the sun a fading sliver on the horizon. After I checked that no teenagers were around, I would head home to sleep. I could only hope that Hatch had already found the missing man and hadn't yet called me.

I basked in the quiet of the woods as sweat gathered at the small of my back. Soon, the only light was moonlight shining through the cracks in the canopy. After a couple of hours of searching with no results, I turned to head home when a twig snapped. I froze. If the noise had come from wildlife, I should've heard it coming.

No, this was someone sneaking around. For the first time in four years on this job, I pulled my sidearm. Then I flashed my Maglite on a man's face.

Eyes scrunched up at the blinding light, Rico stepped out of the woods with both hands in the air. One of them held a camera. "Don't shoot."

I lowered the gun and light. "Rico, are you trying to interfere in a police investigation?"

His gulp was audible. "No, ma'am."

"Then why have I seen you three times today?"

"A happy coincidence?"

I narrowed my eyes. "I think not."

"It's just..." His voice deflated. "A missing person is such a good story for my channel. It's viral material."

Ah, so *that* was it. "I can't let you interfere with an ongoing investigation."

I didn't intend to discuss a missing person with the local modern-age gossip. No, what Rico did was worse. He talked to the world, and his "coverage" of my investigation could do lasting damage.

When he protested, I said, "No. This is nonnegotiable. Go home or I'll arrest you."

He frowned and turned away.

A low whistle echoed around us.

Rico backed up to stand beside me. "Did you hear that?" he whispered.

I nodded and glimpsed his display screen showing heat signatures. He was well-equipped with a thermal image camera.

"Let me see that." I holstered my gun and grabbed the camera. Human-shaped hot spots showed fifty yards ahead of us. Then they disappeared. "Is there a cave up there?"

"Probably. A lot of caves around the springs."

I shot off a quick text to Shad with a location pin. *May need backup.* Then I ran, Rico right behind me. It was reckless, but if I didn't move quickly, I feared I would lose where the figures disappeared.

I slowed when we neared the location. Nothing unusual. I ascended the trail as it veered to the right and grew wider behind a thorny bush. On the other side was a stone overhang above a cave opening.

I handed the camera back to Rico and risked scanning the ground with my Maglite. Boot prints. A lot of them.

I attached the flashlight to my belt and pulled out my phone. I texted Shad to come quickly, providing another location pin.

"Stay here," I said to Rico.

I unholstered my firearm and stepped into the cave's narrow entrance. My shoulders grazed the cool stone as I made my way through several sharp turns. Ahead, a soft light lit the ground. Around the last corner, water trickled and echoed in a large chamber illuminated by battery-operated torch lights. I padded farther inside with my sidearm ready. Large rock formations littered the back. To the right was a pool of water. To the left was another tunnel, larger than the last. The other side of the pool had a sandy inlet covered in shadow, but something strange caught my attention. I grabbed the Maglite and pointed it to the other side of the water. I sucked in a breath. A bare leg wearing a heavy hiking boot poked out from the rocks.

I surveilled the area before holstering my gun, then stepped to the narrowest part of the pool, where I jumped to the other side.

Wet clothes clung to a man, who lay on his side, his face turned away from the light. I rolled him over and my heart pounded.

Bassinger.

I checked his pulse. Strong. Relief flooded my body.

I grabbed my phone. No service. Great. I needed to get Bassinger out of the cave, but I couldn't get him across the pool of water on my own.

I rubbed Bassinger's sternum. He winced and groaned. A good sign. Then I saw blood surrounding a hole in his shirt. I pulled the shirt up and checked his abdomen for a wound. There wasn't one. I tried his back. Nothing. Even the dirt beneath him was uniform in color with no bloody dark spots.

None of this made sense.

A shot rang out. The force punched my back, shoving me onto Bassinger. I groaned. Through my Kevlar vest, the shot had hurt like a jab from a heavyweight boxer.

Another shot. I ducked. Rock chipped off the wall.

An angry voice echoed around the chamber. Or maybe two voices. It was hard to tell through the additional shots. The cacophony of sounds echoed throughout the cave. It was impossible to pinpoint the location of the shooter.

I needed cover.

I pulled my Beretta out and scooted toward the water.

Another shot.

My leg!

I rolled over the edge into the pool.

The water was frigid. My limbs froze and I sank fast. The pool felt bottomless.

The shooter yelled, but his words were garbled through the water.

I couldn't stay underwater, but I needed to pop up where the shooter wouldn't expect me. The shooter must have come from the tunnel at the back of the cave. I would try there first.

My limbs struggled to move, and my chest burned as I ran low on oxygen. I pushed through the cold. With one hand, I pushed on the rock ledge and broke the surface—and aimed.

The shooter had taken cover behind a rock formation. The only visible part of him was his hand holding the gun.

I aimed and squeezed my trigger.

The shooter went down, wailing and cursing.

My weapon was still aimed in the area of the shooter, and I pulled myself out of the water. I froze when I realized another man faced me.

"You, get on the ground!" The order had come from *behind* the other man.

Shad.

The small, frail man in front of me dropped to the ground.

"Chief, you good?" Shad called out, striding along the cave's edge.

"Yeah. I'm good."

Shad kicked the gun away from a seething and wounded Sebastian.

The small man squeaked, "I didn't do anything!"

"Claude?" Shad asked.

The clerk from the inn sniffed. "I told him he went too far. He was yelling like a crazy person outside the inn last night. He's always trying to get me killed, but I'm done. He said we hadn't gotten enough, so he—"

Sebastian threw a fist into Claude's side. "Shut up!"

Sebastian's involvement didn't surprise me, but Claude's was a shock. Then again, my gut had told me this morning that something was off with the hotel clerk.

I helped Shad secure our suspects.

Shad stared at my leg. "Chief, were you shot?" He pulled out his phone and cursed. "No reception."

I reached down, stuck my finger in a pea-sized hole in my pants, and yanked. The fabric gave with a rip.

No wound. Just like Bassinger.

"What happened?" Shad asked.

Before I could respond, Bassinger stirred and gingerly sat up. The man's dark eye circles and pale skin from his recent videos were gone. He glanced wide-eyed around the cave, then put a hand to his stomach.

"You're okay," I said. "I'm Chief Simpkins, and this is Officer Redfern. We're here to get you home."

Shad gestured at the two sitting in the dirt. "Recognize these men?"

Bassinger nodded. "Yeah. They brought me here. And when I wouldn't give them more money—as if ten thousand dollars wasn't enough—that one shot me." He lifted his shirt, searching for a wound. Nothing.

My mind raced. "Bassinger, did you get in the water?"

He nodded again.

"Shad, can I borrow your pocketknife?"

My deputy tossed it over. I flicked the blade open to prick my finger. When a small bead of blood emerged, I dipped the finger beneath the water's surface. The blood disappeared and so did the cut.

"No way," I whispered in disbelief.

Shad gasped. "I'd heard the legends as a kid."

"Me too," Rico said from behind me.

I turned. He had his phone up, recording.

"Turn that off!"

Rico slid the phone into his pocket.

"Chief, what do we do about this?" Shad asked.

Rico whispered, "This magic spring is worth billions of dollars."

I shook my head. The town enjoyed the extra money from the Branson tourists, but that was at a manageable level. What would happen if word got out about this?

"We could charge people," Shad said.

"Or we could bottle it," Rico added. "Sell it on the internet."

"No," I said.

"Why not?" Rico and Shad asked in unison. The mania showing in their eyes was all too familiar. Toni had looked the same.

I needed to get out of this cave. "Listen, let's table this. I've got a missing person to return, men to book, and reports to write."

Shad and Rico glanced at each other, then nodded.

Back at the station, Shad and I booked the two men, and after Bassinger gave his statement, Rico took him to get cleaned up.

As the sun rose, a heavy dread weighed me down. I had spent the night detailing the scam and the events at the springs in my report.

Turned out Claude and Sebastian had been running their operation since the day the first bus arrived from Branson. In return for access to a hidden spring with miraculous healing effects, people like Bassinger were told to bring a duffle bag with money, leave it under their seat on the bus, then they were given a hunter-orange Deer Stand Café cap to wear on the hiking trail. Claude would pick them out of the crowd, blindfold them, and guide them to the cave.

My stomach soured at the thought of it all. In my report, I had wanted to omit the facts about the spring, but this was no different from lying. If the news of the spring became public knowledge, could I stand to watch anyone profit from the desperation of others?

I shoved my chair away from the desk and stood at the window. I glanced down at the text I'd just typed, my finger hovering over the Send button.

I'm interested in the job. Send details.

It was my chance. No more Mayor Doyle, no more chasing teens in the dark, and no more Mystic Springs. If Shad's and Rico's reactions to using the springs for profit represented the town's feelings, then I had no place here. For four years, I had tried and failed to fit in. The problem was me. I was the wrong caliber for this town.

Shad knocked. He held a cup of coffee aloft in offering.

I waved him in and sat.

He placed the paper cup on the desk. "Did you get any sleep?"

"No. You?"

He shook his head and sat down. "Can you believe those two have been getting away with this for two years? If they had a buyer on each busload of tourists, that would be millions of dollars. But how did they find the cave in the first place?"

"I can answer that," I said. "Turns out Claude was a nervous talker and sang during his ride to the station. Said he found a map in the inn's basement. Apparently, the building used to be a speakeasy, with lots of hidden treasures collecting dust down there. Claude mentioned the map to his cousin Sebastian, who came up with the plan."

"Wow. Claude and Sebastian are kin?" Shad shook his head. "Didn't see that coming."

Shad was attempting to be funny, but I couldn't muster a smile. "Shad, about the cave."

He put up a hand. "You were right."

I stared at him.

"Those two men were profiting off the desperate—the ones likely drowning in medical bills and frantic for a cure. Claude and Sebastian didn't care about that." Shad sneered. "Makes me sick."

I wanted to believe him, but this was too big.

"Oh, and one more thing." Shad tapped his phone and slid it to me.

On the screen was Rico's YouTube channel.

"Rico Cerna, with my new series highlighting the influential people of Mystic Springs. First up is someone newer to the town, but her position is better suited for an outsider, at least in my opinion. She shows the locals the law is impartial, which isn't easy in a small town. Our Chief of Police, Sam Simpkins, truly looks out for every resident of Mystic Springs."

The screen showed clips from yesterday's investigation, along with pictures of me at various community events.

I swallowed hard and handed Shad his phone back as I steeled my resolve. "We need to keep knowledge of the spring from the general public."

"Agreed."

"It's our duty to help people. *For free.* Do you think we could get Bassinger and Rico to keep an eye out for people seeking help? I'm talking about people who are sick. Not those looking for a facelift—or a cure for bunions."

Shad smiled. "Yeah, I think they would absolutely be on board. I'll call now."

Before I sunk back in my chair, I highlighted and deleted the details in my report concerning the spring's special power. This omission felt surprisingly good.

I picked up my phone and hit delete on my unsent text.

Mystic Springs was stuck with me. I wasn't going anywhere anytime soon.

R. A. WESLEY

R. A. Wesley was first published in 1993, if you count when the local newspaper ran kids' scary stories during October. She grew up an Air Force brat but spent most of her time in Utah. R. A. has a wandering spirit and has traveled to places like Thailand, Spain, England, and even worked on a cruise ship. She is now settled in the Midwest with her hilarious husband and two sassy kids. When she isn't narrating books to her kids, she can be seen with one earbud in, catching up on audiobooks.

Tell R. A. what she should read next at
https://www.instagram.com/r.a.wesley
Or email: RAWesley.books@gmail.com

WHAT'S INSIDE

DAVE SWANZ

MORNING SUNLIGHT BREAKS in through Dave's bedroom window. It creeps up his sleeping body, assaulting his eyes with an unusual intensity. He wrinkles his face in protest.

"Holy crap, that's way too bright." He flips away from the vicious attack, grabs a pillow, and clamps it down over his face. He was up too late talking and playing video games with Chuckie, his best friend since kindergarten.

He struggles to get a full breath—the pillow smells weird, like a Flamin' Hot Cheeto. He jams his hand between the pillow and pillow casing. Rustling around, he acquires the prize. Dave pulls it out and admires the familiar bright red-orange coloring.

Sitting up, he heaves the pillow at the window and shouts, "Heck yeah!" He flips the stale Cheeto into his mouth and chomps down.

He stares at his alarm clock. "Seven o'clock!" His stomach hurts, his heart races, his hands are clammy, his forehead feels hot, and his head hurts.

"No. It's too early."

He flops his shirtless, fourteen-year-old body back onto the bed with enough drama to make a three-year-old envious. He kicks off the blanket, revealing he fell asleep in his basketball shorts and socks.

His eyes dart to the clock's lower right-hand corner. He curls his lips into a smile, and his eyes widen. "It's Saturday," he whispers. "It's not a school day." His stomach feels better, his heart stops racing, his hands are dry, he's no longer hot, and his head feels fine.

With the agility of a WWE wrestler, he launches out of bed, landing in front of a full-length mirror. A poster of Hulk Hogan —a birthday present from his dad on his tenth birthday—hangs on the wall to the left of the mirror. Dave flexes his scrawny muscles in victory, mimicking the figure in the poster.

In his best growling Hulk Hogan voice, he says, "And then God created a set of twenty-four-inch pythons, brother."

Dave grabs a crumpled T-shirt off the back of a chair, slips his feet into old, faded shoes, and stumbles out of his room and down the stairs.

Popping into the kitchen, he finds his older sister sitting at the breakfast table, dressed for work, hovering over a cup of coffee, and fidgeting with her name tag. She flips the tag from the front with the name *Taylor*, to the back, which says *Property of Deer Stand Café*.

"Hey, Smiley. You're up early."

She grabs her coffee cup and glares at him. "Stop calling me Smiley."

Dave opens the fridge door, then repositions food, looking for his caffeine. He spots his savior—Diet Coke. A nefarious person has placed a sticky note on it. *Don't drink this. Have some orange juice instead. Love, Mom.* Frowning, he grabs the sticky note and slaps it on the pitcher of orange juice. "Ha, good try, Mom." The fridge door slams shut as he pops the tab.

"Hey, Smiley. Did you see what Mom's trying to pull on me?"

"Does it look like I care?"

"Dang, sis, what's got you down today?" He places the can on the kitchen table, pulls back a chair, and plops down. He grabs a slice of toast from a plate in front of his sister and slathers it with butter. "I thought you liked working at the café?"

Taylor tilts her head and stares at her coffee cup. "I do. I just thought I would be further in my life journey. I'm nineteen, you know. I shouldn't be in this small town. I should be in St. Louis or Kansas City, living the good life and doing exciting things."

Dave takes a massive bite of his toast. Crumbs fall from his mouth. "If you want excitement, you can tag along with me and Chuckie—help us geode hunt at the spring. That's exciting."

A banging at the back kitchen door grabs their attention.

Taylor shakes her head. "I'm not hanging out with a couple fourteen-year-olds looking for stupid rocks." She pushes away from the table, stands up, and grabs her Deer Stand Café vest and matching deer antler headband.

She opens the back door, and Dave glimpses Chuckie's goofy smile. Chuckie steps in, dressed in flip-flops, blue jeans, and a cartoon T-shirt that's too tight for his fluffy physique.

Chuckie bows to Taylor. "Good morning, milady."

She steps past him. "Stop it. It's too early for that creepy stuff."

"As you wish," Chuckie says as he sits beside Dave.

"Hope you guys don't drown in the spring," she says as she heads out.

Chuckie turns to Dave. "Bro, your sister is so hot. I think she likes me."

Dave waves at the closed door. "Love you too, Smiley."

Dave and Chuckie grab their backpacks, jump on their bikes, and head north through town, toward the spring they intend to hunt.

After finding five nice geodes while walking along the side of the creek, Dave and Chuckie continue north, then skid to a stop beside the actual spring they are going to hunt.

Chuckie scans the area. "Are you sure we should be geode hunting *in* the spring?"

"We found some good geodes down the creek. Just think what different kinds might be at the bottom of the spring. The source, bro. We might find some that really make our summer." Dave strides closer to the spring. "If we find the right ones here, we can make enough money for our new bikes in no time."

Chuckie follows Dave. "Bro, I just want to go on record as saying this is a bad idea."

Dave reaches the spring's hole. A deep blue shimmering pool stands before them. They both stare into the crystal-clear water. Dave puts his hand on Chuckie's shoulder. "Bro, don't be a wimp. Jump in there and find us some geodes."

"Why do *I* have to go?" Chuckie protests. "It was your bright idea."

"Exactly. I'm the brains of the operation, and you're the brawn." Dave pushes him toward the pool. "Now go get us some money."

Chuckie splashes in and swims out a few feet. He maneuvers his body to face back toward Dave. "Man, it's a good thing your sister is hot, otherwise we wouldn't be friends." Chuckie dives down.

As Dave watches his friend disappear under the surface, he begins to wonder if he should be down there with him.

Bubbles percolate to the surface before Chuckie pops back up. "I see some nice ones, but they're about twenty feet down." He dives under again. This time, he resurfaces with two nice specimens. "There's a weird cluster of 'em over to one side—almost at the bottom."

Dave wades out to grab the two from his friend. "That's weird. All the ones we've found so far have been individual. You sure they're geodes?"

"I think so." Chuckie goes under again.

Dave returns to his backpack and places the two geodes with the other five they had already found. He turns to look for Chuckie, who hasn't resurfaced yet. A massive burst of bubbles erupts in the pool.

Dave dives in and maneuvers his way down. Chuckie struggles frantically, but he's making no headway. He is suspended. Dave swims down to the bottom to see if his foot is caught on the rocks but sees no sign he's stuck. He grabs Chuckie by the waist and tries to pull him up, only for them both to be pulled farther down. Nothing is around them but the crystal-clear water of the spring.

Finally, Dave breaks free of his invisible bonds and kicks as hard as possible to bring them both to the surface. He drags his friend out of the pool and to the shore, then drops him on the grass.

Dave's heart is pounding. He leans over Chuckie and slaps his face. "You okay, bro?"

Chuckie spits out water and gasps for air. "Ouch!" He rubs his cheek. "I almost died. Did you see that?"

Dave moves Chuckie's chin from side to side. "You look fine.

Don't be such a weenie." Dave grabs the cluster of four rocks from his friend's grasp and moves to his backpack. "Good job holding onto the geodes, dude."

Chuckie struggles to his feet. "Bro, I saw it all. Bright lights. My life flashing before me. My mom yelling at me about clean underwear."

Dave breaks apart the cluster of weird geodes and places the separated ones in the backpack with the others. "Stop being dramatic, sissy. Mount up. We gotta get to the souvenir shop and get Mrs. Brockman to buy 'em."

———

Chuckie and Dave cruise to the Springs and Things Souvenir Shop. They drop their bikes and bound up the three steps onto the porch with the backpack of geodes. Dave grabs the handle to go in, but Chuckie slumps down on the top step.

Chuckie waves Dave off. "Bro, I'm tired from almost dying. I'm just gonna sit here and catch my breath."

Dave frowns, wondering if his buddy might be in shock or something. He kneels beside him and places a hand on his shoulder.

Chuckie leans forward and takes a deep breath. He pulls up his pant legs to reveal a rash in the shape of a hand on each ankle. "They've been itchy since we left the springs, bro. That can't be good, right?"

Dave's response is interrupted as a car with Illinois license plates pulls into the gravel parking lot. A mom, dad, and their maybe ten-year-old daughter get out and walk past them into the shop. Dave and Chuckie can see the tension on the family's faces as they pass by.

Dave gets up and walks into the shop behind the family. He turns to see Chuckie lean back and close his eyes. He shouts to Chuckie, "Stay! Good boy."

Dave finds the owner at the counter. "Hey, Mrs. Brockman. I've got a couple more geodes for you to buy. Found some cool, weird ones at the bottom of the spring."

Mrs. Brockman shakes her head. "Sorry, Dave, I can't take any more uncut geodes. They aren't selling very well. If you can get them cut open so we can see what's inside, I would be willing to buy more. You might want to talk to Judd and see if he can help you."

Dave pushes the door open and plops down beside Chuckie. "It's a no-go," he says as he gives the backpack to his friend. "Mrs. Brockman doesn't want any more unopened geodes. She said we could ask Judd. Maybe he's got something in his shed to help us."

Dave and Chuckie turn their attention to the storefront as they see the door fling open and the little girl storm out. The boys hear her father yelling at her through the open door.

"Lyric, get back in here!"

Lyric turns back. "No! I don't want to be in there if I can't get a geode. I'll wait in the car."

Chuckie looks at the girl, hearing the irritation in her voice. Chuckie pulls out one of the geodes from the backpack. "Dads, am I right? You can have this one. Your dad'll need a hammer to open it for you."

"Thanks," Lyric says, taking the geode. She rushes to the car and hops in the back seat. A couple seconds later, her dad and mom follow her. The dad forces the door open, yelling after the little girl. He gets everyone situated in the car, then drives off.

Dave looks at his friend. "Grab your stuff, bro. We're going to Judd's Deer Stand Café."

The boys hop on their bikes and pedal the five blocks west to the café.

With the backpack hanging off Chuckie's shoulder, the boys stride into the café and up to the owner, Judd Rusbridge.

Judd, a tall, gangly man dressed in camo clothing, a camo hat, and a camo apron, all embossed with The Deer Stand Café and Honky Tonk logo, is serving coffee to out-of-state visitors and telling a story about the springs.

Judd smiles as he eyes the two boys. "And speaking of the good people of our town, here are the two best geode hunters in the county. You folks need a genuine Missouri geode, these are the gentleman to know."

Dave pulls Judd to the side. "Hey, Judd, is there any way we can use the shop out back to crack open some of our geodes?"

Judd adjusts his hat. "Sure, boys. That should be okay. Just clean up when you're done." He walks back to his customers.

Dave's sister, Taylor, is bussing tables but steps over to the boys. "What are you two idiots doing?"

Chuckie holds up the backpack of geodes. "We're going to whack open some geodes and get filthy rich. May I whack one open for you, milady?"

Taylor steps back. "Eww, no! Why are you so weird?" She

points at Dave. "Don't do anything stupid." She goes back to bussing tables.

Chuckie slaps Dave on the back. "Dang, bro, is your sister hot or what?"

Dave and Chuckie bust in through the side door of the forty-foot-long shed. They flip on the overhead lights to illuminate an array of eclectic decor. Various types of guns are displayed on the wall to their left—shotguns of every gauge, rifles of every caliber, and numerous pistols. Mounts of deer heads and turkey feathers are scattered among the guns. Fishing equipment and mounts of fish in different poses decorate a second wall.

A third wall contains an array of shop tools. Hammers and saws hang in an orderly fashion, while bigger equipment stands in rows along the bottom of the wall.

A sturdy, overbuilt workbench sits in the middle of the shop. They dump their geodes on the benchtop. Chuckie grabs a hammer from the tool wall and rushes it back to the table. He picks a nice round geode from the spoils, raises the hammer above his head, and brings it down with enough force to crack it open. It smashes into several sections. Sparkly purple and green pieces litter the table.

"Heck yeah!" Chuckie blurts out. "That's what I'm talking about."

Dave grabs one of the weird-looking geodes they found at the bottom of the spring. He places it in the middle of the table, then he snatches Chuckie's hammer, winds up, and takes a big swing. He crashes the hammer down on its victim. The rock careens across the table, over the edge, and crashes to the concrete floor.

Chuckie strides over to the geode and picks it up. "Not a mark on it. What a wimpy arm."

Determined not to look like a wimp, Dave goes to the tool wall, chooses an even bigger, eight-pound hammer, and returns to the bench with the stride of a confident man.

Dave motions Chuckie out of the way. "Take a step back, junior. I don't want to hurt you when this thing shatters into a million pieces." Dave stretches, exaggerating his windup.

The mighty blow doesn't cause any damage but instead sends the rock blasting off across the benchtop, skipping across the floor, and slamming into the far wall.

"Oh my." Chuckie puts his hands on his cheeks. "How will we ever pick up so many geode pieces? It'll take all day."

Dave goes to retrieve the rock. "Whatever, bro." He picks it up. "Huh. Not a scratch on it." He grabs Chuckie by the shoulder. "We need to see if Judd will let us use his wet saw to cut this thing open."

The boys rush through the café, dodging customers as they find Judd regaling a table of new customers with an old joke.

"Hey, Judd, is there any way we could talk you into letting us use the wet saw in the shed to cut open a tough geode?" Dave asks.

Judd turns from his customers and scans the boys' faces. He steps to the side of the table, places his hand on an older customer's shoulder, and gives a little squeeze. "Do these boys look responsible enough to you?"

The older gentleman nods his head. "It should be fine. They can't get into too much trouble being unsupervised, right?"

Taylor steps up to the table. "Don't worry, they'll be supervised." She turns the boys around and escorts them to the shed.

Taylor carries out the wet saw. Water in the reservoir sloshes about as she sets it up on the benchtop. "You two idiots better not get me fired," she says as she plugs in the machine.

Dave places the stone on the wet saw's platform. "You won't get fired for helping us." He flips the switch and the machine squeals to life, then he pushes the stone toward the blade.

At first, the teeth easily bite into the stone, but then sparks fly as if the stone is made of metal. Suddenly, the blade catches and rips the rock from Dave's grasp, sending it crashing to the other side of the shed.

Chuckie runs to retrieve the stone. "Holy crap, Dave! You suck."

Taylor yanks the stone from Chuckie. "You idiots, let me do that." She pushes the stone to the blade. Sparks fly again as she applies pressure. This time, the blade's teeth bite so hard that the rock is ripped from her grip and sent flying high enough to hit a shop light hanging from the ceiling. Plastic housing and glass rain down to the garage floor.

Dave pats Taylor's shoulder and points to the mess. "*That's* why you're gonna get fired."

Chuckie retrieves the stone and hands it back to Taylor. "Your stone, milady."

Taylor snatches the stone. She points to the tool wall. "Go get us some hard hats, goggles, and clamps," she commands Chuckie.

All three don their safety equipment. Taylor uses a clamp to secure the rock. This time, she doesn't force the blade through the rock but makes an eighth-inch-deep cut all the way around it. She places the rock on the benchtop, grabs the larger hammer, and swings it down hard enough to shatter the geode's outside rock shell. They all stare at what's left.

A small, shiny, black... something.

Dave hesitates a moment, his heart pounding, then he picks up the object and brushes it clean. He holds it under the bench lamp at the end of the table. "What do you guys think it could be?" The heat from the lamp warms the black... something. "It looks like it's covered in fish scales."

It moves in Dave's hand. Startled, he drops it onto the benchtop.

The three watch in amazement as the shiny object tilts one way and then the other as the scales bristle and move. A tiny, clawed hand emerges, followed by glimmering black wings. At last, a small creature uncurls. It stretches its legs like a shiny, black cat with wings. With bright, glowing red eyes, it stands and stares at the group before emitting a stream of fire from its mouth.

The three scatter and dive out of the way.

"Holy crap, Dave, what've you done?" Chuckie shouts.

Emitting a high-pitched scream, the creature fully extends its wings and takes flight. It hovers briefly over the benchtop before flying to the shop lights in the rafters.

The creature dive-bombs them, and Dave rolls out of the way. "It's not my fault! You're the one who found it."

Chuckie ducks out of the way. "Dude, it's totally your fault. I said it was a bad idea."

The creature lands on one of the rafters. From its roost, it surveys its surroundings.

"Would you two stop bickering!" Taylor shouts. "We need to catch it before it gets outside."

Dave stares at her. "Catch it? We need to get the heck out of here."

The creature plunges from the rafter, spewing fire as it makes a strafing run. The benchtop catches fire as the dragon—it has to be a dragon—returns to the rafters.

Dave scrambles from the table and grabs a fire extinguisher from the tool wall. He pulls the pin, points the black nozzle at the fire, and squeezes the trigger. A puff of white engulfs the flames on the table. Smoke rises.

Dave turns to Chuckie. "Grab a fishing net off the wall. We'll distract it, and when it makes another dive, use the net to catch it." Dave grabs Taylor and shoves her out into the open.

Chuckie dashes to the fishing wall and grabs one of several hanging nets. He positions himself at the end of the smoldering table.

In the middle of the shop, Taylor waves her hands and shouts at the dragon. "Hey, ugly. Come get ya some."

The dragon screeches as it leaps into its next attack run.

Taylor ducks out of the way at the last second as Chuckie tosses the net over the creature.

"I got it!" Chuckie shouts. "I got the little sucker."

The dragon's bright red eyes stare at Chuckie. It spits a broad stream of fire that disintegrates the netting. The dragon then escapes to the rafters again.

Before the dragon can rain fire upon them, the three rush to the bench and dive under its protective top.

Taylor points at Dave. "Go get Judd. Tell him we need help."

Dave darts to the door and stumbles out. As the creature zooms toward him, he slams the door shut in time to trap it inside.

Dave bursts into the café and slides to a stop beside Judd.

Judd eyes him. "Whoa there. What's got you all worked up? You got all your fingers, right?"

"We need you out at the shed, Judd."

Judd turns to his customers. "If you'll excuse me, I'll return to finish that story in a second." Judd follows close behind Dave.

Dave leads Judd into the shed. Judd sees the smoldering benchtop. "What in tarnation is going on in here?"

Dave, Taylor, and Chuckie all gather behind Judd, as if the man could protect them. The creature swoops at Judd's head, spewing fire. The flame hits his hat, setting it ablaze.

Taylor grabs the fire extinguisher and puts out the fire on Judd's hat. "Take cover!" Taylor shouts.

They all crowd under the bench. Judd watches the circling creature. "Aww crap. Not again." He turns his attention to the boys. "You boys have all your fingers?"

Dave stares at Judd. "There's a dragon flying around, and your question is if we have all our fingers?"

Judd takes off his hat and checks for any remaining embers. "Yeah. I'm the one who gave you boys permission to use the wet saw. If you cut your fingers off, that'd be on me." He puts his hat back on and points to the creature. "If a dragon kills you... not my fault."

Judd crawls from beneath the bench and rushes to the gun wall. He grabs a 12-gauge shotgun and a box of shells marked *Blue Magic*. He loads the magazine, and one in the chamber, then slides back under the bench with Dave and the others.

Dave grabs Judd's arm. "What'd you mean when you said *aww crap, not again?*"

Ignoring the question, Judd places his hand on Dave's shoulder. "Listen, I need you to ride to the Mystic Visions shop and get Miss Flaminia. Tell her to bring the crystal balls *on* the wall. She'll know what to do. Go!"

Judd points the shotgun at the creature and pulls the trigger. Blue lightning from the hit knocks the dragon back, giving Dave time to bolt for the door.

———

Panting, Dave bursts in through the front door of Mystic Visions. Sweat pours down the side of his face. "Balls to the wall!" he shouts.

Inside the shop, a large, old-looking wooden table occupies the middle of the room. Flaminia Tempest, the enigmatic owner of the occult shop, exuding an aura of mystique and allure, sits at her cluttered table, shuffling tarot cards with practiced ease. Her face, framed by cascading black locks tied back elegantly with a glimmering gold band, captivates with her unconventional beauty. Her dark, piercing eyes seem to hold the secrets of the universe.

"What are you doing?" Flaminia matches Dave's intensity.

"Judd told me to tell you *balls to the wall*, and you'd know what to do." Dave forces out the words between gasps for breath.

"Do you mean crystal balls *on* the wall?" Flaminia counters.

"Maybe. It could be that," Dave says.

Flaminia shakes her head. "Dang. Not again. How many are there?"

"Just the one," Dave says, surprised.

Flaminia points to a row of crystal balls lining the top

perimeter of the room. Many are red, several are green, and the rest are clear. "Use the library ladder and retrieve a crystal ball, please."

Dave pushes the ladder into position and scrambles up to grab a glowing red one.

"No, no. Not the red one. That's full already. Grab a clear one."

Dave returns the red one, snatches a clear one, and slides down the ladder. He rushes to Flaminia, stopping at her table.

She searches through her tarot cards and grabs The World card. "This will do the trick." Her black, jewel-inlaid silk robe whisks silently about her as she follows Dave out the door.

Dave and Flaminia throw open the shed door and scramble in just in time to see Judd loading the shotgun.

Judd motions to them to hide under the workbench with him, Taylor, and Chuckie. "Welcome to the party, Flaminia," Judd says with a wink and a smile. Then he shouts, "Taylor, get that net on it!"

Taylor rushes out and nabs the creature in her net, but it drags her skidding across the floor. The net handle slips through her grasp.

"Crap. I forgot how strong those things are," Judd says as he levels the gun and pulls the trigger.

"Just like 2017 all over again!" Flaminia shouts.

"You've seen this before?" Dave asks.

"Maybe," Judd and Flaminia respond in unison.

"What is that thing?" Taylor shouts.

"When the Spanish Conquistadors traveled through this

area, they called them Dragón Pequeños, which means little dragon," Flaminia says.

Dave watches the weird creature as it flutters above. "They've known about these things for that long?"

Flaminia ignores his question and points to Taylor. "You, douse the dragon with the fire extinguisher when we get it in position. The CO_2 will cool it, and I can capture it." She takes the crystal ball from Dave and pulls *The World* tarot card from her pocket.

She motions to Judd. "Shoot it. Aim for its wings to bring it down far enough that the boys can grab the handle."

Flaminia cracks open the crystal ball, revealing it's full of a thick, viscous gel.

Judd pops up and gets the dragon in his sights. *Bam!* The first shot explodes in a burst of blue lightning, hitting the creature's left wing and forcing it a few feet lower. A quick pump ejects the spent shell and replaces it with a fresh one. *Bam!* The second shot hits the right wing, with the same effect. The dragon is forced lower.

Dave and Chuckie are now able to grab the fishing net handle. They use all of their fourteen-year-old strength to drag it toward Taylor.

She aims the nozzle at the dragon and squeezes the extinguisher's trigger. A stream of white nitrogen engulfs the small creature. Its wings slow down and curl around its body. The dragon thuds to the shed's floor, paralyzed by the nitrogen, as Flaminia predicted.

Flaminia writes a magic spell on the tarot card and places it into the viscous gel of the left half of the crystal ball. She scoops up the dragon from the net and plunges it into the right half. Gel oozes out as she squeezes both halves of the crystal ball together.

She chants an incantation as she places the crystal ball on the benchtop.

As Flaminia's chant reaches its crescendo, an intense, bright white light flashes where the two halves of the crystal ball come together. Like welding two metal pieces together, Flaminia seals the two crystal ball halves with her incantation. Smoke billows along the connection line as the bright, arcing light floods and illuminates the shed's interior.

Judd turns his back to Flaminia to face the kids. "You guys might want to turn and close your eyes."

Dave hears Flaminia's faint chant. He peeks around to see the intensity of the light diminish, then disappear.

The light in the shed has returned to normal by the time the others open their eyes.

The crystal ball smolders on the benchtop, now glowing bright red. The color shields what's inside from prying eyes.

Judd strides over to Flaminia with a smile. "Hell yeah! Just like 2017. But that time there were three of 'em. Glad there was only one this time."

Judd turns to the boys with just as big a smile. "You boys clean this place up before you leave. Oh, and put any other *unique* geodes back where you found 'em."

Flaminia collects her belongings, tucking the full crystal ball securely under her arm. With a purposeful stride, she approaches Dave, Chuckie, and Taylor, meeting their gazes with her penetrating stare. With a graceful sweep of her hand, she passes over their auras, a silent observer of energies unseen. "May the geode you gave away to the little girl hold on to its mystical secrets," she murmurs cryptically as she exits the shed, leaving her words lingering in the air.

Dave turns to his sister and Chuckie. "How freaking awesome was that?" He punches Chuckie in the arm. "Smiley, you thought you had to be in a big city to have excitement. I told you you'd have fun with me and Chuckie."

Chuckie grabs a dustpan, garbage can, and a couple of brooms. He bows to Taylor and passes her a broom. "Your cleaning device, milady."

Taylor smiles. "You two are still idiots."

DAVE SWANZ

Dave Swanz writes screenplays and short stories that start innocent enough but take a sharp left turn when they ask, "What if?" He then races down that path to find out. Dave was raised on a Northeast South Dakota dairy farm surrounded by wide-open prairie, which gave his imagination enough space so the characters in his head could run free. He came to writing later in life and, with help from Writers of Warrensburg, wrangled the characters running free in his head and gave them a home on the page. He now lives with his wife, Anna, in Missouri.

IVY

TAMMY CUMPTON

YOGA WAS HARD. And as a middle-aged woman, Dilly Tuttle was trying her hardest to hold the pose for longer than five seconds. But soon, she spotted where a robin had recently laid an egg in a clump of dried grass on the ground. It rested about ten feet from where she was standing. She was sure the egg was a sign from the gods that there was to be another harvest at her family's hidden mystical garden today. Every month, like clockwork, she would see a sign that a harvest was coming.

Dilly hurried inside to gather her trip supplies. She packed her bag with water, food for breakfast and lunch, and her magical harvesting supplies. One piece she needed more than anything was her treasured bag of holding. As a magical bag that held an insurmountable number of things, it would never get bigger or heavier.

She looked at the clock. Ten a.m. She planned on being back before dark, but the harvesting took time, and it would be close.

Dilly covered her slightly tan skin in sunscreen and bug spray, then dressed in her hiking jeans, a button shirt, and thick socks. Slipping on her hiking boots, she tried to think about anything she might have forgotten.

Her mother's words of wisdom rang in her head. "Just do what you can, and that will be enough." Dilly had found this to be completely true.

As Dilly shut the front door of her home and began her trek to the spring, she thought of the magical harvests she had been doing since she could remember. Dilly Tuttle's family had been going to the garden by the spring for decades, and, most likely, people like her family had tended it for centuries. Her parents had placed and maintained a small area to eat, with a picnic table, at about the halfway point to the spring. The garden at the end of the path, beside the spring, produced exotic and rare plants that people couldn't find anywhere else in the region. Fresh durian was almost always on the picking list.

All the harvests had been a secret because of the fear that other people would ruin it. Once her parents had died, Dilly worked alone. She had no interest in hiring someone to work for her in her home, even now that she was getting on in years. She would never be able to trust that they wouldn't betray her and follow her to the garden one day.

For too many years, Dilly got knocks on her door in the middle of the night. All because the local town folk in Mystic Springs thought she and her family were witches. Some silly person somewhere in history had made up stories about witches only working their magic at night. Which is what Dilly liked to tell everyone who showed up at her place after eleven p.m. She liked to have her bedtime around then, so she put up a sign at the front of her driveway: "All plant sales must be complete by 10:45 p.m. No later."

The truth was, her mother and father had been witches their entire lives, as had Dilly. So many of the witches, and families with magical abilities, had moved away from Mystic Springs. But they failed when living away from this area. Too many in the public came to realize who they were and objected to the magical beings fabricating what they needed to make themselves look better.

The Tuttles were not frauds or liars. When customers requested an item, they were told to wait till the order could be filled. The waiting times varied and always made the customers a little bit wary. They suspected the family used the time until delivery to import the exotic fruits instead of raising them nearby.

When Dilly had finally had enough of customers' distrust and the nighttime harassments, she converted the family business to online orders only.

Today, Dilly started down the footpath her ancestors had laid out over time. Sweat dripped down her face and collected on her shirt's collar. The memories of all the times in her life walking this trail were her special treat—a sweet secret that she and her ancestors had kept for decades. She remembered pure excitement and joy coursing through her veins when her mother or father announced a harvest day.

Then Dilly had run along ahead of her family, and on the way home she had lagged behind, feeling the exhaustion of a harvesting deep in her bones. Some of her happiest times were on this path and in the garden at the end of it.

Dilly frowned slightly. She had no children. So, she would never share those memories with her own child. She had learned years ago, in a relationship that had long passed, that she could not biologically have a child. Her significant other had told her she was broken, a cruel statement Dilly had believed for many years. She wasn't broken, but her heart was when he had finally left her—alone. Dilly found out after he'd left that she was much stronger than she'd ever imagined. She was happier, too.

She was most comfortable in her own skin just being outside. It was deep in the forest surrounding the spring that she would find all the coolest things. Once she found a skull of a deer with antlers fully intact and completely cleaned, just sitting there for Dilly to pick up and take home. Her mother had thought this find was just as neat, and insisted on displaying it, where it still hung on the porch today.

―――――――――

The last half of the journey flew fast. She was there by 10:30 a.m., in plenty of time to do the thanking ritual before she harvested. She saw the garden ahead and started chanting the prayer in her mind. *Today, we give thanks. Thanks for these godly gifts. Thank you, dear gods and goddesses.*

After arriving at the garden, she strolled through and admired the variety of fruits and vegetables, noticing a few that looked very strange. Closest to the spring, plants grew that required more shade and less light. Alongside those plants were new plants, different from the others. They were large plants blooming with petals, with fruits hanging down that Dilly had never seen.

Dilly tried to imagine what these fruits could be, and who would benefit from this special gift. She could often tell what gifts went together for an order based on how strange the request was. Today, there was breadfruit, and some durian plants that had a few fruits each. She was quite confused when, next to these plants, she found a small pile of what looked like socks. They were growing out of a plant resembling a bean plant. Dilly went closer and confirmed there actually were a dozen crisp, white cotton socks. Dilly sniffed the air near this bounty, enjoying their fresh smell. It reminded her of clothes that had been left outside, hanging on the line to dry, but were forgotten till the morning.

She picked one of the small socks and held it up to examine. Next to the sock plant was what appeared to be a plant that Dilly knew as Dutchman's breeches. But this one was much larger. Instead of the usual blooms resembling tiny pairs of old-fashioned underwear, this plant was covered in what looked like children's underwear. The kind only a small child would wear. She pondered why these fully organic things were going to be requested.

Dilly found the rest of the plants holding a whole outfit of clothes. Their fruits had opened up like flowers to reveal a pair of pants, a long-sleeved shirt, and a short-sleeved shirt. More plants contained similar outfits, including two pairs of shoes. She found three already-harvested plants, one big plant that looked like it should have contained another outfit, one for shoes, and another was an underwear plant. Like the others, these missing clothes would be fully organic, grown by the waters of the mystical spring.

Dilly approached the altar, to prepare for the ritual of thank-ing, and she saw burnt matches all over the altar. Another person must have been here. She finished the ritual and her harvest, packed up her bag of holding, and put all the clothes on top of the fruits—that way they wouldn't get squished.

As she walked out from under the trees beside the spring, she turned and spoke aloud. "Please do not take more than you need. And do not tell anyone about this place. Because next time I might not be so nice." She didn't hear anyone else in the garden, but that didn't mean no one was watching.

She was all the way back to the picnic table and eating lunch when she heard something. A shuffling sound, on the path leading back the way she had just come. Dilly rose from her seat and put her bag on the table. Walking quietly, she moved slowly, trying not to shuffle her feet, so as not to scare whatever it was. Nothing was down the path, so she turned on her heels and walked back toward her table.

When Dilly returned, she saw her bag open on the ground. She knew she had left it on the table. There was no wind today to have blown it off. She found a stick about a meter long. Poking the bag with the stick, she watched the bag move slightly. Something was in there. She gathered up her courage and said, "Come on out, I know you are in there." Dilly waited as fear and excitement warred within her. She hoped for a cat, but it was a small child. An olive-skinned girl climbed out of the bag wearing fruit-stained clothes, which appeared to be the clothes from the garden. The girl stared up with wide blue eyes at Dilly, watermelon juice dripping from her hair. Dilly couldn't help but feel bad for her.

The little girl spoke softly, tears welling up in her eyes. "When I climbed inside the bag, I fell and knocked over the pile of these big balls that were sticky when they broke open. And now I'm sticky! I'm sorry."

The watermelons? Dilly believed her, and she responded like her mother had responded to Dilly as a child. "Well, are you alright? That probably didn't feel great."

And the little girl looked confused. "Yeah, but you aren't mad? 'Cause it's a mess in there." She motioned to the bag.

"It's fine as long as you are alright. What is your name? Mine is Dilly."

"My name is Ivy." The girl's giggle matched her happy look. "Dilly is a silly name."

"I always thought that too. Do you know your last name, or

your mom's name?" Dilly was curious to see if this was a child of a family from a neighboring farm.

Ivy replied, "I don't know, but I came from there." The girl pointed back the way both of them had traveled.

Dilly frowned. She'd known there was another farm way past the other side of the creek, but she had no idea who lived there and if there were children. Dilly decided the best thing to do was take the girl into town to see the chief of police. She rarely went into town at all, but because of the special circumstances, Dilly knew this was the correct solution.

"Come, child. Together, we'll figure out who you belong with."

Dilly and the child walked to Dilly's farm. Throwing the harvesting bag on the table and grabbing her keys and purse, Dilly hurried back out the door and ushered the small girl to the beat-up old truck in her driveway.

When Dilly got to the truck, she realized this child was of such an age and size that she would need some kind of car safety seat. But Dilly didn't have one, so she decided to drive extra carefully with the girl buckled in with a seat belt. Ivy, now silent, leaned against the window, looking out with wide eyes. She didn't say anything for the rest of the ride.

Dilly pulled up to the police station and offered the girl her hand to walk inside.

Smiling, the girl scooted across the seat to Dilly's open door and said, "Thank you."

Although the police station was just a few miles from the farm, Dilly hoped the chief wouldn't notice her lack of a car seat.

The police chief, Sam Simpkins, who was barely old enough to vote, manned the front desk today. She had some pretty big shoes to fill—the old police chief had been in Mystic Springs for a long time.

"Hi, Chief Simpkins. I have an issue here I could use your help with." Dilly stepped to the front desk with the child hiding behind her. She then pulled the child forward by her hand to show the officer.

There were two loud bangs from a couple of car doors outside, then a loud fight erupted from the entryway. The scuffle spilled into the office, and the chief jumped up to separate the couple.

Dilly said, "Chief Simpkins, you can take care of these people first. We will be right in the waiting room." Dilly pulled the child away from the fight and went into the tiny waiting room just off of the entryway. It was usually for taking reports. There were missing person pictures on the wall behind the bench. Dilly turned around and looked at all the different faces. None matched the girl's appearance.

Nearly thirty minutes later, the police chief came out and beckoned Dilly and Ivy into her office. They sat in front of the chief's desk, then Dilly explained she had found the girl while on a hike around her property.

The chief showed concern. "What's your name?" she asked the child.

"Ivy, and this is Dilly," the girl said, motioning to Dilly.

The chief and Dilly smiled at each other.

Dilly said, "Oh, we already know each other. I used to bring the chief locally sourced loofahs."

Sam seemed to consider this. "The local emergency foster home is full up, and I am just way too busy to take care of her."

Dilly didn't give it a second thought. "She can stay with me. I have a spare bed in the study that I can make up for her." Maybe Dilly wasn't a people person, but something told her Ivy would be fine with being at the farm.

Sam got up and walked around to the front of her desk. She

leaned her slight frame against the desk, smiled, and said, "Okay, I'll have some papers drawn up and faxed over. You can come back and sign them tomorrow."

Dilly and Ivy smiled at each other. They headed to the door, with Ivy holding Dilly's hand and practically pulling her along.

Instead of worrying about this new little life in her hands, Dilly decided to focus on putting away the harvest waiting for her at home. She would pretend the child was an assistant sent from the gods to help her in her business for a while.

Once home, Dilly explained she needed to put away the things she had collected. She walked through the kitchen to the canning porch, where she kept her two large freezers. She was sure the child would get bored and go explore the house, which would have been just fine with Dilly. Instead, rapt with attention, Ivy watched Dilly put away the fruits.

Dilly pulled from the bag the clothes that were covered in watermelon juice. She was about to pull out the rest of the fruit when she realized that Ivy, standing slouched against the doorway, looked wilted. She asked, "Are you hungry?"

Ivy nodded.

Dilly took her to the kitchen. "What do you want to eat? I have grilled cheese, or SpaghettiOs, or whatever you see that you want."

Ivy just shrugged. "I don't know. Can you pick?"

Dilly grabbed the can opener and the medium pot and got to work on dinner.

The juice-and-fruit-covered clothes were all going in the washing machine. Ivy could see Dilly from where she sat, waiting for her meal to cool down. Ivy watched Dilly pulling out the clothing and fruits. With each item Dilly pulled out of the bag of holding, Ivy asked, "What's that?"

While Ivy ate, Dilly explained each item. There was a

special reason for each one. "This white eggplant is for Mrs. Rogers. She uses them for special dishes." Or, "All these water-melons are for the farmer down the road. He didn't get his crop out in time, and he needs to have them at his roadside stand."

Ivy nodded with each item, apparently filing them away in her brain.

After Dilly got all the items put away, she decided Ivy needed to have a bath. The child was sticking to everything she touched. Dilly asked, "You know how to take a bath? You'll have to go upstairs."

"Yeah," the girl said, sounding determined, her small face set in concentration to walk up the stairs.

"Okay, I'll get the tub ready and get you a towel and washcloth."

No questions from Ivy, so that meant she knew what to do, right? Dilly was sure it would be so easy for Ivy to take her own bath.

Ten minutes later, Dilly knocked on the bathroom door and asked, "Are you done yet, girly?" She opened the door a little. Ivy didn't answer, but Dilly could hear movement.

Then a quiet voice said, "Uh, I might be?"

Dilly suspected Ivy would *not* be done yet. Opening the door all the way, she peered into the bathroom. The girl had gotten into the tub fully clothed. She had put the pink body wash in her hair, and the bottle of shampoo hadn't been touched. This poor girl wasn't old enough to take her own bath. Hiding a laugh, Dilly dove into getting the girl ready for a real bath.

Dilly frowned slightly, then smiled at Ivy to show her it was alright. "Okay, I see, there were some misunderstandings in what we do here. You see, we take off our clothes, then we get in the tub. Let's stand up, and we can fix some stuff. And then you will be all clean!" Dilly had Ivy stand up and helped her remove the soaking-wet clothes. Then Dilly drained the tub.

Ivy started crying and climbed up on the bathtub edge. "No! I don't want to go!"

Dilly replied, "No, honey, the drain doesn't take humans away. It only takes away the water. See?" She motioned to the now empty tub.

This time, Dilly had Ivy sit in the tub, and then every time Dilly did something, she told Ivy what they were doing and why they needed to do it. "We are gonna wash your hair. We use a little bit of soap, then we rinse the soap out."

Ivy played with the soap bubbles while Dilly washed her hair. Dilly had the child hold the washcloth, then said, "Let's play a game. You hold the washcloth, and when I point to one of my body parts, you wash that body part on *your* body." Dilly showed her how to wash her arm as an example.

Ivy loved bath time. But Dilly realized it was getting late, and she said, "I know you wanna spend hours in here, but you are starting to *raisin up*." Dilly didn't think this statement would be such a big deal, but Ivy burst into tears and howled.

"Oh no! My hands are old! Am I going to be old now?"

Dilly covered her face with her arm and coughed to cover up her laugh. "Oh no, honey. Wrinkling is just our body's way of getting a better grip when we are in water for a long time."

Ivy stopped crying instantly and said, "Oh." She stood up to get out.

Bedtime was easy in comparison. Dilly made up the second bedroom for Ivy. Dilly pulled the comforter down from the top of the bed and motioned for Ivy to get in. Tucking the covers up to Ivy's chin, she sat down by the bed and pulled out her favorite book from under her bed.

She showed Ivy the book. "Do you want a story before you go to sleep?"

Ivy held out her hands to look at it. She thumbed through it, closed the book, and looked at Dilly with a solemn expression on her tiny face. "I am very tired," she said softly. "Maybe tomorrow?"

Dilly nodded and stood up.

"Please don't go yet. Not until I go to sleep."

Dilly sat by the bed silently while Ivy lay still. Ten minutes after they had started bedtime, Ivy's breathing became deep and even. Dilly slowly stood and walked out of the room. As she headed off to bed, she listed all the things she needed to do tomorrow that she hadn't gotten done today.

Chickens and running water filled her dreams until a little girl splashed through the water and grabbed Dilly's hand. Immediately, she woke up.

In the early morning light, there wasn't much to see. But, with a start, Dilly spotted Ivy on the end of her bed, facing away, kicking her feet back and forth, and quietly singing, "Silly Dilly, silly Dilly, silly Dilly."

When Ivy turned and noticed Dilly was awake, she said, "Oh good! I'm hungry." The girl hopped down, skipped into the kitchen, and then back again. "You snore," she said with a huge smile. Ivy squealed and backed away, barely avoiding getting hit by the pillow Dilly threw at her.

For the next five minutes, Dilly listed everything in her house that was for breakfast, yet nothing sounded good to Ivy.

Dilly thought back to yesterday, when Ivy had eaten anything given to her. Today, though, Ivy seemed to be a completely different child. Opening the freezer, Dilly went through an additional list of possible breakfast items, but Ivy pointed to the ice cream instead. Dilly said, "No. Real food first, then sweets."

"What if I eat it in a waffle cone?" Ivy asked deadpan, and then cracked a smile.

Dilly broke a smile too and asked if the girl wanted waffles. Ivy agreed, and Dilly got to work. By the end of the morning, Ivy was ready to go outside. While running water for the dishes, the two discussed the rules for going outside.

"Always ask if you want to go out there," Dilly cautioned. "And if you see an animal, do not try to pet it. Walk away and find me."

Ivy promised she would, and Dilly joked that she shouldn't get in anyone's van for candy or a puppy.

Ivy gave her a funny look.

"What?" Dilly questioned. "Don't you know what candy is? Or a puppy?"

"Yeah, I know what those are, but what is a van?"

Dilly explained. "It's actually a vehicle like a car or truck, but it carries more people."

"So, they take kids away in vans?" Ivy asked slowly, like that was the strangest thing she had ever heard.

"No, not all the time," Dilly said hurriedly. "Sometimes it's a car, a truck, or anything like that. They will use anything to pick up people to take away." Now she was unsure if the child should go at all. Ivy might have been taken from somewhere, perhaps right out of her own backyard.

Before Dilly could stop her, though, Ivy was out the door and down the sidewalk in seconds.

I do live in the middle of nowhere, Dilly thought for her own comfort as she busied herself doing dishes, making sure the herbs and other plants got separated out into different bundles for selling. After about five minutes, Dilly finished her chores, so she went outside to check on Ivy.

Ivy was squatting, just staring at the nest Dilly had seen on the ground yesterday. When Dilly approached, she noticed something had changed. The nest now had two eggs in it. "Where did the other egg come from?"

"That beautiful mama bird laid the egg here just a couple minutes ago," Ivy said to Dilly with a huge smile.

Dilly almost fainted. This was definitely a sign of another harvest, and she could not ignore it. So, Dilly told Ivy they had to get ready and head out to the garden to harvest again.

Dilly explained they had to go right now, but Ivy shuffled her feet. Dilly could tell by her behavior, Ivy just wanted to play. So, Dilly made it a game. "Hey, Ivy, let's list all the things we will need for our walk today."

Ivy lit up at this and said, "Okay! I know, we need waffles. And maybe a drink?"

Dilly smiled at this.

As she gathered the things they would need, Dilly shouted at Ivy, asking what else they might need.

In another room, Ivy didn't give an answer, but she called out, "Dilly?"

"Yes, sweetie?" Dilly asked as she walked into the room. Ivy turned around, and Dilly couldn't help but smile. Ivy had a pair of sunglasses on, grinning. Dilly held out the bag of holding, and the girl took off the glasses and put them in.

On the path to the garden, Ivy was helpful by carrying all the extra things.

When they arrived at the garden, Dilly saw it was completely full again, with all new things this time. Even though she knew they would harvest just as much as they needed, Dilly saw there was way too much for them to get done. So, she started off with the big plants, then the ones she had to dig up, and then she moved on to the fruit plants she could just stand and pick.

Ivy was happy to see a bunch of clothes plants, so Dilly told her she could get started harvesting those. When they had harvested almost all the plants, Dilly realized the sun would set soon. She gathered Ivy's clothes and put them in the bag of holding. Dilly grabbed two candles and a match and put them in her apron pocket. She had been this late before, and she knew the path was difficult to navigate safely with no light. So, she had learned to keep her candles at the ready in case darkness came on her stroll back from the mystical garden.

Because it was June, darkness arrived around eight p.m. But Dilly and Ivy weren't even back to the picnic table when Dilly stumbled over a rock and twisted her ankle. Pain shot up through her ankle and she fell to the ground. The bag of holding fell out of her hand and bounced along the path ahead of her. She cried out, "My ankle! Oh, this is *not* good."

Dilly looked up to see Ivy sprint away from her as fast as her little legs could take her. She cried for the girl to come back. Then she hollered for a good ten minutes. Finally, she sat silently. It wasn't cold out now, but it would be by morning.

Dilly frowned as she remembered her meeting to sign papers. She had completely forgotten about it. How was she to take care of Ivy now?

Unexpectedly, help arrived. Dilly cried when the emergency crew Ivy had called carried her back to the house and then to an ambulance. The entire event was just straight-up embarrassing. She was a grown person who had tripped and fallen. And then she couldn't get up. The thought crossed her mind that she was just too old to live alone and might need some help. Ivy knew how to dial the phone, Dilly realized. It hit Dilly then that this had to be Ivy's gift from the Springs, her ability to help Dilly in any way possible.

In the emergency room, Ivy waited quietly while doctors treated Dilly. Then Ivy came to her. "I kept this safe so I could give it to you."

It was the bag of holding. Ivy had recognized its importance to Dilly and had protected it for her.

That's when it dawned on Dilly. This girl *was* her help. The garden had given her a small helper who could be her family. Ivy and Dilly could help each other grow as people together. Someday, Ivy would care for the garden as Dilly and those before her had. And, when Ivy was much older and alone, Dilly hoped the garden would grow something or someone as precious as this child it had gifted her.

TAMMY CUMPTON

Tammy Cumpton is a single parent of a curious, confident, creative daughter. The two of them spend their time enjoying nature and the many animals on their small family farm. Her writing styles and topics vary from story to story, but it's always fantasy fiction. Magic has always held a special place in her life. Tammy looks forward to writing her next story. Her short story, Ivy, is Tammy's first publication.

THE BLIND DATE

SCOTT UMPHREY

GARY DIDN'T MEET many women, so he followed a friend's advice and signed up for a dating service. The lady he had a semi-match with was named Samantha. It was a fluke that she was the police chief of Mystic Springs, the small town where he lived. At first, he was freaked out by the idea, but then he was intrigued, though he was not sure why. Was it the power? A woman in uniform?

He chose the fanciest restaurant in town for their first date, hoping to impress her. The Speakeasy, an old bootlegger's cave from the prohibition era, was fancied up with restaurant amenities.

He left his date's name, along with a ten-dollar bill, with the hostess so that she would bring his date to the table, and he wouldn't have to mingle with the masses. This was a trick he'd learned in business that really impressed clients.

He chose a table far from the bar so that they could talk.

He thought about gulping down a glass of wine before she got there. That way, when he drank his second glass of wine, it would seem to be his first glass. He liked the idea, so he started to motion the waitress, but then he saw the hostess leading his date to his table. So much for that idea.

Samantha wasn't wearing her uniform. Instead, she wore a white dress that stopped just above the knees. Gary was pretty sure she didn't wear a dress to the police station. As she approached, he noticed she was a little more heavyset than her picture had led him to believe.

He stood, smoothed his pants, and greeted her. "Samantha?"

She flashed a cute smile. "Yes."

"I'm Gary. Nice to meet you." Should he go in for a hug? No, too much. Shake hands? Too formal. Fist bump? Absolutely. He held out his fist.

She didn't seem to know how to handle this and squeezed his fist twice like a clown honking the bulb of a horn. He smiled at her awkwardness. The hostess pulled out Samantha's chair—nice touch—and Gary and Samantha sat.

Gary started, "I—"

"How did—" Samantha interrupted.

They both laughed and stopped to let the other continue. After a moment, Samantha started again. "How—"

"I am glad—" Gary interrupted.

They stopped again and both uttered stilted laughs. As they waited awkwardly, Gary was aware of the sounds from the kitchen and the murmurs of diners echoing off the cave walls.

Gary flagged down a waitress. "We're ready to order drinks." Without asking Samantha what she wanted, he leaned forward to give the waitress their order.

The waitress stopped him. "I will get your waiter, sir."

Damn. He wanted a drink.

"Is something wrong?" Samantha asked.

"No, no." Thinking quickly, he said, "I was just wanting to get you a drink, Samantha... if that's what you wanted."

"Call me Sam. All my friends do. Normally, I am not a big drinker, but tonight I'm a little nervous, so I might like some wine."

Yes, now he could get down to business. Gary ran a finger along the inside collar of his shirt—it was wet. He felt slightly dizzy and was ready for his wine. The cave was damp, which didn't help. Also, it was quite noisy with sounds of scooching chairs and patrons entering and exiting the restaurant. He had taken his mental health medicine that morning—one Klonopin and one Lexapro—but by 3:30 p.m., he'd felt anxious and dizzy, so he'd taken another Klonopin. It probably didn't help that he'd washed the pill down with a couple fingers of whiskey—with water—as he'd left the apartment.

Gary watched for the waiter, but the cave was barely illuminated by flickering oil lamps strung across the ceiling, making it hard to see. Suddenly, the waiter was standing next to Gary. He was dressed in artist black, including a black apron, and wore a bun. Gary was not impressed with his hairdo.

Man Bun announced, "*Bonjour. Je m'appelle* Jeoffry and I will be your server tonight."

Gary rolled his eyes.

"Can I get you anything from the bar?"

Gary turned to Sam. "Can I order for us? They have a Pink Catawba you will love."

She answered tentatively. "Okay."

"Great." Gary turned back to Man Bun. "We'll have two Pink Catawbas."

"Very well. I'll be right back with your drinks."

Gary rubbed his hands together. "Now we're cooking."

Sam stood up. "I'm going to the little ladies' room."

"Sure, I'll be right here." Gary grimaced at his stupid

comment. Of course he'd be here. Where else would he be? He watched her figure as she headed to the restroom. Not bad.

The waiter returned with a bottle and glasses, then poured a sample into Gary's glass, expecting him to taste the wine. But instead, Gary finished it off in three big gulps. He smacked his lips and held the glass out for more. "I do like me some Catawba."

The waiter rolled his eyes and filled Gary's glass, then filled Sam's glass and retreated.

Gary gazed toward the bathroom. The coast was clear, so he took a large gulp... of Sam's wine. She would never know.

As Sam approached the table, she noticed Gary had a little less hair than his picture showed. In fact, he had quite a comb-over job. "Ah, our wine is here."

"Yes. I waited for you."

"Oh, thanks, but that wasn't necessary. Drink up. I'll wait for mine."

"What do you mean? It's right here."

Sam waited to see if he would catch on, but he didn't. "Well... I need to see it delivered."

"Delivered?"

"Yeah. I'm afraid so."

Gary frowned. "Alright." Then he stood and draped a cloth napkin over his arm and picked up her drink. He walked several paces away, then spun and deposited the drink on the table. "There. Your drink, milady."

"No, you aren't getting it. Delivered from the bartender. Nothing personal, but when I worked in the city, I can't tell you how many women I saw roofied. I just don't take chances."

Apparently, Gary finally understood. He nodded and took the drink back to the bar. She watched him drink her wine as he walked. He appeared to explain the problem to the bartender and handed the bartender her drink. Gary came back to the table muttering something about getting charged for an extra glass of wine, but Sam ignored his comment.

When the bartender delivered Sam's fresh drink, Gary motioned to the drink. "Your fresh, un-poisoned wine."

Sam swirled her glass and held it up to the light.

Gary let out a grunt. "Huh."

Sam let this go and sniffed her wine. She smiled at the wine's floral aroma.

Gary said, "You're quite the wine connoisseur. I'll show you how to drink wine." He grabbed his glass's stem and almost spilled his wine. He took a big gulp, dribbling some on his chin, and then wiped it off with his napkin.

Ignoring him, Sam finally tasted her wine, savoring it. "Wow. That's good." Again, she held the glass back up to admire the color.

He held his glass up, mimicking her ritual. "Yeah. Mine's good too. Frankly, I have a hard time telling wines apart. For me, they all lead to the same result: a good buzz." Then Gary apparently decided to change the subject. "Are you working on any big cases now?"

Sam shifted uncomfortably in her chair. "Well, we do have the Russell Bagshaw disappearance that we're working on, but, of course, I can't talk about it."

"Oh no, of course not. I was just making small talk. I don't want you to get in trouble for talking about a case. Do you think he was murdered?"

Sam stared at him, incredulous. "Didn't you hear a word I just said? I can't talk about it."

"Oh sure, I understand."

They both stopped talking because the waiter had arrived with two big ice waters, with Mystic Springs logos on the glasses, and two menus tucked under his arm. "I'll let you two look at these. We do have a special tonight: *Duck à l'Orange*. White wine, vinegar, and fresh citrus create layers of tangy flavor. I'll be back to answer any questions." And with that, he was gone.

Gary's forehead was sweating now, and he wiped it with his handkerchief.

Sam asked, "Are you okay, Gary? You look a little white."

"Oh, I'm okay," he assured her with a wave of his hand. "Once I get some food in me, I'll be fine. Are you hungry?"

Sam hesitated, then decided to share her thoughts. "I was a little nervous when I first came, so I wasn't hungry, but the smells and the sight of warm rolls on tables—I could eat now." She took a drink of wine.

"Good," Gary said, and they both picked up their menus.

Sam noticed Gary's menu was shaking in his hands. He must be nervous. Why was he nervous? Has he done something wrong? Or was it just Sam's natural inclination—being a cop?

Gary seemed to notice his menu shaking, then he laid it flat on the table. They both perused their menus. The waiter arrived. "Are you ready to order?"

Instead of letting Sam go first, Gary started to order, which Sam thought was a little rude. "I'll have the broasted chicken with a baked potato. Butter on the baked potato with sour cream on the side. And she'll have the lamb chop with garlic mashed potatoes." Gary nodded at the waiter, apparently satisfied with his ordering job.

Sam stared, amazed. Did he just order for her? What was going on? She still wasn't sure what she wanted, but she sure as hell didn't want the lamb chops.

This was all very odd. Sam guessed it would be okay if this were a 1950s movie where the man ordered for the little woman. But it wasn't the 1950s, and it wasn't a movie in a fancy restaurant. They were eating in a bootlegger's cave where she expected bats to fly in her hair soon.

"Hey," Sam whispered, trying not to make a scene. "How do you know what I want?"

Gary stiffened like he didn't know how to answer. "Well... I just... thought I was doing the right thing, ordering for my date."

"The right thing?"

"Yeah. Right that a man should order for a woman."

"Not in this day and age," Sam retorted.

The waiter crossed out Sam's previous order and stood ready to take her new order.

"I wanted a salad, but after all this, I need a little protein."

The waiter offered, "We have a Southwest salad that has grilled chicken on it. Would that be okay?"

Sam said, "Oh, that sounds delicious. Can I have ranch dressing?"

"Sure... but it comes with a great Southwestern Ranch that I suggest you try. It is basically ranch and salsa mixed together."

"That sounds terrific."

"Very well. I will get this in." The waiter left the table.

Sam rolled her shoulders and took a deep breath.

When Gary started to explain, she stopped him with her hand. "Water under the bridge." She took a big gulp of wine.

Gary forced a smile and took a sip of wine. "If you'll excuse me, I need to go to the little boy's room."

As Gary headed off to the bathroom, he noticed that his left pinky and ring fingers were vibrating—a sign that he was starting to have a panic attack. Blood was withdrawing from his hands and arms and into his trunk. This was so that if a limb was bitten off by a saber-toothed tiger, or a date, he would not bleed to death.

Passing the bar, which exhibited cigarette burns and was made from Benny's Ten Pound Nail crates brought to a high polish, he found the dark hallway to the bathroom. Many restaurant and bar restrooms had cute names, like Lass or Laddy, Roosters or Hens, or Standers or Squatters. Sober, most men could usually figure these out, but drunk, Gary was often stymied. Fortunately, he entered the men's room. He knew because there were no foreign machines on the wall dispensing feminine hygiene products.

He sat on a toilet in a stall and massaged his left hand, trying to get the blood flowing back into it. After a while, he dug out his wallet and took out a crisply folded square of paper. He balanced it on his closed knees and gently unfolded the square and removed a Klonopin. He swallowed it dry. It stuck in his throat. He gagged, trying to cough it up, but it didn't budge. He rushed to the sink and scooped water into his mouth. He got water all over his pants, but the pill finally went down.

Crap. Now she would think he wet himself. He tried drying the front of his khaki Dockers with paper towels, but the towels were brown ones that didn't absorb much water. He rubbed and rubbed, but it made no difference.

He started losing his balance, so he grabbed the sink countertop, dropped the paper towels on the floor, and headed back to the table.

In the dark hallway, a server had left a large tray near the kitchen door, stacked with dishes cleared from tables. On the tray were several unfinished glasses of wine.

He checked to see if anyone was watching. He reached for the fullest glass as someone rounded the corner. He continued raising his hand past the wine glasses and feathered the hair on the side of his head. It was an old lady on her way to the restroom. Whew. Close call. When she was gone, he once again reached for the glass and gulped most of it down.

"Ah." Gary finished the glass. A waitress came by in a hurry, probably to check on an order for a big-tipping table.

When she had passed, he reached for another glass and finished it off. Oh good, much sweeter. Gary now felt fortified with his fresh buzz and much more confident about his blind date.

While Gary was in the bathroom, Sam took the opportunity to look around the cave. Glass shelves holding liquor, backed by mirrors, were behind a bar. Sam had been here before, but only in an official capacity. It was nice to have a break from her date. Between her anxiety and the fried smell that could never seem to be exhausted from the cave, she felt queasy.

Gary arrived back at the table. "So, what does a normal day look like for you?" He leaned back, stretched his legs out, draped his left arm over the chair, and tucked his hand in his waistband.

"Well," Sam started, "there really is no such thing as a normal day. Usually, whatever is going on in the community dictates our work practices. And then in our spare time, we fit in paperwork. What about you?"

"What about me?"

Sam took another drink of wine. "What does a normal day look like for you?"

"Oh, yeah. Well, a normal day for me is just trying not to kill a sixth grader."

Sam had no idea what he meant and didn't really want to know.

Gary leaned forward. "Do you want to know a teaching secret of mine?"

She raised her brows. "Sure."

"On the first day of school, I pick the snottiest kid and I shoot him in the head and place his body in front of my desk."

Sam stared, unsure of what to make of this.

"Then during the year, when it comes time for students to hand in their homework, they have to step *over* the body to place the homework on my desk. The body is a reminder that they should behave."

"That's terrible," Sam exclaimed.

Gary leaned back, his eyes widening. "Of course, I don't *really* do this... it's just a joke I came up with years ago that I tell my non-teacher friends, to freak them out. What's wrong with you that you believe this?"

Sam said, "I know it's *supposed* to be a joke, but it's in no way funny, and it's very inappropriate."

They sat in awkward silence, listening to the tinkling of glasses, forks, and knives. Finally, Gary said, "I hope we can laugh."

"What?"

"Well, I mean, I... well, maybe this hasn't gone the way I had hoped... or maybe the way you expected. I don't always say the right thing."

This was an understatement. Sam simply nodded.

Gary sighed. "Maybe we can start again?"

Sam considered this. He had already done and said several dumb things, things that should be a warning, and maybe even, on a first date, a reason to run. On the other hand, she had been so lonely lately that, for some unknown reason, she entertained his treaty.

He was waiting for a response.

"What the hell. Just please don't tell any more stories about harming children."

Gary exhaled loudly, apparently relieved. "I promise. Would you like a second glass of wine now?"

Sam considered this, then again said, "What the hell. Sure."

Gary looked elated. He raised his hand and hollered, "*Garçon*," pronouncing the ç like a g, Steve Martin style.

Sam rolled her eyes and smiled.

The waiter strolled over, and Gary started ordering Sam another glass of wine, but he must've learned his lesson. He stopped mid-sentence and motioned toward Sam.

"I think I would like another glass of wine."

"The same?" the waiter asked.

She smiled. "Yes."

The waiter turned to Gary. "And for you?"

Gary covered his wine glass with his hand and said, "Oh no, only one glass of wine for me, then it's ice water to sober up—so I can drive home."

"Very well." The waiter left.

Sam smiled at him. "That's the first sensible thing I've heard you say all night."

Gary removed his hand from the wine glass and took a small sip of the Pink Catawba.

Now Sam felt a little more like they were a part of the merrymaking crowd. When her wine arrived, they toasted and chatted just like everyone else. They talked of each other's lives, their dreams, and goals. Now that they weren't trying so hard, they were able to relax into pleasant conversation.

Soon their dinners came. Gary was famished. He picked up his broasted chicken and started tearing into it with his teeth. A disappointed look from Sam convinced him to set it down and use his knife and fork to remove the meat from the bone.

Sam stabbed her salad, apparently deciding to eat a couple of forkfuls of just greens before adding protein. The southwest salad had strips of spiced tortilla on top of the salsa/ranch dressing. The wine must have made her hungry. She chewed quickly and swallowed. She prepared another forkful of spinach and took a breath, but the breath didn't come. She dropped her fork. It hit her plate, then the table, and then bounced on the cave's stone floor.

Alarmed, Gary dropped his fork into his potato.

Sam gripped her throat with both hands.

Gary stared, wondering if there was a problem.

She jumped up, dumping her chair over. She also bumped her lap against the table, knocking salad out of her bowl and spilling her wine.

It was only with much skill that Gary was able to swoop up his wine and keep it from spilling. Once he'd seen to the safety of his wine, he stood and asked, "Did you burn yourself? Was your food too hot?"

She threw her right hand over her shoulder, trying to slap her own back. When that didn't work, she picked up her chair. She spun it around so the back of it faced her, took two steps back, then rushed the chair.

Gary was afraid she might hurt herself, so he stepped

forward and swatted the chair out of the way. She tumbled and landed on the cave's cement floor. Gary helped her up.

"She's choking!" a patron hollered.

Someone else yelled, "You gotta do the Heimlich on her!"

Of course, the Heimlich maneuver! Gary had seen it done on sitcoms. How hard could it be?

He grabbed Sam by the shoulders and spun her quickly. He wrapped his arms around her chest, pinning her arms to her sides, grabbed both breasts and squeezed. Hmm, bigger and fuller than expected. He sniffed. Something sure smelled good. Lavender? Maybe her perfume or shampoo. She struggled to free herself, but he clutched harder. He alternated squeezing and relaxing his arms wrapped around her chest. He squeezed and squeezed but she would not breathe.

A crowd had gathered around, trying to help, but no one seemed to know what to do. Sam turned her head, her mouth opening and closing like a fish out of water.

"Help!" Gary screamed. "She's choking, and I can't help her." He was all out of ideas. He sure could use a drink.

Man Bun shoved his way through the crowd, pushed Gary aside, and approached Sam from behind. The waiter wrapped his arms around her. He balled one fist, inserted it into the palm of his other hand, and closed his palm around the fist. He lifted upward, thrusting his balled fist into her stomach, below her ribcage. He lifted her off the ground. A green, flat piece of lettuce shot from her mouth and flew across the room. She inhaled deeply, then panted several times like a dog.

The waiter—still holding her—spoke into her ear. "Breathe in through your nose and out through your mouth." The waiter looked at Gary. "She's hyperventilating."

Soon her breathing slowed. The waiter still held her as she

tried speaking between breaths. "Oh... God... couldn't... breathe."

The waiter loosened his grip, and Gary stepped forward, unsteady on his feet, to hold her, but she pushed him away. "You... I... couldn't... breathe."

"I know, I know," Gary reassured her. "You're okay now."

The waiter grabbed Sam's glass of water. "Here, take a sip." He held the back of her head, and she grabbed the glass with both hands and took several tentative sips—it was like she was afraid she would choke. She was breathing more normally now.

She confessed, "I haven't... not been able to breathe... like that... before. My air was... entirely cut off."

"You're okay," Gary reassured her again.

"The lettuce... must have been flat over my windpipe. I was horrified."

The crowd started to disperse, and the waiter and Gary motioned Sam back to her seat—she was shaky on her feet. Gary bent down to pick up her chair, lost his balance, and crashed to one knee. Between the whisky, the Klonopin, the Lexapro, and the several glasses of wine, he was on the verge of blacking out. He was going to feel that knee tomorrow.

Sam picked up her chair herself and Gary limped back to his seat.

"And you... all you did was fondle my breasts. I should arrest you."

"No. I tried to help you. I did what I thought I was supposed to do."

"Well, you didn't. You just groped me."

Gary didn't know what to say—she was pretty much right. He'd been trying to perform the Heimlich maneuver, which he thought was easy to do, having seen it on TV so often over the years.

"And you knocked the chair out of the way when I tried to self-administer the Heimlich maneuver."

"I thought you were... I don't know... trying to self-harm."

"Self-harm? I was trying to save my own life."

"Well, I didn't know that."

She shook her head. "I want to go."

Trying to salvage the evening, Gary said, "But you haven't finished your salad."

"Are you kidding? I may never eat again. After what just happened, I don't want to put anything in my mouth. I might choke. I just want to go home." A tear streamed down her cheek.

Gary stood. "Sure, sure. I understand. Let me pay the bill, then we can go. I'll be right back." He found the waiter at the register. When the waiter turned to him, he said, "Uh, we need to get going."

"Yes. Let me get your bill."

"I appreciate it."

When the waiter returned with the bill, Gary paid and gave him an average tip. As the waiter took the money, Gary pressed a ten-dollar bill in his palm and said, "And this is for you. You know, for helping save my date."

"Oh, sir. That's not necessary. It's my job."

"Yeah, I know all that, but I can't help but think how... inadequately I performed."

"I am trained to do the Heimlich maneuver. I've done it several times over the years. That's part of my job—the safety of my customers—not just serving you food."

"Well, that's very admirable, but I still want you to have this. You deserve it."

"Just doing my job, sir." The waiter handed the bill back.

Sam waited for Gary at the table. She felt like she had been put through the wringer. When Gary returned, she was standing and ready to go.

"Sorry. I had to pay."

"I know. I'm just ready to go."

Gary offered the crook of his arm. She wondered if he was providing support for her, or vice versa.

Outside, the night was warm. Sam's police cruiser sat directly in front of The Speakeasy, no more than ten feet away.

"Where's your car?" Gary asked.

Sam frowned. "Are you sure you're okay to drive?"

Gary brushed away her worries with a wave of the hand. "Oh, sure." He pointed at the cruiser. "Ah, there it is." He hurried between her and the cruiser's door. A little unsteady, he leaned back against her car and crossed his legs.

Sam just wanted to get in the car and go home.

"Would you like me to drive you home?" Gary asked.

Sam shook her head and motioned for him to move. "No way."

Gary didn't move. "Uh, it sure has been... I mean a lovely night. Do you mind if I call you?"

She suppressed a laugh. "You've got to be kidding."

"Why?"

Sam began listing his shortcomings while enumerating them on her fingers. She bent down her index finger. "One, for starters, you ordered for me. Two," pulling down the second finger, "you wet your pants. Three, you ate your dinner with your fingers." Pulling down the pinky finger, "Four. You drank too much or took way too many drugs—your pupils have been dilated all night. Five," going to the thumb, "you may or may not have tried to drug me. And now I must go to the other hand. Six, you almost let me choke to death."

Gary looked flabbergasted. He blinked and stared off into the distance, then moved from in front of the car door.

Sam sighed. Maybe she'd been too hard on Gary. She reached out to comfort him.

He flung aside her hand. "Well, you're not so great a catch yourself." Mimicking her finger counting, he bent down his index finger. "One, you didn't know how to fist bump. Two, your use of 'little ladies' room' makes you sound like a ten-year-old. Three," bending his ring finger, "you're a wine snob with your swirling, sniffing, tasting, and smacking of lips. Four, you believed I killed school children. And five," having run out of fingers, he bent down his thumb, "ah...." Apparently, he couldn't think of a fifth one, so he crossed his arms and stood stoically.

Sam looked at her shoes for a moment. "I didn't... well, I guess I was kind of hard on you."

Gary didn't respond but continued standing there, frowning with his arms crossed.

Sam opened the car door but then stopped. She turned to Gary and nodded. "Get in."

"What?"

"Get in. I'm driving you home."

Gary waved her off. "Nah, nah. That's okay. I—"

"It's not a request, it's an order."

Gary saluted, "Yes ma'am." He hurried around to the other side of the cruiser and got in.

Once they were inside the cruiser, he said, "I really appreciate—"

Sam stopped him with a look.

Gary rode silently with his hands in his lap.

After some directions, Sam pulled up to Gary's apartment.

"I would invite you in—"

"Not necessary."

Gary got out and shut the door.

As Gary walked away, Sam gripped the steering wheel, her emotions reeling. She grimaced, then pushed the button to lower the passenger window. "Yes!"

Gary returned to the car and leaned in. "Yes, what?"

"You can call me."

As Sam slowly pulled away, she saw Gary smile and execute a fist pump. Then she heard him say, "You still got it, old boy."

SCOTT UMPHREY

Scott Umphrey, a writer of memoirs and short stories, grew up on Missouri's rivers, lakes, and streams. He loves sharing his mostly true anecdotes with listeners and readers who relate to his everyday experiences turned into laugh-out-loud stories. He has held many audiences spellbound at open mics and readings. In his spare time, he enjoys boating, playing guitar, and researching the Civil War. He lives with his wife and music performing partner, Kathy, in West Central Missouri, where they play local concerts.

NATURE'S DIADEM

ANNI MEUSCHKE

BRIELLE HAD NEVER BEEN in a real forest before. Parks and small patches of trees, but this was something totally different. It was striking. Gone was the sound of passing cars and human activity. All of it swallowed up by the trees and barriers of brush and leaves. The silence made her every step incredibly loud, the leaves crunching like thunder. But soon, the air came to life with birdsong. The boughs swayed peacefully and leaves rustled all around her in the breeze. The green of summer was still strong, only just beginning to tinge with yellow and orange. The world was awake in a way she had never experienced before. Books and movies could never do it justice. Sunlight speared through the canopy and dappled everything in shifting shadows.

The ground was uneven, stones jutting out, bushes sprawled wherever they pleased. No hard pavement to keep a pace, and plenty to trip on.

Brielle drank in the air that seemed to be getting more delicious with every step. Where were the springs? She hoped she was going the right way.

The shriek of crashing metal snapped her from basking in the calm.

Brielle hesitated as she listened to a scratching sound, unsure if she should interfere, then went forward curiously. An animal trap lay nestled against the trunk of a tree. Inside, a cat scrabbled at the wire walls. Brielle approached carefully, gazing at the creature's black and white markings and round yellow eyes.

"What's going on here?" Brielle wondered aloud, searching the trap, moving a hand toward it.

"Hey! Don't let it out!"

Brielle started at the voice and twisted about to see who it was.

A young man approached, his blonde hair a rough tussle on his head and brow furrowed seriously over bright blue eyes. "This is part of a cat population control effort. I've got to take this guy to the vet now."

"Oh, I'm sorry." Brielle blinked at him, then turned back to the cat with new understanding. "A TNR? Or are you rehoming?" She'd never seen a trap-neuter-release program in action before.

The boy's eyes gained a curious light as he stared at her, realizing she understood the mission. "That's up to the vet, whether it's too feral or not."

He kneeled beside the cage. "It's alright, little one, we're going to help you," he soothed, though he only got a low growl in return.

Brielle studied him curiously, but relaxed as she noticed cat food in the bottom of the trap and saw how genuine he was with the animal. She stepped back to let him do his work, watching with fascination. She'd always wondered how rescuers handled a trapped animal.

He draped a blanket over the cage, and the growls inside fell silent. He then turned to her and offered an awkward smile. "I'm Gavin. You must be new here."

She nodded. "I just got off the bus earlier today. I'm Brielle."

He fixed the blanket more squarely over the cage. "Good to meet you. Here to see the springs?"

She answered honestly. "Kind of, but this whole area seems really nice." She watched him for another moment before blurting out, "Do you need help?"

Again, his gaze flicked to her in surprise. "Do you want to?"

When she nodded, he uttered a small "hmm" as though unexpectedly impressed. "Alright, you take one side, but don't put your fingers between the holes. Some of these cats are merciless." He waited for her to grasp the other end of the cage before hoisting it up. Then he led her along a narrow path back to a truck waiting on a dirt road.

Once they'd placed the cage in the truck, he dusted his hands and collected another blanket from the back. "Thank you," he said, nodding back to the woods. "I have a lot more to check if you want to come along."

Brielle brightened, pleased to be of service. "I'd love to help." First day in town and already committing to some community service? Yes, please.

She mused over this newfound purpose as she followed him back into the trees. As she did, she looked about in quiet awe of her surroundings. All the trees looked healthy, the plant life thriving. And based on the amount of prints she was finding on the trails, so were the animals.

Now that he wasn't carrying a cage, Gavin seemed to walk like every single step had to be carefully planned. He sidestepped as much as he could to avoid stepping anywhere that wasn't already bare soil or rock. He barely seemed to bend even the grass as he went along.

Gavin glanced back at her, apparently aware of her fascination. "Are you, like, a naturalist or biologist or something?"

Her cheeks flushed as she realized how odd she might look being so fascinated with the forest. "Um, no. I'm not anything right now but a cashier. I'm just a nature... enthusiast?" Brielle had given hundreds of hours to documentaries and books, just to be stuck with a fascination she'd never called upon until now.

"Me too." He nodded as the path began to thicken with rocks. "Watch your step through here," he warned, pointing out the moss grown over the stones. "Looks harmless, but I've cut myself more here than with the cats."

Brielle chuckled and obediently watched her step.

Over the next few minutes, he pointed out a field where deer often bedded down and a tree with scratches where a bear must have left his mark a long time ago.

"Did you go to school for this?" she asked him, impressed that he knew so much about this land.

"School? No, I couldn't afford it. Still can't. I just..." Gavin considered his words as he looked up at a barking squirrel, "watch. You can learn a lot just by watching."

Thoroughly impressed and slightly jealous, Brielle followed him through the paths he knew so well. She listened, enchanted, as he spoke of all that he had seen here and guided them back to the truck with cage after cage. She was so enthralled that she didn't dare complain that the hiking was getting difficult. Not even when she slipped on the stones he had warned her of and scratched her hand. She hadn't the slightest idea how many miles they'd trekked or how many hours they'd spent.

Finally, back at the truck, she was dirty and scuffed. Her legs promised to be sore for at least a week. But she beamed with pride as she looked at the cages in the back.

"Where now?" Brielle asked eagerly. The sun was on its downward track now, but she wasn't ready to stop.

"To the vet," Gavin said with a flourish and a smile as he opened the driver's door. "Do you want to see that, too?"

Brielle nodded eagerly.

"Are they going to be open right now?" Brielle asked as they pulled in.

"Not to the public," Gavin said. "They closed an hour ago. But someone will still be inside, giving medicine, checking up on the animals, stuff like that. They'll let us in if we go through the back."

She stepped out with him and hovered by the door as he knocked. She jumped when the door quickly opened. The scent of animals and cleaning supplies spilled out.

A lovely dark-skinned woman smiled at them. "Gavin! You're early! How many today?"

There was a huge grin in Gavin's tone as he answered proudly. "Four!"

"Only *four*?" The woman sounded delighted. "You're doing God's work, Gavin!"

He laughed. "No, ma'am, that's your job!"

She had a sweet, heart-shaped face and lines around her eyes that evidenced a lot of smiles. Her gaze moved to Brielle, and Brielle got the full sense that this woman was perhaps the kindest she would ever meet.

"Hello there," she said, her tone warm and curious. "I'm sorry, I don't recognize you."

"This is Brielle," Gavin said. "She helped me out today."

"Really?" She raised her brows in surprise as she looked at Brielle. "How kind of you!"

"This is Anita Dunsten, our very own veterinarian," Gavin said. "She's the angel helping me with all of these strays."

Anita wagged her finger at him. "Ain't no one an angel here but you!" she offered Brielle a hand. "Gavin doesn't usually ask for any help. You must be very interesting!"

Brielle blushed as she shook Anita's hand. "I don't know about that. I just happened to be in the right place at the right time."

"Oh?" Anita glanced curiously at Gavin.

"She's fresh off the bus," he explained. "I found her at one of my cat traps, and she offered to help."

Anita stepped outside. "Well, that's just wonderful. Nice to know we have some *good* tourists around here, not just looking to dirty up our town. Too many tourists lately just here to chase ghosts."

Gavin sighed and rolled his eyes. "Rico." He showed Anita where the cats were, and they started taking them inside.

Brielle carefully listened to their conversation. Rico's podcast was the whole reason Brielle knew about this place, but Anita and Gavin talked like he wasn't doing them a service. "I hope those tourists aren't messing with the water," Brielle said.

"Of course they are," Anita said as she lifted up a cage. "It's the whole reason most people come here. Of course, our water *is* the best." Her eyes twinkled. "I just wish they had a little more respect for our residents and didn't leave their trash scattered in the forest and whatnot." She sighed and shook her head. "Any-way, enough griping. Let's get these kitties unloaded, and I'll take care of them."

Brielle helped move the cages into the clinic. She listened

politely as the pair made small talk and waited patiently when they were leaving. Was everyone here so warm and kind?

The sun was low in the sky by the time they headed back outside, giving final farewells to Anita.

"How's your hand?" Gavin asked Brielle as the door closed behind them.

Brielle blinked at him and flexed her hand on impulse. She had nearly forgotten the scratches after slipping on the rocks. "It's fine. I'll have to clean it really good whenever I get back."

He tilted his head at her and held out his hand. "May I see it?"

She started to assure him again as she let him look, but trailed off as he was staring at her scratches with such profound intensity. She couldn't decide what he was thinking. His brow cinched together seriously, then he stood eerily still for several seconds.

"Gavin...?"

He blinked at her, then gave a small sigh through his nose. "If you don't have any other plans, there's one more thing I could show you."

Brielle stared at him, confused.

"The spring," he explained. "There's still a couple hours of light, if you want to see it."

"Oh," Brielle glanced at the sky, then back to him. "Is it far?" Her legs were tired, and she wanted to clean her hand soon.

"Not very," he promised. "I can get us there in a few minutes, and you can rinse your hand in the spring."

There was something so sincere and imploring about the way he said this, like it would be so special. And she had to admit, she definitely wanted to see it. "Okay."

He smiled and patted his truck. "Let's go then!"

Within a few minutes, he parked once again by the forest.

They got out, and he led her up a path she had not taken before. She adopted his style of walking again, setting her feet carefully where he set his.

"We're nearly there," he promised as her pace slowed.

"The spring?"

"Yes, the spring." He gave her a look that made her think he was picking his words. "Have you seen it yet?"

"No, not yet," Brielle said, getting more curious at how serious he was.

"Have you heard about it?"

"Of course. It's kinda famous."

"What do you think of the legend?" he asked.

"That it's magic?" Brielle thought to be careful of her words, too, not wanting to offend him. "I don't know that I believe that, but I'm sure it's beautiful."

He gave an amused grunt. "It *is* beautiful," he said as he walked.

She looked up as she heard babbling water, and soon they stepped through a gap in the trees.

Her eyes widened as she beheld the scene before her. It was the kind of thing you could only see in movies. The water rushed endlessly before them, crystal clear, twinkling in the setting sunlight, rippling in its roam over a rocky bottom. In awe, Brielle moved closer and peered in. Minnows flitted along, and crawdads crawled along the stream bed. A freshwater mussel poked out from the coarse sand. Moss was growing on the bigger stones, and the roots of the surrounding forest seemed to stretch right to the very edge of the water.

"Oh... oh wow," she breathed. "This is the cleanest water I've ever seen!"

Gavin smiled as he followed her to the edge. "It's amazing,

alright. If you follow this stream up, there's a rock face with a little waterfall. Up there is where the spring begins."

"Wow!" Brielle couldn't hide her excitement. This really was the town's best-kept secret. "And it's this clean throughout?" She searched the water, hunting along its edge for any other treasures of wonder in its depths.

He smiled, looking pleased that she admired it so much. "Sure is. I do some cleaning here and there, but the water handles itself pretty well."

"This is... *gosh*, just so gorgeous! I love this. Can I see the spring?" She turned to him and was surprised to see him hesitate. Her excitement curbed. Maybe she was getting too ahead of herself—this was such a special place, and maybe he didn't want to share.

He tipped his head, and she couldn't read his expression as he studied her. His mouth was pressed in a firm line, his brow pulled together, but his gaze was more curious. Finally, he tipped his head to the sky and ran a hand through his hair.

"Come here," Gavin said, taking a seat on the bank. "Let's wash your hand."

It almost seemed wrong to put her dirty and scratched hand in something so otherwise perfect. But Brielle came over, sat with him, and dipped her hands in. If nothing else, the cold of the water would soothe the dull pain in her palm. A few seconds passed as she let the wound soak, as per Gavin's instruction, then blinked down at her hands. The water wasn't cold enough to make her feel numb, yet the pain was lessening.

She stared as the red irritation faded, and the scratches sealed themselves back up. Any grit left in the wound slipped out as though pushed, and in seconds her skin was fully restored.

Stunned, Brielle slowly flexed her hand, wondering if it

might start hurting again. This couldn't be real—things like this didn't happen in real life.

Yet her hand flexed and moved normally. And completely without pain.

Beside herself, Brielle looked to Gavin, who smiled innocently at her.

———

Five days later, Brielle left her room and stepped out into a cool early-morning, rolled-in fog. She confidently walked the same path she had since her first day here. She had stopped wearing her large hiking boots out here, as it felt less intrusive to the forest, so now she wore slip-on shoes. It certainly made her strides lighter as she minded her every step the way Gavin had taught her. Searching every day for cats with him, and navigating this forest so frequently, made her positive she could reach the spot they had agreed to meet—atop the rockface where the spring overflowed into a waterfall. A place she now knew was called Seldom Seen, a name she adored.

She felt light on her feet as she walked, excited for whatever new things she might learn or see. She passed over plenty of animal tracks in the moist ground, many small cat prints, but also raccoon and fox, and what might have been a horse or mule being ridden up this way in the last couple of days. The forest was so quiet, as if the fog muffled every sound. It took extra effort with the limited visibility, but once she reached the water, Brielle held her head higher with pride that she could now traverse the forest by herself with no problems. She made her way up around the falls to be on top of it and looked around with a smile, in awe of the swell of water spilling so quietly over the edge. The gray world complimented and deepened the green and hints of red showing among the leaves.

She spotted a red tabby cat farther down on the opposite side, lapping at the water. Brielle furrowed her brow at it, wondering why it hadn't been caught yet.

She chose a place to sit near the edge of the water.

"Hello again," she said, greeting the water like an old friend. She dipped her hand in to wet her hot, sweaty neck. A small splash sounded behind her, making her turn to glance again after the cat, but it had vanished.

She tipped her head back, traced more water over her forehead, and closed her eyes, breathing in the cool air. Ideas of staying in Mystic Springs already filled her mind. This beautiful, homey town, filled with friendly people, was so quiet, so peaceful, so—

She blinked open her eyes and jerked forward to peer over the edge as the sound of crashing foliage came from below the falls. What on earth could be making so much noise?

With wide eyes, she tracked the shuddering branches as something approached. Her gut twisted in disgust as a man ripped himself from the surrounding trees, toppling over and crumpling bushes and rolling stones from their places in his wake. He was huffing and puffing, but he lit up with an ugly, triumphant grin when he saw the water.

"Finally!" His voice pierced the quiet. "See if you can ignore me now, Rico, when I ruin your precious water." His clunky shoes ripped at the ground and sank into the mud as he approached the water's edge.

A sour feeling grew in Brielle's stomach as she watched with suspicion. He dropped a backpack, dug out a water bottle, filled it up, and stuffed it back into his pack.

He started to stand up, stumbling and cursing as the mud sucked at his shoes, slapping him back down to his knees. He spat and glared, then heaved himself up. He scooped out some mud and flung it into the crystal-clear water, creating an ugly brown cloud.

He paused for a moment as he noticed what he'd created, then a slow smirk crawled up his face. He threw in another fistful of slop, then began laughing and flinging anything he could reach. Like a wild chimpanzee, he threw stones and branches into the water. He tore up the ground, then moved into the water, splashing about and kicking up the bottom of the stream.

Brielle sighed deep inside as she watched him, her anger rising, but her lips seemed glued together. She didn't want to yell down at him, assuming it would only land herself in trouble. This was not a man she could reason with.

The man panted and laughed, apparently pleased to cause such a disgrace. He grabbed at his pants and unzipped.

Brielle winced and looked away, not wanting to see him do what she thought he was going to do. And it was here that she noticed the water at her side was trembling where it had previously been entirely smooth.

The man's voice came from below. "What the...?"

His change of tone made her glance down again. His hand was still on his zipper, but he hadn't gotten much further. The water was trembling around him as well, and then frothing. He started to step back to climb out, but before he could lift one boot, the water began to move skyward.

Rising of itself in defiance of gravity, the water heaped up high to tower over the man. He gawked at it with a blend of shock and horror. He twisted to run, but he couldn't manage more than a frantic scramble before the pillar of water lunged forward and snatched him up as if he were little more than a ragdoll.

Unable to tear her eyes away, Brielle watched in horror as the man struggled. The water condensed into a massive ball, bowling him about and rendering him unable to swim or breach the surface. His limbs flailed but didn't even splash. The water lowered itself back down, staying over his struggling body until he stopped moving. The mass that once was a human quickly got smaller, breaking up as if being dissolved, and the water settled back into its previous state. The stream began running as before, back to calm and tranquil, with absolutely nothing in it. No branches that had been thrown, no extra stones—crystal clear again. Not a scrap of clothing. Even the backpack was gone. If it weren't for the toppled bushes and footprints—footprints that were rapidly disappearing—it would be like nothing had happened at all.

Brielle realized she had stopped breathing. She was suddenly aware of how close to the water she was. She jerked back from it, scrambling to her feet, and backed several steps away from it. Panic rose quickly behind her eyes.

What should she do? Should she tell someone? Someone just *died* right in front of her!

Brielle turned to run, then let out a scream when she slammed straight into a human chest. It took her a second to recognize him.

"Gavin!" she shrieked, grabbing his hand. "Come on! We have to go. The water... it just attacked!" She yanked him around to plunge into the forest and run back to civilization.

But Gavin didn't run. He stayed planted where he was. "I know. Calm down."

"No! Didn't you see that? The water just killed somebody!"

Brielle tugged him again, glancing past him at the water, afraid it might lurch out after them at any moment.

"Brielle." His voice was calm and reassuring, as if he was trying to soothe a child. "Calm down."

"What? No!" Brielle tugged again, breathing hard, and finally *looked* at him for the first time. How could he be so...? Did he not see? "B-but you... and h-he... and i-it... w-wait..." Her eyes widened. "Gavin...?"

He offered a smile. "Just calm down. It's alright."

Brielle felt a chill rise up her spine. He'd seen it happen—he must have. And he thought nothing of it? "B-b..." she stuttered, her legs shaking as she stepped back and let go of his hand. "H-how? Why?"

"I told you already," Gavin chuckled, going over to where she had just been sitting. "I don't know why it's like this, but it's not a bad thing."

"But it just killed someone, Gavin!"

"I know. It defended itself."

Brielle's mind raced, spinning over questions and tripping on fear. "But I thought it was good. Mystical even. It healed me!"

He looked back at her quizzically as he kneeled by the spring and trailed his fingers into it. "Well, yeah? Mystical doesn't mean benevolent."

Brielle stared at him as her ears began ringing, a cold hand grasping her spine. Realization dawned on her. This had happened before. What if the spring had done this to her at the first meeting? Would Gavin have even batted an eye? How many times had the spring done this? How many people had met this fate?

How far did the spring's power go? Would the trees that fed on the water reach down and catch her? The very air she breathed was filled with mist and condensation—would the air itself attack her, breaking down her lungs and killing her from the inside? Her neck began to burn, and she remembered having wiped the very same water on her neck to cool off. With a shriek, she scrubbed hard at the back of her neck and then her forehead with her shirt to get the water off. She imagined the very roots of the trees surging up and snagging her feet.

"Brielle!"

She jolted and looked back to Gavin, trembling.

He sighed as he looked at her sympathetically. "The water *defended* itself, Brielle. Come on, you saw what that guy was doing. It's just what happens in nature. You mess around, and you die."

Brielle shook her head. "N-not like *that!*"

"Look," he said, *"good* doesn't really exist in nature—you know that—and neither does bad. You're thinking of the water as if it's something holy, but it's not. It's just nature—living, active nature."

Brielle stared at him, his words trickling into her mind and gradually slowing her thoughts down. She flicked her gaze back to the water, now as peaceful as ever.

Gavin followed her gaze, smiling. "You have to take the bad along with the good. Appreciate it *and* fear it, like anything else in life. You treat it well, and you can expect the same."

Her stomach unclenched as her fear faded. He was right... that man had behaved like an animal. Did that mean death? As far as the rules of nature, *yes.* Would she think of it as anything less than a tragedy if he had foolishly hung over the side of a railing and fallen into a ravine? *No.* Maybe this *was* deserved. And she was only afraid because, naturally, the response to a sudden death was fear. But... the water *had* decided to heal *her.* She must have done something right.

The clicking of keys filled Brielle's ears as she scanned the screen in front of her, flicking over information for her research paper. Her overhead light was glaring now that the sun had long since disappeared below the skyline. She sighed quietly through her nose as she finished her last sentence, then she glanced at the time.

Satisfied with the amount of work she'd done tonight, she closed up her laptop and set it aside. She stretched her legs out from underneath her and groaned as the cramps eased, then she stood. She swept her gaze across the room to get a glance at the thousands of lights in the city down below as she stretched her arms up high and let down her hair.

New York was almost as pretty as Bangkok.

Leaving her books on reading pH levels and pamphlets describing bodies of water in Southeast Asia on her breakfast bar, she crossed her white tile floor. She tapped a button on her wall to turn out the lights as she went to make ready for bed.

Throwing down the blankets to slide in with her silk pajamas, Brielle heard her phone ping. Once she got settled, she checked the screen.

Can't wait to see you tomorrow! Have so much to catch up on! Have a safe flight!

Brielle smiled at Gavin's message. Two years of continued schooling for an advanced degree in hydrology. Two years since she last saw Mystic Springs.

She tapped a reply.

Can't wait to see you, too!

ANNI MEUSCHKE

Anni Meuschke is a naturalist at heart who loves spending time enjoying a cup of coffee while observing the outdoors. She loves to write and is currently working on her first novel, though she spends much of her downtime doing animal art portraits and private commissions alike. Her short story, Nature's Diadem, is her first published piece.

Her art projects can be found on her Facebook page:
Sparks and Feathers – Artwork

THE PSYCHIC'S PARTNER

BARBY BIRD

FLAMINIA'S THIN, pale arms prickled as she stepped from the air-conditioned comfort of Mystic Visions onto the creaky wooden porch. A person did not need to be a psychic, or a meteorologist for that matter, to know that the first day of fall in the Ozark Mountains was to be a scorcher. It was already eighty-eight degrees at nine o'clock in the morning. Flaminia glided down the creaky, multi-colored steps, fanning herself with a local tourism brochure. A recent bypass had rerouted travelers—and their dollars—around Mystic Springs. Her little enterprise was now the only psychic parlor in town, yet it somehow still provided her with a comfortable living.

Despite the muggy air, today felt light. Different. An odd current pulsated in the air. Not that this was bad. It usually meant a message would soon come to her. Flaminia never knew who or what the communication would concern. It could be good news—or a terrible prediction. A person just had to wait until the spirits were ready to make their revelations.

Down the street, a mirage of heat waves already shimmered above the pavement. It was early in the day for that, but this seemed to go hand-in-hand with the odd current flowing through the small town. Flaminia closed her dark brown eyes, hoping to get a better feeling of the revelations she knew would soon arrive. The scorching sun soothingly bathed her face, but a few more minutes would be all she could handle before melting. She opened her eyes to see Judd Rusbridge drive by in his time-worn Chevy pickup truck, a fishing rod and rifle rested in the rack in the back window. With an hour until her first appointment, Flaminia had time to grab a bite to eat at Judd's hole-in-the-wall place, The Deer Stand Café and Honky-Tonk. The place was popular, and the food was good. Of course, Judd wouldn't wait on her. He never did. Flaminia had always sensed a deep-rooted pain behind his stand-offish attitude toward her. Nonbelievers could be uncomfortable with her skill set.

The much-appreciated air conditioning of The Deer Stand swirled over Flaminia and stirred her colorful flowing skirts. During the day, customers could find delicious home-style food. By nightfall, the place would become a rowdy place to grab a beer and listen to a live country and western band. This morning, the café buzzed with locals and a few tourists conversing about the latest gossip. The town loved its gossip.

Flaminia glanced around the busy room, spotting the last available stool at the counter. She squeezed through the hungry clientele and worked her way to the seat, a wobbly, red-and-chrome stool. Judd's sister, Alice, scurried by with a wave and a wink, indicating she would be with Flaminia as soon as she could. The psychic cautiously spun on her rickety perch, hoping it would manage the turn. She studied the occupants of the bustling café. Mary Ellen, Judd's mother, laughed with a table full of good ol' boys. The woman loved flirting. Her husband had been gone for several years now, and rumor had it that Mary Ellen loved to entertain gentlemen callers on the weekends. That was Mystic Springs's gossip for you.

"Let me guess. Coffee and a Danish?"

Flaminia carefully rotated on her stool to see Alice's toothy smile. "Yes, the usual, Alice. Thank you."

Once the coffee and Danish were delivered, the plump waitress scurried on to other customers. Flaminia looked up from her first sip of coffee, instantly noticing Judd's eyes locked on her through the pass-through window in the kitchen. He quickly looked away, but Flaminia saw him turn crimson before he moved out of sight.

He is a strange one. But who am I to call someone strange?"

———

Flaminia's ten o'clock turned out to be two single sisters from Kansas City on a weekend getaway. She told them the usual. Good fortune was about to come their way. Handsome strangers would cross their paths. Their careers were going in a promising direction. She made it a point to never tell her customers about the darkness that might come their way. But in this morning's readings, she thankfully saw no darkness in the future for these two women. After the reading, she expertly ran through her sales pitch and sold the women two vials of healing spring water and rose quartz crystals with instructions to wear them every day. The quartz would open their hearts to love. Her pitch was an easy one, and the women gladly graced Flaminia's palm with cash.

Later in the day, as Flaminia strolled through a shaded grove of trees, the air turned refreshingly cool. A carpet of pine needles quieted her steps. To an outside observer, she would have appeared to float magically down the tranquil woodsy path as her long skirts flowed about in the breeze. But there were no observers in her private forest. Shortly, she reached a rusty gate. A handmade "No Trespassing" sign dangled from it in a cockeyed fashion. The Mystic Visions owner pushed the rickety gate open and gently closed it.

Perhaps she should replace the gate before it completely fell apart. Or not. It had been there for many generations, and disturbing the setting felt slightly wrong. Flaminia would have to hire someone to fix the gate, but she wanted no one in this private, mysterious area of her forest. Her forty acres backed up to a national park. No one could ever live or build behind her property, which added to her privacy.

Mystic Visions had at one time been a true mom-and-pop grocery store owned by Flaminia's parents. But a period of fewer tourists in town resulted in dropping sales, and the little store could not survive with just local purchases. The difficult decision was made to sell the business. Before this could happen, Flaminia's parents died in a tragic automobile crash. They had been on a backroad barely traveled, and the accident was not discovered until the next day.

Flaminia was thirty-five at the time and their only child. Visions were always a part of her life. She'd heard whispers that her grandmother had the "sight." But she never understood why they came to her, or what they fully meant.

Then, a vision of her parents in a mangled car wreck caused a panic.

Flaminia's parents had been headed back from a trip to Birmingham, Alabama, in search of a house to live in once they retired from the store. She had pleaded with them to travel no farther than Kennett, Missouri, that night. Her parents had even agreed to the proposed overnight stop.

Yet that night and into the next day, Flaminia's gut feeling signaling doom had burned as if on fire, and she'd feared it was spot on.

It was.

Early that afternoon, Flaminia had gotten the news that her parents and their wrecked car had been found. She assumed that her father, being a typical tightwad, couldn't justify paying hard-earned money on a motel, and had driven on. The dreaded confirmation of their deaths completely upended her world. She was the last of her family, and her life could never be the same.

Then one day, she came to an epiphany. Her vision of her parents lying dead in a ditch meant that her gut feelings or guesses amounted to more than luck. She possessed a *gift*. One that she could develop and use to make a living.

But at that moment in time, Flaminia, still grieving, worried this gift might also bear the weight of a sad, sick curse.

Flamina carried two clear gallon jugs to fill with the precious spring water. This was all she could handle at one time. She used glass containers because plastic ones meant contaminants could leach into the water. The spring water was too pure to risk that. After filling the jugs, she sat down on the rock bench she had built years ago. A faint breeze tickled the chimes she had placed nearby over the spot where she had buried the ashes of her parents. It was peaceful here, and the perfect sanctuary to meditate, reflect, and reminisce. So many memories.

Flaminia thought back to the time when she'd first dreamed she could use her gift to support herself. As an aspiring entrepreneur, she had sold the grocery inventory. Then she remodeled the building's interior to provide a room for readings, with a small retail area, and her living quarters in the back. The place was humble but well-suited to her needs. A fresh coat of bright orange paint on the exterior, colorful stairs, and a wooden sign hung by chains displaying "Mystic Visions" had put her in the psychic business. Nearly twenty years of telling fortunes and reading palms had provided her with modest financial security.

She counted herself lucky the local springs still drew a few tourists to the small rural town. Rico Cerna's constant posting on his YouTube and Instagram accounts brought many of them to Flaminia's establishment. People loved to learn more about the magical, healing waters and appreciated the retelling of the area's legends.

Some of her clients seemed a bit strange to her, and some were desperate to find answers to their questions about their life —or afterlife. Flaminia tried to help the assortment of people who called on her services. Years of experience had taught her to keep her own counsel on any darkness she may encounter during readings. There was no sense in upsetting and alarming her clients. That would not be good for bringing in returning customers, nor would it result in positive Yelp reviews. Besides, what could those facing dark times do? Could anyone change fate?

A fault running underneath Flaminia's property delivered three springs of naturally carbonated water to the surface. Two of these springs had slowed in production over the years, but her favorite still faithfully provided her with an abundance of water flavored by a billion years of remarkable geology below her land. This spring she called Otoe, in honor of the Natives who had used its effervescent waters for healing before the Indian Removal Act of 1830 forced them from the land. Flaminia's great-grandfather was part Ojibwe, and she believed the ancient spirits would enjoy the fact that the property was owned once again by a gifted one with Native blood. It was her land to protect. No one else knew of these springs. She'd fenced the property years ago to keep out nosey Nellies.

A soft wind tickled the wind chimes again. Flaminia turned her face to the sun, eyes closed. Then blackness....

It was a small shore covered in trees, roots, and thick foliage, and Flaminia took care with her footing. A rock embankment rose high on one side of her with clear water on the other. The embankment was too steep to climb, and the water too deep to wade. She looked around, contemplating how to get up the cliff. Distant laughter from above disturbed the quiet. She glanced up to the top edge of the embankment. At that moment, Flaminia saw the undercarriage of a car soaring over the edge of the ridge directly over her head. The vehicle came down slowly, as if moving in slow motion. As her gaze followed the car through its flight, she thought how unusual it was for an airborne vehicle to move in that manner. The car hit the water with a thunderous smack. Flaminia studied the back of the sedan as the churning water swallowed it. It was clear the vehicle was some sort of police car. The light bar on top flashed red and blue before going dark as the cruiser sank deeper and deeper into its watery grave. In only a few seconds, the car disappeared from sight, as if it had never been there. Gentle waves lapping against the surrounding bank and a few ripples glistening in the sun were the only indications the water had been disturbed.

Flaminia lay on the ground. Water had spilled from one of the jugs, and damp earth clung to her face as she sat up. What a waste of the precious spring water. She could refill the jug, but she hoped the lost water wasn't a bad sign. She rose and seated herself on the bench, replaying the vision in her mind. A terrific feeling of dread overcame her as she realized she had, in this last minute, possibly seen someone die in her vision—just as she had with her parents. It seemed like she could do nothing.

Was this more than just an unreliable vision? There was something about that police car. With a gasp, Flaminia realized it must have been the squad car of the missing police chief, Russell Bagshaw.

But would anyone believe her?

Flaminia knew she had to try. She gathered up her skirts and the one full jug of water and scurried down the path home.

Flaminia recited the details of her vision to Samantha Simpkins, the town's replacement police chief. She insisted the Mystic Springs police force—all two of them—look in local bodies of water for the missing lawman.

The chief studied the distressed psychic. "Look, Flaminia, I would like to say I believe you." Chief Simpkins's youthful face showed her skepticism. "Surely you understand how odd your request sounds. Searching local bodies of water for a missing lawman based only on a vision you had?"

Flaminia opened her mouth, but the chief didn't give her a chance to speak.

"Even if this event truly happened, it's still only Shad and me in the department. We don't have the manpower to go poking around every body of water." The chief looked down at the floor of her office. "If I ask the county or state to help with this, I'll become a laughingstock."

"But—"

"Listen, Flaminia. I want to find Chief Bagshaw as much as the next person. I really do. But put yourself in my shoes."

"Samantha, I understand how crazy my vision sounds. But you must know I'm not making this up." Not wanting to keep insisting to the point of getting on the chief's bad side, Flaminia stood and crossed to the department's front door. She turned to add another plea, only to see *both* officers staring at her. Great. Now the chief would tell the younger officer how the town's psychic was a crackpot.

Flaminia ambled down the sidewalk as she wondered who to go to for assistance next. Maybe she'd think better after a stop for the Rueben sandwich she was craving. The Deer Stand Café had the best Rueben around, so Judd's it would be. For lunch. The live music, drunken hillbillies, and rednecks galore who filled the building later in the evening? Definitely not her scene.

Just as it had been earlier in the day, the air conditioning was welcome. The outdoor temperature had been climbing all day and the heat index had to be over one hundred degrees. So, the cool air produced goosebumps as it moved across Flaminia's damp skin. She chose a booth against the wall and out of the sun. She pulled the little menu from its clip holder, though she already knew what she wanted—the Rueben and a tall glass of ice water. Turning the menu over, she perused the list of delicious desserts. A shadow appeared at her side. She was surprised to see Judd wearing a camo apron with a green order pad in one hand and a pen in the other.

"Flaminia, what can I get ya?" Judd's voice was abrupt.

"Hello, Judd." Flaminia greeted him politely. "I will have a half Rueben sandwich and ice water with lemon."

Judd scratched down the order and quickly retreated to the drink station. When he approached her table with the water, he asked, "Was there something else, Flaminia?"

She surprised them both by grabbing his arm. She looked into his shocked eyes and whispered, "Please don't cry, Daddy. You can hug my teddy bear. Wally will dry your tears."

Judd's face whitened. The glass of water crashed to the floor.

Judd would not look at Flaminia as he cleaned the broken glass and mopped up the water. When he reappeared with the sandwich, he placed the plate on the table, along with a fresh glass of water. Then he sat himself in the booth on the seat opposite Flaminia.

Clasping his hands, he looked at her with tears in his eyes and asked, "How did you know?" His voice became a whisper. "Those were the last words my daughter ever spoke to me."

Flaminia looked at Judd's tears. How could she explain this in a manner he could understand? He had always made sure to let Flaminia know that the idea of her having a *gift* was, in his words, "hogwash." She had secretly been hurt by his skepticism a time or two, but she never indicated that fact to Judd.

After showing Judd she knew his daughter's last words, Flaminia hoped he would take her vision of the missing police chief seriously. Judd could do what he wished with the knowledge. He could believe her or not.

"First, Judd, I am so sorry. I cannot imagine what the pain of losing a child does to an individual."

Judd's eyes focused on his clasped hands resting on the table. "Flaminia, I'm ready to hear what you have to say. I don't understand how you could possibly know what Clara said to me at the hospital. We were alone. No one else was in that room. Not even her mother. So, tell me how you know."

The psychic reached across the table and put her hands over Judd's. "Sometimes I just know things. Sometimes I have visions. And sometimes I hear things. They might happen together or separately. In this case, Judd, I saw and heard your daughter say the words. I saw you sitting by her hospital bed. You were crying. Then the vision ended." Flaminia gave his hands a soft squeeze. "That may not be what you wanted to hear. But this isn't hocus-pocus or witchcraft. It is just something I have been gifted with. It could even be called a curse, because, at times, the knowledge is painful to receive. Do you understand? Does this make any sense to you?"

Judd was silent. Then he locked eyes with her. "No, it does not. Maybe I can't ever understand this. Maybe I will just have to trust you and your gift." Judd's hands trembled. "This is quite a stretch for me, but I don't doubt you. Can you tell me anything else? Is she okay?"

"That is something I typically never know. But she seemed... serene." Flaminia released Judd's hands and reached for her sandwich. "The dead don't usually reach out to me. Well, not until this morning, anyway."

Judd raised an eyebrow. "What happened this morning?"

Flaminia's well-endowed chest rose with a heavy sigh. Judd seemed sincerely interested, so she continued, "I went to the back area of my property. Suddenly, I blacked out from a vision. This vision was unique. I am certain it was in the past because I believe Police Chief Russell Bagshaw was in it."

Judd's baby blues widened. "Chief's been missing for eight months. Everyone thinks he must have run off. His bank account was drained, and rumor was that he was seeing a stripper named Trixie over in Springfield."

"I don't think he did, Judd. I think he is still very close to here, under a body of water in his cruiser. That's what I saw today. Well, at least I saw his car."

The honky-tonk owner looked stunned. "Holy crapoly. Are you serious?"

Flaminia nodded. "I tried talking to Chief Simpkins immediately after my vision. She sympathized, but she told me it would be too embarrassing for her to tell anyone about my gift. She felt she would be laughed out of town if she gave me even an ounce of credibility." Flaminia's shoulders sagged. "I don't know why I'm telling you this. You probably think I'm crazy, too."

"After what you just told me about Clara, I can't help but give you some leeway. Maybe even help you out." Judd hooked his thumbs in his camo suspenders with a satisfied grin. "What if I could help you solve the disappearance of the chief and his car? You describe the body of water he's in, and I can find it!"

"It's not that easy. I mostly just saw his car going over a tall cliff and a small stretch of a tiny beach. I heard laughing. Then the car went flying, splashed into the water, and that was it."

"Well, I have fished just about every body of water around here. Can you tell me about the road he was on? Could you describe this tiny beach or cliff?"

Flaminia knitted her brows and closed her eyes, her usual trance-like state for extreme concentration. "The road is isolated. No, it's not a road. It's more like a path or trail. A "No Trespassing" sign hangs on a chain on one side of the path. The grass is tall. There are lots of trees on either side. Thick trees. The squad car stops just before the edge of a cliff. It is very quiet except for distant laughter. Then there is a yell that sounds masculine. An argument permeates the seclusion of the area. I hear doors and maybe a trunk shutting. Then the car goes over a steep cliff that looks like a solid rock wall. The car splashes in the water."

Flaminia drew in a deep breath. "That's it, Judd. That's all I see."

She waited patiently while he took his time processing the information. "I think I know where you're talking about. It's the old Lover's Leap. That was the go-to place for necking and drinking. My last year of high school, it got closed up after a kid jumped off the bluff and broke his back. His family tried to sue the landowner, but I don't think anything ever came of that." Judd slid out of the booth. "Come on, Flaminia, we're going for a ride."

Judd's truck was like riding in the back of a lumber wagon, but at least the air conditioning worked. Neither of them spoke. Both were eager to see if Flaminia's vision matched Judd's memory.

"Keep your eyes peeled, Flaminia. The path should be on your right. When I was a kid, there were posts on either side of the road. But they may be gone by now."

A half hour had passed when Flaminia yelled, "Stop! Look!"

Judd slammed on the brakes, causing them both to lurch towards the windshield.

"See that? Right here. To the left of that spruce tree."

Squinting, Judd apparently saw what Flaminia had pointed to, a post leaning at a forty-five-degree angle. About eight feet to the left of the post was a second post with a chain hanging from it. A nearly invisible grassy connection between the road and the posts could easily be missed. Judd backed up his truck and turned onto the almost imperceptible path. They exited the truck and walked over to the rusty chain. Following it, they found a weather-beaten "No Trespassing" sign lying on the ground.

"Well, Flaminia, so far, your vision is spot on. Let's find out what's beyond this point." They climbed back into the truck.

They went forward until fallen limbs blocked the rising road. Flaminia waited in the cool truck while Judd moved the large branches with ease.

He returned to the cab. "Does this area look familiar, Flaminia?"

She studied the forest. "I'm sure this is it."

Tall grass on the path waved in the light breeze that made it through the trees. Eventually, the path widened a bit and then ended at the brink of a cliff. Judd slammed on his brakes and again nearly put them through the windshield. The ground in front of them disappeared. The enormous expanse of Oho Spring stretched out below. Wide-eyed, they turned to each other.

Judd said, "That drop-off is closer than I remember!"

"That was a little too close for me, Judd. If you're trying to give me a heart attack, mission almost completed."

"I'd have appreciated it if you'd used your extrasensory perspiration abilities to say, 'Hey, stop. Cliff ahead.'"

The two laughed nervously at the near mishap. Judd backed his truck up several feet and turned it around for good measure. It wouldn't be any good for them to be at the bottom of a spring. The two exited the battered truck. Judd watched as Flaminia strode about the small clearing, inducing her trance-like state again to call up her memory.

She walked to where Judd sat on the tailgate. "This is exactly what I saw this morning. I am afraid to look over the edge of the cliff, afraid of what we might see."

Judd nodded in agreement. "Well, we came this far. We need to do this. We need to look over the edge."

Flaminia wouldn't say she was afraid of heights, but the idea of looking over a one-hundred-foot cliff wasn't soothing.

Judd's hand slipped into hers. "You ready?"

She nodded and let Judd lead her over to the edge. Deciduous trees with vibrant yellows, reds and oranges were breathtaking against the green cedars.

Using more caution than was probably necessary, the two peered over the edge. The water in the center of the large pool was a deep blue. A light breeze made small waves lap up against a small beach at the bottom of the cliff. Flaminia recognized this beach. She met Judd's eyes and nodded. They looked again out over the water that sparkled with the late afternoon sun. Soon, darkness would settle in, as the days were getting shorter. Raising her hand to shade her eyes, Flaminia examined the water. She gasped and grabbed Judd by the arm. "Look straight down! Do you see it? There's a car in the water!"

Judd stared at the bubbling, sun-glared spring water. "Well, that *could* be something."

"*Could* be? What part of 'a car in the water' don't you see, for Pete's sake?"

After standing there for a few minutes, Judd nudged Flaminia's elbow. "I think it's time we called for help."

Trooper Harrison of the Highway Patrol Investigative Division, an old hunting buddy of Chief Bagshaw's, promptly took the lead as soon as the vehicle reached the shore. After an excruciating wait, he pulled his head from the car. "That's Russ, alright. He's handcuffed to the steering wheel." The trooper frowned. "I've never seen anything like this. The body is so pristine, I'd swear he entered this car moments ago. Looks like we might have a fountain of youth here."

Harrison reached over the body and grabbed a bag from the front seat. He rummaged through the bag. "We've got Russell's passport, his empty wallet, a one-way plane ticket to Mexico in his name, and even some gift-wrapped women's lingerie. I'd venture to guess the lingerie means he didn't plan on being alone. Figure he was aiming to take a trip—before somebody made other plans for him."

The sun shone hot and bright on the beach of Playa del Carmen. Trixie, now known as Aubriella, sipped from a champagne flute filled with magical spring water from Mystic Springs, Missouri. A wide-brimmed hat shaded her face, but any passerby could easily see her expression of ecstasy as she was overcome with the caress of youth rolling through her.

BARBY BIRD

Barby is a passionate and avid reader who has recently made her mark with her first anthology contribution. She delights in crafting suspenseful murder/mystery stories that keep readers on the edge of their seats. Family is her top priority, and she cherishes every moment spent with them. Barby's hobbies include writing, reading, hiking, and traveling. She is also a dedicated metaphysical practitioner, running her own online business, "Tranquil Journey." Residing in mid-Missouri, Barby shares her life with her loving and hilarious husband and their beautiful yellow lab, Judy, who is always up for an adventure.

THANK YOU!

We hope you have enjoyed reading **Mystic Springs: A Collection of Anomalies**.

If so, you'll also love **Hawthorn Creek: A Collection of Secrets**, another short-story anthology we published, with fourteen engaging stories about secrets hidden in the small town of Hawthorn Creek, a town not too distant from Mystic Springs, come to think of it.

Our group, Writers of Warrensburg (in Warrensburg, Missouri, co-administrated by Goldie Edwards and Stan C. Smith) includes authors of all genres, which is reflected in the variety of stories in this collection. Our goal is to help our members develop their writing skills, marketing skills, and a general authorly mindset. All proceeds from sales of the eBook version of *Mystic Springs* are used to facilitate these efforts.

To learn more about our group, the authors contributing to this anthology, and how this short story collection came about, please visit our website:

https://writersofwsbg.weebly.com

Finally, if you have enjoyed this book, we'd love it if you would take a moment to post an honest review on Amazon. Reader reviews are important to the success of books like this one.

Thank you!